**Lindsay McKenna** is proud to have served her country in the US Navy as an aerographer's mate third class—also known as a weather forecaster. She was a pioneer in the military romance subgenre and loves to combine heart-pounding action with soulful and poignant romance. True to her military roots, she is the originator of the long-running and reader-favorite Morgan's Mercenaries series. She does extensive hands-on research, including flying in aircraft such as a P3-B Orion sub-hunter and a B-52 bomber. She was the first romance writer to sign her books in the Pentagon bookstore. Visit her online at lindsaymckenna.com.

# LINDSAY McKENNA

# WOLF HAVEN

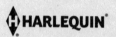

ISBN-13: 978-1-335-18998-1

Wolf Haven

First published in 2014.
This edition published in 2020.

This edition published by arrangement with Harlequin Books S.A.

For questions and comments about the quality of this book, please contact us at CustomerService@Harlequin.com.

Harlequin Enterprises ULC
22 Adelaide St. West, 40th Floor
Toronto, Ontario M5H 4E3, Canada
www.Harlequin.com

Printed in U.S.A.

Recycling programs for this product may not exist in your area.

# WOLF HAVEN

To Frances Ann Overton,
one of my wonderful and inspiring readers,
who has done so much for so many others. She is a role
model as a special-education teacher in Kanab, Utah.
Thank you for all you do, Frances. You have the
biggest heart of anyone I've ever met. The children under
your care are very blessed to have you in their lives.

And

To Murray and Debbie Shields, owners of Eco-Treks,
Toronto, Canada. You two truly inspire those who go
on your offered trips a chance to reconnect with the
beauty of our planet in so many wonderful ways. Thank
you for allowing us to be with you at the Fraser River
Bald Eagle Festival near Mission, British Columbia,
Canada, November 2013. As photographers, we got so
many wonderful photos of these incredible raptors. I
recommend your tours to everyone around the world! You
are a heart-centered couple who truly bring back the *wild*
in *wildlife*, for beautiful hikes through rugged country,
great for photographers, birders or those in need of
healing with Mother Earth and all her relations.
Thank you!

# CHAPTER ONE

SKY PASCAL MOANED, tossing in her sleep on the hotel bed. Her stomach was in knots, with the pain radiating outward. She flinched and drew her legs up toward her body. The vibration of the Black Hawk helicopter surrounded her. She could smell the sweat from the bodies of the air crewmen on this flight to Forward Operating Base, or FOB, Charlie. The odor of the kerosene aviation fuel was always present.

She'd been asked to fly along with Dr. Aaron Zimmerman to take a look at an Army soldier who was thought to have appendicitis. They had been over at a different FOB when the call came in. The FOBs were only forty miles from one another, and they were the closest medical team that could respond.

Now the vibration of the Hawk skittered through her. Sky was on the metal deck of the medevac helicopter as it raced through the darkness to reach the soldier.

She was an emergency-room trained R.N. and Zimmerman, who sat near the door, was a surgeon, specializing in internal medicine. Two other combat medic crewmen, whom she could not see, were nearby. The two pilots to her left were wearing night-vision goggles.

The tension was so thick it felt like a wet blanket around her hunched shoulders. Her mind raced.

She was assigned to the Army hospital at Bagram Air Base near Kabul, Afghanistan. A first lieutenant, she had three years under her belt in the U.S. Navy. It wasn't un-

usual for different military services to have personnel assigned to the huge, busy hospital. She loved her job in the
E.R. Sky was good in a crisis—cool and calm. That was
why Zimmerman had asked her to go with him as he visited the outlying FOBs. If he had to perform surgery on
the spot at the FOB, he wanted someone like her with him.

But now her mouth was dry, and her heart was skipping
beats in her chest. She was dressed in Navy fatigues, the
"blueberries" coloring standing out starkly against others
who wore desert-hued uniforms. Glad to have the forty-
pound Kevlar vest on, Sky lived for missions like this.
They were exciting and scary as hell.

She knew there was danger with any helo flight. The
Black Hawk Army pilots, who were from the black-ops
Night Stalker squadron, were flying high enough so the
Taliban couldn't send grenade launchers up at them. However, the Stinger missiles were always a threat. One could
blow them out of the sky regardless of their altitude. Sky
was a knot of excitement and fear, adrenaline leaking
through her bloodstream.

She couldn't see through the darkness because she
wasn't wearing night-vision goggles. Only the four crew
members were wearing NVGs. The flight wasn't long to
FOB Charlie, located three miles from the Pakistan border.
There were only two platoons at the Army base.

Sky was told this particular FOB was an essential stop-
gap measure to halt or slow down the Taliban and al Qaeda
soldiers trying to sneak into Afghanistan. FOB Charlie
was an important deterrent.

Zimmerman had warned her beforehand that this would
be a dangerous mission because of the FOB's location. Sky
had leaped at the chance. Maybe she was bored. But that
couldn't possibly be. She lived on the same dicey border
of stress and pressure in the E.R. Night and day, men and

women were brought in chewed up by the weapons of war. She felt no small amount of pride in being part of the E.R. team who helped save those lives. Now she was going to help a young soldier with appendicitis.

The sound of the engines changed on the Black Hawk. Sky felt a sudden lurch, the nose suddenly dropping. She inhaled sharply, throwing out her hand on one of the litters against the wall. Wearing a helmet, she heard the tense, short exchanges between the two pilots.

Something was wrong.

She caught a whiff of what smelled like burning oil entering the cabin. Her pulse ratcheted up.

A sudden shrieking, screaming noise blasted through the cabin of the Black Hawk. The bird banked sharply right and plunged downward. It happened so fast. The thumping of the blades. Being thrown up against the skin, striking her head hard on the bulkhead, nearly losing consciousness. Suddenly, they were upside down. She hadn't been able to wear the seat belt. The other crewmen were thrown around, as well. Yelling and sharp orders from the pilot filled the ears of her helmet.

They were falling out of the sky. The screeching of metal upon metal continued to shriek through the cabin.

Her mouth went dry. Sky bit back a scream. Oh, God, they were going to crash! It was some sort of mechanical malfunction. Her mind swam with terror. Where were they? She couldn't see out the window! Gravity was shoving her hard against the aluminum skin of the Black Hawk. She was scared. She was going to die!

SKY REARED UP in the bed, screaming. The sound echoed about the small hotel room. Sweat leaked down her temples. Her ginger, shoulder-length hair swung around her face, momentarily blinding her as she threw her hands out, as if to stop herself from falling. Her legs were entangled in the sheets. She breathed in heaving sobs as she opened her eyes, trying to get rid of the sensation of the plummeting helicopter she rode down in the crash.

Still reeling from her nightmare, Sky lurched jerkily out of the bed and fell onto the carpeted floor. Landing with an *oomph,* her head slamming into the floor, she snapped wide-awake. She groaned, drawing up her hands, covering her face, lying flat on her belly, unable to move.

If she closed her eyes, she saw the crash behind her eyelids. If she opened her eyes, she could still smell the burning oil in the cabin, feel the helo vibrating like a wild, wounded thing around her. She heard the terse commands and tightness in the pilots' voices up in the cockpit as they wrestled to stop the bird from augering into the Afghanistan mountains.

Her nostrils flared, and she felt the sweat running down her face. Her breath came out in explosive gasps. Her heart pounded. *Oh, God... Oh, God... I'm here. Not there. I'm here. I survived... God, I survived....* And she kept up the litany in her head, unable to erase the coming crash. Or what happened after that.

Sky pushed her trembling fingers into the tight weave of the carpet, trying to orient herself to here and now.

Why wouldn't the images go away? Why wouldn't she stop feeling the Black Hawk shivering and whumping around her? *Get up! Get up!*

Sobbing for air, Sky forced her paralyzed body to move. Her nightgown was soaked with sweat. Shaky and unsteady, she got to her knees and slowly straightened her long fingers against her curved thighs. It was nearly dawn, the light leaking in around the drapes of the Wyoming Inn. Looking over at the bed stand, she saw the red numbers: 5:20 a.m.

Pushing the damp strands of her hair off her face, Sky

hung her head, trying to steady her breathing. At the Balboa Naval Hospital in San Diego, this was what they'd taught her when she'd get anxiety reactions or a full-blown panic attack. She'd been a broken shell of a human being when she'd been rescued by a SEAL team two weeks after being captured. They'd brought her fractured soul and tortured body to Bagram hospital, where she'd been an E.R. nurse.

Whispering her name, she held on to it. *Skylar Pascal. First Lieutenant. U.S. Navy.* She repeated her name again and again. She had to concentrate on her physical body. Damp palms moved down the soft cotton of her damp gown. She forced her attention to the temperature in the room on an early-June morning. Focused on any sounds she might hear, like the ticking of the clock. Finally…finally…the sensations of riding the helo down into a crash left her. The terror of thinking she was going to die in that moment eased, as did the harsh gasps tearing out of her mouth.

Slowly, Sky lifted her hands, threading her fingers through her long, straight hair. She reveled in its silkiness. Feeling how soft and sleek it was compared to the nightmare's smells, sounds and sensations. *Ground. Ground. Get back in your body, Sky.* Her throat tightened, and tears jammed into her eyes. No longer did she see the movielike frames of the nightmare. Relief shattered through her as the hot tears fell down her cheeks.

Pulling her thick hair off her shoulders, the bulk of it falling between her shoulder blades, Sky didn't even try to stop the tears. Her therapist, Commander Olivia Hartfield, a specialist in PTSD at Balboa Naval Hospital, had told her they were good. It would help to cleanse her, help her emotionally stabilize. Above all, she'd told Sky, never fight crying. Let the tears flow. They were healing. Sky wiped the perspiration off her wrinkled brow. Gulping, her mouth dry, she wanted water.

*Water.*

Opening her eyes, Sky let the word filter through her and bring up the soul-destroying sensations and what they did to her. *Water.* Once, she'd loved water, loved swimming, loved walking in the rain, running outside to feel the fury of a thunderstorm as a child. Not anymore. Water was her enemy. Water had nearly killed her. But she was thirsty.

The nightmare was leaving her, and Sky looked around. She was in a small hotel room in Jackson Hole, Wyoming. She had a job interview at 9:00 a.m. She frowned, and her heart began a slow beat, underscoring her trepidation. Sky absently touched her heart. She desperately needed this job. She'd gone through so many of them and had been either fired outright or let go with apologetic sympathy. Either way, she was unemployed when she had to find a way to survive and work like everyone else.

*Water.*

As she forced herself to stand, her knees felt wobbly. Sky sat down on the bed, understanding she was having an adrenaline crash. It made her weak. Made her unable to do much of anything until it passed. Her mouth felt dry and cracked. *Thirsty.* She was so thirsty. Sky couldn't stand to see a pitcher of water. Shaking her head, she forced herself to lie down. Usually, once she had a nightmare, she could go back to sleep. Since Afghanistan, since the Black Hawk crash, she was lucky to get two or three hours a night. Sky closed her eyes and didn't even try to pick up the sheets off the floor. All she wanted to do was escape into sleep. There, she didn't have to feel anything. There, Sky could go away for just a little while....

THE ALARM STARTLED Sky out of her badly needed sleep. She jerked up, the noise sending her into panic. Heart crashing, she quickly pushed the buzzer on the clock, and it stopped shrieking at her. Looking up, she saw sunlight around the curtains. She'd set the clock for 7:00 a.m.

*I have to get up. Get moving...*

Glancing at the sheets and blanket strewn across the floor, she felt guilty. Sky got up and walked slowly toward the bathroom. She smelled of fear sweat. As she ran her hand down her cotton nightgown, she felt the dampness from the nightmare. She would wash her hair, as well. Today she needed to be presentable. Needed to look normal. Whatever *normal* meant.

She'd never be normal again. After turning on the water for a bath, she closed the bathroom door. This was the hardest thing to do: take a bath. Water meant suffocation and dying. It meant terror beyond anything she'd ever experienced. Olivia had worked long and hard with her that six months she was recovering. Worked to get her to take a bath. Sky would never take a shower again. *Not ever.* It would remind her of the torture she'd endured. At first, she'd wash only with a cloth and water in a steel bowl. In six months, she'd graduated from a bowl of water to taking a bath with a small amount of water in the tub. It was progress, Olivia said, congratulating her for her courage to challenge the very thing that had nearly killed her.

As Sky turned off the faucets and slowly put one foot into the tub and then the other, she got herself to focus on her coming job interview. She was to see Iris Mason, owner of the Elk Horn Ranch, at 9:00 a.m. *This morning.* Somehow, Sky would find the strength it'd take to gut through that interview. She needed the job. Would she get it? Or would Iris Mason see right through her and turn her down as so many other employers already had?

GRAYSON McCOY WAS walking from the main office of the Elk Horn Ranch after talking with Iris Mason when he saw a silver Kia Sorento SUV pull up in front. He'd settled his black SEAL baseball cap on his short brown hair and slowed a little. The early-June morning was near freezing, not uncommon at this time of year for this part of Wyoming. To the east rose the jagged, tooth-shaped Teton Mountains, their slopes glazed with white snow.

Because he'd been a SEAL for seven years, he was alert and watchful. Iris, the owner of the Elk Horn Ranch, had been excited about a woman named Skylar Pascal, who was coming to interview for a job. It wasn't just any job, either. Gray wasn't sure he wanted to work with a woman at the wildlife center. He'd been hired a year ago because his mother, Isabel McCoy, was a noted wolf biologist and wildlife expert. Iris had wanted to create a one-hundred-acre wildlife preserve on the Elk Horn for their dude-ranch families who came every year for a vacation.

Further, Iris, who always had an eye on saving the planet, wanted part of the refuge for timber wolves and to bring them back to the States. His mother had told him about this job, and Iris had hired him on the spot.

The green grass beneath his cowboy boots was thick with dew as he slowed. Across the dirt road stood the log cabin. He watched with a little more interest as a woman dressed in a tasteful, coffee-brown pantsuit with a white blouse emerged from the SUV. His eyes narrowed speculatively as he absorbed her.

Being a SEAL, he had the ability to see all the details, which was always important. She was young, mid-twenties, with long, beautiful, ginger-brown hair that swung gently around her shoulders. The way she squared them, the way she walked, made Gray think she had a military background. Military people walked a certain way: shoulders back and proud, a straight spine, the chin slightly tilted upward. This woman was probably around five foot ten or so. Long, lean and damned graceful. She had a white leather purse she pulled over her left shoulder. Another sign of being in the military. Gray smiled to himself. It left the right arm free to salute with, and women in the military always carried their purses on their left shoulder as a result.

He didn't want to be swayed, but when she lifted her chin and looked around—looked at *him*—his heart unexpectedly thumped once. It was a crazy reaction and surprising to Gray. He had been emotionally numbed out for a long time...ever since Julia's murder.

Frowning, Gray slammed the door shut on his aching past. Instead, he zeroed in on the woman's square face, her high cheekbones and wide-spaced blue eyes. Damn, she was good-looking as hell. A ten in his book. Yet his SEAL senses warned him that something wasn't right about her. Nothing appeared out of place, but his finely honed intuition was never wrong. It had saved his life way too many times to count over in Afghanistan when he was with SEAL Team 3.

Not close enough to really dig into her eyes to ferret out what he sensed, Gray saw her mouth was full. Even lush. Brushed with pink lipstick. Her cheekbones were high. He wondered if she had Native American blood in her. There was keen intelligence in Skylar's eyes, and Gray applauded that. Iris wouldn't hire someone for the wildlife center who didn't have a lot on the ball. His heart stirred for the first time in two years. What was it about this woman that was making him feel once again?

Gray rubbed his recently shaved chin. Skylar Pascal dressed conservatively. Even her footwear showed that. She wore no heels, just commonsense white leather shoes. Sunlight glinted off her plain gold earrings and a practical watch wrapped around her slender right wrist. He liked the way her hair glinted with red, brown and blond highlights as the early-morning sunlight slanted across the narrow valley. His fingers positively itched to tunnel through that shining, thick mass.

Gray turned away, snorting to himself. He headed down the path toward the one-story redbrick building not far away. The sign above the two main double glass doors read: Elk Horn Wildlife Center. He'd helped lay those bricks to create the building as well as the sidewalk he traversed. Glad to have his black nylon goose-down jacket on, he saw his breath turn white in the freezing air. The sky was a light blue, cloudless, and he loved this quiet time of the day.

His heart turned back to Skylar Pascal. Who was she? Iris had her résumé on her desk, but hadn't offered it to him. She'd interviewed ten people so far, and none had met her criteria. Iris was in her seventies and knew what she wanted.

She'd single-handedly built the Elk Horn into one of the most economically successful ranches in the valley. Iris was like a sweet, silver-haired grandmother to him. That nurturing exuded from her. Iris and her second husband, Timothy, along with her son, Rudd, and the rest of her family, ran the ranch.

Halting, Gray partly turned to see Skylar Pascal disappearing inside the office door. He wondered obliquely how her interview would fare with Iris Mason.

Iris had the skill of a SEAL when it came to ferreting out a person and looking behind their game face. That was one of the many things Gray liked about the woman. She saw far and deep into a person. She'd seen him, and he hadn't tried to hide who and what he was. He'd been a wounded military contractor who had lost his wife to Russian mafia drug runners in Peru two years ago. He'd been flown home physically wounded and emotionally devastated by the experience. And when he'd interviewed with Iris, she'd seen him, warts and all. Every question she'd asked, Gray answered truthfully and without hesitation. Iris liked his honesty. And she'd hired him on the spot.

Gray wondered what Iris would think of Skylar Pascal. She appeared elegant, beautiful and confident to him. But he knew from his twenty-nine years of living that looks were deceiving. Iris had a hunting-dog nose for people, for their foibles, their weaknesses and their strengths. She'd certainly dismantled him in a hurry during his interview. But Gray hadn't been threatened by Iris or her questions. And he had been a SEAL where one's honor, never telling a lie, worked in his favor during that two-hour interview with Iris.

As he wandered toward the center, Gray found himself wishing that Skylar Pascal would pass the test. He didn't know why. He really had wanted a male assistant, not a woman. But his desire was based upon a very brutal experience that would live with him until the day he died.

Iris had been rather upbeat about this woman coming in for the interview. She was an R.N., and Iris wanted someone with that degree here at the ranch. He found it synchronistic Julia had been an R.N., too. Shrugging, he put it all out of his mind. He had no say in who Iris hired or fired. He was just grateful she'd hired him because in doing so, Iris had given him his life back whether she knew it or not.

"THANKS FOR COMING," Iris said, gesturing for Skylar to sit down in front of her desk after shaking her hand. "Can I get you something to drink? Coffee? Tea?"

Sky sat down, placing the purse in her lap. Her heart was beating so hard she wondered if the older woman could hear it. "No, thank you. I'm fine."

"Just ate?" Iris asked, smiling briefly as she sat down.

"Yes, ma'am, I did." Well, it wasn't a lie. Sky had had coffee and some toast. It was all her tense, tight stomach would hold. When she got nervous like this, if she ate too much, she'd get sick. Not what she wanted to happen this morning.

Iris tilted her head and studied the woman. "Ma'am?" She tapped the résumé beneath her hand. "Must be your Navy training coming out?"

"Yes, ma'am," Sky murmured. She liked the maternal energy she felt around Iris Mason. The elder was about five feet five inches tall, with merry-looking blue eyes that missed nothing. Her silver hair was up in an askew knot on the top of her head. On the corner of the desk was a beat-up straw hat that she probably wore when outside.

"You don't need to call me 'ma'am.' Do you like to be called Skylar?"

"Actually, if you don't mind, most people call me Sky."

Iris nodded. "Pretty name, either way." She frowned and went over her résumé. At certain points, Iris had a red circle next to the item. "You were in the Navy after you graduated from college. What pushed you that direction, Sky?"

"My father had been in the Marine Corps for four years. He always talked enthusiastically about the military and how it made him a man." She shrugged, her hands damp on her purse. "I loved all his stories about the Marine Corps. I thought it would be a good fit." Sky tried to keep her voice low and even. Inwardly, she was taut with anxiety. Luckily, there were lots of windows and light around her. Sky couldn't stand closed-in places. It would send her into a full-blown panic attack. Or a dreaded flashback.

"So you did this out of duty to your country?"

"I wanted to be of service. My specialty is emergency-room medicine. I thought I could be of more help at the front lines." She shrugged a little shyly. "Maybe save some lives…"

Nodding, Iris said, "I like people who like to serve. Here on our ranch, we get six dude-ranch families in every week from June first to September first. I like people who want to help others." She squinted her eyes and studied Sky. "Did you get that service gene from your mother or your father?"

Sky tried to smile. "My mother."

"Tell me about her."

Sky felt suddenly exposed. Normally, interviews were straightforward and about only her job. Iris, however, seemed to have another agenda. Why? "My mother, Balin, is a full-blood Cheyenne. From the time I could remember, she taught me about generosity, being accountable and helping others. She has always been my role model."

Iris nodded. "Native Americans have a high ethical code, and you are lucky you have a mother like that to raise you in those traditions."

"Yes, Ms. Mason, I think so."

"Call me Iris," she said. "I don't stand much on ceremony around here. Okay?"

Sky relaxed slightly. "Of course, Iris."

Tapping the résumé with her pen, Iris said, "The job I'm looking to fill requires someone who is a multitasker of sorts, Sky. I need an R.N. here who can take care of bumps, bruises and scrapes our ranch guests get. I need a babysitter from time to time because some families bring in very young children. Even babies. And they need to be watched and cared for. Then there is my wildlife center. I need to hire an assistant to help Grayson McCoy, who runs it. That means cleaning up poop from the wild animals and doing any other dirty, grimy job that needs to be done. We have two timber wolves, for starters. Gray's mother, Isabel McCoy, is a world expert on wolf behavior. How are you around kids, babies and animals?"

Sky felt some of her tension bleed off. "I love children, Iris. Babies especially. And animals always lift my spirit."

"Good. What about playing nursemaid to the kids if they get a cut or bruise?"

"My E.R. background can take care of just about anything that comes up without any problem."

"Are you afraid to work around wild animals?"

*No. Just human animals.* Sky compressed her lips and shook her head. "I'm not afraid of animals, Iris."

"With your Native American blood, I'm guessing that nature and anything livin' in it would appeal to you?"

"I love being outdoors," Sky whispered, suddenly emotional. She felt the sting of tears in her eyes and forced them back. "I live to breathe fresh air, feel the wind on my face, the warmth of sun on my skin. I love all animals. I respect them." And in the two weeks she'd endured torture, it had been in a cold, damp, airless room without any windows.

"Thought you might," Iris said with a grin. "It's in your blood. In your bones."

"Yes," Sky said with a slight smile.

"How are you at getting along with men?"

The question startled Sky. She saw the bulldog set of Iris's expression. "Why…er…fine. I was in the military, and although I was a nurse, I worked around far more men than women without any problem."

"I see." Iris tapped the résumé. "If you were doing so well in the Navy, why'd you leave it, Sky?"

Her throat tightened. Her fingers clenched the leather purse in her lap. Sky was about to give her a standard, pat answer, but something warned her to be honest with Iris.

Was it because the woman was so nurturing and warm? "Well," she choked out, "I actually received an honorable medical discharge. I—I didn't want to leave the Navy, but I had to."

Iris sat up, studying her in the thickening silence. "Can you tell me why you received that kind of a discharge? Did you have some kind of health condition that wouldn't allow you to continue being a Navy nurse?"

Sky knew in her heart that the job was hers if she just came clean. There was something magical about Iris Mason. The feeling that she wouldn't hold the truth against her gave Sky the courage to answer her.

# CHAPTER TWO

SKY TOOK A deep breath. Iris was the only other person, besides her parents, that she would tell. Too afraid of judgment from others, Sky evaded and avoided the truth at every turn with everyone. Even her father, who had told her to grow up and take it like a man. She licked her lower lip, and the words came out in a strained whisper.

"I was in a helicopter crash and was one of the two survivors. I was then captured by the Taliban." Her brows dipped, and she closed her eyes for a moment, all the terrifying emotions welling up inside her as she brought it all back. "I—uh… I was tortured for two weeks before a SEAL rescue team found me." Lifting her head, Sky tried to steel herself for a reaction similar to her father's. Instead, she saw nothing but sympathy in Iris Mason's wrinkled face.

"I'm so sorry," Iris said, her voice heavy with regret. "Do you have any physical problems because of it?"

Sky shook her head. "No…none. I'm a hard worker, Iris. I love outdoor, physical work. It actually helps me.…"

Iris nodded, frowning and giving her a patient look. "It took a lot of courage to tell me this."

Her fingers knotted a frayed thread on the edge of her purse. "Yes, ma'am… I mean… Iris." Sky wanted to cry because Iris's reaction was the same as her mother's. It gave her the courage to look up and meet the elder's darkened gaze. "You should know," she went on, "that I have

PTSD. The six months I was at Balboa Naval Hospital I received therapy for it."

Iris nodded. "You'll be glad to know you have company here on the ranch. Gray McCoy, the man who runs my wildlife center, is an ex–Navy SEAL. He has PTSD, too."

Sky's eyes widened, and she stared over the desk at Iris. "Really?" He was in the military. In the Navy. She knew a lot about the SEALs because so often these operators were wounded in action and arrived at her E.R. at Bagram. They were true heroes in her eyes. Men made of flesh and bone with lions' hearts. She'd treated them over the years and had come to admire and respect them for their courage, their grit and toughness.

"Really," Iris murmured. "Can you still operate with people, around children and babies, with your PTSD?"

"Yes, I can."

"What can't you do?"

Sky liked her question. "I, um, don't do well in dark, enclosed spaces that have no fresh air."

"Crowds?"

Sky shrugged. "I don't like going into a movie or restaurant that's full of people."

"Would six dude-ranch families be too much for you to be around?"

"No." And Sky's mouth drew up a little. "Besides, I love kids. And babies. I never feel anxiety around them. Just…crowds."

"I like your honesty, Sky. It becomes you."

"Thank you. I feel as if I can trust you. I don't know why, but I do. I don't want to be hired without you knowing that…."

"I've got a small office in back," Iris said, pointing behind her. "I was thinking it could be used as a medical office."

"Does it have at least one window?"

She nodded. "Has two. That work for you?"

"Yes, that would work. Thank you."

"What kind of symptoms do you have, Sky?"

"Nightmares," she admitted, scowling. "I have them a lot, and I wake up screaming."

"Well, Gray and you have another thing in common—nightmares."

Sky almost felt as if she already knew this man. "I feel for him," she said. "I wouldn't wish this on anyone."

"Do you lose a lot of sleep because of it?"

"I get between three and five hours of sleep a night." Sky shrugged. "I'm a nurse, and I hate taking drugs. I refuse to take sleep medication. My mother told me a long time ago that dreams were a way of healing ourselves, and I believe her. If I take sleep meds, I don't dream. I guess I'd rather tough through the nightmares because sooner or later, the trauma will defuse itself through them, and I'll be free. I hope."

"You and I hate drugs," Iris murmured, amusement in her eyes. "I have no problem with you having nightmares and not wanting to take meds to knock you out."

"Good."

"Any other symptoms I should know about?"

"I get panic attacks if I'm in a small, dark room."

"What else?"

Sky bit down on her lower lip, her lashes sweeping downward. Iris was acting as if none of this bothered her. Was she really contemplating hiring her? How much should she divulge? Fear gnawed at her. "I get anxiety when I'm overly stressed."

"Can you give me an example of it, Sky?"

She lifted her lashes and raised her head. "I got hired at a hospital over in Casper when I got released from the

Navy. I found out very quickly I couldn't stand the constant stress of E.R. work like I had before. I get rattled, and I'm no longer cool, calm or collected in that circumstance."

"The stress level around here on a scale of 1 to 10 is a 3. Can you handle that?"

"Sure."

"Good," Iris said. She folded her hands and gave her a gentle look. "I like you, Sky. We try and hire vets around here. Vets have always been good for our ranch because they are hard workers who are responsible, and they're loyal. I see those same qualities in you. I'm okay with your PTSD. We have good health insurance for all our employees. Your wounding came from war. It changes a person sometimes permanently, but you know what? No one can steal your soul from you." She smiled a little. "I'd like to hire you, Sky. I think you'll be a fine addition to our growing staff. How about I take you around and show you our place, the dude-ranch portion, the medical office? After this we'll go over to the wildlife center and you can meet Gray, your boss. How does that sound?"

Sky's heart skittered briefly with joy. It was the first time since her torture that happiness had threaded through her dark depression. "Thank you, Iris. I'd love to come work for you, for the ranch."

Eyes twinkling, Iris slowly stood up and threw the old straw hat on her head. "Kinda thought this might be the perfect environment for you, Sky. You ready to check out your new digs?"

Was she? Euphoria, sweet and strong, soared through Sky. She sat there savoring the hope that came with it. Iris was smiling at her, kindness shining in her eyes. "More than ready, Iris."

"Come on," she urged, waving her hand toward the door.

"Hey, Iris, you wanted to see me?" Gray closed the screen door to the office. His boss was sitting behind her desk.

"Indeed I do. Come on in for a minute."

Gray removed his baseball cap and sat down in front of her desk.

"I'm sorry we missed you this morning. I just hired Sky Pascal. She's an R.N., and I was hoping to have her meet you at the wildlife center."

Gray grimaced. "Sorry. I had to run into town unexpectedly and pick up some supplies from the Horse Emporium."

Waving her hand, Iris said, "I understand. Anyway, we need to have a chat about our latest employee, who will be your assistant."

"Okay." Gray saw some darkness in Iris's normally bright, shining blue eyes.

Iris handed him the résumé. As Gray read through it, she shared the details from the interview she'd had with Sky. When she mentioned the PTSD, his head snapped up, his eyes narrowing intently on her.

"None of this is in her résumé," he said, handing it back to her.

"She came clean with me." And then Iris smiled faintly. "Just like you did during your interview with me."

Gray flashed her a wry look. "I like her already. She's honest."

"That's what I felt. It took a lot for her to discuss the situation with me. It was highly stressful on her."

"What caused her PTSD?" Gray knew nurses would sometimes be at forward operating bases, and they got shelled and attacked by the Taliban. That was enough to give anyone PTSD.

"She told me she was in a helicopter crash and then captured by the Taliban and tortured."

Instantly, Gray's brows went down. He felt suddenly protective of the woman he'd seen this morning. *"What?"* That blew him away.

"Yes," Iris said, going on in a low voice, "she said a SEAL team rescued her two weeks later. She spent six months at Balboa Naval Hospital after that. And then the Navy gave her an honorable medical discharge."

His knuckles whitened around the arms of the chair he sat in. Gut tightening, he felt sick about it. "She looked fine this morning," he muttered. "I saw her drive in and get out of her car."

Iris raised an eyebrow. "Looks are deceiving, Gray. You probably know that better than most of us because of your SEAL training."

Stunned by the information, Gray sat there, a host of raw, painful feelings twisting through his gut. "Yeah, I do know. But, Iris, this is rare. Rare for a woman to be captured and tortured. I mean, I've never heard of it while I was in."

"It was bound to happen," Iris said bluntly. "Women are serving in combat zones now. There are no lines of demarcation any longer."

"I don't deny that," Gray said, scowling. Sky Pascal had looked so clean, untouched and beautiful this morning. God, what must she have gone through? "Did she say what kind of torture?"

"No, and I didn't ask. I felt it was enough she told me. And it took everything for her to say it. She really struggled."

Nodding, Gray felt his throat close up. His mind clicked along at a million miles an hour. "Damn."

"Look, Sky knows you were a SEAL. I told her you two shared one thing in common—PTSD."

"Yeah, that's the truth," he admitted darkly.

"But I need to warn you she has nightmares. Told me she wakes up screaming from them."

His heart ached. For two years, Gray had been numb. Now he was filled with all kinds of emotions, as if his feelings were pulling out of their dormant state and coming to life once again. Reeling from the information, he rasped, "How often?"

"She said pretty often."

"It's still fresh in her," he said. "That's why."

"Last I heard, you were getting nightmares about once every couple of weeks."

"Yeah," he admitted. "But initially, especially the first year after the experience, a person can get nightmares three to six times a week. It's brutal, Iris."

"Guess that's the phase of healing she's in," Iris said. "You up to dealing with this? Because the employee house is where both of you will be living when you're not doing your eight hours of work around here."

"It won't be a problem," Gray assured her.

"Maybe you can be of support?"

"Sure." Pushing his fingers through his short brown hair, Gray added, "I can help, but damn, Iris, I'm not a psychotherapist. I could do more damage to her than help."

"You know," Iris drawled, sitting back in her chair, "the one thing age has taught me is if you come from the heart, it's never wrong. Keep that in mind, Gray. Love of a sister or brother human being is pure light and never damages, but heals." She wagged her finger at him. "I know you haven't practiced much love as a SEAL, but you have a heart, you have feelings, and I believe that you can be there to help Sky if she needs it. Don't you?"

Hell, he was already there, but he wasn't going to tell Iris. He grinned a little. "Yeah, I can do it."

"Good," Iris said gruffly. "I need you to go over with

your truck and pick her up at the Wyoming Inn, where she's staying. Pack up her stuff and bring her back here. She's taking the East bedroom. You've been assigned the West one. I'm going to leave it up to you to get her up to speed on stuff. Any problems, you come to me. Okay?"

"Yes, ma'am," Gray said, rising. He saw the bulldog set of Iris's mouth and knew she was invested in Sky. And why not? From what he'd seen from a distance, Sky was worth fighting for. Worth caring for. Worth protecting.

He could sense all those SEAL feelings coming to life once more within him. When Julia had been murdered in South America, because he'd been unable to protect her, he'd died, too, in a different way. Now he was like a grizzly coming out of winter hibernation, coming back into the light of day. The fact Sky had been tortured twisted him in an unexpected way.

Iris sat there watching him. "I know you're thinking of Julia," she said softly. "Maybe this is a way to help you along with closing that wound within yourself."

Wincing internally, Gray stood there absorbing Iris's words. He'd fallen in love with Julia. He had been a military contractor assigned to protect her. And a year later, when she'd been caught in a cross fire, she had thrown herself in front of him. Taken bullets meant for him, such was her love. The guilt he carried was like an elephant sitting on his chest all the time. To this day, he faulted himself. He and Julia were married, and she'd sacrificed her life for his. Gray's mouth flattened, and he slowly put the baseball cap on his head. "I don't know about that, Iris."

"It's just a thought," she said. "Now, skedaddle. Let me know when you have Sky here and acclimated. I'd like her to start day after tomorrow. Give her a ride around the ranch some morning."

"Roger," he said, leaving. Every time Julia's name was

brought up, it was like a branding iron savagely burned into his heart. The pain was insurmountable. The grief, equally serrating. As he took the wooden steps down to the lawn surrounding the building, he scowled. So far, he'd stuffed all his feelings into his kill box regarding Julia's murder. SEALs learned to completely bury their emotions, leaving them clear-minded and free of distraction so they could operate efficiently. Emotions brought murkiness, indecision and hesitation. It could be a deadly distraction. Unsecured emotions could get a SEAL killed.

A SOFT KNOCK came at Sky's hotel door shortly after lunch. She had opened up her suitcase, packed her toiletries and was getting ready to leave. She looked through the peephole.

A man with a weather-hardened face, his hazel eyes large and intelligent, stood relaxed at the door. Sky had seen him briefly the morning of her interview. Remembering Iris had said she'd send one of her wranglers to help her pack and get to the grocery store, she opened it.

The man wore a black baseball hat, the SEAL symbol embroidered in gold on the front of it. Her heart picked up in beat. He was built like all the other SEALs she'd ever seen at the E.R., lean, hard muscle. Not muscle-bound. She saw the creases at the corners of his eyes, telling her he'd spent a lot of time out in the elements. He had a square face, a nose that had been broken at least once, a scar that ran along the left side of his jaw. His eyes were narrowed upon her, and she could feel him instantly begin to catalog her; that was what SEALs did. They left no stone unturned.

SEALs reminded her of a primal animal in his element of raw survival.

"Ms. Pascal?" he asked in a low voice.

Her gaze moved down his arms. He wore a blue chambray shirt, the sleeves rolled up to just below his elbows. His arms were darkly haired, his hands large, fingers long and capable. She gulped. "Yes. Did Iris send you?"

"Yes, ma'am. I'm Grayson McCoy. I run the wildlife center for Iris." He saw how pale she'd become, her gaze showing her uncertainty. Wanting to put her at ease, not place her on terror alert, he forced a slight smile. "Iris asked me to come over and help you out. I'll take you to the grocery store and anywhere else you might want to go to before you move into the employee house this afternoon."

Her fingers went to her throat. Sky could feel her pulse bounding beneath her fingertips. That was how much this man, this SEAL, affected her. When the corners of his mouth drew up, his game face dissolved. He looked approachable, human. "That would be nice. Thank you, Mr. McCoy."

"Call me Gray. I'm not much on protocol, either," he said. The change in Sky was stunning. Color rushed back to her cheeks. He liked her long, narrow hands. Seeing her pulse on the side of her slender neck, Gray found himself wanting to explore her as a woman. Sky Pascal was a looker. If he'd thought she was beautiful from a distance, she was exquisite now. "Can I help you pack or carry your suitcase down to your car, Ms. Pascal?"

Flustered, Sky saw the intense look he gave her. She might be all of twenty-six, but she knew when a man was appreciating her as a woman. For a moment, she was tongue-tied, which wasn't like her at all before her capture. Since then, broken psychologically by the torture, she'd become shy and unsure of herself, her old self murdered by the Taliban. "Just call me Sky." She stepped aside and gestured him into the well-appointed room. "I have one suitcase."

Gray nodded deferentially and entered the room, feeling the woman's nervousness. She wore the same pantsuit, looking quietly elegant. He watched as she quickly closed the door, noting her hands trembled. Purposely backing up so he wasn't crowding her, Gray couldn't stop liking what he saw. The sunlight was pouring into the window, and her ginger hair shone with gold and red highlights. It swung clean and shining across her shoulders. "Iris said she'd have me pay for the room. She doesn't want you paying for it."

"That was very kind of her. Thank you." Her heart was going crazy in her chest. Gray McCoy reminded her of a lethal snow leopard, never hearing him come until it was too late. He had that distinctive SEAL walk, one of complete silence. Sky hadn't been interested in a man for a long time. Now her body was behaving as if it had a mind of its own. She could feel her breasts tightening, feeling the heat of his gaze.

What was wrong with her? Was the stress too much? And yet, Sky didn't feel anxious. Oddly, she felt protected by Gray. It was a sense, an energy. Nothing overt or obvious. Maybe it was the care she saw burning in his hazel eyes that missed nothing. She noticed how he gentled his tone of voice, as if dealing with a hyper wild horse. On some days, that was exactly how Sky felt. Bad days. On good ones, she was emotionally stable. *But not today.*

"Here," he said, stepping forward, placing his hand around the handle of the suitcase, his chest barely brushing her shoulder, "let me get that for you."

Sky stepped out of the way, her shoulder tingling wildly in the wake of Gray accidentally brushing against her. He smelled of sunshine, pine and a hint of sage that grew so prolifically in other parts of Wyoming. A man's smell. Masculine. It made her ache. Sky hadn't felt sexual in such a long time. She'd thought the capture had killed her femininity. Apparently not. At least, not with Gray McCoy, who stood patiently waiting with her suitcase in his hand. As a nurse, she was good at small talk. Now words just jammed up in her throat, and she couldn't get anything out of her mouth. Sky missed that ability because in the past, she'd been able to gently communicate with men who were in excruciating pain and calm them with her voice and touch.

Picking up her purse, she said, "I'm ready." When he smiled a little, one corner of his mouth hooking upward, his green, gold and brown eyes soothing, she felt a sheet of heat wind through her like a warm spring day.

Gray opened the door and stepped out, holding it for her. "Do you, by the way, have any jeans or work clothes with you?"

"I don't."

"No worries," he assured her, shutting the door. "We'll stop by the Horse Emporium on the way out of town. They have men's and women's work clothes. Iris wants you to start the day after tomorrow at 9:00 a.m." He looked down at her. "That work for you?"

"Yes."

Gray saw her hesitate, sort of looking like a deer in headlights, paralyzed. He knew PTSD could do it to a person when they were becoming overwhelmed with too much information, and they couldn't process it as quickly as other people. "What would you like to do first?" He knew how important it was to hand back the control to her. It would ease her anxiety.

Sky gave him a look of apology. "I'm sorry. I'm just stressed. I wasn't really thinking I'd get the job."

Gray smiled. "Iris knows what she wants. And she likes you a lot. Had nothing but praise for you when she told me she hired you." He watched her begin to relax, some of the tension leaving her face. Did Sky know how beautiful she was? Was she in a relationship? Iris never said.

"Thanks for understanding."

"Follow me," Gray urged quietly, heading down the hall toward the elevator.

Sky felt pleasure watching this man walk with such silent grace. The breadth of his shoulders, his well-sprung chest narrowing into a flat, hard belly and narrow hips. The Levi's hugged his long, thick thighs, telling her he spent a great deal of time in the saddle. As they waited for the elevator, she said, "Iris mentioned you were in the Navy like me."

"I was a SEAL."

"What team?"

"ST3." He angled his head to see if she understood the terminology.

"I patched up a few ST3 operators the years I was at Bagram," she said softly.

"You never saw me," he said wryly, holding open the elevator door for her to enter first. "In a way, now I'm sorry you didn't."

"No, I never saw you in my E.R.," she noted wryly. There was something about Gray McCoy that was allowing her to relax for the first time since being released from the hospital. Maybe it was his easygoing way, the warmth and care she saw burning in his eyes toward her. Or? Again, she felt him silently appreciating her as a woman. It lifted her spirits. Sky swore masculine heat radiated off his body. And she felt she could trust him. Maybe because he was an ex-SEAL? Her experiences with them had always been positive in the past. Why not now?

# *CHAPTER THREE*

SKY WORRIED THAT Gray McCoy would ask her too many questions about her stint in the Navy. But to her relief, he didn't say another word. He was quiet as he drove her over in his truck to Albertson's, the main grocery store for Jackson Hole. They would pick up her SUV at the inn afterward. He walked quietly behind her, reminding her of a guard dog watching over his mistress. She pushed the cart around, gathering the food for her dinners. Like a silent shadow, he wasn't one for small talk, but then, SEALs were a very closed-mouth bunch anyway. As she went to the vegetable section, Sky saw Gray's face grow amused.

"Are you vegan?" he wondered, watching her put a lot of green stuff into her cart.

"No. Why?"

Shrugging amiably, Gray enjoyed watching Sky's grace as she moved. He liked following her, the sway of her hips inciting a cauldron of heat in his lower body. She had healing hands with long, tapered fingers. "Employees have a house on the ranch. There's a full kitchen, living room, an office with a computer, and there's two bathrooms. Since I was the only one living there, I made meals every night." He gave her a hopeful look. "I was going to ask if you wanted to cook, and then I'd take the next night and make us a meal."

Sky laughed a little. It felt so good to laugh! "Let's see if I'm following this. You're afraid I'm going to make rabbit food when you're a strapping wrangler who's wanting a beefsteak instead?"

God, she looked incredibly desirable when she smiled. Really smiled. A smile that went straight into those shining dark blue eyes with huge black pupils. Those ginger lashes were long and emphasized the cobalt color of her eyes. Gray had the good grace to look down at his dusty boots for a moment. When he lifted his head, his mouth twitched with a smile. "You're pretty good. Is that your nurse's radar in action? Reading a patient?"

A surge of joy tunneled through Sky as she basked in the sunlight of his masculine smile. He'd hooked his thumbs into the pockets of his Levi's, standing with his weight on one boot. He was comfortable in his skin as a man. And he was comfortable with who he was. "It's nurse's radar for sure. Was I right?"

"Yes, you were."

"What do you like to eat?"

"Meat and potatoes. A salad is okay, too."

"Where were you born, Gray?" It was the first time she'd said his name, and it rolled off her tongue like a delicious chocolate. Sky liked the sound of his name. It fit him. Gray was a color that was neutral, a combination of black and white. His dark side was as a shadow warrior in black ops. His light side? Did he have one? Sky thought he did. In time, perhaps he would reveal that side of himself to her.

"Cheyenne, Wyoming."

"Ah, the capital of the limited palate?"

He grinned a little. "Guilty as charged."

Sky leaned against the cart and studied Gray openly for the first time. He didn't seem to mind her looking him over. His cheeks had turned ruddy even beneath his deep tan. There was a little boy hidden in this man's body; she could feel it. Sky bet he had a little boy's awe of the world and that it was magical. Maybe she'd find out later. "I'm kind of a garbage-can eater," she confided. "I'll eat just about anything."

"Where were you born?" he teased.

Laughing softly, Sky said, "Casper, Wyoming."

"Vegan city?"

"Not really. My mother's full-blood Cheyenne, and I was raised on venison and buffalo for the most part. That and a lot of trout. My father is a gourmet chef when he gets in the mood, and growing up, he taught me about spices, sauces and gravies."

"Gravy is definitely something I could get used to."

"Figures. Meat, potatoes and gravy kind of guy."

His straight, dark brows rose. "Is there anything else?"

Sky shook her head and gave him a sour grin. "I don't mind cooking dinner every other night. The real question is, will you eat what I make or starve?"

"I won't starve," Gray assured her. "I probably don't have a gourmet gene in my body, but I'll do my best. My mother always said when food is cooked with love, it always tastes good."

"I like your can-do spirit," Sky teased. "Are you open to Chinese?"

"Sure, as long as there's some meat with it."

"Middle Eastern food?" Because it was a favorite of hers. His smile deepened.

"Yeah, I like lamb, couscous and stuff like that."

"See? This isn't going to be a food nightmare for you like you thought."

Gray enjoyed their repartee. "What's that bok choy you just grabbed used for?"

"It's for wonton soup. The Chinese version of chicken soup. You'll love it."

"As long as it has a healthy amount of meat in it, I'll survive."

Sky smiled and continued down the row of vegetables. "Lots of chicken," she promised.

"Gray!"

A woman's voice floated over the veggie department, and Sky stopped the cart, looking in that direction. A red-haired woman in her early thirties smiled and came their way. Sky saw that she was decidedly pregnant.

"Hey, Val, good to see you," Gray greeted her warmly, grinning as she walked over with her arms full of plastic vegetable sacks.

Val nodded. "Who is this, Gray?" And then she got devilry in her green eyes. "Your new girlfriend?"

Sky felt her cheeks go red hot.

Gray winced. "No. Val McPherson, meet Sky Pascal. Iris just hired her today to be my assistant. She's also an R.N. and will be setting up a small medical office at the ranch."

"Hey, Sky, welcome to Jackson Hole," Val said, shifting all the veggies to one arm and thrusting her hand out toward her.

"Here..." Gray muttered. "Let me..." He took all the sacks from Val.

"Hi," Sky said, liking the woman immediately. "How far along are you?"

Val looked over her shoulder and watched as what had to be her husband rounded the corner. She waved him to come over. He had the cart. Turning, Val placed her hands on her swollen belly. "Seven months and counting."

"That's wonderful," Sky sighed.

"It is now," Val griped. "Morning sickness sucked, I've got to tell you."

Laughing, Sky nodded. "Yeah, it's a real pain. Are you going to have a home birth or go to the hospital?"

Val raised her brows. "I want a home birth, but my husband here—" she grabbed the man's hand and drew him to her side "—is scared out of his mind I'll end up dying at home trying to give birth. Griff? This is Sky Pascal. She's an R.N. and will be working at the Elk Horn Ranch."

Griff doffed his gray Stetson. "Nice to meet you, Sky. You say you're an R.N.?"

"She is," Gray said, reaching over and shaking Griff's hand.

Val grabbed Sky's arm. "Listen, I'm all ears. What's your speciality as an R.N.?"

"Oh, I wasn't in obstetrics. I was an E.R. nurse. Sorry."

"Well, no matter. Did you ever deliver any babies?"

Gray watched Sky's face light up with unabashed joy.

"Yes, I've delivered about forty babies while I was over in Afghanistan."

Val blinked. "You're military?"

"Was," Sky admitted.

"I was in the Air Force. An intel officer."

"I was a first lieutenant in the Navy."

Griff looked at all of them. "Now I'm feeling left out. I'm the only one here who hasn't been in the service."

Gray patted his shoulder. "You'll get over it, Griff." And the two men traded grins.

Val patted Sky's hand. "Listen, we *must* get together. Okay? We'll do lunch over at Mo's Ice Cream Parlor. Best food in town. I'd love to hear about your military experiences."

Sky's smile faded a little. "I'd love to, Val. Maybe when I get my feet under me with my new job over at the ranch?"

"Of course," Val said. She gave Gray a teasing look

and then whispered in her ear so everyone couldn't hear, "He's single...."

Sky wanted to melt into the floor and disappear. "I figured he was since he's living at the employee house like I am," she said.

Val nodded sagely. "You two would make a lovely couple. Well, gotta run! I'm going to be late for my ob-gyn's appointment if I don't get these veggies to the cash register. Gray, see you later." And then Val gave him an evil look. "And you be nice to Sky. No pranks."

Gray managed to look puzzled at her assumption. "Yes, ma'am," he teased back, leaning down and giving Val a swift kiss on the cheek. As Gray straightened, he patted Griff on the back. "Hang in there, McPherson. Two more months..."

Sky watched the warm and affectionate banter among the three of them. Gray's guard had gone down when Val and Griff arrived. They were clearly good friends. She hoped Gray would be that relaxed around her, one day soon. When he looked at her, she felt as giddy as a teenage girl swooning over the football captain who gave her a glance.

Sky wasn't sure what was going on, so many different impressions hitting her. With the PTSD, every sense was heightened, even her intuition. It was almost too much busy activity with Val coming in like a tornado out of nowhere. She saw Gray's smile dissolve and concern appear in his darkening hazel eyes that turned more brown in color.

"You okay?"

Sky collected herself and said, "Yes."

"Iris said you had PTSD like me."

Her stomach tightened. "Uh, yes, I do." *Please, God, don't let him ask me anything about it. Please...*

"Val is high energy," Gray told her in a quiet tone.

"And people with PTSD feel like they've been blasted by a bomb around a person like that. You're looking a little exhausted."

Rattled by his insight, Sky grimaced. "God, am I *that* readable? I hope Val didn't notice. I really like her, and she was very nice."

Without thinking, Gray placed a thick strand of hair behind her ear. It had been an unthinking reaction. An intimate act between a man and woman. He cursed himself because no woman had drawn him out like this since Julia. What was it about Sky that invited his touch? His fingers fairly itched to feel that thick, loose, shining hair of hers. He wanted to smell it, run the strands against his cheek and feel the silkiness of it, of her. He saw the shocked response in her expression after his hand fell to his side. Her eyes went huge, and her lush lips parted.

"Sorry," he muttered, frowning. "It won't happen again."

Sky's ear tingled in the wake of his touch. Her heart was thudding in her chest. Her lower body flexed. Sky knew what that meant. Before her capture, she'd had two other healthy relationships in her life. She enjoyed sex immensely and had grieved over the loss of it later.

The look in Gray's eyes had warmed as he'd caught the strand on his finger and eased it behind her ear. She felt him wanting her. Man to woman. And he looked properly sorry that he'd done it when she'd overreacted to his gesture.

"No," Sky whispered quickly, "it's not you, Gray. It's me. I'm just jumpy when someone makes a fast move toward me with their hand."

Now Gray felt like a jerk. *She was tortured, you asshole.* He had no idea what had been done to Sky. He had to be careful with her.

"Listen," he said, holding her gaze, "I am really sorry, Sky. I didn't think. I'll try and watch myself so I don't accidentally scare the hell out of you."

"No…it's me. It's okay. I—I just have to learn to not overreact like this, that's all."

Nodding, Gray forced a slight smile to help her defuse her wariness. Sky was so readable, unlike SEALs, who had the best poker faces in the world. "You got a deal." He had no desire to push her about her experience. In time, maybe she'd trust him enough with that volatile and terrifying ordeal. Until then, he was going to try to make damn sure he never startled her as he just had. "So," he said, trying to sound light and teasing, "do you have enough vegetables now? The fridge is only so big."

Sky managed a slight smile. "Yes, I'm done shopping."

"Would you like a bouquet of flowers?" Gray wondered as they walked toward the front of the store. "Kind of a welcome to Elk Horn Ranch?" He noticed how she gazed longingly toward the area where the bouquets were kept.

"No…not right now. I'm really short on cash at the moment. Maybe in a few weeks."

Gray cursed silently. He was like a bull in a china shop with her. If she was looking for a job, she probably had very little money, if any, to live on. "Well," he told her sternly, pulling out his wallet, "you're not paying for any of this."

"But—"

Gray flashed her a dark look. "Listen, consider this a celebration gift that you got a job." He slid the bills into her hand and said, "I'll be right back."

Shocked again over his generosity, Sky had purposely chosen only rice, beans and vegetables because she couldn't afford expensive meat. She had only twenty dollars left to her name. And a maxed-out credit card. As she got in line at the cash register, she watched Gray walk into the flower section. He moved through the pails of flowers like a cougar hunting prey. Finally, he chose a large bouquet and turned, walking toward her. The look on his face showed her he had his game face on once again. As he drew closer, however, the hardness in his eyes thawed, and she saw that gold-and-green warmth shining in them again. For her.

"What do you think?" he asked, handing her the bouquet.

Sky was dazzled. The flowers were pink and white oriental lilies, yellow Asian lilies, fragrant white roses and red Gerbera daisies. Seeing the price, she said, "They're beautiful, Gray, but they cost too much."

"I'm buying," he informed her. "Do you like them?" He held her upturned gaze. Her mouth was driving him crazy. Her lips were full, soft, and God, he wanted to taste them beneath his mouth.

"Are you sure?" Because since being discharged by the hospital, she'd not been able to keep a job, and her nest egg was dwindling away as she had to buy a car to get around in, pay for insurance and buy food.

"Listen, you've been going through a rough patch. The least I can do is something that will bring that beautiful look to your eyes." He lowered his voice, and it turned gritty and intimate. "I want to see you smile again, Sky."

Their last stop was the Horse Emporium. Gray introduced her to Andy, the owner. It was a busy place where ranchers bought their hay, straw and grain. Sky found the women's section in the clothing area of the main store. Gray was shooting the breeze with Andy at the counter, catching up on what was going on in the valley.

She looked at the price tags on the sale jeans. She simply didn't have the money. Feeling shame, Sky worried her lower lip. Gray had already sprung for food, and she wasn't about to ask him for any more money. Nor did she expect him to pay for her needs. She'd just have to wait.

"Problem?"

Sky sucked in a quick breath, hearing Gray's low voice nearby. She snapped her head up, and he was standing across from where the women's jeans were hung on the rack. "You scared the hell out of me!" she whispered, giving him a distraught look. Blinking, Sky placed her hand against her throat, trying to control her reaction.

"Bad habit," he said apologetically. Gray looked toward the counter. "I saw you standing over here, and you looked upset." He met her wide, fearful gaze. "I'll make you a loan so you can buy what you need, Sky." He held up his hand when she started to protest. "Look, we all need help every once in a while." He dug into his wallet. "I'll put it on the credit card. It won't be due for thirty days. Iris pays us every two weeks, so you can easily pay me back." Gray searched her tense features. "Okay?" He said it softly. With understanding.

He watched as she battled back tears. Gray cursed inwardly. He was a sucker for any kid or woman who cried. Sky had turned away, taking a sharp swipe at her eyes. Moving around the rack, Gray gently laid his hands on her tense shoulders, not wanting to scare her again.

"Sky, it's okay. What are friends for? If we can't help one another out in bad times, what does that make us?" He gently turned her around, her eyes downcast, her hands knotted against her heart, knuckles white.

"I—I've just never been this poor," she uttered, unable to look at Gray. His hands were so warm and large on her shoulders. They felt good. Steadying. When he laid his hands on her, a soothing calm overtook Sky. "I—I just don't know how to thank you, Gray."

"You can pay me back by buying everything you need, Sky. I make a very good salary, and I'm not hurting for money, so use it. Okay?"

Sky wished she wasn't so emotional. It just wasn't like her. All her calm, cool collectedness was gone now, it seemed. In its place were razor-sharp emotions, many of them tearing her inwardly apart. She felt Gray's care, his strength and something else. Something she couldn't define even though she wanted to. His mouth was so strong, and his lips were pulled into a faint smile. The tenderness he exhibited surprised her. She just wasn't used to someone caring for her like this.

"Okay," she said, her voice strained. "I'll pay back every penny. I promise."

"I have no doubt, Sky. So, go ahead and buy what you need." Damn, he wanted to touch Sky everywhere. He wanted to smell her, taste her, touch her, love her. Gray knew he could give Sky the security he knew had been destroyed within her by the torture. And God help him, his protectiveness was at an all-time high with her. He'd confront anyone who got near her with any intent to harm her. That was the SEAL in him, a part of him that would always exist regardless of whether he was out in the civilian world or not. Once a SEAL, always a SEAL.

EXHAUSTION WAS LAPPING at Sky as she got to see her new home. Gray unlocked the employees' house, a two-story redbrick building with a dark green painted metal roof. Her bedroom was amazing. The East bedroom, as Iris called it, reminded Sky of the 1930s era. A rainbow quilt lay over the queen-size bed. There were brass head-and footboards, as well. The furniture was all handmade out of walnut. An air of femininity permeated the room. The cream-colored walls reflected ample light, and Sky loved it. The room was so large it contained even enough space for a desk, chair and stained-glass lamp.

Gray helped carry all her purchases from the Horse Emporium into her bedroom. And then he placed all her groceries into the fridge or the large pantry. As Sky quietly shut the door, she felt weary. It had been a long, stressful day. She didn't even have the energy to put all her jeans and other clothing items away. All she wanted to do was lie down on that heavenly bed. And she did, promptly falling asleep.

WHEN GRAY QUIETLY opened Sky's bedroom door at 6:00 p.m., he saw that she was still sleeping. His heart lurched in his chest as he saw how fragile she appeared on the large bed, her hand near her cheek as she slept on her side. It hurt to see she had drawn her body up into a fetal position of protection.

Mouth thinning, he closed the door and walked down the hall to the kitchen. He would make dinner for them tonight. He'd just returned from talking with Iris and giving her feedback on Sky's lack of money. Tomorrow Iris was going to advance her two weeks' pay, and that would help de-stress Sky to a degree.

Gray knew she liked salads. He liked meat. Deciding to bake some chicken breasts, he noodled through all the veggies and chose the ones he recognized. A chef he was not. But he could make Sky a nice salad to go with the baked chicken. He also knew how to make rice, so that would be in the mix, too.

Unable to explain the happiness filtering through him as he focused on the food, Gray realized it was because Sky had unexpectedly walked into his life. As he worked, he kept one ear keyed on the hall for a door opening. How long would Sky sleep? No one understood the tentacles of PTSD unless they'd experienced it themselves.

His mind flew from one terrible atrocity that had been done to her to another. When he'd appeared quietly in front of her at the Horse Emporium, she'd nearly lost her composure. Cobbling together all her actions and reactions, Gray had seen recent pink scars around each of her wrists. Granted, he knew the Taliban often skinned an enemy alive, cutting and pulling an inch of skin off the back or front of their body each day. The victim eventually bled to death or had a massive infection, and sepsis killed them. He'd not seen any scars along Sky's shoulders. She'd worn a blouse that he could look beneath just enough to see her shoulders were clear of any scarring.

His brows fell, and his mouth compressed as he ran through torture procedures. As a SEAL, he'd gone through SERE—Survival, Evasion, Resistance and Escape—and had every kind of torture experience.

He poured the brown rice into a long Pyrex dish and added water. As he picked up the chicken breasts, his hand halted with the meat midway to the dish.

*No, can't be! No fucking way!*

Gray turned, staring down the hall, his heart picking up in heavy beat. A SEAL could control his physical body unlike any other person on the face of the earth. When he was on a mission, his heart rate was slow, his blood pressure normal even though danger and threat surrounded him and his team. But now, as he stared down the dimly lit hall that led to the bedrooms, he felt nausea. And terror.

*It can't be. It just can't be...*

Hissing a curse, Gray placed the chicken breasts into the rice and then covered it with a piece of foil. Washing his hands with soap and water, Gray slowly dried them off, not wanting to admit that he knew without ever being told what kind of torture Sky had endured.

She'd been waterboarded. The scars on her wrists verified it. A person was laid on their back on a wooden board the length of their body, their wrists and ankles manacled to hold them down. The board was canted slightly, so a person's head was below their chest. A strap was then placed across their brow so they couldn't move their head as the water was poured slowly into their nostrils. The terror of drowning made them panic and jerk at the restraints, causing deep scarring. And Sky's wrists proved it to Gray. He cursed beneath his breath, wanting to vomit.

## CHAPTER FOUR

GRAY TRIED TO put a choke chain on his emotions when Sky sleepily appeared down the hall near 7:00 p.m. His anger had simmered nonstop when he put the pieces of her torture together. Waterboarding broke a person psychologically and emotionally. And it didn't take long to do it.

As he moved the dinner plates and flatware to the oak table in the dining room, he savagely stuffed all his feelings into his kill box. Until he could verify what he thought was true, Gray could only conjecture. And looking at Sky's drowsy features, her hair mussed around her face, she appeared damned fragile. Too fragile to talk about something he knew was terrifying for her.

"Hey," he called, laying out the flatware, "did you have a good nap?"

Sky yawned and rubbed her face as she walked toward the open area that housed the kitchen, dining room and living room. The cathedral ceiling made the place feel airy and large.

"I did, thanks. Sorry I slept so long. Something smells good." She halted at the edge of the kitchen where Gray was working. Her mind was spongy. It had been so long since she'd slept so deeply and without interruption. They'd returned from town at 2:00 p.m. Looking at the clock up on the wall, Sky realized she'd slept a solid five hours.

"I threw together what I know," Gray warned her with

an amused look, pulling out the salad dressing from the fridge. He handed it to her. "I even made you a salad."

Touched, Sky took the bottle of dressing. Their fingers briefly met. Warmth sheeted up her hand and into her arm. There was just something calm and soothing about being around Gray. He moved with a masculine grace around the galley kitchen. Sky couldn't take her gaze off him. He was handsome in a rugged kind of way, his face hard and weathered by working outdoors as a SEAL. "This will do fine," she said, turning and taking it to the table.

"You have good timing," he said, putting on the oven mitts that were really too small for his large hands. Opening the oven, he drew out the chicken-and-rice dish.

"I guess I do. Can I help you at all? Get some water or something to drink with our meal?"

"Nah, I'll get it. Why don't you take a seat? My turn to serve you." He set the dish on a trivet in the center of the rectangular table. Gray had put one plate at one end of the table and the other plate to the right of it. He wanted Sky close, not far away from him. He watched as she chose the seat on the side of the table. Her movements were slow, and he could see how cloudy her eyes were from the sleep. *Good sleep. Badly needed sleep.* Gray was always grateful when he could sleep without nightmares. At least Sky hadn't had one yet.

Sky pulled the white linen napkin and placed it across her lap. If nothing else, Gray was quick and efficient. In no time, he'd put the steaming, delicious-smelling dish in front of her. He got rid of the oven mitts, dropping them on the granite counter, and pulled her salad from the fridge.

Sitting down, Gray placed the bowl near her plate. Her eyes widened a little as she stared at it.

"Is something wrong?"

She smiled a little. "That's a huge salad, Gray. I'm not

sure I can eat all of it." Moved by his thoughtfulness, Sky saw he'd sprinkled tomatoes, sliced carrots and celery across the top of the greens.

"You're underweight," he growled, slipping a chicken breast onto his plate. He gave her one, as well.

"I just don't have much appetite," Sky protested, apology in her voice. She eyed the chicken breast and then spooned the fluffy brown rice onto her plate. It all smelled so good, though. She was wildly aware of how close she was to Gray. He wasn't wearing his game face, either, and that helped her relax. She watched him enthusiastically dig into the meal and wished her appetite would return.

"Eat what you can," Gray urged her gently. "In time, your PTSD symptoms will start to lessen, and you'll be a little more hungry." He saw the stressed look on her face as she stared at all the food on her plate.

"It hasn't been that long," Sky admitted, picking up the fork and knife, cutting into the juicy chicken breast. "I have good days and bad days."

"That's to be expected. You're in the primary healing phase right now." Gray wanted to change topics, give Sky something to look forward to. "We're going to be riding a half a day, starting tomorrow morning," he said. "Iris wants me to take you around the ranch and start getting you acquainted with the property."

Maybe that would urge Sky to eat. When her eyes widened, he felt himself go hot with longing. Much to his chagrin, he felt himself growing hard. What a helluva situation. Gray forced control over himself. His desire for her wasn't smart under the circumstances, yet this was the first time since losing Julia that he was actually interested in another woman sexually. Hell, this was going to be tougher than he'd anticipated being around Sky. After her ordeal, she wouldn't be thinking about him in that way. Not at all.

"Seriously? Horseback riding?" Her heart opened with excitement.

"Yep," Gray said, noticing she was beginning to eat. "You need to get the layout of the ranch. Then we'll be back by lunch, and I'll give you the grand tour of the wildlife center I run."

"This sounds like a dream," Sky said softly.

*You're a dream.* But Gray kept the comment to himself, forcing himself to pay attention to his dinner and not Sky. Her cheeks had become infused with a pink color. Her eyes were such dark blue pools. Gray felt as if he could drown in them. And in her. His body was going crazy, and he wasn't thinking clearly around Sky. *Why?*

"I think you've got the best job in the world," Sky said. "You work with animals."

He smiled a little, hearing the breathy quality of her voice. "My mother is a world expert of wolves. She's got a degree in wildlife biology. I was raised around wolves and all kinds of other North American animals while growing up. She's the one who suggested I try out for the job a year ago. I was lucky enough to get it."

"What a charmed childhood," she sighed.

"I was very lucky," Gray agreed. He watched her begin to relax. The tension disappeared from the skin across her broad cheekbones, her Native American heritage on display. He found himself like a thief, wanting to absorb her into him. Sky's blue eyes were slightly tilted, giving her an exotic or mysterious look. "What about you, Sky? Tell me about your parents."

"My mother stays at home. She has a small cottage business and creates one-of-a-kind gorgeous elk-and deerskin bags. She beads them." Sky turned pensive. "She taught me to bead when I was about ten years old. She makes incredibly intricate flower designs."

"And your father?" Gray saw her enthusiasm wane a little.

"My father was in the Marine Corps for four years. When he got out, he went to cooking school for four years and became a chef. Then he came back here to Wyoming and met my mom."

"I'll bet he was proud of your Navy service."

Shrugging, Sky picked at her salad. "I guess."

"Was he unhappy you didn't join the Marine Corps instead?" There was a lot of challenge and testing between the Navy and the Corps.

"No, not really."

Gray frowned. "You look sad, Sky."

"I must be really easy to read." She cut him a glance. When his mouth curved faintly, all she could think about in that moment was gently touching that full lower lip of his and exploring it with her index finger. Gray had a beautiful mouth. And her instinct told her he would be a good kisser.

"SEAL intuition at work," Gray teased, wanting to keep her relaxed and open. "Was I wrong?"

Shaking her head, Sky muttered, "No."

"I imagine your parents were beside themselves when they found out you'd been captured." He saw her brows dip, her fork suspended in midair for a moment.

"Yes, I found out later after they transferred me back stateside, and I could talk to them via phone, that they had been sick with worry."

"Were they able to come out and visit you while you were recovering in the hospital?" Gray had been wounded before and knew how boring and lonely it was to be in a hospital half a globe away from his family.

"I—I didn't encourage them to come and see me at Balboa Naval Hospital." She gave a small shrug. "I was an emotional basket case, Gray. I just wasn't myself... I felt so out of control."

Sky was closing up on him. Though he wanted to reach out and touch her, give her some care, Gray forced his hands to remain right where they were. Time to switch topics. "The first time I got wounded," Gray confided quietly, "I woke up and found myself at Landstuhl Regional Medical Center in Germany."

"Gunshot wound?" Sky winced inwardly when he nodded. Gray seemed so strong and vital, as if nothing could harm him. Yet as she saw the darker brown in his eyes, she began to understand that when he was emotionally upset about something, that color was more prominent.

"Yeah." Gray finished off his chicken breast and the rest of the rice. Pushing the plate aside, he said, "I was with a good team. Kell Ballard was the lead petty officer. We were going in to rescue an American doctor who'd gotten kidnapped by the Taliban. It was a night mission, and I took a bullet to the left arm during the op. Kell saved my life. I was bleeding like a stuck hog from a torn artery, and he got a tourniquet around my arm. I don't remember much after that, passing out."

Taking in a slow, ragged breath, Sky understood those types of wounds. "I saw my fair share of them at Bagram." She lifted her gaze and held his turbulent-looking eyes. "Do you have any residual issues from the wound?"

"No, not enough to get me medically discharged from the Navy," he admitted.

"Did you like being a SEAL?"

"I liked being a shooter, and I was good at what I did." He didn't want to go any further with his life as a SEAL. Gray patted his thigh. "Later, I took another bullet. It took out fifty percent of my femur in the area where it struck. Even though I healed up, my leg was never going to be as strong as before and take the weight and beating it could before. My days with the SEALs were over at that point."

"I'm so sorry," Sky whispered, seeing the sadness in his eyes. "SEALs are special. They're a tight group of men. I'm sure your platoon were like brothers to you."

"They still are," Gray said, always feeling the loss. "We stay in touch with one another to this day."

Sky began to eat again. "So, you've been out for just a year? After being discharged, you got the job here?"

It was his turn to feel under a microscope. Gray clasped his hands on the table. "I got out three years ago." Hoping to avoid more questions, he added, "I took a contractor's job down in Peru for a little while. After that, I came home to Wyoming. My mother had been working with Iris Mason on the wildlife-center concept. She suggested me to run the facility for Iris, and the rest is history."

Sky sensed trepidation and grief around Gray. It was mirrored deep in his eyes. Nothing obvious. But there was a heaviness, much like a deep, untended wound in him. "Were you worried about finding a job when you got discharged? I know I was."

"Like every vet, yes, I was. I was worried about my money I'd saved drying up while I tried to find something. If I hadn't had my mother's lead on this job, I'm not sure how long it would have taken to find work. Did you have the same problem?"

Groaning, Sky nodded. "I left the hospital and drove home to my parents' place. I tried working as an R.N. at the local hospital, but the stress was too much for me." She hitched her shoulder and whispered, "It was my PTSD. After that, I tried for any job that would hire me. I worked at a fast-food place, but again, the stress made me quit. I just couldn't handle it, Gray."

"PTSD does that," he agreed gently, seeing the shame in her expression.

"My mother understood. But my father doesn't to this day. He said it was all up in my head."

Anger flared within Gray. He stared disbelievingly at her. "He said that?" Tension thrummed within him as he saw the devastation in Sky's eyes. She could hide nothing from him.

"Yes. I just stood there looking at my dad, stunned. Wondering if he'd ever been tortured…ever been so scared of dying…" And she pulled her lower lip between her teeth, worrying it.

"I know what it's like to be scared," he said.

"You were a SEAL. You guys are always in danger. What you do could get you killed on any given day."

Gray nodded. "Right on. But it's different for you, Sky. I don't think most women in the military ever think about the possibility of capture." *Or being tortured.* He wanted to tread lightly on the subject, but felt starved to know exactly what had happened to Sky.

The only physical clues he could find were new, pink scars around her wrists. If she'd been waterboarded, Gray would bet his life she also had scars around her ankles. They tied the person down on a wooden board, cuffing their wrists and ankles. And knowing the Taliban like he did, they probably threw chains around her extremities, not caring if her flesh was ripped bloody as they dropped a cloth on her face and then poured water through it, suffocating her in the process.

Sky moved her fingers in an aggravated motion through her loose hair. "No… I never, ever thought about capture or—" her voice lowered with pain "—torture."

He could see he'd pushed her far enough. There would be other days maybe, when Sky was emotionally stronger, that he could approach the topic with her again. "Hey, I made some chocolate pudding for dessert." He rose in one fluid motion, picking up their plates. Giving her a warm smile, he asked, "Interested?"

His smile was like hot sunlight through her icy gut and heavily beating heart. Just talking about her capture sent adrenaline spiking into her bloodstream, still too fresh, like an open wound in her soul.

"Come on. You did a good job of eating," Gray coaxed her. Indeed, she'd finished half the chicken breast, most of the rice and all of the salad. Not bad for someone who said they weren't hungry. Gray gave her a pleading look and saw her resistance melt.

"Well… I'll try a little…."

"I'm sorry I upset you," Gray murmured, meaning it. "I'll be back in a minute. Would you like some coffee? Water? Tea?"

*Water.* Sky jerked inwardly. Even the word made her feel terror. Sky was unhappy with her overreactions, and yet she couldn't stop or control them. "Coffee."

"Cream? Sugar?"

"Both."

"You like it sweet and blond."

Rallying beneath his warm teasing, she felt Gray's caressing care and protectiveness descending over her like an invisible blanket. The sensation was so comforting that Sky took a long, deep breath, feeling the adrenaline fading in her bloodstream. She began to relax. "That's a Navy saying."

"Yep, sure is," he said.

Sky watched him work quickly and efficiently in the kitchen. There was never a wasted motion to Gray. Shockingly, she felt sexually hungry. It was a welcome sign that showed her she was healing from the capture. Sky had given up ever feeling normal in any way again. She wondered if Gray was in a relationship. Val had told her he was single. It was beyond her to think Gray would be eligible. Why was she thinking in that direction at all? He was her boss. It wasn't good to mix personal with professional, and Sky needed this job too much to risk it.

"Here you go." Gray leaned over, handing her a white mug of steaming coffee. He placed a small bowl of chocolate pudding in front of her. He sat down, wrapping his hands around his mug.

"Thanks." Sky sipped the sweet coffee. "You're a much better cook than you led me to believe."

"I reached my limit tonight, believe me."

"I think people are more than what they believe they are," she said, picking up the spoon and tasting the rich chocolate pudding.

"You're a philosopher, too."

Coloring, Sky gave him a pained look. "Me? No."

"You have good insight into people. Maybe because you're a nurse?"

"My mother is the deep philosopher," Sky assured him. "And yes, you can't be around wounded or sick people and not employ a little psychology." She slid her fingers around the mug, absorbing the warmth. "That and a lot of compassion."

Gray nodded and sipped his coffee. They talked as if they were old, longtime friends. Their connection reminded him of his days with his SEAL buddies. Maybe it was because Sky was a people person, loved helping others and clearly was compassionate. When a person cared, others knew it. He tried not to glance down at her hands because every time he did, he tried to imagine what they would feel like grazing his flesh. Completely inappropriate. Foolhardy. Crazy. "Maybe one of these days, you can return to the field of nursing," he said.

"I honestly want to," Sky admitted. "Maybe E.R. is too much for me now. I was thinking of switching to obstetrics. I love babies and children so much," she said, her voice growing soft. "In school, I learned all areas of nursing. I would just have to be oriented to the obstetrics unit and have some in-house classroom training, but I think it's what I'd like to do someday. I could look into it when I feel I can handle being back in a hospital setting."

"Well, you'll have babies and children galore around here," Gray said, smiling.

Sky smiled dreamily. "I just love the babies. Holding them. Smelling their sweet smell, watching them watch the world around them…"

"Why didn't you go into obstetrics in the first place?" Gray wondered.

"At the time I was a risk taker," Sky admitted, shaking her head. "My father was a chef at a big cattle ranch, and I grew up around horses and wranglers and cattle. I was a real wild child, barefoot, daring, and I loved challenges."

Gray felt her happiness and saw it reflected in the pools of her eyes. "You'll do your fair share of riding around here."

"Bring it on."

"Maybe this job will help bring you out of the closet you got put into," Gray said. "Riding in nature to me is a dream come true. I'd rather be outside than indoors."

"I feel the same way," Sky agreed, finishing her coffee. She felt tired again, knowing that she was sleep deprived. "Can I help you clean up in the kitchen? Wash dishes?"

"No," Gray said, standing. "We have a dishwasher, and I'll take care of things out here."

Standing, Sky looked around the living room. There

was a large television on the wall, comfortable chairs and a coffee table between two huge leather couches. "Listen, I'm turning in early."

"You need more sleep," Gray agreed.

"What time do we go riding tomorrow morning?"

Gray smiled a little after putting the cups in the sink. "I'm up at 5:00 a.m. to feed the animals, but you don't have to be. Why don't I meet you here for breakfast at 8:00? Then we can get our horses saddled and take off."

"I love the idea of spending time in the saddle." Sky felt her heart open, fierce emotions flooding her. "Gray... you've been so kind. Thank you for everything...."

Gray leaned against the counter, arms across his chest. Right now Sky appeared vulnerable. He knew the look because he'd seen it in other SEALs and had gone through it himself. It was when a person had chronic sleep deprivation, was stressed to the max and had no downtime to recoup. "Listen," he said, "your first order of business is to get rested up. That's number one. We'll take your days ahead one at a time, Sky. Fair enough?"

"Yes." She worried her lower lip and started to turn away. Then she halted and forced herself to meet his shadowed gaze. "Gray? I might have nightmares—"

"Don't worry. I have them, too."

"I might wake you. I scream..."

He wanted to kill the bastards who had done this to her. Forcing his reaction deep so she couldn't possibly sense it, he rasped, "I'm here if you need me. Okay? You don't have to go through this alone anymore, Sky. Got it?"

# *CHAPTER FIVE*

THE NIGHTMARE BEGAN INSIDIOUSLY, like it always did. The blackness surrounded Sky. She felt the icy coldness of the Hindu Kush night as the Taliban dragged her and Dr. Aaron Zimmerman from the crash to a nearby cave. Everything was so dark. Sky was semiconscious, blood running down from beneath the helmet she wore, blinding her left eye. She heard the enemy speaking in Pashto, the words angry and sharp. Felt the men who half dragged her tighten their grip like talons around her upper arms until she cried out in pain.

She was thrown into a cage, barely large enough for a small bathroom. The doctor was dropped beside her. Gasping, pain in her head, unable to see anything, Sky heard the rattle of a chain and then what sounded like a padlock being closed. And then the Taliban's voices drifted away. Fear rolled through. Her whole body ached from the crash. The Black Hawk had autorotated down a thousand feet, dropping out of the black night. Something happened as the bird hit the earth, suddenly flipping, the screech of metal tearing through the cabin.

Sky was thrown to the ceiling, blacking out for a moment. She vaguely remembered the sounds of shrieking metal being torn around her, a roar entering the cabin. One moment she was in the chopper; the next, she felt herself flying through the air. She'd landed outside it, slammed into the earth, knocked out.

"Aaron!" she rasped, finding his shoulder. God, if only she could see! "Aaron! Answer me! Where are you injured?" She wiped the warm blood away from her left eye, blinking, trying to see, but it was pitch-black. Her heart was pounding, and she was shaking with adrenaline.

Aaron groaned. "M-my leg. Busted…"

"Which one?"

"L-left… Shit…we're in trouble, Sky…."

Didn't she know it. "Be still," she said, her voice shaky as she swiftly ran her hands as if she were reading braille down his body to his left leg. Her heart stopped when her fingers ran into his femur, which was sticking out of his pants. This was bad. Really bad. He had an open fracture, the bone broken and splintered, tearing through thick thigh muscles and breaking out of his skin and the material of his camos. Sky felt the warmth of blood pumping strongly out from beneath her fingertips as she tried to get a mental picture of how bad the injury was. Breathing in gasps, Sky realized Aaron would never survive if she couldn't get him medical help right away. Without light, she couldn't find the artery that had been torn and was pouring blood out of his body.

"Hold on," she whispered. Quickly, she took off her heavy jacket. Sky always kept a small Buck knife in the pocket, just in case. Her fingers were shaking so badly, she could hardly pick up the knife. Finally, she did. Blindly, Sky cut her jacket front open so that she was able to create a canvas strip of cloth three inches wide.

"I'm creating a tourniquet, Aaron. Hold on…" She found his upper thigh, shoving the strip of cloth beneath it.

Aaron groaned.

"I'm sorry," Sky whispered brokenly. If only she had some morphine to stop his pain, but she had nothing. Their medical bags had been in the helicopter and there was no telling where they were now.

Quickly, Sky pulled the strap of cloth as tight as she could around his thigh. Aaron groaned. But it was weaker-sounding. He was bleeding out. She *had* to save his life! He would die in less than three minutes if she didn't get the tourniquet in place. With all her strength Sky pulled the strap hard, knowing it would cause Aaron more pain.

He made no sound.

Her breath hitched. *No. Oh, God, no!* Tightening the tourniquet even more, trying to stop the flow of blood from his torn artery, Sky fought back a sob. Her hands shook as she held it as tightly as she could. She was gasping so loudly she couldn't hear anything else. Her heart jumped in her chest. She held the tourniquet tight, praying it would work. The muscles in her arms were shaking now, not used to such brute physical demands on them for so long. If she let the tourniquet go, Aaron would bleed out and die.

Sky blinked. Someone with a small lantern appeared out of the utter darkness. The shadow of the Taliban soldier, his bearded face, the turban he wore and his narrowed eyes upon her, sent a sheet of terror through Sky.

"Help us!" she called, her voice breaking. "He's bleeding out! I need medical help. Please?" Her shaking voice echoed and reechoed in the cave. She watched as he set the lantern down. Soon two other men joined him. Their deeply shadowed faces were filled with hatred. She felt fear as never before. Hunched over Aaron's leg, Sky sensed they were both going to die.

The one soldier, the tall, thin one, opened the wooden door. Their prison was makeshift at best, nothing but thin tree saplings bound together with rope every foot or so to create the cage. If she'd realized that, Sky could have thrown herself against the structure and maybe escaped to get help. But it was too late now.

The soldier leaned over her, curving his fingers like a painful claw into the shoulder of her uniform. He snarled something and yanked her upward. Sky was slammed into the rocky wall behind her, breath whooshing out of her. Dazed, she tried to get up as the other two soldiers entered. To her horror, one of them put a gun to Aaron's head.

The pistol barked.

Sky screamed. She lurched to her feet, attacking the soldier who had murdered Aaron.

In one swift motion, the soldier backhanded her. Sky saw stars behind her closed lids, felt herself flying through the air. And then she lost consciousness.

IT WAS DARK. Sky whimpered. She was somewhere else, not in the cave. She could feel a mud wall as her fingers moved through the darkness across the rough material. Her body ached. Her head felt as if it would split in two. Where was she? What time was it? And then, remembering Aaron's murder, she began to cry out softly in grief. Aaron had saved hundreds of men's lives with his dedication as a surgeon at Bagram. Sky crouched on her knees, her face buried in her hands, sobbing.

Light suddenly flicked on overhead.

Jerking her head up, Sky held up her hand to shade her eyes from the sudden light. It was a lone, naked electric lightbulb hanging far above her. Wildly, she looked around now that she could see her prison. It was a mud room. She saw what looked like a narrow wood table, water buckets nearby, and chains piled at the four corners of the table. There was a heavy wooden door to her left. The only escape. There were no windows. Her mouth was dry. She was so thirsty that she crawled over to the one wooden bucket, quickly sluicing water into her cupped hands, drinking noisily.

The door pushed open.

Sky gasped, crouched over the bucket, her eyes widening as two men entered. These were different men than her original captors. One of them, a short, pudgy man with a well-trimmed black beard, entered first. He wore typical Afghan clothing, a rolled wool cap over his long, matted hair. The second man, taller and with hatred in his eyes, shut the door behind them.

Sky didn't know what to expect. Adrenaline began pouring into her bloodstream as she watched the tall Taliban soldier swiftly come around the table. He reached down, grabbing her by the shoulder, forcing her to stand.

Sky's legs were wobbly. She gave a cry as his fingers sank deep into her shoulder, forcing her against him so she wouldn't fall.

"Be gentle," the pudgy man said softly in accented English, giving her an oily smile. "We don't want her skin broken." He held her wide, frightened eyes. "Take her to the table," he ordered.

Blinking, Sky froze. The man spoke English very well. Her mind became paralyzed as she was dragged toward the table. Sky tried to fight. The soldier's hands were like iron, and her struggles were useless.

"I am called Kambiz. What is your name, please?" he inquired solicitously, smiling at her.

Sky breathed raggedly, staring at the man across from the table. She knew she had to give her name, rank and serial number. And she did. He looked pleased and pulled out a small notebook and pen. Patiently, he wrote everything down.

"Continue to be cooperative, Lieutenant Pascal, and you won't have to suffer," he told her. Giving her an apologetic look, he said, "Now, I must ask you to not struggle. Jahid will have no choice but to hurt you." He smiled a little more. "Your choice."

Sky moaned and tried to free herself from the man's grasp. She could feel her terror amp up as she stared at the fat man with the oily smile. She could feel his hatred of her behind that thick-lipped smile. "You can't do this! There are Geneva Conventions you must follow. I won't let you throw me on that table!"

In an instant, Jahid picked her up bodily and threw her on the table with stunning force. Sky gave a cry. Oh, God, were they going to rape her? She fought back. Every time she did, the soldier slapped her, stunning her. She felt the icy coldness as he jerked the cuffs of her shirt up to expose her wrists.

Kambiz scuttled around, holding her down on the table as Jahid jerked off her boots and then her socks. In moments, she lay gasping. The wood was smooth beneath her back. She fought to get up. Kambiz cursed and held her down. Chains rattled. Jahid quickly slipped them around her wrists and ankles. In moments, Sky was chained to the table, on her back, breath exploding out of her. The chains bit into her sensitive flesh, rough and icy cold. She shook with terror. What were they going to do to her?

"Now," Kambiz muttered, angry at her resistance, "I am going to put this leather strap across your forehead."

Sky's terror and adrenaline blotted out her ability to think. Shame that she was unable to defend herself against these two men leaked through her. The soft leather strap, once in place across her brow, was tightened down until it was painful. She could not move her head one way or another. Further, she realized the board was canted downward just enough so her head was slightly below the rest of her body.

"Please," she cried hoarsely, "don't do this! Let me go!"

The pudgy man patted her shoulder gently. "Now, now, Lieutenant Pascal. As I told you before, if you tell me what I want to know, I'll tell my friend Jahid to release you so you can get off this table. We will give you water and feed you."

Kambiz dragged over a tall stool and situated himself close to her. He rearranged his long brown wool vest around himself, making himself comfortable.

She heard the Taliban soldier named Jahid move around to her left. What was going to happen? What were they going to do to her? Kambiz pulled a cloth from his pocket and laid it across his thigh with some pomp and flash.

"Now, Lieutenant," he began, smiling down at her, "tell me why you were in that helicopter that crashed?"

Sky's training warred with her terror and vulnerability. She saw the glint in Jahid's eyes as he leaned forward, smiling down at her.

"I—I was with Dr. Zimmerman. I'm a surgery nurse. We were on a flight to save a man's life. The soldier had appendicitis, and he needed emergency help."

"Very good," Kambiz praised, pulling out his notebook and writing down the information.

Sky became aware that Jahid held a bottle of water in his hand, waiting. Waiting for what? Her breath came in ragged gasps. The humiliation of being chained in front of them burned through her.

"Where were you flying to? What base?"

Sky shook her head. "I can only give you my name, rank and serial number." She quavered as the man's small eyes narrowed thoughtfully.

"Pity," Kambiz murmured. He put his notebook and pen into the pocket of his vest. And then he stretched forward, laying the cloth across her face. "Lieutenant, I don't like doing this to you, but if you refuse to answer my questions, you must know there is a price to pay."

Sky's panic arced as the cloth covered her face. She didn't know what to expect next. Suddenly, water rained down on her nostrils in a slow, continuous dribble. It quickly soaked the cloth. The water poured into her flared nostrils and she opened her mouth.

Gasping, Sky strained, trying to stop it, unable to move her head to avoid the water. The chains bit savagely into her wrists and ankles as she tried to escape. The water kept coming, funneling into her nostrils. Sky choked. She gasped. Coughed violently, water sputtering out of her nose and mouth. Oh, God, she was suffocating beneath that stream of water! Screaming, her spine arching upward, the chains biting deep into her flesh, she was drowning! Grayness began to move in front of her eyes. The water kept flowing into her nose. Oh, God, she was going to die!

GRAY WAS ROUSTED from sleep by Sky's screams drifting across the hall. *What the hell?* Wearing only a set of boxer shorts, he staggered out of bed and threw open the door. What time was it? He saw milky streams of moonlight down the hall from the living-room area as he ran across it to Sky's room.

Flipping on the light, he halted once inside Sky's room. *Jesus.* Sky was on the wooden floor, her legs tangled up in the sheet and blanket. She was on her back, her eyes glazed and unseeing, fighting off an invisible enemy, arms flying, legs kicking outward. Breathing hard, Gray quickly crouched near her, but not so close to get struck by her flailing arms and legs.

"Sky," he called. "Sky? It's all right. It's Gray McCoy. You're not there. You're here. Listen to me, will you?" Oh, he knew the virulence of flashbacks. Knew that Sky was caught up in her torture, saw it in the stretch and tension in her contorted face. His heart caved in with anguish. Gray wanted to scoop Sky up, hold her hard and safe. But that wasn't how it worked. If he touched her, he could deepen the hold of the nightmare that had trapped her within its terrible embrace. She could think he was the enemy.

She was gasping and choking, jerking her head from side to side. If he had any doubts that she'd been waterboarded, they were gone now. Her reactions were consistent with that kind of torture.

"Sky? Sky, it's Gray. Listen to me, will you? You're safe. You're not back there. You're here with me in Wyoming. Come on. Listen to my voice. Let it lead you out of that nightmare you're caught up in. Please? Listen to me?"

Gray spoke in a low, urgent tone to Sky, hoping like hell he could reach her, break the hold of the flashback that had her in its steel grip.

It hurt to watch her struggle. Her chest was heaving beneath her white cotton nightgown. The fabric had hitched halfway up her thighs, her lower legs caught in the sheet as she tried to kick out. Reaching out, Gray swiftly unraveled the tight bonds of the sheet from around her lower legs. Gray kept up the singsong litany. He wanted to kill those bastards who had done this to her.

Slowly, over ten minutes, Gray began to see Sky calming. Began to see the glazed look slowly leaving her wide, terror-filled eyes. Her hair was matted with sweat, the strands thick and twisted around her head. How badly he wanted to protect Sky.

"It's going to be okay," he said over and over.

Sky kept hearing a man's low, urgent voice in the background. Finally, she recognized it. Instantly, she homed in on it as she fought, choked and screamed, trying to evade the water pouring down her nostrils.

Her legs were free! It broke the grip of the nightmare. She floated somewhere in between the paralyzing terror and Gray's voice growing stronger, calling her back to safety.

Slowly, the adrenaline left her shaking body. She coughed violently, feeling the swell of water in her nose tunneling down into her throat, eventually receding. Sky stopped seeing the tiny mud hut room, stopped feeling the cold, wet wooden board beneath her body.

Blinking rapidly, she realized she was no longer there. She saw a crystal light in the center of a ceiling above her. She was warm. She sobbed for breath, raised her hands. She was no longer cuffed to the table. The pain, the blood flowing across her wrists had been very real. As she stared at her wrists in front of her face, she noticed the many long, pink, jagged scars around them.

"Sky? It's Gray. Turn and look at me. Come on."

His low voice was so close. Sky slowly turned her head, staring up into his worried, narrowed eyes. He was crouched near her head, his arms draped over his knees, watching her. There was anger deep in his eyes. Yet a sense of safety poured off him toward her; it was undeniable. Gagging, Sky fought the hold of the nightmare. She was here. She wasn't there. She was safe! Hot tears jammed into her eyes. Tears of relief.

"Sky? I'm going to slide my arms around you. Can I hold you?" Gray watched the tears spilling down her tense cheeks. Her flesh was waxen. It ripped at his heart. He had to do something to get her out of that toxic nightmare.

She rolled slowly to her side and struggled to sit up. She pressed her hand against her tightly shut eyes. Terrible, gutting sounds tore out of her.

Gray didn't wait for an answer. He moved in quickly, sliding his arms around her shaking shoulders and beneath her bent knees. In moments, he picked her up and carried her out of the bedroom and into the darkened living room. She collapsed against him, her face pressed and buried against his naked chest, her fingers digging convulsively into his shoulder, as if trying to hide. Gray understood.

The thin wash of moonlight gave him enough light to see where he was going. Sitting down in one corner of the leather couch, Gray settled Sky across his lap. He pulled a bright orange afghan from the top of the couch and hauled it across her, feeling how cold she was. She was a quivering mass in his arms. Her sobs serrated his pounding heart as he pulled her tightly against him, his arms around her, just holding her. Holding her safe in a world gone insane around her.

He tried not to be influenced by the sweet smell of her hair as he tucked her head beneath his jaw. Tried not to allow the soft firmness of her body against his to stir up his own male needs. Tears always made him feel so damned helpless, but at least Sky could release the terror.

Rocking her gently in his arms, he rasped against her ear, "It's all right, Sky. You're safe now. You're with me. I won't let anyone hurt you now, baby. It's all right. You're safe…."

## CHAPTER SIX

WITHOUT THINKING, GRAY began to run his hand across Sky's tangled, damp hair in an effort to calm her. He felt so damned bad for Sky as she cried in his arms. Her warm tears moistened the hair across his chest. Her fingers spasmed, opening and closing against his flesh. If anyone ever thought that waterboarding wasn't torture, they were so full of shit. The proof was huddled in his arms. Sky physically shook, emotionally and mentally broken by the torture. Gray had no idea how many times it had happened, either. The more they did it, the more broken the human being became, splintered and fractured.

"It's all right, Sky," he murmured against her ear. "It's going to be okay. Get it out. Let it go." And then Gray grimaced. He was the last person a woman would want around when she was crying.

When Julia cried, which wasn't often, he'd get up and leave the hut at the Peruvian village. He just couldn't handle it then. But now… This was different. He'd matured, fast. And Sky was a military vet like himself. She'd paid the ultimate price of war. She was a nurse, someone who helped save people's lives, and she should never have been put in this situation in the first place. But she had been. There was no defined front in Afghanistan, and that left all women serving in the military just as exposed as the men. Gray knew the statistics, that a hundred and fifty women had died in combat in Iraq and Afghanistan, untrained and yet out on the frontier of combat.

Gray smoothed her hair, allowing his hand to trail across her hunched, trembling shoulders, moving slowly down her long spine. Every time he caressed her, Sky relaxed a little bit more against him.

Sky needed a lot of care right now, and Gray didn't mind giving it to her. What would have happened if he hadn't been here to interrupt her grisly nightmare? How many times had they occurred and Sky had had no one to help her or talk her down?

Without thinking, Gray pressed a soft kiss to her hair, tightening his embrace a little, absorbing the continued trembling of her body. Sky's weeping slowed and she finally grew quiet within his embrace. Gray could feel her naked vulnerability, her trust. It humbled him, since he couldn't help but want her in other ways. She didn't deserve that kind of reaction from him at all. Instead, Gray forced himself to focus on giving back to Sky, not taking. Too much had been taken from her already.

Sky finally unclenched her hand against his chest and wiped her face with her shaking fingers. Gray caught her hand, holding it within his own. Her hand was so small and white against his large, darkly tanned one. Pressing her hand against his chest, he whispered, "It's going to be all right, Sky. You're past the worst of it. Just rest. I'll be here. I won't let you be alone right now. I'll stay with you as long as you want…."

Gray's roughened words spilled through Sky's fractured emotional state. Eyes tightly shut, her cheek resting on the damp, silky hair across his chest, she felt his male strength gently surrounding her, making her feel safe. His voice soothed her, and with each ragged breath she took,

this new calm chased away the virulent terror still holding her in its invisible grasp.

Gray's presence brought her back. They shared a common military background. Somewhere in her fragmented
mind, Sky wondered if Gray had ever been tortured. It
was as if he understood on levels she could never give
voice to. And he was here for her. Present. Like a big, bad
guard dog.

He was a large man, and she felt so small leaning against
him. Gray was holding her gently as he might hold a hurt
child. The PTSD, the waterboarding, had stripped her of
her own internal strength. Whereas before she had always
been the calm, quiet, strong one in charge of the E.R. at
Bagram, she now felt as if she were constantly unravel-
ing. Sky had been unable, thus far, to put up boundaries
on her wild, rampant feelings, to stop them or not allow
them to run her life as they did now.

If she'd been worried Gray wouldn't understand, or that
he'd be disgusted with her as her father had been, she
was relieved. Sky had had several episodes of the same
nightmare at home, her father aggravated with her, but
she didn't feel anything exuding from Gray right now except care and protection. Sky never thought in a million
years she'd ever be the recipient of a SEAL's guardianship.
Right now she was like a starved animal lapping up anything Gray could give to her in the way of emotional support. There was no judgment emanating from him. Every
time Gray's large hand gently trailed across her hair and
down her back, Sky felt a little more stable. A little more
calm. His mouth lingered near her brow, the warmth of
his moist breath flowing across her face. There was such
tenderness in this man. She'd never experienced it quite
like this. Gray was not only soothing her, but Sky also felt
as if his presence were actually, in some miraculous way,

feeding her strength she presently didn't have. Feeding her hope. Tending to her torn soul.

"Better now?" he asked, feeling her sigh in response in his arms. Gray felt her head bob once, felt her unclench her hand and her long fingers smooth out across his upper chest. His flesh leaped and burned beneath her hesitant, innocent touch. He knew Sky wasn't sexually coming on to him. She was lost in the ugly morass of her injured emotions. Gray shut his eyes tightly, resting his jaw against her hair, holding her a little tighter for a moment.

Sky cleared her throat that ached with tension. "I—I'm sorry…."

"Hush. It's okay, Sky. I know what you went through. I'm just glad I was nearby when the flashback happened."

Sky frowned, her mouth compressed. Shame flowed through her. "You shouldn't have to see this. Or hear me…" In the hospital when she had the nightmares, they gave her an antianxiety drug to calm her down. Her screams woke up everyone else. She shared a six-bed unit with other wounded vets. If she didn't have the nightmares, then one of them would. No one ever got quality sleep in that unit.

A chuckle rumbled up through Gray's chest. She hungrily absorbed the sound of it, felt his hand slide along her jaw, tenderly smooth strands behind her ear. God, how pitiful she was. She was so starved for his continuing light caresses. So utterly needy, it shamed her. She was a nurse, the one to bestow care upon those who so desperately needed it. Now she was in their position.

"Hey, we're vets. We've seen combat. SEALs never leave anyone behind, baby. I'm not leaving you behind. Okay?"

*Baby.* The endearment renewed her hope. A broken sigh escaped from her taut lips. Gray continued to shower her with his attention. How many times in her life as a nurse had she done similarly for her vets who lay broken and hurting in her hospital ward? So many that Sky had lost count.

Gray eased back again, no doubt seeing the tears. "Good tears this time?" he asked, his throat tightening. She looked up at him, feeling her world shift. The corners of his mouth lifted. "Talk to me, Sky."

Her throat ached with tension from the rawness of her earlier screams. "Y-yes, good tears." His dark eyes changed and grew kind. Sky leaned against his chest, the soothing sound of his slow heartbeat continuing to calm her. She had no strength with which to move. She didn't want to anyway.

"How can I help you, Sky?"

His words sank into her heart, and she swallowed hard. "What you're doing right now," she whispered brokenly.

Gray nodded and slid his hand down her back. "It helps to talk about it, Sky. Maybe not right now, but later. I'm a good listener. I've been in combat. I've had friends captured and tortured. I know a little bit of what you're going through because of them."

Something broke inside Sky. She realized Gray cared deeply. The low tenor of his voice vibrated through her, giving her the courage she'd lacked for a long time. Opening her eyes, Sky stared out into the darkened living room. Thin, milky streams of moonlight made the window and other areas where the beams struck look gray instead of dark. "I was in a Black Hawk crash. They were flying me and a surgeon to a forward operating base near the Pakistan border. An Army soldier had acute appendicitis and needed immediate emergency surgery." Sky swallowed and emotionally gathered herself. She told him about the crash, being captured and of Aaron being shot in the head. When she got to her torture, she rasped, "They threw me on a board, covered my face with a cloth and poured water into my nose." She felt his arms tighten around her, as if trying to protect her from the terrifying torture. Words failed her. The shame and humiliation were right there, eating away at her.

Gray closed his eyes, battling his rage. He forced his emotions deep, opened his eyes and asked in a low tone, "Do you know how many times you were waterboarded?"

Sky shook her head. "I was a captive for two weeks. Th-they would come in two days between each waterboarding bout and do it again. They'd cuff me to that damned table… I lost count. All I know is that by the time the SEAL team came, I was a shadow of myself. They found me quivering in a corner, no clothes on… I—I really don't remember much after that, Gray. Someone put a blanket around me. The next thing I knew, he lifted me up and carried me in his arms. He got me out of that horrid room. I could breathe fresh air. I heard a helicopter nearby, and that's the last thing I recall. I woke up in Landstuhl a few days later."

Sky swallowed hard tears in her voice. "Gray… I didn't even get to thank the SEALs who rescued me. I feel bad about that. Those guys risked their lives for me…."

"I can find out for you," he reassured her, pressing a chaste kiss to her brow. "That's ST3's territory you were in. I'll make a call and get the intel. I know you'd probably like to email them, and they'd feel good hearing from you. Okay?" Because it could be part of her ongoing healing process.

Sky wearily nodded, pressing her cheek against his warm, hard chest. The soft, silky hair tickled her chin and nose. Gray's scent was evergreen soap and his own unique male scent. Inhaling it, Sky felt as if she were inhaling life. "Th-thank you. It would mean so much for me to do at least that much for them. They're all heroes in my eyes."

Gray stared into the darkness, his mind moving at light speed. Sky had been waterboarded a lot. It was an ineffective way to gather intel, that he knew. It had been proved that when a prisoner thought he was dying of suffocation, he would say anything to get the waterboarding to stop. And Gray was sure Sky had told them what they wanted to know. God, she was only a nurse! She wasn't privy to black-ops movements. She didn't carry a security clearance. All that was above her pay grade. Then why the hell had they done this to her? To what end?

"You went from Landstuhl to Balboa Naval Hospital to heal up?" he asked.

Nodding, Sky opened her eyes. "I spent six months there. The first month—" she grimaced "—I was on a cocktail of drugs. Emotionally, I was a basket case."

"Baby, anyone who'd gone through what you did would be, too."

"It tore me apart." Shaking her head, Sky sponged in Gray's quiet strength, his warmth and his attentiveness. He understood. All SEALs went through SERE, where they were all waterboarded to show them what it was like. But because of her military classification, she never had to take that dreaded course. Maybe if she had, she'd have been more mentally prepared, not taken by the shock and terror of it. Maybe…

"You've come a long way in a short time, Sky, with those kinds of experiences behind you." Gray held her desolate gaze. "You realize that, don't you? You're functioning at a high level despite it."

"I feel so damn weak, Gray. I feel like I'm set back every time I have that same flashback."

"That's going to change," Gray promised her quietly, curving his fingers against her cheek. "You're with someone who knows the score. I'm here for you. I won't walk away from you, either, so don't think you're taking advantage of me." He smiled a little as he watched hope flare to life in her shadowed eyes. "We'll take this one day at a time. What you have to do is tell me when the stress is getting to you. I can take you out of the line of fire, and you can come back here to the house and rest. Ramp down."

"But won't Iris be upset if that happens? She's paying me for eight hours of work a day." She saw Gray give her a very male smile.

"Technically, Sky, you work for me. Iris cuts the paychecks every two weeks. If I tell you to go back here to rest, you do it. Iris would understand anyway. She's hired a number of returning vets from Iraq and Afghanistan in the past. She's no stranger to PTSD and what it does to us. I know she wouldn't be upset with you, so don't you be."

Sky nodded. "Okay. I get it."

"Feel like moving? I can make us some tea. Or you tell me what you need." Gray didn't want her to leave him. She fit beautifully against him, her soft, womanly curves meshing against his hard angles. He didn't want to stop touching her here and there, but he knew he had to. There was a difference between care and making love to this woman. He couldn't cross that line with Sky.

Stirring, Sky sat up, pushing her tangled hair off her face. "I need to get a bath. I reek." She wrinkled her nose and gave Gray an apologetic look. Touching the damp nightgown she wore, she added, "I'll take a bath, change into a dry nightgown and then I need to try to go to sleep. Thank you, though, for the offer of the tea." *Thank you for saving my life tonight.* Without thinking, Sky placed her hand against his square jaw, leaned over and pressed a chaste kiss against his sandpapery cheek. And then she forced herself to her feet, her knees mushy from fear. Gray held her arm until she got steady enough to walk slowly toward the hall.

He watched her slow progress, worry clouding his expression. His cheek tingled hotly in the wake of her lush lips kissing him. It took everything he had not to enclose her with his arms once more and turn and trap that mouth of hers. He watched her move robotically, her stride tentative, unsure of her balance. Once she reached the hall, Sky put out her hand, using the wall to help guide her toward the bathroom.

Gray wanted to help her, but he understood her need to try to get stronger despite her injuries. And he didn't want to enable her. It was a fine balance to walk with her.

The door to the bathroom opened and then quietly closed. With the sound of water running in the bathroom, he sat there, elbows resting on his thighs, hands clasped between them. Gray shook his head, feeling the rage and injustice of her torture by the Taliban. He'd contact the senior chief of ST3 and find out the SEALs who were involved in Sky's rescue. And he'd talk to the men who had found her. She wasn't telling him everything. If he was going to help her, he had to know the whole story.

Gray slowly got to his feet, very aware of his erection. When Sky had unexpectedly kissed him, he'd gone hot and burned with sudden need for her. Only seconds later did he realize she'd kissed him out of gratitude, not out of desire. His body had its own miniature brain, and sure enough, he'd hardened beneath her entirely innocent gesture. What Gray didn't want was for Sky to feel he was a sexual predator, using her flashbacks as a way to get to her. She hadn't said she'd been raped. But he needed to know one way or another. Tomorrow morning, he'd place that call to his old SEAL team in Coronado.

# CHAPTER SEVEN

"GRAYSON, HOW ARE YOU, brother?"

"Hey, Jag, good to hear your voice." Gray smiled as he stood near the door to the wildlife center. It was nearly 8:00 a.m., and he had put in a call to the senior chief of ST3 at Coronado. The senior had given him the contact number of the SEAL who had led Sky's rescue mission. Gray knew him well, Petty Officer First Class Ryan Stark. He had been a shooter in his squadron, and Gray had been with him when Kell Ballard, the LPO, had headed up the team. When Kell left, Ryan took his place. Everyone knew him as Jag, for *jaguar,* because Stark was as silent and deadly as the legendary South American cat.

"How's life in Wyoming? Last email I got from you was two months go. Did you get snowed in?" Jag teased and laughed heartily.

Gray could feel his stomach knotting. "No, just busy putting the final touches on the wildlife center I'm running. Look, I got permission from the senior back at Coronado to ask you about a rescue mission you headed up."

"Sure. What do you need to know?"

Gray knew all their ops were top secret. But ex-SEALs or retired SEALs were sometimes cut some slack if there was a personal stake in needing to know. "Your rescue of Lieutenant Skylar Pascal. Do you remember it? It was about eight months ago?"

"I couldn't forget it if I wanted to," Jag growled. "How did you get wind about this op?"

Mouth quirking, Gray walked around the corner of the building where he was out of sight of everyone. No one was around on the cold, sunny morning, but he didn't want this conversation being overheard. He filled Jag in that Sky was going to be his assistant.

"Now, I know a couple of things," Gray went on in a quiet tone. "She was in a Black Hawk crash, and there were two survivors. The doc was shot in the head later in a cave, leaving her the lone survivor. The Taliban held Sky for two weeks and she was waterboarded."

"You know a whole helluva lot," Jag muttered.

"Not enough, though. I need your eyes on this, Jag. You were there. You pulled the op. What else can you tell me about that mission?" Gray held his breath, trying to prepare himself.

"It was a nightmare, man. Me and my team took down four Taliban guarding that Afghan house. We captured two others. The Taliban was hiding her in plain sight in a border village. We got inside the house, found this small room locked. I shot off the lock and kicked the door open. It was dark and smelled bad. Real bad. I aimed my rifle around with the light beneath it and spotted something in the corner of the room. At first, I thought it was just a pile of old, ratty wool blankets. There was a table in the center of the room with chains on each corner of it. I flashed my light around and there was blood all over the freakin' place. There was vomit, shit and urine. The place smelled bad, man. When I went over to the blankets, I used the toe of my boot to nudge it, and it moved. Scared the hell outta me. I leaped back, ready to fire at it, thinking a Taliban was hiding under it."

"But it was Sky?" Gray pressed grimly, his eyes narrowing, his gut knotted so tight it hurt.

"Yes, it was. She was naked, hair matted and filthy dirty. I tried to ask her name but she was dazed and in deep shock. All she could do was huddle, arms wrapped around herself, shaking. It was really bad, Gray. Never seen anything like it."

Mouth tightening, Gray rasped, "What else? I need to know all of it."

"I knelt down beside her and put my rifle aside, told her who I was. Told her we were there to rescue her. I saw her one wrist, Gray, and man, it was ground up like fresh, raw hamburger. And then as I slowly pulled the blanket off her back to examine her for other wounds, I caught sight of her left ankle." Jag blew out a breath, his voice deepening. "She had blood poisoning from those chains they were wrapping around her ankles and wrists. Red stripes were running halfway up both her calves. She had a high fever, shaking with chills, and was completely out of it. She didn't respond to me. They fucking broke her, Gray. And I mean in the worst kind of way. One of my other guys, a combat medic, came over and he about lost it as he quickly examined her for other wounds. She was so filthy, bloody and was sicker than hell."

"Had she been raped?" Gray closed his eyes, steeling himself.

"We didn't know at the time. When we got her to Bagram hospital, I talked to one of the doctors in the E.R. who admitted her. He said she hadn't been raped. Shit, they'd done just about everything else to her. The doc wasn't sure she was going to make it. Lieutenant Pascal had a fever of a hundred and five degrees with a very advanced case of sepsis, blood poisoning. She was severely undernourished and dehydrated, Gray. Literally, nothing but skin over her bones. I don't think those bastards fed her at all. The corpsman gave me a clean blanket from his rucksack, and I wrapped her up in it and picked her up, got her the hell out of there. She went unconscious on me while I was carrying her toward the helo. The corpsman put an IV in each of her arms on the flight into Bagram. None of us were sure she was going to make it. She was in pitiful condition, Gray."

"Did you get the bastards who did this to her?"

Jag laughed darkly. "Sure did. A little fat man and a tall, skinny bastard. We took 'em prisoner. Later the CIA boys at J-bad, Jalalabad, took them in custody. And after the spooks learned what they'd done to Lieutenant Pascal… Well, let's just say those two got what they doled out to her in spades."

"I'd like to kill them," Gray snarled.

"Hey, man, no worries. I heard about four weeks later that they were found dead from trying to escape. I didn't ask how. It just made me feel good those two sonofabitches were dead for how they treated that Navy officer."

"Anything else?"

"No, that's it. It's enough," Jag said wearily. "You say she's with you now? How is she?"

Gray snorted and started pacing the length of the building. "Considering everything you just told me, she appeared normal to me and to everyone else around here."

"Man, that's unbelievable she's rebounded like that. She's got a real set of balls."

Gray wasn't so sure. "She had a flashback last night, screamed and woke me up. I eventually talked her awake, and she told me about her capture. But I knew there was more. Sky is a very strong woman to have handled everything that's happened to her and still be able to function in society."

"Man, I'll tell you, busting into that room and the rank odor that hit us, the smell of her rotting, infected flesh..."

Nausea burned in his throat. Gray swallowed hard, his voice hoarse. "Did the spooks ever tell you if they learned anything from those two bastards? Why they did this to her?"

"Yeah. I met one of the spooks about six weeks later over at the J-bad chow hall. We were flown up there as part of a task force on an op going down that night. I asked him the same question. The little fat guy said they thought she was a spy."

Grunting, Gray halted and took a deep breath. "Lying bastards."

"Hell, yeah. The spook said they'd tortured Lieutenant Pascal just to get even with all Americans. One American was as good as another, as far as they were concerned. Didn't matter if it was a man or woman."

Rage flowed through Gray, his hand tightening on his cell phone. "Hey, I owe you on this, Jag. Thanks for letting me know the rest of the story."

"No problem, man. It's good to hear she not only survived, but she's thriving, too. I'd never have believed it myself, seeing her in that state."

Nodding, Gray said, "It gives me a lot of hope I can help her walk the rest of the way."

"Seriously, Sky's in good hands with you, brother. But...are you up for it? Are you over Julia's death?"

"Some days I think I am, and others, no. It comes and goes."

"What happened down there in South America with you and her?"

Pushing his fingers through his military-short hair, Gray halted and rasped, "Losing Julia down there took a piece of my soul. One of these days we'll sit down over

some beers, and I'll tell you the rest of the story. Fair
enough?"

"Fair enough. Look, stay in touch a little more closely,
okay? I like hearing from you. And if there's anything else
I can do to help you and this gal, let me know."

Gray was grateful for Stark's information. He clicked
off his cell and stuffed it into his goose-down nylon jacket.
Standing, hands on his hips, he surveyed the quiet morning. The Elk Horn Ranch was huge. Low ground fog hung
across the wide, green pastures. He saw some mule deer
hedging a tree line in the distance, hurrying back to their
sleeping areas for the day. Shaking his head to clear it,
Gray glanced down at his watch. It was exactly 0800. Time
to go see how Sky was this morning. Probably feeling like
hell after that episode last night.

Gray moved silently down the wall of the building, his
worry front and center. He now understood she was a lot
stronger than she appeared. Sky had to be tired from battling the PTSD all the time. He knew in himself, it was a
twenty-four-hour-a-day battle. Now, three years out of the
teams, the symptoms had ratcheted down. Plus, he was
getting help from Dr. Jordana McPherson in Jackson Hole
for his high cortisol, which was part and parcel of PTSD.

Mouth taut, Gray turned the corner and walked down
the redbrick sidewalk toward the employee house. His
heart started to thud harder in his chest. Gray found himself emotionally involved with Sky. It was part his natural
inclination to protect someone weaker than himself. The
other part? Shaking his head, he felt suspended between
the past in South America and the present.

Jesus, whatever was happening between him and Sky
was organic. It had a damned life of its own, and he didn't
feel completely in control of it or himself. More than anything, Gray would not allow himself to want her. Sky was

healing. She needed support. How the hell was he going to continue to separate those two issues within himself? With a soft curse, Gray lifted his ball cap off his head and then settled it back on, pulling the bill low over his narrowed eyes. What the hell was he going to do?

The scent of bacon frying hit Gray's flaring nostrils as he quietly entered the house. Sky was in the kitchen, dressed in a pair of jeans, wearing one of her long-sleeved pink tops, her hair clean and shining. Gray felt his body react. When she lifted her head, his heart slammed into a strong beat. Gray hoped she'd slept deep and long. There were faint shadows beneath her deep blue eyes. His gaze fell to her lips, and they parted as he homed in on them. There was a sizzling connection between them, burning him up, turning him inside out with hunger for her.

"Hey," he greeted her, taking off his cap and hooking it on a peg near the door, "you look pretty good this morning."

Sky felt her knees go a little weak beneath the intense look Gray gave her. He was clean-shaven this morning, and he looked way too good in his tight-fitting Levi's that showed off his sculpted, hard thighs. Nervous beneath his inspection, unsure of how he was going to react to her this morning after last night's debacle, she asked, "Have you eaten yet?"

Gray sauntered into the kitchen, pulled down a mug and poured coffee into it. "No. I was waiting for you to get up." He liked the way the Levi's outlined her butt. She had a very, very nice one along with long, coltish legs to go with it. Gray nearly burned his tongue as he sipped the coffee. Scowling, he had to get out of the kitchen. Get away from Sky because he wanted to turn her away from the stove, where she was frying the bacon, slide his arms around her and kiss her senseless. He knew he could do that. Knew he could give her the kind of pleasure she likely had never experienced. Maybe it was his SEAL confidence. Maybe it was the fact he'd had a lot of women as a SEAL before finding Julia and falling in love for the first time in his life.

"What time did you get up?" Sky asked, transferring the bacon to a basket lined with paper towels.

"0430." He watched her like the starving wolf he was. Sky was all grace, her long hands and fingers once more reminding him she was a healer. "You?"

"0700." She smiled a little. "I feel like I'm back in the military."

He grinned a little, resting his hips against the counter. He enjoyed watching her work at the stove. "You okay with it, or do you want me to give you civilian time instead?"

"No, I'm fine with it. How many eggs do you want?"

"You feel up to doing this?" Gray demanded, concerned. Sky's face was clear and so were her eyes. It was a change from how she'd looked last night.

"Yes." She cut him a sideways glance. "I'm not fragile, Gray. I'm healing."

"I get overprotective sometimes," he apologized. "I'll take six eggs, please."

"You're a SEAL. Why wouldn't you be that way?" Her eyes met his. "And thank you for what you did last night." *I needed you. I was falling apart.*

"I'll do it every time, Sky. No one should go through this alone."

Her hands trembled a bit as she broke the eggs into a bowl and then added salt and pepper. "You have PTSD," she said softly, whisking the eggs and seasoning together in the bowl. "Did you go through it alone?"

Gray nodded. "Yeah."

Sky's heart tore open. "Well, if you have a nightmare and it wakes me up, I'm coming in to hold you like you held me last night. No questions asked. I can be there for you, too."

He watched as she poured the mixture into a large black skillet without physical reaction. The idea of Sky holding him sent scalding heat through Gray. It was what he was trying to avoid with her.

"That might not be a good idea," he cautioned her quietly. When she looked up briefly, he said, "As a SEAL, I have powerful muscle memory. You can't touch me when I'm in the throes of a nightmare, Sky. I'll strike out. I might hurt you badly, never realize it until later." His mouth flattened, and he gave her a dark look. "That's the last thing I'd ever want to do to you. You've suffered enough pain for one lifetime."

"You forget, Gray, I was an R.N. for three years at the Bagram hospital. Plenty of SEALs and other black-ops guys went through my ward. Trust me, I know not to go running to their bedside when they're trapped in a flashback."

He'd forgotten about that and met her wry smile. "Good to know." Because some part of him would die if he *ever* hurt Sky by accident.

"You didn't touch me last night," Sky said, stirring the fluffing eggs in the skillet with a fork. "You talked me down. Your voice, your care, penetrated that nightmare of mine last night. You knew how to handle the situation, and so do I."

Gray sauntered over to take the basket of bacon from the counter while she put the scrambled eggs in another bowl. "I knew better than to try and reach out and touch you," he agreed, his shoulder barely grazing hers as he stretched across her to grab the basket.

Sky followed Gray over to the table and sat down with the bowl. Her shoulder tingled pleasantly in the wake of their accidental meeting with one another. "We're a sad lot, aren't we? Military vets with PTSD?"

Gray pulled the toast from the toaster. "Look at it this way, Sky. We are stronger than we would be without the other." He gave her an amused look and handed her the toast he had buttered. Just getting to contact her fingers momentarily sent a sizzle of heat up through his hand. She grimaced, but the softness in her eyes remained.

"I'm glad you're here." Sky shook her head and handed him the bowl after putting some scrambled eggs on her plate. "Iris gave me a chance knowing I'm damaged, not whole. You didn't blink an eye over my issues for obvious reasons." More softly, she added almost shyly, "You haven't judged me, and for that, I'll always be grateful to you."

Gray placed a huge amount of scrambled eggs onto his plate and set the bowl aside, leaving some in there in case Sky wanted more later. "I'll never judge you, Sky," he said. *Not ever.* Not after what Jag had confided in him. Gray doubted seriously if Sky could remember the bulk of those two weeks in captivity. Other military men, who had managed to survive torture, had told him it was a blank slate in their minds. He hoped like hell it was a blank slate in Sky's mind because he couldn't stand the thought of her remembering.

Sky wanted to move on from the topic centering on her. She was always uncomfortable talking about her capture. She picked at her eggs. Gray, on the other hand, ate voraciously. He'd put half the bacon on his plate and had two more pieces of bread in the toaster. "Are we still going to ride this morning?"

"Yes. I've got two geldings saddled in the main barn. When we get done here, I'll carry a pack on my back with water and some protein bars. We'll head out to the areas where we take the families who come to the dude ranch. You need to know the trail system and the fastest way back here in case a child or adult gets injured."

"Sounds reasonable." Sky's appetite increased, and she reached for the blueberry preserves. "Do you have an idea of injury statistics among the guests?"

"Not many, from what I know," Gray murmured. There was a flush spreading across her cheeks. He didn't blame Sky for not wanting to talk about her wounds. "The horses we have are matched to the rider. And Iris is set on having good, patient and quiet horses for the guests. We've never had a death or even a bad injury from someone riding one of our dude horses."

"So, kids cutting their hand or knee? Falling-and-bruising-themselves sort of thing?"

Gray nodded. "That's about the extent of it. Sometimes one of the guests has forgotten to bring his or her medication, though. Iris wants the most popular meds available for them here at the ranch, if possible."

"Or could we run down to the drugstore in Jackson Hole and pick up a duplicate prescription for them?"

"Exactly. It happens more than you think."

"People get distracted. They forget. It's tough to remember a med every day or taking it a couple of times a day," Sky offered.

"You're such a marshmallow, Ms. Pascal."

His teasing had her grinning. The light in Gray's eyes made her feel good, feel desired. The way his sculpted mouth moved into that lazy smile of his sent sheets of heat and hunger through her. "Consider me a steel fist in a velvet glove, Mr. McCoy. Just because I don't look tough doesn't mean I'm not strong. You just don't see it."

"How did you get to be so strong?" he wondered, becoming serious. Gray liked the laughter shining on her face. He wanted to see Sky laugh more often.

Sky shrugged. "I grew up on a cattle ranch, Gray. I hated shoes. My mother liked me running barefoot. I always rode a horse bareback, never with a saddle. I'd run for miles just for the sheer love of feeling the wind on my face and playing with my long hair."

Gray could picture Sky as an exuberant child. And he saw that elfin look in her expression to match it. "Your mother's a strong woman, isn't she?"

"The backbone of our family," Sky agreed. "As a child, I matured really fast because of how life is given and taken away from you on a ranch." She gave him a wry look. "I didn't have other kids to play with, so I was out in nature and on my own. I spun fantasies lying on my back in a meadow, watching clouds drift by. I closed my eyes, and I smelled the earth, and it was like perfume to me. My days were magical in a way because my mother encouraged me to be independent and resourceful from the time I learned to walk."

"And that's where your strength came from." Gray could envision her as a child, that shining ginger hair of hers long, flying behind her as she raced barefoot across a flower-strewn meadow.

"Yes," Sky said softly. "I loved my time growing up here in Wyoming. I loved discovering and defining myself by exploring, climbing, hiking and watching the birds and animals around me."

Gray felt woven into her world of magic. Swallowing hard, he nodded, wanting to show her how he felt. Wanting to kiss her full, parted lips, taste her, run his hands over her from her head down to her feet. He got ahold of himself and poured them coffee.

"Do you think it's due to your Indian heritage?" he finally asked, sitting back down. "That gives you this inner strength?"

Sky tilted her head and drowned in Gray's green-and-gold eyes. The invisible connection between them was palpable. He was masculine, thoughtful, and his eyes never left hers. She could feel Gray wanting her, man to woman. Swallowing against her tightening throat, she couldn't handle him and her own healing process together. A sadness filtered through her because Sky was so powerfully drawn to Gray. She craved him in every way. If nothing else, she was far enough along in her own healing to begin to awaken sexually once again. And for that, she was grateful.

"My mother tells me I'm like her grandmother. She was a healer, too. She was a medicine woman for her people." Sky lifted her fingers, moving strands of hair away from her face, watching Gray's eyes darken over her unconscious gesture. "My grandmother was so very strong and confident. I never saw myself like her at all because I cried over little things, things that touched my heart. I never saw my grandmother cry. She was so stern, like a bulwark. She was indomitable."

"I like you just the way you are," Gray said, his voice low. He couldn't be this close to Sky and not absorb her like the heat of sunlight was absorbed by the rich, fertile earth. "Crying is a good thing. And you don't need to be stern."

One corner of her mouth lifted as she raised her head and looked out the window. "When I became a Navy officer, I hated the sternness. I remembered how my grandmother was, and I was forced to behave like that around her, up to a point. I didn't really like being an officer, Gray." She looked over at him. "I loved being there for the men and women who were sick or injured. I just wanted to ease their pain, their suffering. I really disliked being a manager of people." She wrinkled her nose. "So now you know the real truth."

"I can see that in you," he offered. Sky was a healer, like her grandmother, but a softer, more approachable version. All Sky wanted to do was help others. It was in her DNA. "There are plenty of animals over at the wildlife center that will enjoy having you around. They all respond to a loving touch." Hell, he responded now to her touch. Now Gray just wanted to hear her laugh. And God, he wanted to love her.

Pushing back his chair, he drank the last of his coffee and set the mug down. "Come on. It's time to show you around the Elk Horn Ranch."

## CHAPTER EIGHT

THE PLEASANT CREAK of leather as Sky rode the buckskin quarter horse soothed the constant anxiety that was a part of her life since capture. They had ridden down a dude trail toward a set of two hills that rose out of the flat plain. At 9:00 a.m. the sun was warming and taking off the deep chill of near-freezing temperatures in the valley. Above her, the sky was light blue. A few high clouds, which looked like strands of a woman's long hair unfurling across the sky, made her smile. She tried not to allow Gray's quiet masculine presence to deluge her opening senses. It was so easy to ride near him, their legs occasionally touching as their horses ambled along at a steady walk.

She glanced over at his profile. He wore his SEAL baseball cap, the bill low over his eyes. Gray was constantly looking around, and she understood it was part of who he was. SEALs lived or died by how alert they were to the subtleties around them. His large, gloved hand rested on his thick right thigh, the leather reins of the horse in his left hand. He'd traded in his black goose-down coat for a denim jacket that hugged his broad shoulders and emphasized his powerful chest. Sky found it disconcerting that she had such natural beauty around her on this quiet, frosty morning, and her heart and her body instead were focused on Gray. He'd done nothing to lure her to him. Nothing overt. She tugged at her thin leather riding gloves, glad Gray had borrowed a pair from Iris earlier for her.

Gray rode a tall, rangy black half Thoroughbred and half quarter horse gelding known as Shadow. Man and horse looked supremely confident, and Gray rode with an ease of someone born to saddle. They were a matched pair. Shadow's small, fine ears were constantly twitching, listening, and the horse was just as alert as his rider.

All Sky wanted to do was enjoy the outing. It was a gift to her, and she slowly inhaled the pine-scented air deep into her lungs. The hills just ahead of them were covered thickly with fir. She enjoyed the sway of her gelding, Charley, between her legs, simply relaxing and allowing the day and the man beside her to infuse her with happiness. If Gray knew how much she was drawn to him, Sky was sure he'd be shocked. Having no explanation for her unexpected feelings toward him, Sky wondered if it was because of Gray holding and caring for her last night. That had to be it, she decided. She pulled the green baseball cap a little lower over her eyes as the eastern sun's slats shot bright and blinding through the pine trees in their direction. Gray had given her the cap. On the front of it was embroidered Wildlife Center in gold thread with a wolf emblazoned upon it.

Gray pointed toward the trail that led between the two hills. "This is a nice trail, usually one we reserve for adults, not children, because you can see it takes us an hour to get out this far. Most kids have never ridden a horse before, and we try to keep them to less than about thirty minutes so they don't end up with bowed legs and sore butts."

Sky grinned and chuckled. "That's good thinking."

Gray liked her smile. "We use it as part of a picnic ride. When we get into the hills, you'll see a nice area to your right where we have hitching posts and picnic tables. Usually, on Wednesday or Thursday, we plan a lunch out here for our guests."

"It's beautiful," she breathed. Literally, Sky felt as if the energy of the area, the pristine beauty, was pumping new life into her. Until just now, she hadn't realized how badly she needed to get back into nature. It had been such a strong part of her growing-up years.

"You look happy," Gray observed, seeing luster shining in her blue eyes. Sky had pulled her thick, long hair into a ponytail. Her cheeks were flushed, and he saw no tension in her face at all. He was beginning to realize how much she needed this type of work to relax. Gray understood that the PTSD kept her in a constant state of anxiety. It had him, too, until Dr. McPherson had given him an alternative medication that had stopped the cortisol from remaining constantly in his bloodstream. Now he was at peace, no longer amped up on twenty-four-hour-a-day anxiety. For Sky, however, until he could persuade her to get to Jordana for treatment, Gray knew she would always remain in her hypervigilant state. Only two things could dull this sharp-edged hormone within her, and that would be brute exercise or getting out into nature. Both had helped him, so he understood on a deeper level what was happening with her this morning. His heart swelled with silent joy. Gray felt helpless to stop desiring Sky. He knew she didn't realize how attractive, how necessary, she'd suddenly become to his life. Gray had no explanation for it, either, except that his two-year-long depression and grief over Julia's murder was finally lifting. And he was starting to come alive once more.

Charley got frisky, tossed his head and snorted. Sky laughed a little, sharing her horse's joy of the cold morning. "You have no idea what this outing is doing for me. I grew up riding horses, and this is like going back to that time." She gave a breathy laugh. "I almost feel normal, if you want the truth." Sky suddenly felt so free, a feeling she hadn't had in a long time.

"Your anxiety levels are down." They rode close enough that Gray could have reached out and grazed her cheek. That mouth of hers sent dark longing through him, and he wanted to feel those lips beneath his. Something told him deep in his SEAL intuition that Sky was a very passionate lover and enjoyed the man who had her attention. That sinner's mouth of hers made him burn with longing for her.

"Anxiety." Sky's brows fell, and her mouth compressed. "I hate it, Gray. I wake up with it. I go to sleep with it. I always feel on guard, threatened, and jump at my shadow sometimes. It's not pretty," she muttered, shaking her head.

"I understand." Without thinking, Gray reached out, touching her jacket-clad shoulder for a moment. Damn! He scowled, unhappy with himself until he saw the reaction on Sky's face. Her eyes had widened, those black pupils growing large, her soft lips parting. Did he see what he thought he saw? Desire in Sky's eyes… Swallowing hard, Gray forced his hand back to his thigh.

"Do you have it, too?" she asked, feeling her skin suddenly heat up beneath his brief touch. Sky felt her breasts tighten, felt her nipples hardening and brushing against her soft cotton bra. The man could incite a riot in her body.

"Yeah, I did." Gray looked away for a moment. They were entering the shadowy area between the two hills. The trail was wide and solid in front of them. It would curve soon, and the silence within the area would be even more soothing to Sky. He turned and looked over at her, seeing lingering want in her eyes. Did Sky realize it? "I used to have it just like you. I was going to talk to you about it, but now's as good a time as any."

"You said you *used* to have it? How did you get rid of it, Gray?" Sky had been told by her therapist she would have anxiety forever. Oh, over time, it would lessen, but never disappear entirely. The anxiety was like a living animal within her, a separate hormonal entity that she was at constant war with. It was always trying to wrest control from her and send her emotions rocketing out from beneath her grip. And she hated it because instead of not reacting to a nonthreat, her anxiety made everything a threat to her, pumping gobs of adrenaline into her bloodstream, making her go shaky and feel scared.

"Yeah." Gray gave her a reassuring smile. "Dr. Jordana McPherson is an expert in PTSD symptoms. I went and saw her a year ago, and she gave me a saliva test. It showed my cortisol levels were off the charts and said it wasn't unusual for someone like me who was in black ops for nearly a decade. I lived with that anxiety and controlled it constantly. She gave me what she called an 'adaptogen' for thirty days and damned if it didn't work. The fourth day I was taking it, my anxiety disappeared. I couldn't believe it."

Sky's eyes widened enormously as she heard his story. "Seriously? It *stopped* your anxiety symptoms?"

Nodding, Gray smiled a little. "Every one of them."

"Do you have to take this adaptogen all the time?"

"No. Only for thirty days. What it does is plug the cortisol receptors, Sky. In doing that, it stops the cortisol from moving into our bloodstream. And then you feel peace. Finally." He saw such burning hope mirrored in her eyes.

"But…my therapist never told me about this at the hospital."

Gray shrugged. "Jordana is on cutting-edge technology where PTSD is concerned. She said this adaptogen is considered alternative medicine. Frankly, I don't care what the hell the medical establishment calls it. It worked, and I've been free of anxiety ever since then."

With a ragged sigh, Sky whispered, "I'd give *anything* to get rid of my anxiety. I know it's hormone based. I hate feeling on edge twenty-four hours a day. It's so wearing physically and emotionally on me. I see threat everywhere, Gray. Things that never scared me or sent adrenaline crashing into my system do now. I found out after I got out of the hospital and was driving home to Wyoming to stay with my parents that I was in a constant state of panic. I would stop at a truck stop to go to the restroom. If a trucker just looked at me, I went into panic and anxiety. The bathroom stalls were so small and enclosed that I could hardly force myself into one." Sky shook her head, giving him a sad look. "I was so totaled emotionally by all these things that by the time I got home, I was absolutely physically exhausted."

Gray felt bad for her. "That's how it goes, unfortunately."

"When I got home, my mother told me to go hike and get back into nature. She said it would help, and it did." Sky's voice dropped with pain. "But it didn't stop the nightmares. My dad was so upset by them. It's part of what drove me out of their house. He said it was all in my head, that I could stop them if I really wanted to." Sky felt tears burn in her eyes and forced them away. "I—I tried to tell him I had no control over them, but he never believed me."

Gray winced internally, seeing the serrating anguish in her eyes and hearing it in her voice. "He didn't know what happened to you. He didn't realize," he said.

"I couldn't tell him, Gray. Only you, my therapist and my mother know what happened to me during captivity." Sky gave him a pleading look. "I only told you because I know SEALs have PTSD given they are constantly on dangerous missions and see horrible, horrible things. I knew you'd understand."

Damn. Gray found himself aching to stop the horses, lean over and pull Sky into his arms and hold her. The stark look of raw terror was clear in her expression, in the quaver of her low voice. "You didn't tell your father anything?"

Shaking her head, Sky looked down at the saddle horn, ashamed. "N-no, I couldn't. He distrusted me. And honestly, there's a lot I don't remember about it to this day."

Breathing a sigh of relief, Gray murmured, "That's not all bad, Sky."

"The therapist said it was locked in my memory. Said my brain would decide if or when I'd recall any, some or all of it."

"Do you remember much beyond what you told me?" Gray held a breath, hoping like hell it was erased in Sky's memory.

"After the first day of waterboarding, everything is a blank. I don't know why… It just was… I remember pieces, the SEALs breaking down the door to rescue me. I remember a man's voice. I remembered his touch on my shoulder. I saw the care in his eyes. I heard it in his voice, but that's all."

Gray's mouth thinned. He couldn't tell Sky he'd talked to Jag, the SEAL whom she had seen, who had been gentle toward her in that filthy torture room. "I know SEALs who don't remember to this day bad things that happened to them, Sky. Maybe your memory, your brain, is protecting you."

"I'm not sure, Gray. My therapist told me the nightmares were about what the brain has refused to give me memories about. I hate the nightmares." She flashed him an apologetic look. "They drove my dad crazy. I kept waking my parents up almost every night. It was pretty bad."

And she'd had no one to hold her safe, to talk her down, Gray thought, feeling anger stirring toward her callous father. He knew most people didn't have a clue about how PTSD affected a person after they'd survived a trauma. All they saw was a highly unstable, angry and irritable person who seemed to switch personalities on them. Yeah, he'd been there, done that. And he knew her parents were probably feeling pretty inept and helpless to give Sky what she needed in order to start healing. "People don't understand PTSD," he told her, regret in his voice as he swung his gaze toward the curve they were approaching. "I'm sure your parents love you but they feel helpless."

Nodding, Sky said, "Yes, exactly. My mother wanted me to go to a medicine woman she knows and get a series of sweat-lodge ceremonies to help me heal, but it just wasn't my way." Sky watched him with a hopeful look. "But what you said about Dr. McPherson? If you could give me her phone number when we get back, I'd really like to call for an appointment."

"Be happy to," Gray said. "You'll like Jordana. She's a lot like you, very caring and compassionate."

Feeling heat sweep up her neck and into her face, Sky felt chagrin. The expression in Gray's eyes was a mix of care, concern and desire. This living connection throbbed between them, wild, almost out of control. It affected her physically as well as emotionally. "I need to do something. I can't use you as a crutch, Gray."

The somberness of her statement hit Gray hard. "Listen," he told her in a growl, "don't go there, Sky. I am someone you can lean on while you're getting your feet under you again. I told you last night I wouldn't leave you or walk away when you had those nightmares, and I won't. It makes no difference to me if you have them every night or once a week. I'll be there for you." And then he forced a slight smile. "Hell, you'd do the same for me, wouldn't you?"

Sky gave a mirthful smile and touched her cheek that felt so hot beneath his dark inspection. "Of course I would. I did it for the men and women in my hospital ward. I'd do it for you."

"No matter how often, right?" He drilled her with a hard look because he had to bring this home to Sky that she was worth saving. Worth caring for. Worth helping her to survive this.

"Without question," Sky murmured.

"Well," he told her, "that's how I feel toward you, Sky. The same commitment you gave your patients who were in your ward recovering from wounds is the same one I have toward you. It's no different, baby. Okay?" And Gray held her glistening blue gaze. His passionate, growling words had brought tears to her eyes. He watched her fight them back, swallow a couple of times and then control them.

*Baby.* Sky trembled inwardly, and it wasn't from fear. It was naked, burning need making her body react. Gray had called her by that endearment last night. The word had such power to her, had such a profound healing effect on her raw emotional state. "That makes sense," she admitted. "I—I just don't want to become a burden to you, Gray. I work for you. I want to be of help to you at the wildlife center."

He held up his hand. "Look," he coaxed, "I know that. Iris knows that. But she and I both know you need a little time and space to heal, too, Sky. And we're okay with it, and you need to be, too. Fair enough?" He added a slight smile. Gray watched Sky bow her head for a moment and tuck her lower lip between her teeth, worrying it. He reached out, his hand settling on her shoulder. "It's all right, Sky. You're a fighter, and you're doing a helluva job of landing on your feet again. You're so used to helping others. Now let us help you through this rough patch."

He curled his fingers around her shoulder, giving her a small, gentle shake.

"Some days I feel strong, Gray. And there's other days when I feel like my feet have been knocked out from beneath me."

"And on those days when you're feeling like you're flailing around, tell me, all right? Because I'll know not to pile too many demands on you. It comes down to communication, Sky, and I need that from you."

"You'll have it. Thanks for understanding."

Gray's horse suddenly snorted and planted his feet, nearly unseating him.

Sky's horse grunted and did the same.

"What?" Sky whispered, her gaze anchored on the corner of the trail. She heard sounds and couldn't make them out around the corner. "What's going on?"

With a hiss, Gray leaned down and hauled the .300 Win Mag rifle out of the leather sheath beneath his right leg. "Grizzly. Keep your horse under control," he rasped as he unsafed the rifle and put a round in the chamber.

The horses were skittish, wanting to turn around and run away. Gray held his horse in tight check, using the reins and his legs to force the gelding to remain where he was.

Sky's whole world amped up with sheer adrenaline flooding her bloodstream. She couldn't see the bear, but she heard growls and snarls drifting around the corner. "What do you want me to do?" She had no weapon on her. Gray had locked and loaded the rifle, the butt resting on his right thigh, his entire focus on the curve of the trail.

"Stay close. Grizzlies this time of year are starving because they've come out of six months of hibernation. They're aggressive. Stay behind me, Sky."

"Yes," she whispered, holding the horse's reins, forcing

the buckskin to stand his ground. Thank God she knew how to ride.

"Follow me," Gray whispered, his gaze locked forward, his gloved hand around the rifle. A .300 Win Mag was one of the SEAL rifles of choice for snipers. Gray had never been a sniper, but he knew how to handle this powerful weapon. He never rode anywhere without this rifle in a sheath beneath his right leg. Grizzlies were plentiful in this area and were the apex predator in the valley.

As he forced his balking horse around the corner, Gray lifted his chin and looked up on the thickly wooded hill. Shit! A large, dark brown male grizzly tore into the hillside. A white wolf was snapping at him, growling and snarling, trying to stop him from digging into a burrow that was obviously her home.

Gray cursed again softly. He felt Sky's horse near his, and he whispered, "The grizzly's found a mother wolf's den. Chances are, she has pups in there. This is going to get messy, Sky. Stay close."

A scream lurched into Sky's throat. She saw the white female wolf barrel in and leap at the grizzly's head. The bear was digging into the soft, muddy hillside with five-inch claws, dirt flying all over the place. The wolf slammed into the bear, biting down savagely on the bruin's broad, thick head. The grizzly reared out of the hole, roaring. It slapped at the wolf, its claws sinking deep into the animal's side.

Sky winced as the wolf screamed and yelped. Tears slammed into her eyes as she watched in horror the blood spurting from the wolf's side, turning her white fur red.

The grizzly growled, grabbed the wolf with both front paws and bit down into her back, slicing through her spinal column.

A short shriek filled the area. Sky cried out as the white

wolf suddenly went limp between the bear's massive paws. At the same time, she heard the deep boom of Gray's Win Mag.

The bear woofed and jerked around toward them. His small black eyes were surrounded by red, making him look like an evil monster.

Gray fired the rifle again.

The bullet hit inches from the bear's rear legs. Her horse reared, trying to get away from her, panicked with the smell of the grizzly's scent in the air. An eight-hundred-pound bruin could kill a horse. Easily. Not to mention, a human. As she struggled, Sky noticed Gray's calm and focus. He had a choke hold on his gelding's bit, the horse standing and shaking as he fired a third time.

The grizzly looked back at the opened wolf lair and then glared at them.

Gray fired again.

This time, the bear suddenly lunged forward, galloping up across the hill and disappearing over the crown of it.

Sky let go of a held breath. She hadn't even realized she'd been holding it. Tears blurred her vision. "Oh, my God, Gray, there are three pups that are dead outside the den!" she cried out, jabbing her index finger up toward the lair.

Dismounting quickly, Gray handed her the reins to his horse. "Stay here. That grizzly probably won't reappear, but I'm not taking any chances. It could circle behind us and attack us."

She grabbed the reins to his horse, unable to stop her tears. Three small pups, two of them white and one gray, so very tiny, lay unmoving outside the half-destroyed den. Sky felt her heart ripping open. She watched Gray move with lethal swiftness up the hillside. The area was still muddy and wet from the last of the winter snow. He held the rifle in his right hand, searching around, always looking for the bear to possibly return for his kills.

Gray gazed down at the slaughter. Was the bruin going after what was left of the den? Gray laid the rifle down, close enough to reach in case he needed it again. Getting down on his hands and knees, he moved into the den. Were there any pups left?

He pulled out the dry dirt the grizzly had been digging into. Moving it with both hands, he heard a little wolf yip. Gray pulled a small flashlight he always carried on him out of his pocket and flicked it on, peering inside.

Three little wolf pups, one white, one black and one gray, were all piled up into a little fuzzy hair ball at the very end of the den. This was what the bear had been after: the rest of the white wolf's pups who were still alive. These three blind little survivors had crawled to the back, trying instinctively to escape death. And they had.

Gray pulled out of the den and looked around. So far, the bear hadn't returned. He looked down the hill at Sky. She was white-faced. The carnage was probably triggering all kinds of silent terror within her.

"Hey, Sky," he called, "dismount and tie those horses up. Then come up here. I need your help getting these three wolf pups out. They're alive and okay."

# CHAPTER NINE

"OH, MY GOD," Sky breathed, kneeling down next to Gray in front of the destroyed wolf den. "They're so precious!"

Gray heard the well of emotion in her voice. He'd pulled all three pups out, filling his large, gloved hands. "They're lucky little things. They were probably born three days ago. Their eyes won't open for another two weeks." He twisted his head, catching her wide-eyed gaze as she stared down at them with a maternal look on her face. "Which one do you want?" He offered the squirming, mewing pups. "Pick one and then we'll carry them down to the horses."

There was sudden light in Sky's flawless eyes as she leaned forward, their heads nearly touching. Her fingers curled around the pup on the top, the white one.

"I'll take her," she whispered unsteadily, gently holding the tiny white baby between her hands. Sky gently stroked the pup's tiny, pug-nosed face. The pup's little skull was broad, as if her black nose were smashed up against her tightly closed eyes. "I've never seen a wolf pup before," Sky breathed softly. "What should I do, Gray? How should I hold her?"

Gray smiled as he stuffed the black wolf pup into one pocket and the gray pup into the other. They would remain warm and safe there for now. "Hold that little tyke for now, but once we get on the trail, I'll hold the pup for you until you mount up. Then I'll slide her into your jacket pocket.

She'll be warm and protected there until we can get her back to the center." Gray looked around, always alert, always sensing. The bear would be back sooner or later. He'd have a meal of the mother wolf and her luckless three pups. Gray didn't want to tell Sky that. She was shaken enough by this tragic and unexpected event.

"Okay," she whispered, her whole focus on the squirming little pup who made mewing sounds, nuzzling and butting her head into her jacket, looking for what Sky thought might be her mother's milk.

Gray slid his hand beneath Sky's elbow and helped her stand. "Let's get going." He picked up the rifle and urged her ahead of him. Gray searched the crown of the hill above them. He could sense that grizzly was waiting nearby. Out of sight, but still a danger to them. Gray didn't want the bear coming back before they had left. He turned, seeing that Sky had made it down to the trail and was standing by the unsettled, nervous horses.

Hurrying down the hill, dodging trees, Gray walked over to his nervous gelding, whose ears were flicking restlessly back and forth. The black horse's nostrils were flared wide, drinking in the surrounding scents. Gray slid the rifle into the sheath. He and the horses knew the bear was nearby, just waiting. He moved between the horses and gently took the white wolf pup from Sky's hands.

"Mount up," he told her, pulling the looped knot free from the tree she'd tied the buckskin's reins around.

Excitedly, Sky mounted and took the reins. She opened up her left pocket. Gray carefully deposited the whimpering little pup into it and then buttoned it closed. "Okay, we're good to go."

Sky watched Gray mount. He reached down and pulled the rifle out of the sheath once more, unsafed it, putting another round into the chamber. She gulped. "Do you think the bear will attack us?"

"I'm just being careful," he told her, turning his horse around. They'd go back the way they came. "Come on. I want you to ride in front of me, Sky. I'll bring up the rear."

Sky nodded and felt that powerful sense of safety wash over her. Gray was in SEAL mode, alert and protective. His face was hard and unreadable, his hazel eyes narrowed and piercing. Sky urged her buckskin into a ground-eating walk. She didn't want the horse to trot, fearing it would be upsetting to the poor little wolf pup who'd just been orphaned.

Once they were clear of the hills, Gray took his cell phone and called Rudd Mason, the manager, who had luckily come into the office earlier than usual this time of morning.

Sky listened to the conversation. Every once in a while, she'd open the button on the pocket flap and peer into it. The little white wolf pup was sleeping. She'd taken off her gloves and, with her index finger, softly stroked the pup. The baby jerked and whimpered.

"It's going to be all right," Sky soothed softly to her. She didn't know if the pup was a he or she, but it felt female to her. She heard Gray end the call.

"Rudd will alert Wyoming Fish and Game," he told her, tucking the cell into an upper pocket of his jacket.

"Does that mean they'll come and get them?"

"No." Gray smiled. He had put the rifle away once they were half a mile from the hill region. "I'm licensed by the state of Wyoming to keep wild animals and medically care for them. These three pups will be allowed to remain with us. We'll be responsible for them."

Happiness flooded Sky. "That's wonderful! I was so afraid they'd be taken away." She saw amusement glimmering in Gray's eyes. There was more green to them right now, and she was coming to realize when he was happy, that was the primary color she saw.

"Don't be so quick to be happy. You do realize that pups feed two to four times a day from their mother? That means you and I are going to be sleeping and waking up during the night to take care of them."

"I'll love every second of it."

"I figured you would," he groused, smiling fully. There was excitement dancing in Sky's eyes. Her cheeks flushed, hope radiant in her face. As much as Gray lamented that a wolf mother and three of her pups had been killed, this unexpected situation could turn out to be a gift to Sky. She needed something to focus on other than herself. Gray felt his own heart open wide because he saw her happy for the first time. And God knew he wanted to make Sky happy.

Gray rubbed his jaw in thought. "We're going to probably have a state wildlife agent visit us this afternoon. He'll want to check out the pups, take their photos, get their sex and make sure they're healthy."

"Then what?"

"We'll be given permission to care for them."

Sky could barely contain her joy. "Can we name them, Gray? Or does the state give them a number or something?"

"Sure you can give them names. So you think that white pup is a female?"

"I know it," she said, sure of herself.

"How do you know it?"

"A feeling." She shrugged. "I've lived my life on my intuition. I'm not stopping now." She gave him a grin.

"You're a SEAL in disguise, then," Gray murmured.

"Oh, I know you guys run on it. It saves lives."

"Got that right." Gray opened up each pocket and

peered in, checking out the other two pups. They were both asleep, and that was good.

"What about milk, Gray? Do they drink cow's milk?"

"No way. Iris has some goats, and we'll use their milk along with some other ingredients that need to be added to their special formula. It won't be wolf milk, but it will be close enough. Plus, we can add vitamins and minerals to help them along. By the time they're weaned off milk, they're going to be fat little guys and girls," he said.

"Do you have baby bottles for wolves?"

"No, but I can rig up a couple of bottles."

"Teach me everything you know. I really want to learn, Gray."

He chuckled. "You're certainly going to earn your money by being my assistant," he warned her. "For the next couple of weeks until they get their eyes open, they're blind and helpless. They're going to rely on us to keep them warm, to feed and potty them."

"I'm ready," Sky said, feeling more whole than ever before. Maybe it was the boyish look in Gray's expression or the way that chiseled mouth of his curved faintly into a smile that did it. Maybe the wolf pups. She felt excitement instead of anxiety. Hope instead of dread and darkness.

Gray nodded, one corner of his mouth hitching upward. "Yes, I think you are."

WHILE GRAY MIXED the formula with warm goat's milk, Sky sat in a small room that had two large windows. The floor was made of tile, and on it Gray had put a wooden crate with a fleece blanket in it. Above hung a sunlamp that would provide the pups the extra warmth they would need when wrapped up in that fleece to sleep. Sky squirmed inwardly, her hands stroking and loving the three blind wolf pups in her lap. They were making little whimpering sounds, opening their tiny mouths, showing their little tongues and looking around for what she thought was their mother.

Even though she was in a small room, one that Gray referred to as the maternity ward of the huge center, Sky didn't feel claustrophobic. Maybe it was the fact there were two large windows. One showed the landscape east of the center, the green, rolling pastures and the two hills in the background. The other window overlooked the huge expanse of the center itself.

Already, as she babysat the pups, Rudd and Iris Mason had come over to see them. Iris was beside herself with joy, continually patting the fat little pups with latex gloves on to protect them from human bacteria. Rudd grinned and shook his head. He was Iris's adopted son. And shortly after that, Kamaria Sheridan, who was Rudd's daughter, came over with her husband, Wes Sheridan. In her arms was a two-year-old little boy, Joseph. It had been touching to Sky to watch Kam work with her son, who was mesmerized by the squirming puppies. The wolf pups didn't feel threatened. Every time they heard a voice, they lifted their heads, their blind eyes moving toward the sound. They missed nothing because their wild instincts were online.

"Okay," Gray said, slipping into the room and closing the door behind him. "Chow time." Sky had a soft pink blanket across her lap, and she'd created a nest out of it so the pups were safe and secure. They were whimpering almost nonstop now.

"They're hungry," he said with a grin, handing her a small glass bottle with a tiny rubber nipple on it. Inside was the warm formula. "Pick up your favorite, the white one."

Sky did so after putting on a pair of latex rubber gloves. It was important, Gray told her, to always wear gloves because that way, human bacteria would not transfer through to the pup's mouth and cause health issues. The first ten days were critical, and after that, the gloves could be removed. Gray used his hands to show her how to keep the pup's back legs positioned on her lap and carefully hold her hand beneath its belly. This made it easy for the pup to lift her head to receive the bottle.

"Good," he praised, kneeling beside her. "Take the bottle in your right hand and then squeeze the nipple just a bit so a drop of milk appears at the end. Then move it gently against the pup's mouth. She'll do the rest," he said.

Nervously, Sky did this. She wanted Gray to trust her, and she was eager to learn how to feed the babies. No sooner had the drop of milk hanging off the nipple touched the baby's mouth than the pup lurched forward, latching her tiny muzzle noisily around the nipple. She sucked hard, her tiny little front feet moving and pushing her head against Sky's hand.

"Ohhh," Sky whispered, giving Gray a glance, "this is so precious." She felt him pat her shoulder.

"You're doing fine," Gray praised, watching Sky's face utterly change. There was such a maternal look in her expression that made him go hot with longing. In that moment, she looked at peace. Sky had transcended her own suffering and was focused entirely on caring for the squirming baby in her hand. Her lips were softly parted, mouth curved, her eyes shining with absolute euphoria. Gray knew the feeling. He kept his hand on her shoulder. "You're doing great. That pup isn't missing a drop."

Sky was wildly aware of Gray's hand resting lightly on her shoulder. It felt so natural. He was a large man in comparison to her, and his closeness was comforting, his long fingers curving over her shoulder as if to steady her. Or maybe to silently coax and feed her confidence. "She is starving!" Sky whispered. Very soon, the bottle was empty. She handed it to Gray. "Another?"

"That's enough for now. The pup's digestive system will probably react, and she'll get diarrhea for a bit. It's just part of how this goes." He took the pup and chose the black one next, settling it into Sky's awaiting hand. "That's enough milk to keep the pup from being hungry. If Mom was here, her little belly would look like the Goodyear blimp." He grinned, handing her another filled bottle.

Sky felt as if she were in a special haven for the next half hour as Gray led her through the process of feeding each pup. And when she was done with each, Gray took the pup, gently placed it on its back and checked for the sex of the individual.

"You were right about the white one," he murmured, taking the third pup and checking it. "Two girls and a boy. This gray one is male." He glanced up into her eyes, lost in the cobalt blue and gold he found in them. "Nice call, Sky."

Gray was so close, so male, and she inhaled his scent. It automatically made her lower body contract with need. "Thanks," she said, her voice wispy. "I feel like I'm in a dream, Gray. I don't want this to end. We should call this place Wolf Haven."

He chuckled and slowly rose to his full height. "I like it. We'll rename the maternity ward with it. And no worries. You're not going to feel very dreamy after two or three nights of getting up in the middle of the night to feed them. You and I will take turns, but it's still going to play hell on our sleep cycle for a while. Sleep deprivation for both of us."

Gray walked over to the box he'd made for the pups, rearranging the blanket and cuddling the pups together because that was what they would do in the wild. The pups piled up on one another with full bellies and became sleepy. Gray brought the lightweight blanket over them and then turned on the sunlamp above the box. He had a thermometer inside their box to keep track of how warm it would get.

"They'll be warm enough that way?" Sky asked, standing and folding the small blanket and setting it aside on a nearby table.

"Yep. But at first, I'll come in every hour and check the temperature. You don't want it too hot, or we'll dehydrate the little critters."

"Then I'll follow you around like a shadow," Sky promised. "I want to know what you know."

Gray rested his hands on his hips, watching as Sky came over to look at how he'd arranged the blanket over the pups beneath it. "You will," he promised.

"Did your mother teach you how to do this?"

"Yes, she did. I grew up with wild animals living all around me. My mom is a sucker for babies, and I can remember at age seven sitting in a rocking chair with a baby porcupine in my arms, feeding it with a bottle of milk." Gray smiled fondly.

"What a wonderful childhood."

"Don't be jealous," Gray teased as she came over to stand near him. She was watching the pups moving beneath the blanket. "You had a pretty nice childhood yourself, growing up here in Wyoming."

"Yes, but I never got to feed the babies."

Gray knew instinctively Sky would be a wonderful mother. Just the way she held the pups, the tenderness of her expression, the rapture in her eyes, said it all. He found himself starving for her to touch him in the same way. He was about to say something when he recognized Tom Harvey from Fish and Game coming in through the front doors. He touched Sky's shoulder. "Here's Tom. Why don't you hang around and you can see what goes on?"

"Thanks," Sky said, watching a lean, short man in dark green gabardine slacks and a long-sleeved tan shirt walk through the facility. She didn't want Gray's hand to leave her shoulder, but it did. Even now, as happy as she was, Sky was wildly aware of every little touch. He fed her, pure and simple. And whether he knew it or not, he was nourishing her soul with invisible strength, helping her rebuild.

SKY STUMBLED BLINDLY out of her room. The alarm had gone off near her head, snapping her out of a deep, badly needed sleep. It was 3:00 a.m. Three hours ago, she assumed Gray had been awakened by his alarm clock and had gone through the motions of warming the wolf milk formula.

She'd pushed her hair out of her face, dressed in a thick pink fisherman's-knit sweater, her Levi's and boots. Gray had thoughtfully left a light on in the kitchen so she wouldn't kill herself getting from her bedroom and through the living room. Rubbing her eyes, Sky felt drugged. She'd gone to bed around 9:00 p.m., utterly exhausted. And she'd slept deeply. No nightmare. *Thank God.* She was always grateful when she didn't have one.

After pouring the formula into the bottles, she placed the lid down on the warmer. It would take ten minutes to warm the formula to just the right temperature for the babies. Her heart expanded with joy as she scrubbed her face, trying to get rid of the drowsiness.

The house was quiet. Moonlight drifted in, lending a ghostly look to the windows on the west side of the house. Should she make coffee? If she did, Sky would never go back to sleep. And there was nothing to do at 3:00 a.m.

No, she'd just tough it out, but God, she'd been sleeping so well....

"Get over it, Pascal. Chin up," she growled to herself. Walking out to the porch area, she pulled on her thick down jacket, pulled a knit cap over her loose hair, grabbed her gloves and zipped up. Nights in June at this time of year could be below freezing.

Sky turned and looked out the window. Gray had left the lights on over at the center across the street. Solar lighting had been thoughtfully built in along the winding red-brick walk, so she didn't need a flashlight.

In no time, the formula bottles were warm and ready. Sky quickly dried them off, put them in a small warm-up pouch and hurriedly carried it over to the center. When she reached the maternity room, she flipped on the light. After shedding her jacket, gloves and hat, she eagerly knelt down by the box. She ran her fingertips along the top of it, feeling the warmth of the sunlamp.

She peeled back the pink fleece blanket, and a smile tugged at her lips. The pups had all moved into one corner, piled up around one another, their little bodies twitching or jerking every now and again.

"You are sooooo cute," she cooed softly, picking up the black one on top. "Come on, sweetie. It's time to eat," she whispered, replacing the blanket over the other pups. Slowly rising, Sky watched as the little female yawned, her tiny paws moving upward as if to stretch while in the palm of her latex-protected hand. "What are we going to name all of you?" Sky asked. She sat down in the rocker and brought over the small blanket across her lap. Gently laying the pup down, she pulled out the bottle of formula.

To her amazement, the little pup whined and started moving quickly toward the sounds. Laughing lightly, Sky scooped up the pup, brought her back to her lap and began to feed her. The baby made growling, grunting sounds, her little paws pressing eagerly into Sky's hand as she strongly suckled, gulping down that formula. Sky was amazed at the strength of the tyke.

"I wish you could tell me your name," Sky whispered to the wolf pup. Her hair was thick and scruffy, sticking up here and there. When she was done feeding her, Sky smoothed her fur into place, emulating a mother's tongue, hopefully. Gray had said it was important to do the things a mama wolf would do routinely with her brood.

In no time, Sky had fed all three pups. Their little tummies were rounded slightly, and she gathered them all into their corner. The pups promptly snuggled into one another and fell asleep, full and satisfied. Once she tucked them in, Sky removed her gloves and dropped them into a nearby wastebasket.

She looked at her watch. Forty minutes had flown by, and now she was wide-awake. Glancing out the window, she noticed how the Wyoming night was dark and quiet. Time for her to go back to bed.

After cleaning up the kitchen and preparing the formula for Gray's 6:00 a.m. feeding, Sky walked quietly back to her bedroom. Gray slept right across the hall. Sky hesitated before pushing open her door and quietly shutting it behind her. She shed her clothes, climbed back into her flannel nightgown and slipped into bed. Before Sky knew it, she had fallen asleep.

THE SMELL OF bacon frying slowly awoke Sky. Groaning, she turned over in her warm bed, the covers pleasantly heavy around her. As she forced her eyes open, she realized it was morning. She stretched and looked at the bed stand. It was 8:00 a.m., time to get up.

How were the puppies? She would be feeding them

in an hour. Frowning, she went to pull out a clean set of Levi's and a red long-sleeved shirt from the dresser. Hurrying to the bathroom, Sky turned on the faucets to take a bath. Always, running water sent her into anxiety. But not this morning. What had changed?

As she quickly took a nice, hot bath with her favorite almond soap from Herbaria, Sky hurried through dressing. By 8:30 a.m., she was walking down the hall toward the kitchen, where Gray was making breakfast. She swallowed convulsively. This morning he hadn't shaved yet, the darkness of the beard lending shadowed qualities to his strong-boned face. He wore a light blue chambray shirt, Levi's and his scuffed, scarred cowboy boots.

"Morning," he greeted her, transferring the bacon to an awaiting basket. Gray glanced over at Sky as she entered the kitchen to pour herself some coffee.

"It is," she said, smiling over at him. "Do you want more coffee?"

"Please." Gray poured a mixture of eggs, red and green peppers and shredded cheddar cheese into the hot iron skillet. "You up for an omelet with me this morning?" He liked the way those Levi's fit her tall, slender body. She had really nice hips, the type a man could grab hold of and— Gray short-circuited his sexual thoughts about Sky.

This morning, her face was clear, her eyes sparkling, and no sign of tension was in her expression, either. She'd left her hair down, the ends slightly damp and curling across her shoulders. Sky was so damned natural, as if completely unaware of how gorgeous she was.

"Sounds wonderful, thanks. Is there anything I can do?"

"Throw some bread in the toaster?"

"Jam?"

"In the fridge. Strawberry for me. Blueberry probably for you." His mouth curved faintly. Already he was getting used to what Sky liked. Gray found himself wanting to please her. "How'd the 3:00 a.m. feeding go?"

"Great," she sighed. "I just love holding them."

"You're a natural mother," he teased. Gray liked the quiet efficiency as they worked seamlessly around one another. Sky had set the table and then walked over to near the stove. She rested her hips against the counter, her hands around the mug.

"You fed them at 6:00 a.m.?"

Gray nodded. "Yeah. They're doing great."

"I was sleeping so deeply at three when that alarm went off, I just groaned. Hope you didn't hear it." She grinned over at him. Sky liked the way his mouth moved in response. Heat sheeted through her.

"I heard nothing. Dead to the world," Gray murmured. He took the omelet, which was huge, and placed it on a platter. "Let's go eat."

Sky sat down and watched Gray slice the omelet in half. "No…just a third of it, Gray. Please…"

"You're too skinny, Sky. You need to eat more."

Making a sound of protest, she gave up as he transferred it to her plate. "Do you always get your way?"

"Usually."

Sky snorted. The toast popped and she buttered the pieces, giving one to Gray. "I *am* eating more."

Gray knew pushing Sky would be a stressor on her, so he relented and said, "Yes, you are."

"I suppose you give those wolf pups the same talking-to?" she asked, laughing. Never had Sky felt so free. So… happy. And as Gray slathered the strawberry jam across his toast, she stared at his large hands. He had long fingers, calluses beneath each of them. There were large veins on the backs of his hands that were dusted with dark hair. He had working hands. He was a man who liked thrusting them into the soil or wrestling a fence post into place. *Or touching me.* What would his fingers feel like sliding across her skin? Cupping her breasts...

Gulping at where her mind had suddenly gone, Sky was shocked at herself. Gray was a powerful male influence over her and she gave herself an internal shake. The past few days had been like heaven. A reprieve. Gray had held her. And God help her, Sky wanted to explore more of him. In every possible way. He'd turned her world upside down and inside out. He hadn't done it on purpose. It had just happened, as if an organic and natural outgrowth was occurring between them. She felt out of control, and yet they were so solid and smooth in one another's presence, as if they had been living together like this for years. Sky had never had this happen before. Surely, it was due to her capture, her emotions torn and skewed. Desperate to get herself healed, she knew that she was no prize to be around. Her father had already made that clear. His words had wounded her all over again.

*"Who will have you, Sky? If you keep acting like a crazy person, you'll be alone all your life. You need to snap out of it and get a life."*

## CHAPTER TEN

"HOW IS SKY DOING?" Iris Mason asked as Gray stepped into her greenhouse. She'd asked her son, Rudd, to call over to the wildlife center to ask him to drop by for a visit.

The sun shone bright into the large glass building as Gray took off his baseball cap. Iris was sitting at her baker's table, transplanting a group of young lettuce plants into much larger pots. Gray knew she liked to raise organic vegetables, but in this part of Wyoming, there wasn't a ninety-day growing season, and so gardening was out unless one built a greenhouse, as Iris had done.

He walked over to her table to observe her work in progress. Her straw hat was in place as usual, her silver hair escaping out from beneath it, reminding Gray of a hen sitting on her eggs in a messy nest.

"So far, so good," Gray said. He pulled up another wooden stool and sat near the table so they could talk. It had been two weeks since Iris had hired Sky, and he knew she always checked up on her new charges. And since Sky worked for him, he was the go-to guy to get the answers.

Iris patted the rich soil around one of her romaine lettuce plants, her gloves dark and damp from working on thirty pots she had neatly sitting in a row in front of her. "I was over there yesterday at the center when Sky was feeding the wolf pups. She seemed happy."

Hell, he was happy, but Gray swallowed his personal

comment. "I think the work is helping her with the PTSD symptoms, Iris."

Nodding, she pursed her lips and slid him a glance. "Does she have nightmares?"

"Only one so far," Gray said, rubbing his hands along the tops of his thighs.

"Sky told me she had them a lot. So, that's unusual? You have PTSD, and that's why I'm asking you about this."

"She warned me she had them very often, a number of times a week, but I haven't see that happen so far." He shrugged. "Sometimes nightmares come and go in cycles for no reason, Iris. Or they're triggered by an outer event, like a smell, a noise or something that's related to the trauma the person experienced." And Gray hoped like hell Sky continued to sleep deeply and peacefully throughout each night.

"Did you suggest she go to Jordana for treatment of her PTSD?"

"Yes, I did." Gray rubbed his chin. "I spoke to her about it last week and she said she was going to call Jordana today after she fed the pups."

"Good."

Gray frowned. He felt as if Iris was withholding something from him. "What's wrong?"

"Nothing," Iris murmured, setting the pot aside. She took off her dirty gloves and laid them on the table. "Rudd got a call three days ago from Sky's father, Alex Pascal. He demanded to talk to Sky."

Gray scowled. "Okay." He wasn't surprised that her family wanted to keep in touch with Sky no matter how strained relations were right now.

"Rudd put the call through to the employee house phone. Sky either wasn't there or refused to call him back, I guess. Were you aware one way or another about this call?"

"No. Sky never mentioned it to me."

"The message went through three days ago. Was she behaving differently that day?"

Gray thought back. "Yeah, she acted upset but never shared anything with me. I thought she might be having a bad day and wrote it off as nothing more than that."

"Well," Iris said grimly, "Alex Pascal called back this morning, and he was pissed off and raging at Rudd. He accused my son of not alerting Sky that he wanted to talk to his daughter. I have no control over whether Sky returns his calls or not."

Gray saw the anger banked in Iris's watery blue eyes. She was one of the matriarchs of the valley and well respected. Iris was easygoing on the surface, but beneath it, she was a tough, Wyoming-bred woman. "Sorry to hear that. Do you want me to ask Sky about it and get back to you?"

"No." Iris pulled off her straw hat and moved her fingers through her messy hair, trying to tame it into some semblance of order. "From the times I've worked with Sky, she seemed very settled and happy here. We got rave reviews by the dude-ranch families who were here last week about her. You know she babysat a couple of very young boys, age three and four?"

Smiling a little, Gray said, "Yeah, she came back to dinner at the house after babysitting them all day, higher than a kite. She loves babies of all kinds, Iris. And she was floating."

"Well, so were their parents. I guess those two redheaded little boys are a real handful. And the parents couldn't believe how nice and respectful they'd become by being with Sky all day. I don't know what she did, but those two troublemakers were sweet as pie, and the parents were tickled pink. Their two boys cried yesterday when they left. They wanted to take Sky home with them."

Gray felt warmth in his heart. Yeah, he felt the same way those two little active boys did about her. Sky was sunlight in his life, automatically lifting him, making him feel lighter, happier. "She's got magic, Iris, no question. What can I say?"

Iris chuckled. "The woman has a touch with young ones. There is no doubt."

"So," Gray said, "back to her father. He's pissed because Sky didn't return his call?"

"I guess. I was wondering if she got the message and ignored it."

"Well, it's pretty hard not to see the red light blinking on the phone. I taught Sky to check it every time she came into the house, in case there was a message on the phone for me."

"So," Iris murmured, "I'm gonna assume she got the message but didn't call her father back."

Gray quirked his mouth. "Most likely scenario." He told Iris the rest of the story of why there was a rift between father and daughter. When he finished, Iris was thundercloud angry.

"You can't be serious, Gray! What father in his right mind, especially one that had been in the military, would tell his suffering daughter that her PTSD symptoms are all in her head?" Iris slapped the table with her hand, snorting and glaring around the greenhouse.

Yep, Iris could get her dander up in a hurry. Gray had seen her fly into her banty-rooster mode from time to time. Fortunately, not at him. She ran a tight ship at the ranch and was fair-handed and fair-minded. But when she saw any kind of injustice, Iris got pissed, and everyone around her knew how she felt. And she always did something about it.

"I'm serious as a heart attack, Iris. The man is blaming her for her PTSD symptoms."

"What a turd," Iris muttered angrily, pushing off the stool. She untied her dark green apron and pulled it away and folded it.

"You want me to find out, don't you?"

She gave him an irritated look. "If you can do it diplomatically. I don't want Sky thinking I'm snooping into her business. I don't want to stress her out over this silly tempest in a teapot, Gray."

"Makes two of us," he reassured her, slipping off the stool. He pulled the cap from his back pocket and settled it on his head. "That it?"

Iris pulled a folded piece of paper from her pocket. "Almost. Ask Sky, when she has time, to set up that little medical dispensary we talked about at her interview. I want you to drive her into town and have her take this list of items to our local drugstore. The owner, Jay Johnson, is expecting her. He's agreed to sell us everything we need at wholesale price. I want Sky to set up a wholesale account with him because we'll need to resupply the dispensary from time to time."

Gray took the long list. "Okay, I can take her over there this afternoon between pup feedings." He saw Iris give him an intense look. Uh-oh—Gray knew that look. When Iris had her mind set on something, he knew to get out of the way. She was like a laser-fired rocket.

"How are *you* getting along with her, Gray? You two compatible over there at the employee house?"

Swallowing a grin, Gray put on his game face. He could feel Iris fishing. "We've divided up all the household duties, and things are working out fine from my perspective. Why?"

"Well," Iris said, plopping her straw hat on her head,

"Kam was over at the center yesterday with her son, Joseph, watching Sky feed the pups. I guess you came in at that time. Kam mentioned to me later that she saw a huge difference in Sky when you came over to see if she needed any help."

"Oh?" Gray frowned.

Iris patted his upper arm like a mother doting on her much-loved child. "When Sky told you she was okay and you left, Kam decided to ask her some questions."

Gray saw a sparkle come to Iris's eyes. "Okay," he muttered, confused.

"Kam is very sure that Sky likes you on a personal level."

"Oh…" Hell, Gray wasn't going there. Not with Iris. He also wanted to protect Sky in the process, too.

"Just *oh?*"

Uncomfortable, Gray put his hands on his hips. "What did Kam think she saw?" He wasn't a SEAL for nothing. Answer a question with a question. Keep the questioner off balance.

"My granddaughter is a very astute observer of people, Gray. I think you know that."

"Yes."

"Well," Iris said, walking slowly toward the door down the aisle, "it was something Sky said to her."

Gray's mouth quirked. "Okay, I'll bite, Iris. What did she say?" His protectiveness was rising in him, much like a porcupine who raised its quills to protect itself. Only Gray couldn't care less about himself; it was Sky he wanted to protect.

Iris gave him a warm look. "Kam thinks she's sweet on you, Gray."

He didn't react and kept up the slow saunter toward the door. "That's what Sky said?"

"Well, no. Kam shared that when you came in, Sky's voice went softer, and she saw something in her eyes. Kam asked her if she had feelings for you."

Gray's jaw twitched as he gritted his teeth.

Iris gave him a one-eyebrow look. "She does."

"Is that Kam's opinion?"

"It was."

Gray could feel Iris looking at him, but he didn't respond, shoving his hands into the pockets of his Levi's. "Then that's Kam's opinion, Iris. I respect her abilities, but you know it's only that—an opinion."

Chuckling indulgently, Iris nodded. "You know, when I saw you two together for the first time, I thought you'd make a fine-looking couple."

Gray wouldn't take the bait.

"And," Iris went on airily, waving her hand, "you have so much in common. You are both military vets. And unfortunately, you both share PTSD." Her voice lowered. "You know, in my seventy-five years, I've found the best relationships have a number of key ingredients in common."

Iris knew about Julia's murder and his efforts to climb out of the hell of grief and depression because of it. Iris never treated her employees like worker bees. No, she embraced them as long-lost children come home again, and she was like a cosmic mother to all of them.

Slanting a glance over at the elder, he said, "Iris, my whole focus this past year was getting the center built and ready for the ranch guests. Now that it's up and running, I'm still working through my past. I like Sky. I know what she's going through, more or less. And she's a good person."

"But?"

Gray wanted to groan out loud. Iris was like a wolverine. Once she latched her jaws on to something, she was not going to let go until she got what she wanted. It made him smile. "But I've got enough to juggle on my plate right now, Iris."

"Hmm, okay..."

Gray knew what that response from Iris meant: she didn't believe him. Well, he was going to let her sit with it. He pushed open the door for her, the sun striking them warmly. At 9:00 a.m., the coolness of the morning was just beginning to burn off.

If he admitted how damn badly he was drawn to Sky, Iris would have a field day. His boss was known as a wily matchmaker in the valley, and Gray didn't feel like getting stampeded by her toward any woman right now. Besides, his priority was to give Sky safe harbor, a place to heal up and continue getting stronger every day. That was Gray's commitment to her. Vets helped one another. It wasn't about sex or anything else. It was about loyalty to your brother or sister soldier, sailor, Marine or airman.

Iris halted and turned, studying him. "Well, whatever is happening between the two of you, it's working, Gray."

He cocked his head. "How so?"

"Isn't it obvious? Sky has had only one nightmare in two weeks. Something is helping her heal. Now—" she poked Gray in the chest with her index finger "—why don't you chew on that for a while, hmm?"

His mouth curved. "Okay, Iris, I'll think about it." He touched the bill of his cap. "I'll see you later."

As he turned and walked away, he spotted Sky emerging from the center. She had probably just finished feeding the pups. When she saw him, she came running toward him, her hair flying across her shoulders. That was unusual, and Gray picked up his stride as they met on the side of the road.

"What's wrong?" he asked her.

Panting, Sky smiled up at his scowling features. "The pups, Gray. Their eyes are opening!" she gushed. "And they have the most beautiful blue eyes! Come on. Come and see." She slid her hand into his, tugging him along.

Gray's heart stopped pounding in his chest. "You scared the hell out of me, Sky. I thought something was wrong."

Laughing liltingly, she pulled him toward the redbrick sidewalk leading up to the main entrance of the center. "I didn't mean to scare you." She gave him a tender look and skipped lightly. "Forgive me?"

"Nothing to forgive," Gray said gruffly, smarting beneath his talk with Iris and Sky's unexpected behavior. He drowned in her ebullience, her hair sun-streaked and gleaming with copper, gold and sable. Gray had to stop himself from tunneling his fingers through that shining mass of hers.

Sky was nearly breathless as she pulled on the protective gloves and then knelt down by the wolf pups' box beneath the warmth of the sunlamp. Gray knelt down nearby, pulling on his gloves.

"Look," Sky whispered in awe, picking up the white pup they'd named Gracie. "She has the most beautiful blue, opaque eyes! I didn't know wolves had blue eyes at birth."

Gray gently held the pup, who squirmed in his palm. "Later, between eight and sixteen weeks, they'll turn yellow. But right now this color of blue will be around for a bit. Sometimes, though, the blue color remains. It's rare. There's been a report of one wolf that has blue eyes at fifteen years old."

Gray couldn't tear his gaze from the joy shining in Sky's face. Her lips were lush, wide with a smile that dived deep into his heart and then scalded his lower body. His defense against Sky was crumbling, and Gray didn't care any longer.

But he still made sure to carefully examine each pup. Their eyes were half-open. He watched them move around in the box, seeing for the first time. Sky sat on her knees, rocked back on her heels, her hands resting on her thighs, mesmerized. His heart opened a little more. Whether Sky realized it or not, these wolf babies were healing her as much as she was healing them.

"Why is Gracie opening and closing her mouth when I hold her? This just started a few days ago," Sky said.

"It's called 'champing,'" Gray murmured. "It's a way of greeting another in a friendly manner. It's a ritualistic greeting."

"So…it's good?"

"Very."

"That makes me feel good." She flashed him an excited smile. "Now I'm officially part of their wolf pack!"

Gray absorbed her blue gaze, her voice going low with barely held emotion. "Yeah, we're part of their pack. Right now they see you as Mama Wolf. You feed them, clean them up and care for them."

"So do you," Sky said.

"I'm the alpha male in their lives. You're seen by them as the alpha female."

"What happens now? With their eyes open, won't they need to get out and explore more?"

Gray nodded. "Yes, they'll get bolder. Usually at four weeks, they're starting to investigate outside their den. I've almost finished the area where we're going to permanently put them. It will be ready in about two weeks. When wolf pups open their eyes, the first thing they do is explore within the den. Most often, the parents are gone and hunting. By four weeks, they're outside running around, sniffing, rolling and playing. When they're tired, they'll go back into the den and sleep."

"I saw you the other day up in that ten-acre section. Is that their new home?"

Gray nodded and slowly rose to his feet. "Yes. Want to come and take a look at it?"

Sky nodded. When Gray held out his hand toward her, she didn't hesitate to slide her fingers into his large calloused palm. She *liked* touching Gray. It didn't happen often. She noticed Gray monitored the amount of strength he used to help her stand up. He seemed reluctant to release her hand, but did anyway. Her heart sped up, but this time it wasn't with adrenaline due to threat. It was a thrill of excitement as his narrowing hazel eyes held hers, a burning, unspoken charge flaring between them. Nervously, Sky looked away and shed her gloves, dropping them into the wastebasket.

"Come on," he urged.

Sky knew that ever since the three wolf pups had been rescued from certain death, Gray had been working nonstop with several wranglers from the ranch to install a ten-foot-high cyclone-wire fence around a ten-acre parcel within the wildlife center. It stood among dozens of tall, towering fir, protected on three sides by thick brush outside the fence. The area was quiet in the morning as Sky walked at Gray's side. The paths were strewn with cedar chips, wide enough for an ATV, an electric power chair or a wheelchair. "I always feel when I'm here, it's like a sacred church in nature," she confided to him quietly.

"I feel the same way."

"And you helped design and build all of this?"

Gray nodded, always looking around. To his right was a path that led to two buffalo, a bull and cow. Off to his left was the thirty-acre parcel that was fenced in for the two wolves they already had. "I did, but the credit goes to my mother, Isabel. She created the blueprint, Iris approved them and the money, and I chose the land it sits on and was the construction manager who oversaw the project."

"It feels as if we're in the middle of nature, not on a ranch."

"That was the whole idea. Iris wanted this built such that the animals felt truly at home and had a lot of land to live on, but also to bring nature to all the guests who come to the ranch."

They walked up a slight knoll. Gray halted. He turned and pointed toward the original wolf enclosure. "The two wolves we have, the alpha male and female, have to be as far away from these three pups as we can make it for them."

"Why? If you put in the pups with them, wouldn't the alpha female accept them?"

Gray frowned and shook his head. "No way. The alpha male would more than likely kill them immediately because they aren't his offspring. That's the problem."

"So these babies have to be raised alone?"

"Yes." The desolation in her expression was profound, and without thinking, Gray reached out and slid his arm around her, giving her a hug. He released her and said, "Don't forget, we're their parents now. And I'm going to have to teach you wolf language and ritual real soon so you can continue to act like Mama Wolf."

"I've heard they have a way of communicating," Sky admitted.

"My mother worked with some of the pioneers of wolf communication, and I grew up watching her and helping her. It's not hard to learn, but you have to understand you're the alpha female, and certain things will have to be taught by you to train these pups accordingly."

"I'm ready to learn, Gray." Sky smiled up at him. The

sunlight slanted silently through the awakening morning. Somewhere deep in the fir there was a gurgling call of a raven.

"You're a fast learner. Tonight we'll go over some of them after dinner." Gray dug out the list from his pocket. "I need to bring you into town this morning, and we'll do that after you take a look at the pups' new world."

Sky was amazed at the work that had been done in two weeks to make the orphaned wolf pups a place to live. In one corner, a huge dirt-and-rock den had been built. It looked so similar to the one the grizzly had torn apart that Sky was amazed by the careful attention to details. Inside the den, though, was a recessed sunlamp that would warm it for the pups because their real mother was no longer there to provide it for them. The den was strewn with cedar chips, something soft for them to lie upon. Tiny cameras had been installed in other recesses, and twenty-four-hour-a-day video would begin. These videos would help wolf biologists understand pup pack behavior, among other things.

The enclosure had trees, stumps and brush within it. Many other places were provided for the pups to play, run and learn how to be a wolf. There was a small pool of water at another end opposite the den, along with water running through a man-made concrete stream so they would always have fresh water and a place to swim and play.

Sky heard the excitement in Gray's deep voice, watched his masculine gestures as he explained the layout to her. It was clear that he'd invested his heart and soul in this project, in managing the wildlife center. She reached out, her fingers curving around his upper arm beneath his jean jacket. Instantly, she felt his biceps contract.

"At one time," she said softly, "you were a warrior in combat keeping our country safe. Now you're a warrior for Mother Nature and protecting all her brethren."

"I'll always be a warrior," Gray agreed, his throat tightening. In that moment, the rapture in Sky's gaze nearly made him lose control. It was so trusting that Gray wanted to plunge himself into her in every possible way and on every possible level. Sky understood him in ways no one ever had, his motivation, where his heart's passion resided. Her answering smile tore at his senses.

"I think the babies will just love this enclosure, Gray. You've been so thoughtful and tried to give them everything they'll need to grow up as well-adjusted wolves."

"That's my hope," Gray breathed, feeling her release his arm. His skin burned pleasantly where she'd touched him. Heat scored up and down his arm. All Sky had to do was look at him in that special way, and Gray became putty in her hands. He came so close to leaning down, cradling the back of her head and kissing her. He could almost taste her.

Gray forced himself to take a step back so Sky was out of his reach. "Come on. We have to get you those medical supplies from Jackson Hole."

## CHAPTER ELEVEN

SKY COULD BARELY contain her excitement of purchasing items for her small medical clinic on the ranch. Gray had dropped her off at the Valley Drugstore, owned by Jay Johnson. She'd spent time with the older man, and she'd set up a wholesale account with him in the office. Gray was over at the Horse Emporium, getting sacks of grain and oats for the many dude-ranch horses. He would swing by when he was done and pick her up. Best of all, he'd invited her to lunch at Mo's Ice Cream Parlor.

Jay walked with her to the front of the busy drugstore and pulled out a small wheeled cart for her. "Just use the list Iris provided and go up and down the aisles and get what you need, Sky. When you've got everything, Donna, our cashier, will add it all up." He pushed the dark-framed glasses up on his long nose. "I'll go over and tell her to give you the wholesale discount so there won't be any problems."

Sky smiled over at Jay. He was in his mid-fifties, thin as a pencil, and reminded her of an accountant. He wore crisp black trousers, a white, short-sleeved shirt and had a thin mustache. "Thanks, Jay. I really appreciate it."

She wheeled her cart to the first long aisle. The drugstore was very busy, and Sky saw a lot of tourists in the building. Probably buying bandages and other items for the hiking trails of the Tetons. Looking down at her list, she got serious about what she needed for her little dispensary.

Sky looked back on the past two weeks and how her life had suddenly changed for the better. Not only had she gotten a job she passionately loved, but now she was going to be able to use her nursing knowledge and get back into medicine, which she missed. Best of all, she'd had only one nightmare in that time, an unbelievable turn from having them three to four times a week. Was it the job? Or was it Gray?

Sky didn't want to look too closely at the connection between her and Gray. They were getting closer every day. His quiet and calm gave her support to continue her fight to heal herself.

Every time Gray smiled, Sky's heart ached with need of an even closer emotional relationship with him. And sometimes, when they traded the wolf pups between one another's hands, and he accidentally brushed her fingers, she ached with hunger.

She'd never forgotten the kisses he'd given her as she lay in his arms that dark and terrifying night after emerging from her nightmare. In a matter of an hour, he'd calmed her. The past two weeks had been a reprieve to Sky. A new window had been thrown open, offering her hope from her symptoms that dogged her heels twenty-four hours a day. The energy she used to control those emotional reactions deep within herself left her exhausted at the end of every day. Now getting eight hours of sleep without waking throughout the night was helping her reclaim who and what she was before the capture. Sky woke up happy and hopeful, something that she'd thought had been destroyed forever within her.

Sky couldn't tell Gray that waking up in that house, knowing he was out in the kitchen every morning making them breakfast, sent a keening ache of so many joyous emotions through her that she lay there awash within their rainbow colors flowing through her.

Sky felt as if she were emerging from a dark, endless tunnel, and the past two weeks had been a journey of unparalleled hope to her. She'd struggled so long by herself, refusing medications to dull her savage emotions. In addition to Gray's support, Iris Mason was like a doting grandmother to her. How many times had Iris come over to the center to visit her? Hugged her? Loved her in a motherly way?

Sky missed her parents, especially her mother. She had weekly phone calls to her, but Sky missed her mother's nurturing and support. Iris had replaced that need in her to a large degree whether she knew it or not. Her father had called her several times, but Sky knew she wasn't feeling strong enough yet to ward off his ideas about her PTSD. She hadn't returned his phone calls.

Getting down on her hands and knees, Sky spotted several types of dressings she wanted to carry at her medical dispensary. She leaned down, reached in and snagged four of the packets.

It was then a shrill warning of threat arced through Sky. She froze, scrambling internally to locate the source of the incoming threat. Turning her head to the left, she saw a pair of shining black cowboy boots standing three feet away from her. Jerking her head up, she gasped.

The man looking down at her was darkly tanned, his brown eyes assessing her like a predator. He wore his black hair long, and it hung across his shoulders. His mouth was thinned, and he was staring at her as if she were a piece of meat.

"I like my women on their hands and knees," he growled, leaning down, sliding his hands through her hair. "What's your name? You're new around here."

Flashes of her captors, the tall, thin Taliban soldier with the long, dirty black hair falling over his shoulders, his dark brown eyes filled with hatred toward her, exploded through her mind.

Sky was no longer in a drugstore. She was back in that suffocating, airless room with the Taliban soldier carrying a bucket of water toward her where she lay strapped down to the wooden board. The flashback was so powerful, Sky fell backward, sprawling out on the floor. The packets of dressing flew into the air. She scrambled to get away from the stranger. Just when she'd found a sliver of hope at rebuilding her life...

GRAY HAD JUST entered the drugstore and saw a tall, lean man standing over Sky, staring down at her. The moment he leaned down and touched her hair, he reacted. Hissing a curse, he sprinted through the drugstore, understanding the danger.

"Hey," Gray snarled, gripping the man's shoulder and pushing him backward, away from Sky. "Get the hell away from her!"

The man snarled a curse while stumbling backward. "Who do you think you are! I'm not through with either of you. And I've got friends who could do some damage," he yelled, his arms flailing as he caught himself before falling.

Gray glared at the man, whom he recognized as Chuck Harper, owner of Ace Trucking. "Leave," he ordered. *"Now."*

Without waiting, Gray turned and devoted his whole focus to Sky, who was on the floor, hyperventilating. Her eyes were glazed over. She wasn't here. She was caught in a flashback. *Dammit!* Gray heard the man curse again and leave.

"Sky? Sky, it's Gray. Listen to me. You're safe. You're here, not there."

God, how badly he wanted to reach out and haul her into his arms. But he didn't dare. She'd made such strides, and one bad encounter could set her off. He ached for her and held his hand out toward her.

Sky's face had leached white, her eyes huge, her mouth contorted in a scream that never left her. She was trapped between him and the cart she had been filling with medical items. Her chest heaved with exertion, and Gray felt her terror.

He couldn't stand her anguished look. She was reliving her torture. He was sure of it with every raw, uneven breath she took.

Gray became aware of a number of people gathering around them. He looked up.

"Leave us," he told them in a growl. "She's all right."

Jay Johnson pushed through the gathering crowd. "Gray, is there anything I can do? Call an ambulance? 911?"

He shook his head. "No. Just get these people away from her. It's the last thing she needs right now." Because it would only make Sky feel suffocated.

"Okay," Jay said and then turned, asking the people to disperse.

Cursing inwardly, Gray wanted to punch Chuck Harper in his smug, narrow face. The bastard was known to stalk young, beautiful women. Those that spurned him disappeared, never to be found again. That or they ended up in the hospital with broken bones. But Harper was smart enough never to be caught. The whole town knew he was a stalker. And what he did with those who were abused by him made Gray want to get up, find the bastard and deck him. He had spotted Sky, walked silently up on her, watching her like a predator before making his move.

And Sky was probably completely unaware of him until it was too late. The shock of someone standing that close to her, confronting her, running his hand through her hair, had sent her back into the past. Without even knowing him, Sky had sensed the threat.

*Sonofabitch!* He'd deal with Harper later. Right now, he had to get Sky to come out of the flashback that held her in its grip. Wrestling with his own emotions, his protectiveness toward Sky, Gray concentrated and shoved his own feelings aside.

SKY HEARD GRAY'S CALM, deep voice calling her back. The more she homed in on the low timbre, the more she felt the grip of the flashback dissolve. Blinking several times, tears running down her cheeks as she sat frozen on the floor, her back against the cart, she finally saw him and not the torture room.

Gray's eyes were a darker brown in color, although she could see the green and gold in the recesses. He was patiently extending his hand toward her. At first, she couldn't understand what he was saying, such was the depth and power of the flashback.

Desperately, Sky wanted the pictures slamming into her from memory of her torture to go away. Disappear. She could feel the white-hot pain in her wrists and ankles. Her bones grinding against the metal chain as she tried to escape the water being systematically poured into her nose. She tried to breathe, her breath exploding from her as she felt herself suffocating and dying beneath the relentless water.

Gray moved closer. His knee near her foot, he inched his hand toward hers. Sky felt the warmth and strength of his fingers curling gently around her own. Her hand was so cold and damp. The heat and warmth he provided brought her back. Suddenly, she was staring into Gray's hard, unreadable face. The sense of fierce protection radiating from him was unmistakable.

Gray tightened his grip around her fingers, which sent a frisson of stability through her. And then Sky realized she was sitting on the floor of the drugstore. People were gawking her way, staring at her openmouthed as they slowly passed. Shame pummeled her. *Oh, God...*

"It's all right, Sky. Look at me."

Sky burned with humiliation, but she lifted her lashes and clung to Gray's tender gaze. "Oh, God, Gray, I blanked out. A-a flashback..."

She pushed her hand through her hair, suddenly nervous, wanting to get up and escape the drugstore. Escape the curious looks.

"It's okay," he soothed, noting the sudden look of a trapped wild animal on her face. Sky searched for the man who had triggered her episode.

"Wh-where is he?" Sky's gaze darted around. "I looked up, and he touched me," she choked out as tears rushed into her eyes. "He looked like one of the Taliban soldiers that hurt me." Her scalp crawled where he'd reached out and slid his hand into her hair.

"Come here, baby. Come on." Gray moved forward and easily lifted her to her feet and into his arms. Sky buried her head against his chest, clinging to him, physically shaking. Gray gently enclosed her with his embrace, kept her pressed against him as she wrestled to stop her sobs. He slid his hand across her silky hair, pressed a kiss to it and rocked her a little, trying to take the edge off her terror.

His heart cleaved open, and Gray no longer tried to tell himself that he wasn't fully invested in Sky. She made him feel more deeply than any woman ever had. And the rampant, tender feelings he held for her suffused him as he surrendered to them without a fight. "It's going to be all right," Gray whispered thickly against her ear. "You're going to get through this, Sky. I'm here. We'll do this together. You and me. You hear me?"

Sky couldn't speak, the lump in her throat preventing it. She rested wearily against Gray's tall, strong body. His arms were so protective-feeling, and it fed her strength to halt the terror ravaging through her. Just his hand gently sliding across her hair, his mouth against her brow, the warm moistness of his breath flowing across her damp cheek, was a balm.

Finally, Sky pulled away. But not far enough to lose contact. His hands settled on her sagging shoulders. "I—I'm okay," she managed. Lifting her hands, she tried to wipe the tears off her cheeks.

"No apologies," Gray growled, looking down. "Don't say you're sorry, Sky, because you couldn't help what happened here. You don't need to apologize to anyone. Not ever again."

Jay Johnson came over. "Is there anything I can do to help you, Sky?"

Sniffing, Sky felt so ashamed. "Thanks, but no, Jay. I—"

Jay held up his hand. "It's okay, Sky. That was Chuck Harper who scared the daylights out of you. He had no right touching you like that. I'm really sorry…" Jay scowled angrily in the direction of the glass door where Harper had left earlier. "He shouldn't have sneaked up on you like that. He has a bad habit of stalking women, you know? He gets off on scaring them."

Gray held on to his rage over Harper. "Jay? Can we give you that list Iris wrote out? Collect the rest of the items for Sky? I'll drop back by here a little later and pick them up. Is that all right with you?"

The owner smiled. "Sure. Anything to help."

Sky looked around. "There's the list," she said, pointing to it on the floor near the cart. Near where she'd been sitting and trying to scramble away from Harper. Swallowing hard, she gave Gray a miserable look, feeling like a failure. He nodded and seemed to understand how she felt. Gray pulled her beneath his right arm, tucking her against him.

"Come on," he urged her. "Let's get out of here. You need some fresh air."

"Yes, fresh air…" Because she felt suffocated in that torture room. No light, no fresh air. She gulped and tried to shore herself up. Sky could feel Gray being a guardian toward her. He pushed open the glass door, and the sunlight fell across her. Outside on the main plaza, life went on as usual. Sky halted and whispered, "My purse… I left it in the cart…"

"I'll get it," Gray told her. He guided her to a wooden bench next to the door. "Sit here. I'll be right back."

Sky wanted to shrink into the wood and disappear. What had those people thought when she'd sprawled out on the floor, looking like a madwoman? Oh, God. And she buried her face in her hands, battling the urge to cry. She sensed someone nearby and lifted her head.

"Here you go," Gray murmured, handing the purse toward her.

"Thanks," Sky whispered, pulling the strap over her left shoulder.

"Feel like walking?"

Nodding, Sky started to rise.

"Take my hand."

Gray's hand was large and beautifully shaped. His fingers were long, his palm thick with calluses. Sky willingly slid her hand into his and allowed him to lift her to her feet. When he automatically placed his arm around her shoulders and drew her close, she sighed raggedly. How did Gray know she needed this?

The boardwalk went all the way around the busy main plaza. Tourists were everywhere, the traffic heavy. Gray walked on the outside, guiding Sky close to the buildings so no one could go on the inside and suddenly come up from behind her, startling her. He kept his stride checked for her sake. Sky rested her head wearily against him, a sign of trust. It made his heart widen with a flood of new emotions, new awareness.

Gray looked around for that bastard, Harper, but didn't see him. Knowing Harper, he'd taken off. Anger burned deep inside him. He wasn't done with the bastard. Pushing all of it away, Gray looked down. Sky's cheeks were starting to flush with color once again. He could see her breathing slow and deep, something that would help her calm herself. Her arm was wrapped tightly around his waist, as if she were afraid he'd let go of her. Gray wouldn't, but only time and being with her would teach Sky she wasn't alone in this PTSD storm that would hit like lightning, out of nowhere, and send her reeling out of balance.

"Do you feel like telling me what happened?" Gray asked her, catching her glance.

Grimacing, Sky whispered, "I was down on my hands and knees, getting some dressings, when this terrible feeling washed over me. It felt frightening." She nervously licked her lower lip. "I—I snapped my head up in the direction I felt the threat, and I saw this man." Sky hesitated, touching her wrinkled brow. "H-he looked like my captor. And he leaned down, his fingers sliding into my hair, holding my head at an angle. And just like that, I was back there, Gray. I was in that terrible, little, suffocating room."

Gray's arm tightened protectively around her, as if he were trying to absorb some of her terror.

"He had no business touching and scaring you like that," Gray growled.

"Wh-who was he?" She shivered, pressing her hand against her breast.

"Chuck Harper. He's the owner of Ace Trucking," Gray said with distaste. "He's a well-known womanizer here in town, Sky." He felt her tremble. If only he could take away her anxiety...

"I—I never met him before." Sky closed her eyes for a moment. "I never want to meet him again. He looks like that Taliban soldier."

Nodding, Gray rasped, "I'll make sure he doesn't ever bother you again, Sky. I promise." His mouth went hard like his eyes. It would be the last time Harper ever approached and touched Sky. *Ever.*

Gray halted at the stoplight. "Want to wander around the square?" he asked her.

"Yes, it feels good just to walk."

Because the walking equated with running away from the enemy. Gray knew that only too well, often waking from a nightmare drenched in sweat, his heart pounding like a sledgehammer in his chest. He'd get up, get dressed and go for a hard run along the main ranch road to the highway and back, a four-mile round-trip. Gray knew that exercise tamped down the high cortisol, and that was why so many who had PTSD were joggers or into hard, constant exercise. Walking was Sky's way of running from the enemy in her mind and memories. Movement equated with freedom. Distance from the epicenter of the torture her brain would never forget.

They walked for nearly an hour until Gray felt Sky become relaxed once more. She was no longer pale. Her eyes looked normal now, although he could see the exhaustion in them. "Better?" he asked, halting in front of the drug-store once more.

She tucked her lower lip between her teeth for a moment and then gave a nod. "Better," she agreed.

"Sit here. I'll go pick up your medical supplies," Gray told her. "They should be ready by now."

It felt good to sit and hide on the bench. The sun felt warm and soothing on her hands and face. Sky avoided people's curious gazes and all eye contact. To look at another human, with the exception of Gray right now, drained Sky. The hyperalert state would last another few hours, and Sky had learned to hide from the world as it happened.

Gray returned with a big bag in his left hand. He smiled down at her, offering her his hand. "Ready to go home?"

*Home.* The word had never sounded better than right now. Sky nodded and took his hand, grateful for his care, his silent understanding. As he tucked her beneath his arm, he guided her into the alley between the two buildings, heading for the public parking-lot area.

Climbing into the truck, Sky felt the heaviness of the experience begin to lift from her as Gray drove them out of town. She twisted her fingers together in her lap, frowning.

"What's got your attention?" Gray wondered, turning onto the highway that led up a long, sloping hill. To his right was the elk refuge, a large fenced-in area where elk were fed during the winter so they wouldn't die by the hundreds during the cold season.

"Um, just worried about what Iris will think. What others who saw me will think. The gossip that will fly around town…"

Gray reached out, gripping her hands and giving them a squeeze. "Iris will understand, no problem. And those other people? All I saw was worry and care and wanting to help you on their faces, Sky. Not judgment of you.

Okay? They cared and they wanted to help you, but didn't know how."

His low voice flowed through her, quiet and strong. She opened her hands and held his. "I—I feel like such a failure, Gray."

"What I saw was a warrior trying to contain her terror and fight it."

Hanging her head, Sky closed her eyes, feeling so much of her pain dissolve. Gray's hand tightened briefly over hers, silently feeding her hope. "I hate flashbacks," she rattled, her voice strained.

"They rip open your soul," he agreed, his voice rough. "It used to take me half a day to a full day to come out of one after it hit me."

"It's the same for me," Sky whispered, lifting her head, looking at his strong, hard profile. There was nothing weak about Gray in any sense of the word. His body was hard, angular and tightly muscled. His whole demeanor was that of a true warrior. Even in civilian clothes, he couldn't hide it in his walk, his posture or the way he was ever alert. There was a quiet, rock-solid confidence in him that was rare. And he stood out to Sky because of it.

"There are phases to it," Gray agreed. "Right now you probably feel pretty naked and want to crawl into the nearest hole and protect yourself."

Sky nodded, her throat aching with unshed tears.

"I'll feed the wolf pups when we get home, so don't worry about that. What I want you to do is go to your bedroom and lie down for a while. Doesn't matter whether you sleep or not, Sky, just rest someplace quiet where you feel secure. All right?"

Gray cut her a quick glance. He could barely stand the bleak look he saw in her muddy blue eyes. All he wanted to do was curl up in that bed with her, tuck her along his long body and hold her tight until she fell asleep in his arms. Gray knew he could do that for Sky.

"Are you sure, Gray? It's my turn to feed them."

"I'm sure. I'll take over the feedings until you tell me you're ready to resume. It's not a problem, so don't give me that look."

He forced a faint smile for her benefit. If nothing else, Sky could be counted on to be there to do the job she'd been assigned. That was just like a military vet: they could be counted on to carry the load assigned to them come hell or high water. And right now, he wanted to give Sky an out and not feel so damn guilty about it.

"Okay," Sky whispered, clearing her throat. "Thank you. I'll make it up, Gray. You aren't always going to have to babysit me."

He laughed. Gray shared a heated look with her. "Someday I want to mean a helluva lot more to you than just a babysitter."

# CHAPTER TWELVE

GRAY NEEDED TO talk with Sky. He'd kept busy helping the wranglers move the hundred-pound grain sacks from the truck to the barn after feeding the wolf pups earlier. By the time he got back to the house to check on Sky, it was 4:00 p.m. Had she lain down and tried to rest? He hoped so.

He moved into the quiet house, but didn't immediately see Sky. As he went silently down the hall, he noticed that her door was open. Peering into the darkened room, he saw Sky sitting on the edge of the bed, leaning over, her face buried in her hands. His heart wrenched. He knocked softly on the doorjamb, not wanting to scare her out of her mind with a sharp knock.

"Hey," he called softly, "want some company?" God knew he wanted to go to her without her permission, but Gray knew better. There were times when he was in this phase of the letdown, when the adrenaline deserted him, when he felt exhausted and wanted no one around.

Sky's hands dropped from her face, and she twisted around. "Yes. Come on in…" Never had she wanted to see anyone more right now than she did him. As he approached, she saw concern glittering in his eyes. He rounded the bed.

The mattress dipped as he sat down, their knees barely grazing one another. Sky's throat ached with tension. Gray's hands were resting on his thighs and she sensed his controlled power. She picked up the scent of alfalfa hay around him along with perspiration and his male scent. A few bits of hay clung to his shirt.

"Were you out helping the wranglers in the barn?" she asked. How badly she wanted to surge into Gray's embrace and let him hold her. She felt so shaky, so needy. She hadn't been like this before her captivity. People leaned on her, not the other way around. Yet as she searched his hard face, it was alive with tenderness toward her. She liked Gray so much, and Sky had been running from admitting it, from her feelings toward him. Right now she needed his quiet steadiness, his understanding.

Gray brushed his shoulders. "Does it show?"

"A little…"

"How are you doing? Did you get any rest?"

Quirking her lips, Sky nodded. "I—uh, went to sleep. And I guess Harper triggered the damned stuff in me." She wiped her face in frustration, turning away, ashamed of herself. Her voice cracked as she whispered unsteadily, "Gray, all I want to do is get better. I hate when things like this happen. On my way from the hospital, when I was coming home to my parents' house, I lost it at a truck stop. There was a man who resembled one of my captors. I panicked," she confided miserably. "I—I managed to get to the women's bathroom, locked the stall door and I fell apart."

*To hell with it.* Gray whispered her name and shifted, sliding his arms around her. She flowed into his arms, and that was when he knew Sky needed this. Needed comforting. She tucked her head beneath his jaw, her hair tickling his chin and cheek. Her arms moved around his waist and she clung tightly to him, face pressed against his chest, as if trying to hide. God, Gray knew what it was like.

"It's going to be all right," he muttered, kissing her hair, rubbing her back gently, trying to get her to relax. "You'll get past this, Sky. You've come such a long way in such a

short amount of time." Gray tunneled his fingers through
her hair, pushing the curtain of strands aside to see her pale
face, her eyes tightly shut. It was her beautiful, lush mouth
compressed that told Gray the amount of pain she was experiencing. "We take this a minute at a time, baby. Sometimes an hour at a time. You're still in the coming-down
phase from that scare with Harper. You know the drill."

Sky barely nodded her head. How warm and strong
Gray's arms felt around her. She'd been so cold, her hands
damp, and now the warm, hard, muscled strength of him
surrounding her helped Sky fight the inner war. "I—I
know," she managed in a broken whisper. Gray's heartbeat was slow and calming beneath her ear. She inhaled
the dampness and sweat from his shirt. The faint fragrance
of pine lingered, overlaid with his male scent, and Sky un-
consciously inhaled it deep into her lungs. Dragging life
into her, not death.

"I try so hard, Gray. This caught me so off guard. My
attention was elsewhere, on getting the medical stuff, not
thinking someone was going to stalk me. God, I felt like
he was hunting me. I felt like a scared, trapped animal."

"I know," Gray whispered hoarsely into her hair, sliding his hand around her jaw, cupping her cheek. "I know."

Sky couldn't explain what happened next. She felt Gray
ease her away, his hand framing her cheek and jaw, the
warm calluses rough and yet, so comforting. She lifted her
lashes and drowned in the brilliant green and gold of his
eyes. He was so close…so close…and Sky leaned forward,
wanting his mouth upon hers. It was instinctive, necessary
to her, and her lashes swept downward as her lips barely
grazed the hard line of his.

Heat shot through Gray like unexpected lightning as
Sky leaned forward. He felt the soft, tentative question
that hung between them as her lips touched his. He hadn't

expected this. Had wanted it, but he hadn't even thought that Sky would want to kiss him as badly as he wanted to kiss her. Especially not now.

In those precious, heated moments spinning like scalding, bubbling heat between them as their lips met, Gray knew. He knew Sky wanted him as much as he wanted her. It was a shock to him, thinking it was only one-sided, that he wanted her on every possible level. Wanted Sky in his arms, wanted her mouth against his, wanted to be buried deep within her, wanted to give her pleasure and to take away the anguish he knew always lived within her.

More than anything, Gray wanted to give Sky a beautiful, momentary reprieve from the war that was always a breath away within her.

He groaned as her lips, so unsure, shyly brushed his mouth. His arms instantly tightened around her. He felt her hand slide up his shirt, his flesh reacting wildly to her tentative response. This was real. So damn real his chest tightened with erupting emotions. Her lips were so incredibly lush as he parted his, sliding against hers, silently letting her know it was all right, that he wanted to kiss her, too.

Somewhere in his exploding senses, Gray knew he had to let Sky take the lead. He couldn't overwhelm her, couldn't know what she wanted. She had to *show* him what she needed from him. His erection grew painful, pressing against the material of his Levi's as she leaned into him, a soft moan vibrating in her slender throat. He slid his hand from her cheek and around the nape of her neck.

He felt Sky dissolve into his arms, surrender completely against him as he controlled his own animal-fierce need of her, man to woman. He hungrily inhaled her sweet scent, the silkiness of her hair brushing against his cheek, and he angled her more deeply into his arms, cradling her, his mouth leisurely exploring hers. He wanted to plunge his tongue into her mouth, slide his hand downward to caress her breast. But was that what Sky really wanted? Gray didn't know and was old enough, wise enough, to put a steel band around those runaway testosterone caveman desires.

Her mouth was so uncertain, and he felt her unsureness. Gray was glad he didn't barge in like a proverbial bull in a china shop, glad that he was monitoring all her signs and signals. For the first time in his life, as he felt her lips part, felt her breath moist against his flesh, felt their mouths mold and meld hotly with one another, Gray experienced an incredible rush of unparalleled joy. Sky's breath was ragged. He could feel her heartbeat leaping against his chest, felt the swell of her breasts pressed against him.

His fingers itched to slide around her back, to envelop her curved, full breast, to feel her within his hand, feel her warmth and life. But Gray stopped himself. That wasn't what Sky was wanting. This wasn't about sex. It was about care and something else that was unexpectedly blossoming between them.

Her mouth was responsive, sliding against his, and she trembled within his arms, as if beginning to awaken from a deep, deep sleep. Her slender fingers moved shyly across his cheek, holding him closer, wanting more of his mouth against hers. Her heartbeat amped up, and he felt the sweet vibration in her throat, telling him she liked kissing him.

Just the way she was lightly caressing his cheek, he knew this wasn't sexual, as much as he wanted it to be. Finally, Gray eased his mouth from her wet, warm lips. Barely opening his eyes, he watched hers slowly open. Even in the grayness of her bedroom he could see the blue of her eyes, the clarity that was in them. Gray sensed Sky wanted him sexually, but was hesitant. It was there, in her eyes. But he knew they couldn't rush this. Someday, they could be together. Maybe.

God, he hoped so.

Sky felt soft and curvy in his arms. So sensitive. So vulnerable. Tenderly, he leaned down, pressing a kiss to each of her eyelids. He felt her hand tighten against his shoulder in response, felt her relax fully in his arms. So trusting. Trusting him to do the right thing for the right reasons. Her cheeks flooded with color once again, and her lips parted, the corners no longer drawn in with pain. He wanted to make Sky happy. Her hand slipped from his shoulder, and he felt her fingers curl softly against the roughness of his chambray shirt, his skin tightening beneath her innocent gesture.

"It's going to get better," Gray promised her, his voice low and roughened with emotion. He lifted his hand and nestled strands of her hair away from her cheek. He sensed Sky's raw, deep need for human touch, contact and safety. And then he saw turmoil come to Sky's blue eyes, saw them glistening and knew she was fighting back tears that wanted to come.

"Listen to me," he growled, cupping her cheek, forcing her to look at him. "It will get better over time, Sky. You need to believe me on this because I've walked the same path you're walking right now. You're stronger than you realize, and that's why I don't want any apology coming from you. Understand? We'll do this together. I'm here for you."

Sky sat out at the table with a cup of hot coffee between her damp, cool hands. Gray had gotten her out of the bedroom and taken her to the kitchen table and sat her down. He'd made fresh coffee and cared for her in ways she'd never dreamed would ever happen to her. When he sat down at her elbow, she slid him a shy look.

"I don't want you to feel like you have to always take care of me when I crash like this."

Gray's chiseled mouth moved into a one-cornered smile. The burning look he gave her made her ache. Sky wasn't an innocent. She knew her body, knew she wanted to make love with Gray. But how could she? Presently, she was the one who was weak and needy, not him. It was unfair to both of them.

"Sky, I've never seen myself as being your babysitter. I told you that earlier. I *want* to be here for you." His lips tingled in memory of that fleeting, gentle kiss she'd given him. Gray wanted more from Sky. And he had the steel patience to wait and see where this relationship with her was going.

Bowing her head, Sky stared down at the cup of steaming coffee. "I just feel like I'm taking advantage of you," she managed, her voice raspy with unshed tears.

"I'll be the first to tell you if I feel that way," he said. The devastation was so clear in Sky's face that Gray wanted to sweep her back into his arms and will it away.

Setting his coffee aside, Gray traced her brow and whispered, "Sky, what I feel for you has nothing to do with being responsible to you as a babysitter. Get that out of your head right now. We have something good between us. I felt it from the moment we met. I just wasn't sure you did. You're in the middle of a fight for your life and sanity. I get that. And there's no way in hell I'm going to do anything but support you the way you want. If you want to be held, I'm here, Sky. If you don't want to be alone, say so, and I'll be at your side. No funny stuff. This isn't about sex. It's about one human caring for another." He stared into her glistening eyes. "Are we clear about this? About you and me?"

Sky pushed the coffee mug away and turned toward

him. Her heart wrenched with hope and anguish. His low voice vibrated through her like a wolf's growl, only it wasn't menacing. It was healing. It told her so much.

"I kissed you," she whispered, her voice barely above a whisper. She saw some of the intensity leave his expression, his mouth lifting a little at the corners.

"Yeah, I know you did. And I liked it, Sky." *And I want more. So damn much more from you...* "Tell me why you did it." He searched her eyes, needing to know if she wanted him or if she just needed a way to get rid of the pain.

Sky rested her brow against his shoulder and closed her eyes, feeling like a coward. "It just felt so right to me, Gray. I—I wasn't sure how you would react... I was scared, but I kissed you anyway." And Sky forced herself to raise her head and look him in the eye. "It felt so right to me in that moment. I have feelings for you." Sky glanced away, trying to find the right words because right now her emotions were wild and howling. "Ever since I saw you, I felt something good and clean between us, too. At first I thought it was me. I thought I was being selfish and needy."

Gray made a sound of protest in his throat and slid his hand beneath her chin and got her to see the tenderness he felt toward her. "Baby, if anything, when you're feeling down and out, you turn away from me. You hide in your room or go somewhere to be alone. You don't really come to me when you're in that state, Sky. Do you see that?" Gray had never wanted her to see it more than right now.

Licking her lower lip, his roughened hand against her cheek, she barely nodded. "I don't want to use you, Gray. Not like that." His brows dipped, and his fingers cupped her cheek and chin a little more. "I have to get strong. I have to fight this. I can't use other people as a crutch. To enable me. That won't get me stronger."

His mouth curved a bit more. He wondered obliquely if her therapist at the Naval hospital had told her that. "This is not a war you can fight alone, Sky. What you see as weak or needy really isn't. Humans, when they're hurt, crawl into one another's arms. They lie down beside them and hold them. They rock them. They whisper words they hope will help heal the other person." Gray hesitated, looked up at the ceiling and then down at her. "You aren't the type to manipulate people, Sky. You were in the military. You're strong and you know how to fight back. And that's what you've been doing ever since this happened to you." His voice softened. "Sky, you need to ask for help. Come to me when you're feeling like you need a hug or to be held." *Or kissed.* His entire body was feeling scorched by her kiss, triggering his need to heal her in another way. Only it was a way that Sky hadn't given him permission to follow up on.

"I'm so used to being alone, Gray. So used to fighting this without any help."

"I know you are. Six months in a military hospital doesn't exactly engender you to run over to the nurses' desk and ask for help. I understand." He threaded his fingers through her hair. "This is different. You're at a new level of dealing with your PTSD. No one ever gets through their life alone, Sky. And you need to reshape whoever told you to gut through and not reach out for help."

She sat digesting his impassioned words. Closing her eyes, she felt herself being wrenched back and forth, listening to her therapist, Olivia, or listening to Gray. Opening her eyes, she forced out, "If you didn't have PTSD, Gray, I probably wouldn't believe you. But you do have it."

"I have very little of it left inside me now," he told her. Watching her eyes, watching the terror in them dissolve with each gentle ministration across her hair, Gray knew what Sky needed. She needed him. He could be her bulwark. He could protect her when things went bad inside her. "I want to be the person you turn to, Sky." Gray grimaced and added, "I know you work for me. I know you're worried that the job and personal stuff will get mixed up and confused between us." His voice grew deep. "But I'm here to tell you it won't. It's easy for me to separate the job from the personal with you. Don't shut me out in the future. Be honest with me about what you need, and don't be afraid to come to me about it."

"Okay," Sky whispered, trying to smile but failing.

"Promise?" he rasped, holding her gaze.

"I—promise."

SKY NEEDED TO go to the center, just to be with the wolf pups. They always fed her a certain kind of calmness. As she sat on her knees, the new pups exploring their large room, their eyes open, she watched them sniff and then tumble and play with one another. They were awkward and bungled along on tiny legs. Every day, their little pug-nosed faces were reshaping themselves. Already, Sky could see their noses begin to form and begin to look a little more like an adult wolf's face.

She sat there, hands on her thighs, smiling and watching them. The pups lifted her into another reality. And it was a respite from hers. Heart opening, she thought of Gray, of his mouth moving gently against her lips. He could have kissed her hard, passionately, but he hadn't. He sensed what her needs were, and the tender movement of his mouth against hers drove her to tears right now. She sniffed and forced them back. Crying all the time wasn't going to help her. The fighting she'd begun after awakening in the hospital was what was needed in order to counteract the symptoms that lived like a hungry monster inside her.

Gracie, the white wolf pup, came leaping over to her. She landed on Sky's lap and struggled up her thigh, her little claws rasping noisily against the denim. Gray had given Sky permission to stop using the latex gloves because the pups were at an age where their immune systems were strong enough to thwart possible human virus or bacteria. Laughing softly, Sky leaned over and cupped her hands beneath the wolf.

"Oh, Gracie, are you hardwired to me? How did you know I was feeling like I needed a puppy hug?" She lifted the pup up and snuggled her against her shoulder and jaw.

Gracie whined and licked her voraciously, wriggling, her thin, whippetlike tail fiercely wagging back and forth.

Closing her eyes, Sky cuddled Gracie. The wolf pup whined and wriggled even more, as if loving her and sharing emotions with her. What was there not to love about these beautiful, wild creatures who trusted her and Gray with their lives?

Sky felt two more puppies leap upon her thighs. She opened her eyes and cupped Gracie in one hand at her side. The black female, Crystal, whined and looked up at Sky with shining blue eyes, wagging her tail. And then the gray male, Chert, rolled off her thigh and into her lap, his little legs up in the air, flailing around. Laughing softly, Sky placed all three pups into her lap and gathered them between her hands.

Gray had said that very soon, they would grow so large she could no longer hold them. Even now they were growing like weeds in a garden. Smiling, Sky leaned down so her hair tickled them. The pups loved playing in her hair, and their little yips of pleasure as they attacked the strands made Sky chuckle. Playing with the babies always lifted her spirits. That and kissing Gray.

As Sky used her arms as a protective enclosure so the pups wouldn't tumble off her legs as they pawed and played in her hair, Sky felt her heart opening in a new direction.

Why had she kissed Gray? The urge had become so strong within her, she was unable to stop from lifting her face and placing her lips against the hard line of his mouth. It had shocked her. But when he gently returned her kiss, her whole soul had melted into his strong, capable hands, and she had relaxed utterly into his embrace. The sense of safety, of care, and of some other unnamed emotion, moved through Sky as she played with the pups.

Her mind revolved around their conversation afterward. She waffled between fear of being needy and wanting Gray in her life. Confused, she wiped her hand across her face, feeling unable to separate them as easily as he said he could. Sky just wasn't there yet. She wanted to be, would struggle to be, but she wasn't right now. Looking down at the pups, who had quieted and were lying next to one another in a pile on her lap, Sky smiled softly, gently petting them. Their thin fur was now fluffy and thick. Every day, the pups were changing and growing. They were so strong physically that it surprised her. Sky wished she had some of their strength, but Gray was right: she was a lot stronger than she realized.

Looking up and through the windows into the central area of the building, Sky missed Gray's strong, silent presence. He was a voice of reason in the storm of her wildly fluctuating emotions. He was the calm to her fury that lived like a rampaging animal within her. His kiss had been like breathing new life, new hope into her.

Did Gray realize how much it had helped her climb out of that basement of horrors that hung like a dark specter at every turn of her day? Sky was sure he did because his ability to monitor her, his experience of knowing what she was going through, was always there. Gray did not judge her, and for that, she was eternally grateful.

Gray… Oh, God, she had feelings she'd never felt for a man before, rising up through her, infusing her heart and healing her soul. Sky was caught up in such a morass of daily battles with her rampant feelings that she couldn't take her attention off them to focus on Gray. Would he understand that? Accept it? Sky was unsure. As long as she was a puppet to these raging PTSD feelings, there was no way she could honestly center on Gray and how he made her feel. All she could do right now was be grateful he was standing beside her while she fought the battle to get better.

## CHAPTER THIRTEEN

It was Sunday afternoon, and the next six families, who came from around the world to the dude ranch, were arriving. Gray had just come from the center when he saw Sky greeting one of the families. She had crouched down in front of a very shy eight-year-old boy with glossy black hair. Iris had let them know that the Bradford family, who had a son with autism, would be arriving today. It was their first time here, and Iris had asked Sky to be a chaperone for the boy, Justin. Gray settled his hands on his hips and, from a distance, watched the small boy nod his head as Sky asked him something. The two parents, both clearly anxious, watched them.

Iris welcomed children with mental challenges with open arms. And in the past year Gray had seen a number of them pass through the weeklong dude-ranch vacations. He was glad Sky was there because she had the ability to draw pitch out of a pine tree.

Sure enough, Gray watched the boy shyly lift his head and look at Sky. He knew autistic children were painfully bashful and often would retreat into a corner and become a shadow. They wouldn't make eye contact. That interaction with people was just too agonizing for them.

Gray snorted and dropped his hands. Hell, PTSD made a person feel the same way, so he was sure that Sky would have a unique entrance into Justin's enclosed world where he felt safe from the outside world. For Sky, it was to retreat into her bedroom. That was safety for her. For autistic children, some faded into the deep recesses of themselves.

As he walked across the street, Gray saw Justin's bright blue gaze cling to Sky, who smiled sweetly at him. Yeah, Sky had that kind of wonderful, warm, nurturing personality. Gray would bet by the end of the week, Justin wouldn't want to leave.

Gray walked over and introduced himself to the parents, Judy and Pete Bradford. He told them about the wildlife center and that they were welcome to come over and go through the one-hundred-acre facility by appointment.

Judy, a blonde with short hair, gripped Gray's arm. "Iris was telling us you have wolf puppies here, Mr. McCoy."

"Yes, ma'am, we do." Gray noticed Judy's sudden pleading look.

"Could you...? I mean...would it be too much to allow Justin to see the puppies?" Her voice rose with hope. "Justin loves wolves. He has pictures of them hanging up on his walls. His bedspread has a wolf on it. You have no idea how many times he's watched National Geographic videos on the wolves in Yellowstone."

Sky glanced up at Gray. She didn't know what he'd do with such a request. Normally, the pups were off-limits to the public. When the word *wolf* was mentioned, even Justin turned, scrunched up his face and looked up at tall Gray McCoy.

Gray rubbed his jaw and faced Sky. "What do you think, Sky? Is Justin well behaved? Would he sit near you if you brought him into Wolf Haven?"

Justin turned, jumping up and down in place, giving Sky a begging look. "Oh, please, Sky! Please let me see them. I love wolfs!"

Sky's smile broadened. "Would you mind sitting next to me, Justin? I'd need you to sit here." She pointed near her thigh. "If you could do that, I'd take you in to where we feed the wolf puppies."

Justin squirmed as if his skin were too tight for him. His mother had dressed him in a pair of jeans and a bright red cowboy shirt with a yellow neckerchief. "I promise! I promise!" he blurted out, shifting from one red cowboy boot to another.

Sky angled an eyebrow, catching Gray's gaze. She saw him give a brief nod. Tilting her head, she said, "Okay, Justin, we'll do it tomorrow after you eat breakfast with your family. Wolf puppies get fed about every four to five hours. The next feeding would be at 11:00 a.m."

Justin gave a yip and went running around his parents several times, wildly waving his arms, excited.

Judy smiled with gratitude. "You have no idea how much our son will love this. Thank you from the bottom of our hearts."

"It's not a problem. I'll have to have you sign consent forms, Mrs. Bradford. And only Sky will take your son into that area. You can remain outside the enclosure, watching through the windows. If you want to take photos without a flash, or video, you can do that."

Judy's eyes filled with tears. She reached out, squeezing his arm. "Thank you, Mr. McCoy. This just means so much to Justin. He'll never stop talking about it."

Gray grinned. "I hear you. We have wolf coloring books over there, some kid videos and other educational items your son might enjoy having, too."

Pete Bradford groaned. "And we thought we had to worry about Justin being bored while we were out here."

Sky slowly stood up, not wanting to startle Justin, who had come back and was leaning against his mother's legs, holding her hand. "Well," Sky told them warmly, "I'll be

Justin's babysitter while you two go on the group rides. We'll have fun here or over at the center."

Judy pressed her hand to her breast and sighed. "I just can't imagine all of this. Our travel agent said the Elk Horn Ranch welcomed children with challenges, but this is just incredible! It's beyond anything we could have ever hoped for."

Gray nodded and slipped his hand beneath Sky's elbow. "We hope you enjoy your time at the ranch. If you'll excuse us, Sky has a few things to take care of with me at our new medical dispensary."

Sky followed him, liking the closeness Gray established between them. A week had passed since her flashback episode. The late-afternoon sun was warm, and the valley was green and beautiful. She lamented his hand slipping away from her elbow. "What's up?"

"Oh, just wanted to rescue you," he murmured, giving her a mischievous grin. He halted at the door that said: MEDICAL OFFICE. "I also wanted to take a look at how you arranged your office." Sky had spent a week getting it in order.

Sky nodded and stepped in. The facility was about four hundred square feet, small but cozy. Gray followed and closed the screen door behind him. Outside, a number of wranglers were showing the arriving six families the cabins they were assigned to. Looking around, he murmured, "Nice."

"I particularly like the examination room," Sky said, pointing to the open door to the right.

Gray craned his neck inside the room and looked around. It was painted in five rainbow colors that swirled lazily around the four walls, and the ceiling was white. Perfect for children. Sky had thoughtfully added a tiny brown stuffed teddy bear that sat on the counter with her stethoscope and blood pressure cuff. "Kids are going to love to come in there," he said, glancing over to where she sat behind her new blond-oak desk.

"I hope so," she said.

"Got everything now?" he asked. The difference in Sky between last week and this week was remarkable. She had slept through every night without incident, awakened every morning looking rested. Gray had worried she might have a kickback on the PTSD, but hadn't so far. She looked good enough to eat in those jeans; she filled them out so well. Today, she'd worn a long-sleeved white cotton shirt and a lightweight brown leather vest with brass buttons down the front of it. The pink neckerchief around her neck was nearly the same color as her cheeks.

"Maybe…" she said, frowning and looking up on the wall opposite the desk. There, she had all the drugs under lock and key. Sky watched him walk like a silent cougar over to her desk. Gray perched his hip on the edge of it, his full attention on her. Instantly, her heart rocketed up in beat, and she felt that wonderful aura of protective energy pour off him toward her.

"I'm sure I'll make some adjustments as I go along," she added, talking more to herself than him.

Gray nodded, clasping his hands on his left thigh hooked over the corner of the desk. "So, you think Justin will sit quietly on your lap when you feed the pups tomorrow?"

"I hope so."

"If he doesn't, you know you'll need to pick him up, take him outside and let him stay with his parents. Then you go back in and feed them."

"Good advice."

"He can watch you feed through the window."

She smiled softly. "You were kind to do that, Gray."

He gave her a rueful grin. "I'm a kind dude every once in a while."

Feeling the heat of his gaze, remembering the night before, Sky felt thickening heat purl in her lower body. "You are," she assured him. "Just because you were once a big, bad SEAL doesn't mean you can't be a compassionate guy who helps others."

"Guilty as charged," Gray said, holding up his hands. He slipped off the desk. "Gotta run. I'm meeting some contractors to talk over the blueprint plans that Iris and Rudd made for that new wolf-pup enclosure."

"They are three lucky little tykes," Sky said.

"They are," he agreed. "I'll see you later." Gray felt damn lucky that Sky had walked into his life, although he kept it to himself.

Sky had just gotten into the employee house when the landline phone rang in the kitchen. Who could be calling? Everyone had cell phones. Closing the door, she hurried over and answered it.

"Sky?"

"Mom!" Her heart pounded with sudden joy. "Why didn't you call me on my cell?" Sky had given her mother both numbers.

"Sorry, honey, I just didn't think. Sky, it's about your father…"

Sky's hand tightened on the phone. She saw the door open, and Gray stepped in. He nodded in her direction and closed the door. "What's happened?" The words came out in a strained whisper.

Gray halted and turned, hearing the sudden fear in Sky's voice.

"He's had a heart attack, Sky. He's okay. He's resting comfortably in the hospital. The doctors said his three main heart arteries were nearly all closed with plaque buildup."

Sky closed her eyes, remembering the last, harsh words her father had said to her. That she was fine, that all this crap in her head was her imagination. Swallowing hard, she whispered, "I-is he going to live?"

Her mom sighed. "Yes, he's going to be fine."

"When did this happen?"

"Early this morning. He woke me up, telling me he felt like a horse was sitting on his chest. He was breathing shallow and his face was gray and sweaty. I got him to the hospital as fast as I could. I'm sorry I didn't call you sooner, but he's just gotten out of surgery. I didn't want you worried or waiting on pins and needles to see if he was going to make it or not. He's okay, Sky. Thank goodness."

Gray walked over. When he barely rested his hands on Sky's shoulders, tension was radiating off her. He wrapped his hands around her shoulders, leaned down and asked, "Is there anything I can do to help?"

Tears burned in her eyes. Sky heard the gruff warmth of Gray's voice near her ear. She shook her head. His hands felt steadying. Comforting.

Gray stepped away, releasing her, and she suddenly felt so alone. It was the PTSD, the anxiety amping up in her, making her feel emotionally unstable. Her mother sounded exhausted. Sky knew she loved her father with every cell of her being. This had to be a terrible blow.

"Maybe you could pray for your father? I know you two had a falling-out before you left, honey."

Hearing the sorrow in her mother's voice, Sky closed her eyes, fighting back her tears. "Y-yeah, he was kinda muleheaded." She heard her mother laugh a little.

"Your father is a mule, no question." Her voice lowered with sympathy. "And he should never have spoken those words to you, Sky. I know how much it hurt you. It drove you away from us...."

Anxiety tore at Sky. "Mom, I really don't want to talk about it. It's in the past. I had to leave, and you know why."

"I do, honey. Listen, your father is resting now. I'm going to stay at the hospital and talk to his cardiologist a little later. I think they're going to keep him in here for observation for two or three days. Once I know, I'll call and let you know. Okay?"

"Yes, that would be fine."

"And how are you doing? I'm sorry I missed my promised call to you last week, but things have been up in the air around here."

Her mother usually called weekly, and Sky always looked forward to it. Once, Sky had been like her Cheyenne mother with her rock-solid confidence. Not now, however. *Not ever again.*

"Don't worry about it. You just focus on Dad, okay? Do you think I should come home?" Sky didn't want to. Still too raw from their heated argument that drove her out of their home.

"No, you stay where you are, honey. I can handle things on this end."

Sky smiled tentatively. "You can handle anything, Mom."

"It's good to hear your voice, daughter. You feel better to me. Maybe lighter? Things must be going well for you at this ranch."

Her mother's voice always buoyed her, fed her hope. "Things are going wonderfully here, Mom."

"I'm so glad, Sky."

"We have wolf pups here, and I'll take a few photos and send them by email to you. Maybe that will cheer you up?"

"I'd like that. So would your dad."

Sky's heart sank. She doubted her father would ever apologize for what he'd said. "Okay, Mom. Give me a call and let me know how Dad is coming along in a few days?"

"I will. Goodbye. I love you, Sky."

Gray had poured himself a cup of coffee and waited until Sky hung up the phone.

"What's up?" he asked.

Wrapping her arms around her chest, Sky turned and told him what had happened.

"Glad he missed that bullet," Gray said, his brows dipping. He gestured toward the coffeepot. "Want a cup?"

"Right now, to tell you the truth, I could use a shot of whiskey." Unable to remain still, she unfolded her arms and walked aimlessly around the living room, her gut alive with anxiety and grief.

"About the only thing we have in the house is a bottle of wine," Gray said, following her. He sat down on the couch, watching her pace.

"I don't touch the stuff," Sky said, battling sudden tears that wanted to come. Why the hell should she cry for her father? After what he'd done to her? Halting, she took a ragged breath, trying to control her wild, escaping emotions. Hating PTSD, hating how her feelings were amplified times ten, she dropped her hands from her face and cast a look down at Gray. He was sitting relaxed at one end of the couch, legs crossed at his ankles, watching her. "I might have PTSD, but I'm not going to self-medicate to stop feeling this terrible anxiety in me."

"Come sit." Gray patted the couch next to where he was.

Swallowing, Sky saw the kindness come to his face, the understanding clearly written in his eyes. Gray knew what it was like. She sat down, inches separating them, remembering him holding her that one night. "God," she muttered, "you must think I'm a mess." Like her father did.

Gray shook his head. "Never, Sky. You know that."

Just his confidence in her soothed some of the aggravation. Twisting her fingers into a knot in her lap, Sky whispered, "I feel like I'm apologizing all the time to you, Gray."

"Don't apologize. It's not necessary. I can understand why you're so conflicted about your dad."

She shut her eyes and tried to distance herself from her anxiety. "It got so my dad would look at me like I was some kind of wild, crazy animal that has escaped out of my cage. And now he's the one who's in pain."

Wincing, Gray shifted the cup and slid his hand across her hunched, tense shoulders. "Was he always critical of you?"

"No." She absorbed his touch, welcomed it, wanted more. Sky fought her need because she felt she was taking advantage of Gray's generosity toward her. He'd kissed and held her last week. Now tonight there was another crisis. She couldn't just fold and fall into his arms. She had to rebuild herself on her own.

"You said your father was in the Marine Corps for four years. Did he see combat?"

"I—I don't know. He never said, and I never asked."

"You don't remember your dad mentioning being in combat?"

She pushed several strands of hair away from her eyes. "Yes, no memory." Twisting a glance toward Gray, she asked, "Why do you ask?"

She began to relax as he slid his hand across her shoulders. "If he had seen combat, maybe he was sitting on a pile of PTSD emotions. By you coming home and showing your own PTSD symptoms, it could have triggered his."

"Ohhh," Sky murmured, frowning, thinking about Gray's words.

"Did your mother ever tell you if your dad had nightmares?"

Rubbing her aching brow, Sky shrugged. "Vaguely... I have to ask her, Gray. I don't really remember." She straightened and lamented his hand drifting away from her shoulder.

"A lot of guys never say anything about it, Sky. No matter what war, whether it was Vietnam or another one, most never talk about it." He'd had good luck meeting Dr. Jordana McPherson, and she'd helped him tame that dark monster inside him. And soon, Gray was going to urge Sky to get help from Jordana. He saw the monster she wrestled with daily. Saw it taking a horrific toll on her entire life.

Sky shut her eyes as if fighting back her reaction. Planting her elbows on her thighs, she buried her face in her hands. "I just never thought about it that way...because he never talked about his time in the Marine Corps."

Grimly, he said, "That's probably a pretty important clue that something did happen to him. Something gave him PTSD."

Shaking her head, the pieces tumbled into place. "Oh, God, if that's so, then my dad didn't have anything left over to help me."

Gray set his cup on the lamp table and moved forward, sliding his arm around her. "You know yourself that eighty percent of your energy is turned inward on trying to control those feelings. I'm sure your dad loves you, but something triggered him, Sky. Probably your nightmares. I'll bet if you call your mother in the next few days after his crisis has passed and ask her, she'll confirm he had nightmares after he came home."

"This makes so much more sense to me now, Gray," she whispered, hungrily absorbing his arm around her shoulders, tucking her close to him. He fed her strength, gave her back a feeling of steadiness. "God knows I really was a mess when I got home. I couldn't sleep. I was restless. I jumped at every shadow. I had so much insomnia. I'd fall asleep during the day and then jerk awake if either of them entered the living room, where I was sleeping on the couch." Sitting up, Sky shook her head. "How could my dad live all those years and never show any of these symptoms, Gray?"

Gray shrugged. "He's a very strong individual, and he probably internalized it. Remember? I told you some PTSD survivors can look normal on the outside. They have the internal strength to stop it from showing on the outside, like others do."

She studied his shadowed face, thinking how strong Gray was. "Were you able to?"

"Hell, no. I had nightmares, insomnia, jumped at my shadow just like you did."

"That makes me feel better in a sick kind of way," Sky murmured wryly, watching his chiseled mouth curve faintly at the corners. Gray squeezed her shoulder. How badly she wanted his mouth on hers again. The healthy part of her that had survived her torture craved him. The unhealthy parts of her made her feel as if she was weak, needy and unable to survive alone in the world.

"I learned to take it an hour, a day, at a time, Sky. You have to, also." He searched her face. "I'm glad your dad is all right. And maybe later you can go home and see him."

"Not now, Gray. I'm too sensitive, too overwhelmed with everything."

He gently skimmed her shoulder and forced himself to release her from his embrace. Gray understood the need for Sky to fight her tears, to keep battling, because the alternative was to give up. And she wasn't one of those people.

"Well, maybe as things quiet down around here and you get a feel for the rhythm of the work, we'll talk sometime."

"About what?"

"Me. And how I got help with my symptoms." He smiled a little, seeing hope flare. "Without drugs," he amended. Something he understood was important to Sky. She didn't see herself, see the fact she'd refused drug treatment for her symptoms and fought a daily battle on sheer guts alone. Yeah, she was her father's daughter, no question. Sky's face, those high cheekbones, broad brow and full lips, came directly from her Cheyenne mother, Balin, who had given her daughter her warrior blood. Fighting his very real need to kiss her, Gray knew he couldn't force their burgeoning relationship in any direction. Sky had to keep leading. She was the one floundering and trying to grasp at the straws of her life after the torture. Gray wanted to support her doing that, not become an impediment, or worse, a distraction, to her.

But damn, he wanted her in every possible way. She intrigued him on every level. All of that had to remain mute and unsaid. At least for now.

## CHAPTER FOURTEEN

IT WAS 3:00 P.M. on Sunday afternoon when Gray climbed into the truck and left for Jackson Hole. The induction of the six families was going off like smooth clockwork, and Rudd Mason had asked him to make a quick run into town for him. They were low on special feed for some of the animals at the wildlife center, and Gray wanted to get it stockpiled so he wouldn't have to take time out from his busy schedule next week to do it.

When he left, he saw Sky with Justin. The young, shy boy had ahold of her hand, and she was walking him over to the center. A warm feeling flooded Gray as he drove down the asphalt two-mile road toward the main highway. No one was immune to Sky's warmth and care. Justin would bloom this week, and Gray was looking forward to seeing the boy come out of his shell.

At the Horse Emporium, Gray dropped in to greet Andy, the owner, as well as pay for his order. The place was deserted on a Sunday afternoon, which wasn't unusual.

"My only wrangler on duty is on a run to another ranch with a large order," Andy told him.

Gray shrugged. "No problem. I know where the sacks are. I'll load them myself."

"Sure?" Andy asked.

"Positive," Gray said, lifting his hand in farewell and leaving out the front door.

After backing the pickup to the wooden dock, Gray

climbed out, took the set of wooden stairs and moved into the huge, cavernous barn that held everything a rancher would need to feed his stock.

Gray had gotten Andy to bring in a line of special food for wild animals, and he knew exactly where it was kept. The barn grew shadowy in the rear, and most of the lights were turned off in order to save electricity. Gray's eyes adjusted, and he found the food sacks. They were a hundred pounds each. He easily hefted one over his broad shoulder and carried it out across the wooden floor of the barn to the truck bed.

Gray never tired of the sweet smell of alfalfa and timothy hay that were baled and sitting fifty feet high in stacks at the rear of the barn. He had one more sack of special feed to go. Glancing at his watch, he saw that it was 4:00 p.m. His mind and heart were centered on Sky. Gray always looked forward to having dinner with her. It was a chance to relax, listen to her day and get to know her a little better than the day before.

The back of his neck prickled. What the hell? It was an old warning signal that had saved his life many times as a SEAL. Gray slowed as he approached the sacks of feed in the corner. His radar went online, and his hearing keyed. Danger. *Where?*

As he turned to look to the left, in the darkness near the feed sacks, Gray heard a sound behind him. Just as he turned, he saw a large man with a three-foot length of metal pipe in his hand. And it was coming down at him.

Gray swung to avoid it.

Too late!

The pipe slammed into him, striking him across the left shoulder. Gray felt the bite of the metal into his flesh. A grunt tore out of him as the powerful pipe knocked him to his knees, sending him sprawling across the floor. He blacked out for a second, his head striking the wood. Instinctively, he scrambled to get up. This time, he felt another pipe slam into him, striking his left side. Pain arced upward, but Gray turned and fought off his attacker.

The man who assaulted him was his size. And there was murder in his eyes as he hauled back to hit him with the pipe again. It was muscle memory that saved him from the next blow. Gray lunged forward, fist striking out. His knuckles hit the flesh of the man's jaw. The man screamed, his hands opening and dropping the pipe.

Sonofabitch! Gray staggered, the pain in his side searing through him. He heard another man running toward him. Whirling around, he noted in the shadows a man wearing an Ace Trucking blue uniform. His mind spun.

Chuck Harper had sent some of his truck drivers to teach him a lesson!

Anger roared through Gray. The pipe in the man's hand came down on him. Using several swift moves known as Close Quarters Defense, he sent the second attacker to the floor with a yelp.

Gray heard the other man get up behind him. Spinning on his heel, the man struck out with his meaty fist. Flesh met flesh. Gray's head exploded. He stumbled, but as he did, he swung upward, catching the man's jaw with a sharp, short jab. Hearing bone crack, Gray fell and rolled, knowing he'd broken the bastard's jaw. His whole body ached as he forced himself to his feet, turning to face his two assailants.

Breathing harshly, Gray's eyes narrowed, his fists cocked and ready. The two men looked at one another. And then they looked down at the pipes lying on the floor between them. "You pick one of those pipes up, and you're dead men," Gray snarled. Because he knew how to kill with his hands. And he would.

Each man hesitated, breathing hard, glaring at one another.

Gray remained on the balls of his feet, crouched, ready. "You tell Harper that I'm coming for him," he growled.

The men backed off. They turned and raced for the side entrance door of the barn.

Gray watched them flee. He grimaced, feeling the bruising welt growing across his left shoulder. Rubbing the area, he turned and walked over to the lengths of pipe on the floor. Stupid bastards weren't wearing gloves. There would be fingerprints on them. Gray smiled tightly as he pulled on his leather gloves.

These two goons were going to be charged with assault and battery by him. Picking up the two pipes, Gray walked out of the barn and to his truck. He set them on the front seat and climbed in. His next stop would be the sheriff's department. And he hoped like hell his friend Cade Garner was on weekend duty. Because when it was all done and over with, Gray would be sending out a deputy to arrest those two men as soon as their fingerprints were run through the system. And even if their prints didn't show up, and Gray felt they would, he'd press charges.

Flexing his fist, his knuckles raw, bleeding and swelling, Gray disregarded the pain. He put his truck in gear and headed for the sheriff's department. Rage simmered in him. Harper had warned him he'd get even. Well, he'd tried. Now it was Gray's turn to strike back, only he'd use law enforcement.

As he drove down the street, his mind hovered on Sky. What if Harper got even with him by hassling her instead? She came into town several days a week to pick up items for Iris or for the center. She definitely wasn't safe.

His instincts kicked in even more. For sure, Harper would try to get even with him for tossing his men in jail

for assault and battery. *Damn.* Gray rubbed his jaw and
cursed softly. He didn't care if Harper came after him. He
had the ability to defend himself. But Sky was another
situation altogether. The last thing she needed was to be
stalked or grabbed by Harper or his goons. *Shit.* What was
he going to do? What was he going to tell her tonight when
he got back to the ranch?

GRAY TRIED TO steel himself for Sky's reaction when he
finally arrived home at 6:00 p.m. Grimly, he climbed out
of the truck and put the sacks in the center. His ribs hurt
like hell.

The sun was just starting to set behind the mighty
Tetons in the west. The warmth of the day was beginning
to recede. He hadn't told anyone what had happened. Not
yet. His worry centered on Sky for any number of reasons. He dreaded saying anything to her because with her
PTSD, it would stress her out enormously, and that was
the last thing he wanted. Rage toward Harper grew within
him as he climbed into the truck and drove it over to the
employee house.

He saw all six families were already in the wrangler
dining room in another building. Sky would be home, their
home of sorts, probably making a late dinner for them. His
heart ached for her. *Damn.* He took off his baseball cap as
he entered the house. The scent of spaghetti sauce filled
the air, and he looked to his left as he entered and closed
the door. Sky was in the kitchen cooking.

Gray knew the side of his face would alert her soon
enough. He'd taken a direct hit from one of the goons. His
face ached nonstop, and the flesh around his cheekbone
and jaw was swollen.

"Hey," he greeted her, dropping his hat on the peg,
"sorry I'm late."

Sky turned and frowned. She was boiling the pasta in a large pot. She saw him scowling as he turned toward her. Instantly, she homed in on his face. "Gray? What's wrong? What happened?" She turned down the fire beneath the pot and set it aside. Wiping her hands on the apron she wore, Sky turned and walked quickly toward him. She lifted her hand, lightly touching the injured area.

Gray wasn't prepared for her soft, cool hand to touch the throbbing area, but he didn't wince. "Got into a fight," he offered. "I'm okay. Really."

Sky looked more closely at his injury. "You're not okay, Gray. I'm a nurse. I have eyes in my head, and this is bad." She stepped away and picked up his right hand, observing his swollen, bruised knuckles. Lifting her eyes, Sky matched his gaze. He seemed unwilling to open up to her. Why? He always had before.

"Look, we'll talk after dinner, okay?" he said, pulling his hand out of hers. "I've been in more fights than I care to think about, and this one wasn't anything." He tried to take the growl out of his voice and lifted his head. "You making spaghetti?"

Reluctantly, Sky stepped away and frowned. She knew SEALs would never admit they were hurting. They fought hurt. Pain was something they easily disregarded. And they didn't lapse into suffering if they were in pain. For them, it was business as usual. She raked him from feet to head. He looked okay otherwise, but Sky felt he was hiding something. What, she didn't know. "Could you tell me what happened?"

Gray muttered, "After dinner? I'm hungry." Well, that was a bald-faced lie. His left shoulder was aching like a bastard, and he desperately wanted to get beneath a hot shower to ease the swelling and bruising he knew was there. Worse, when he moved, the ribs on his left side took off with grinding pain. It hurt to breathe deeply, and Gray feared he'd fractured a couple of them.

As he saw the worry in Sky's blue eyes, the tense set of her lush mouth, he leaned down and pressed a kiss to her hair. "Come on. It smells good. I'll tell you everything later." Above all, Gray wanted Sky to eat. She'd regained some of her lost weight, and he was damned if his aches and pains were enough to halt dinner. He'd survive just fine.

"Well…" she said. "Okay. If you're sure? Your jaw looks like it could use some help."

He slipped his hand around her arm and turned her and headed her back into the kitchen. "Hey, finish the pasta. I'll set the table for us."

Easier said than done. Gray had to reach up into the one cabinet to get the plates. He tried his best not to flinch as he reached. Sky was covertly watching him off and on as she stirred the pasta in the pot. Gray knew he couldn't fool her; she was too damned alert. "How did it go with Justin earlier? Did you take him in to let him see you feed the pups?"

Every warning alarm was going off in Sky as she stood at the stove, stirring the pasta with a long wooden spoon. "Yes, it went fine." She followed Gray with her gaze as he reached up. For a split second, she saw him hesitate. Knowing he was injured beneath his clothing, she compressed her lips. If she didn't know SEALs as well as she did, Sky would call him on it right now. And so, she played along because Gray wasn't going to budge from his position. "Justin sat down beside me, and he watched me feed the pups."

Gray set the plates on the table and sauntered into the kitchen and got the flatware. "Did he behave?"

Sky smiled a little. "He's such a sweet child, Gray. He

was perfect. He was so excited, but he remained still. When I was done feeding them, they all promptly piled into the corner and went to sleep. I let him go over and gently pet Gracie. She was on top of the pile."

Gray nodded, putting down the pink linen and adding the flatware. "What happened then?"

"He started crying, the poor child. He used his little finger to pet Gracie and he just wept."

Gray moved carefully, not wanting to engage his fussy ribs on the left side of his body. He got the salt and pepper and set the pair on the table. "Crying why?"

Shrugging, Sky took the pot off the stove. She carried it to the sink and poured the water and pasta through a colander. "I think it overwhelmed him, Gray. He loves wolves so much, and his little nervous system just couldn't handle the joy of actually getting to touch one."

Gray watched as she placed the empty pot in the other sink. Sky lifted the colander and then put the steaming pasta into a large green ceramic bowl. The sauce was already in another bowl on the counter and he picked it up and took it to the table. "And were you able to hold him when he cried?" Because he knew many autistic children didn't want to be touched or held.

"Yes, he let me hold him."

"Lucky little kid," Gray teased, giving her a warm smile. He'd like to be held by Sky, too, but that couldn't be broached.

Sky brought the bowl of pasta to the table. She straightened and untied the apron, hanging it over another chair. Gray brought over two glasses of water. She watched how he moved, and he was stiff, not fluid. Clamping down on the questions, she took her seat. Gray sat at her elbow. When he lifted the heavy bowl of pasta with his left hand, he flinched slightly. It wasn't much, but she mentally noted it.

After piling a bunch of pasta on his plate and hers, he set it down. Sky picked up the marinara sauce and ladled as much as he wanted on his pasta. She did the same for hers, surrendering over to the fragrant basil in the sauce. Sky added three large meatballs to Gray's plate and to hers.

"What did his parents think when you brought Justin back to them?"

Sky tried to focus on the delicious food she'd cooked. When Gray picked up his fork, the knuckles of his right hand were bruised, swollen and scraped. It upset her. "They were excited that Justin was so talkative. They told me normally, he wouldn't say two words to anyone. Not even to them."

"That's sad," Gray said. He forced himself to eat. Food was fuel. And he'd need to keep eating well so his body would quickly heal itself. Sky's concerned looks in his direction didn't go unnoticed. He kept his game face on because he wasn't about to ruin this meal.

"I think," Sky said, "that as the week goes on, and I'll be babysitting him for a few hours every day, that Justin might just open up a little more. His love of wolves will provide that doorway."

"Have you dealt with autistic kids before?"

Sky nodded. "Yes. When I was stateside on a military base hospital, we saw our fair share of them. Most were boys. The head nurse where I was receiving my E.R. training had a son who was autistic, so it was very helpful to me to understand the situation. No matter which way you cut it, Gray, it's sad. The child is imprisoned in his or her mind. Some can't stand to be touched, held or be around other people." She shook her head. "Inwardly, I cry for

Justin's parents. It must be a special hell for them that he can't show his affection to them."

"It makes you appreciate your own upbringing," he said. He saw how deeply touched Sky was by Justin. Sky had slowed down eating, caught up in Justin's predicament. "Hey," he urged, "eat. You need to regain your weight. Okay?" Gray added an encouraging grin.

"You're right," Sky whispered, then went back to finishing off the food on her plate.

GRAY KNEW IT was time to come clean. He'd poured them coffee after the meal. He'd gotten up earlier, removed the plates and flatware, putting them into the dishwasher and making them coffee. As he sat down at her elbow, he saw the anxiety banked in her eyes. Feeling bad in one way, Gray told Sky what had happened. As he did, her eyes widened, her lips parting with surprise.

"Harper sent them to find me," he told her, moving the mug slowly around between his hands. "It was his way of payback when I yanked him away from you in the drugstore." Gray watched as her cheeks went pale. He wished Sky wasn't so easily upset, but knew it was the PTSD fueling her response.

"I didn't like his energy," she muttered, frowning and looking down at her coffee. "I felt danger around him, Gray, when he touched my hair."

"I know," he said wearily. "Harper has a reputation in the town and should be in jail for what he's done." He risked a look over at her. Sky's eyes grew angry.

"The bastard," she whispered, her fingers tightening around the mug.

"Well," he murmured, "Cade Garner is running those prints on the two that attacked me. If he gets a match, that's good. Even if he doesn't, we're going over Monday morning and finding the two guys at Ace Trucking and throwing their asses in jail for assault and battery against me."

Sky tucked her lower lip between her teeth, feeling anxious. "What will Harper do?"

"Be pissed." And then Gray added quickly, "At me. Not you." He didn't know that for sure, but he didn't want to put Sky on alert. At least, not yet. "I'm hoping that when the charges are slapped against them, and I go through a trial and get them put away, this will be the end of it. Harper is used to pushing his weight around. A lot of people are scared of him, and he knows it. He wins through intimidation tactics." Gray's mouth became a slash. "Only this time, they picked on the wrong man."

"Does Harper know you used to be a SEAL?"

"No. I don't make that common knowledge to anyone. It's just better that way."

"Maybe if Harper had known, he wouldn't have sent his men to attack you," she pointed out.

Gray gave a one-shoulder shrug. "Possibly. But it doesn't matter."

"How beat up are you, Gray?" And Sky stared hard at him. "Really?"

He gave her a small smile. "You're like a wolverine, you know that? You won't let go."

Sky grinned a little. "You can't pull the wool over my eyes, Gray. Now, do you need some fixing up? I noticed you're favoring your left side. Did you get hit in the ribs?"

He gave Sky a full grin. "You're good."

"I'm very good. Do you want me to examine your injuries?"

"Yeah, probably," Gray said. He finished off his coffee. "First, let me get a hot shower. The heat will help."

"You're favoring your left shoulder, too."

Rising slowly, Gray shook his head. "I see I'm not fooling you at all."

"Nope, you're not." Sky pushed her coffee aside and stood. "I'll get some medical supplies. Meet me out here in the living room. When you're done with your shower, come on out, and I'll see what I can do to help you."

"Ibuprofen will do it," he grunted.

"Ah, yes," Sky said, "SEAL candy. Well, we'll see, okay?" She wanted to reach out and hold Gray. He was a man used to pain, used to carrying on regardless. But that wasn't always the smart thing to do. The amusement lingered in his eyes, even though pain was reflected in them, too. She watched him walk. It was clear injury was making him stiffen and favor his left side. *Men.*

"Gray? Do you need some help undressing?" When Sky realized what she'd asked, heat flew up into her face. Gray stopped and slowly turned toward her. This time, she saw a burning look in his eyes that made her knees weak. "I mean," she stumbled helplessly, "you might need help unbuttoning your shirt because of your left side."

His mouth twitched, and light danced in his eyes.

"No, thanks, but I'll tell you what. You ask that question a month from now, okay? And I'll say yes."

Oh! Sky turned, unable to do much of anything except feel embarrassed. Gray chuckled as he sauntered casually down the hall toward the bathroom. The man could make a rock feel sexual. Gray was awakening her on that level, and Sky wasn't sure if that was good news or not. She had enough to handle.

Sky heard the bathroom door quietly shut. Drawing in a deep breath, she became nervous and cleared the rest of the table. How was she going to handle herself and her awakening sexual desire and still remain close to Gray? Suddenly, Sky felt shaky as never before. But it wasn't a bad feeling. She felt excited, felt desire for him on every level of herself. He'd done so much for her. And yet just the thought of running her hands across his naked flesh sent her into a spasm of longing that nearly upended her. The man affected her far more deeply and widely than Sky had ever thought possible. What was she going to do?

# CHAPTER FIFTEEN

GRAY PADDED BAREFOOT down the hall. His hair was damp. His upper body was naked. Sky felt her mouth go dry. He wore a set of clean Levi's. There was something touching about such a strong man not all put together yet, barefoot. Her heart took off as she sat at one end of the couch, the medical supplies next to her.

She'd never seen Gray naked before, and Sky was nearly overwhelmed. His chest was broad and deep, his shoulders strong, as if he could carry the loads of the world upon them. His arms were ropy with muscles, large veins standing out on the backs of his long, calloused hands and lower arms.

Sky knew she was powerfully drawn to him. Her body's response was purely sexual. Sky had never felt such burning desire now coursing hotly through her lower body. Automatically, she pressed her thighs together in response as he rounded the end of the couch. His eyes never left hers, and she could feel that heavy, turgid desire grow in her womb.

The light was low, and as Gray sat down, the medical items between them, Sky's yearning ebbed as she saw the livid, red-and-purple welt across his rib cage. Making a sound of distress, she looked up and noticed a huge swelling bruise across his left shoulder.

"My God," she whispered, automatically reaching out, her fingertips grazing his ribs, "this isn't good, Gray." His flesh was warm and moist from the hot shower. Instinctively, her nostrils flared; the pine of the soap he'd used mingled with moisture that clung to his skin, creating his own unique scent as man.

"It looks bad, but it's not," he growled defensively. Gray's breath stuck in his throat as he felt her soft, cool fingers barely graze his swollen flesh. As crazy as it sounded, wherever Sky examined him with her fingertips, the pain momentarily ceased. She had leaned close, her eyes focused on his ribs.

Automatically, Gray remained very still, absorbing her touch like the starving wolf he really was. Did Sky know how badly he wanted her? His erection instantly came to life as she gently reached out to lightly press the bruised flesh across his ribs here and there. Groaning inwardly, Gray tried to force himself not to respond to her tender ministrations. She was in nurse mode right now.

"I'll be the judge of that," she said. Sky saw Gray had on his game face. She'd seen this so often before with black-ops men who were brought into the Bagram hospital E.R. His eyes were narrowed and never left her face. His mouth, that beautifully shaped male mouth of his she'd kissed earlier, was thinned with pain. If she hadn't had years of experience with these operators, she'd have missed the fact he was in serious pain.

The red, angry bruising across his three ribs was vivid and told her of the power of the pipe smashed against his body. She moved her hands across his moist flesh, feeling the muscles beneath suddenly tighten wherever she examined him. Sky *wanted* to touch Gray. This was an excuse, Sky realized, feeling dampness starting to collect between her thighs. Her body had a mind of its own, she discovered, shocked by it.

"Well?" Gray growled.

Sky sat up, resting her hands on her thighs. "Take in as deep a breath as you can, Gray."

He scowled but did as she asked.

Frowning, Sky tried not to be swayed by his chest expanding, that dark dusting of hair across it. She tried to ignore the thin, dark hair down the middle of his torso and rock-hard abs, the dark, teasing line disappearing beneath the waistline of his Levi's. Her mouth grew dry as she saw the bulge pressing against his jeans. Oh, God, she felt a sudden scalding sensation gripping her, feeling more hot juices gathering within her. Forcing her gaze up, Sky concentrated on his chest.

"Okay," she managed, "that's enough."

"They aren't broke." Gray had seen her gaze drift down. Now Sky was aware he was turned on so damned badly by her examination, he felt trapped in a special hell. Her cheeks went suddenly pink as she lingered for a moment on his obvious erection. *Damn.* Gray wanted to get up, escape and go to his bedroom to suffer in the pain and agony he knew he would feel.

"Most likely severely bruised. They could be wrapped," she murmured, her voice slightly off-key.

Gray shook his head. "Maybe if I have to do heavy lifting like hay bales, but no, I don't want that kind of constriction stopping my movement."

Sky forced herself to meet his eyes, saw the blunt desire in them. Her throat dried up. "Then the very least, tomorrow, get to the E.R. and get them x-rayed?"

"I have to anyway. Cade wants an official hospital report on my injuries for the assault charges he's writing up on those two assholes." Gray watched her face, her eyes. When Sky licked her lip, fire surged through his lower body. Gritting his teeth, he saw how flushed Sky's cheeks had become. She seemed rattled. This was a special torture, and Gray forced himself to sit still, his hands tense on his thighs.

Standing, Sky swallowed convulsively and walked around behind Gray to examine the other bruise that lay across his left shoulder. The light brought out the swelling violet-red bruising where he'd been struck by the pipe. Her stomach tightened as she studied the thick welt.

"This has got to be painful, Gray," she breathed, leaning over. Reaching out, her fingers hovering over his moist flesh, Sky wanted to touch him. She wanted to feel those thick, long muscles across his shoulder tense beneath her fingertips. Chastising herself for her lack of professionalism, she examined the six-inch bruise that curved over his shoulder. Her heart started skipping beats, and she felt suddenly shaky and hungry for Gray.

"Well?" he growled, closing his eyes. If Sky kept touching him like that, he was going to haul her into his arms and kiss her into oblivion.

Sky suddenly pulled her hand away, as if her fingers were on fire. It would be so easy to skim his flesh, explore his powerful back, feel each set of muscles leap and respond to her. She straightened and walked around him. Picking up a small jar of ointment, she opened the lid with shaky fingers.

"This is…um… It's not really traditional medical ointment. But it works well on bruised flesh that isn't open. This is Arnica," she whispered unsteadily. "It's designed to create circulation in the area of the bruise, Gray. I—I can put some on if you want?"

Any excuse to touch him again. Her whole lower body was awake as never before. No man had made her feel like this, that scalding hunger gnawing at her, wanting him inside her, wanting to feel the power of him as a man touching her, evoking all those wonderful, sexual responses from her body. Sky thought her body had died after the torture. She wanted Gray. And as Sky tore her gaze from his erection, there was no question he wanted her. The air between them was charged. Taut. Urgent.

"Yeah, go ahead," Gray muttered, looking away from Sky. Shakily, she quickly put the ointment on and spread it across Gray's shoulder. She felt him draw in a sharp breath as her fingers glided across his swollen flesh.

"I'm sorry," she whispered unsteadily. "I didn't mean to hurt you...."

Grimacing, Gray muttered, "It's all right." His erection was throbbing, hot, turgid and heavy. The woman's fingers skimming across his tight flesh made him grit his teeth even more. For a moment, he had a reprieve when she finished. Could he bear Sky's touch on his ribs? God, he wasn't sure.

Sky sat opposite Gray, their thighs brushing as she gently spread the ointment across his torso. The flash of fire in his eyes, the tension palpable, her mind began to disintegrate. Never had she wanted to explore a man more than she did Gray. He had a beautiful, lean, hard, honed body. There was no fat anywhere on him. Just pure male bone and muscles. As she eased her fingers from his ribs and looked up at him, she knew she was lost. Setting the ointment aside, Sky held his slivered eyes, felt his raw, sexual masculinity fully, absorbing it like the thirsty, starved woman she was.

"Gray..." She barely kept her hands off him. Drowning in his eyes, seeing that spark of awareness of what she wanted, Sky owed him her honesty. Even if Gray turned her down, she had to bare her soul to him. "I—I want..." Her throat closed off. She gave a little moan of frustration because of the fear of rejection.

With a low growl, Gray slid his hand behind her nape,

drawing her against him, his moist breath hot against her cheek, his lips hovering an inch from hers. "I want you, too, Sky. All of you. But you have to tell me you want the same thing…."

It felt as if time had halted and intensified as they stared at one another, so much unspoken passing between them. Sky felt Gray's calloused fingers eliciting tiny electrical shocks across her nape.

Swallowing, she forced out, "Y-yes, I want you, Gray." Tears burned in the backs of her eyes. His mouth flexed into a tender smile.

"And I want you, Sky," he rasped as he leaned down, brushing her mouth, feeling the softness of her lips beneath his demanding ones. Her moan fired through him like a bolt of lightning. Sky leaned forward, placing her hand on his neck, feeling his moist breath as she wantonly deepened their kiss. The moment her tongue boldly moved against his, he thought he'd come right there. Groaning, Gray pulled away from her wet, glistening lips, his eyes shards of heat and desire.

Without a word, he got to his feet and then lifted Sky easily into his arms. He felt her gasp, her arms sliding around his shoulders. His ribs ached but he couldn't care less. She felt so damn good against him as he carried her silently down the hall to his bedroom. Her breasts pressed sweetly against his bare chest. She felt so damn good to him, and they hadn't done a thing. Yet. That was going to change.

Gray nudged the door open with his toe. A stained-glass lamp on the dresser provided enough light. He set Sky on the bed and felt her relax and utterly trust him. As rock hard as he was, as much agony as he was in, Gray wasn't going to go ballistic like a teenager with roaring hormones.

"Listen to me," he said, laying her down, his hip near

hers as he tunneled his fingers through her silky hair.
"You need to tell me what you want, Sky. This has to be
mutual." Gray hated himself for saying it, but the haunted
and hungry look in her eyes made him go on alert. "How
long has it been for you?"

Moistening her lips, she whispered, "Over a year…"
She brought her hands to rest on his arms that pinioned
her to the bed as he leaned over her. The shadows brought
out the harsh angles of his face. She drowned in the fire
she saw in his eyes for her only.

It felt good to be desired once more. Sky enjoyed sex,
enjoyed her body and the pleasures that a man and woman
could share with one another. "I—I thought," she admitted in a strained voice, "…that the torture had killed me in
so many ways…. Sexually, too. I mean—" she rushed on
in an embarrassed whisper "—I felt dead inside, Gray…
until…now…with you…"

It took everything Sky had to admit it. The words, however, unlocked his harsh face. She saw his eyes suddenly
go tender. And as he slid his fingers through her hair, her
scalp delighting in his ministrations, Sky was glad she'd
been honest with Gray.

"Our body has a mind of its own," he agreed wryly,
cupping her cheek, seeing her blue, shadowed eyes grow
wide, seeing them flare with hunger for him. "It's natural
and normal, Sky. I told you earlier, you're healing and this
is proof of it." He leaned over, sliding his mouth against
her parted lips, feeling her return the heat boiling in his
lower body. Her hips moved against him, a silent request,
the best kind of invitation. But he needed to confirm they
were on the same page with one another.

Easing his mouth from hers, their noses nearly touching,
he looked deep into her eyes. There was no fear in them,
no hesitation. He knew when a woman wanted him, and

Sky wanted him. "Are you protected?" he rasped, sliding his hand up her arm.

She shook her head. "N-no. I saw no need..." Sky gave him a shrug.

Yeah, Gray got it in spades. "Okay, it's all right, Sky." He sat up and went over to the dresser and pulled out several condoms. Placing them on the bed stand, he sat back down, watching her carefully. Gray knew PTSD was a fickle bitch at best. He had no idea if her torturers had sexually assaulted her. Sky said she hadn't been raped that she could remember, but that didn't mean they hadn't touched or hurt her. In a way, Gray felt as if he were in a minefield, not knowing if one of his contacts would trigger a full-blown flashback or not. "Look," he began quietly, grazing her hair, stroking it, seeing how much she enjoyed it, "we need to take this slow for all the right reasons. You need to guide me, tell me what feels good to you. Or what doesn't."

She nodded. "I'm scared, too, Gray. I—I don't know how I'll respond." And Sky gave him a pleading look of apology. "I want you to touch me, love me. I want to do the same for you..."

"Baby, this time around is for you. We'll find out what works for you and what doesn't. Let me pleasure you. Some other time, we'll take this next step. Right now, let me love you...."

Her lashes swept downward as Gray leaned over, his lips moving from her temple, lightly down her jaw and across to her neck. He felt her vital pulse beneath his lips. Felt her hands rest upon his shoulders, light and heated. She was moaning softly, pressing her hips against his thigh, her breasts grazing his chest. He wasn't going to last long. Gray lifted his head.

"Let's get undressed," he said. Because he felt like tear-

ing the clothes off Sky's body. His hands ached to cup her
naked breasts, to look at her nipples and taste them in his
mouth. Was she damp? Ready for him or not? His heart
was thudding powerfully in his chest.

Nodding, Sky sat up. She watched as Gray moved
lithely to his bare feet. Her mouth went dry as he pulled
off his Levi's, his erection hard and large. Her entire lower
body felt a rush of fluid, heat and anticipation. In moments,
he was out of his boxer shorts. She wasn't far behind, her
hands shaking, but it wasn't from fear. It was from anticipation. As she dropped the clothes to the floor and moved
to the center of the bed, she saw a feral look of a man appreciating his woman. It made Sky feel soaring hope as
her body automatically responded to his heated male gaze.

Gray could barely breathe. Sky was supple, slender,
her breasts small, the nipples already erect, wanting his
touch. He saw no marks across her body to indicate other
torture, just around her wrists and ankles. Anger warred
with a need to love her, give her pleasure, not pain. Her
legs were so long, her thighs curved and firm, making
his fingers itchy to slide across them and find that secret
spot that lay between them. If he was concerned about her
being afraid of him, Gray didn't see it in her eyes or face.
Instead, he found arousal in her expression, matching his
own. Still, he placed control over himself, knowing he
was entering the unknown with Sky. And Gray knew she
might not even be aware, her memories blocked by her
brain, and until he touched her or did something a certain
way with her, she wouldn't know, either. Until it was too
late for both of them.

As Gray lay down beside her, slipping his arm beneath
her neck, he laughed at himself. With any other woman,
he was never concerned with anything except lust. Lust
and pleasure and satisfaction for him and his partner. With

Sky, her welfare was hovering before his eyes, his heart in the mix, something new for Gray.

He gazed down across her face, whispering, "You are so beautiful, Sky…." And she was. He could see the quiver of her heart between her breasts, slightly off to the left side. Tiny ripples telling him her heart rate was high, expectant and locked into their mutual heat and desire. Sliding his hand down her long torso, following the flare of her hip, Gray was struck by her soft, rounded belly. She was a woman built to carry a baby, no question. He splayed his large hand outward, easing her against the mattress, exposing that soft flesh to his lips and tongue.

He felt Sky tense, her breath a sharp inhalation. But it wasn't a fear reaction, because she tried to twist forward, wanting more of his mouth and lips upon her. Smiling to himself, Gray lingered, moving his tongue around her belly button, hearing Sky moan, her fingers digging into his right shoulder. Her breath became shallow as he moved his lips slowly, teasingly, up the center of her body. Lost in her sweet scent as a woman, feeling the dampness grow on her warm flesh, he kissed the area between her breasts. Releasing her hip, he slid his fingers around her right breast, feeling how taut, how alive it was resting in his calloused palm. Her eyes shuttered closed, her lips parted, and he tasted the hard, pink nipple with his tongue. She went wild beneath him as he drew it into his mouth, suckling her gently, testing her response, wanting to know she felt the pleasure.

His erection pressed deeply against her firm thigh. Sky's hands moved restlessly across his chest, her body becoming sensuous and fluid beneath his hands and mouth. The firm warmth of her against him made him groan with need. He wasn't going to last long, as much as he wished he could. When her fingers wrapped around his hard flesh, he tensed. Lifting his head, Gray took her mouth hard, thrusting his tongue into hers. If he was worried she was a wilting violet, Gray set it all aside. Sky was a bold lover and met him fearlessly on the battleground of desire. As her fingers wrapped around his erection, his mind burned up and dissolved. Grunting, he pushed into her palm, wanting more.

Gray became lost in the heat and wetness of Sky's hungry mouth, their tongues tangling, emulating erotic movement of a man within his woman. He growled and tore his mouth away from hers. In one motion, he gently pulled her fingers from around his throbbing erection.

"Another time, baby," he rasped, drowning in her sapphire dark eyes filled with arousal. And before she could do anything, he slid his hands between her damp thighs, moving his fingers toward that soft, wet entrance. Her back arched, her breasts pressing against him, her eyes closing as a keening sound lodged in her exposed throat. Her thigh tensed as he slid his fingers closer. She was so incredibly ready, it threw him off guard. And when she thrust her hips toward his hand, Gray understood that she was a hungry vixen ready to suck him into herself. He smiled, placing wet kisses along the expanse of her neck and sliding his finger into her.

A soft wail caught in her throat as he captured that beautiful, swollen knot of nerves just inside her wet entrance. Gray felt the tension bolt through her. He touched and encircled that knot, feeling the tightness of her body surround his finger, feeling just how small she really was. Sky wasn't a tall or big-boned woman. She was small, almost petite against his bulk and size. It was important her body was ready to accept him. As he whispered the kisses down across her collarbone, he captured her nipple, feeling it tighten within his mouth.

Stroking her below, he felt her lower body get ready to orgasm. It was the sweetest feeling in the world to have the walls of her body contract suddenly, tightly. He heard her wail as the orgasm ripped through her. Gray suckled her deeply and felt her body writhe, her hips bucking wildly against his hand. She was so incredibly hot, so swift to respond that it nearly made him lose his focus and control.

When he slid a second finger into her, deeper, she groaned and called out his name. Within moments, a second scalding orgasm surrounded him, the tightness making him smile. Sky was mewling and gasping, the orgasm taking her away to that sweet, burning world of mindless pleasure. He felt good, able to prolong the second one.

When she finally sank against him, breathing raggedly, he eased his fingers out of her. He knew she'd be tender and supersensitive for a bit, content to hold her, feel the dampness across her skin, watch that soft flush spread silently up across her body. God, he liked pleasing Sky. Her eyes were closed, her face turned into the pillow, her ginger-colored hair spilled across her shoulders. Her lush lips were parted, a soft smile curving her mouth upward in satisfaction. She was so beautiful to Gray that he burned the memory of that one moment into his mind and heart forever.

Gray waited, stroking her thigh, kissing the silky patch of hair, inhaling her sex and scent deeply into himself. She moved sinuously against him. Yeah, she was ready for another round, no question. This time, Gray rose and placed his knees between her opened thighs. Sliding his hands around her breasts, he saw her barely open her eyes. Her lips parted, and she offered him a soft smile, reaching out for him, her fingers wrapping around his lower arm.

"Please, Gray… God, I need you inside me…now…"

He wasn't going to disappoint Sky. After rolling on

the condom, he moved his thumb across her nipples as he eased himself into her hot, wet entrance. She arched her hips upward. He wasn't prepared for her tightness. His mind was melting; he was throbbing in agony, wanting to come. If he was worried about his size, Sky thrust her hips upward, fearlessly drawing him into her. She gasped and froze. So did he. Gray held her head between his hands, staring deep into her barely opened eyes. Taking her mouth tenderly, he slowly moved in and out of her, getting her body to accept him. Her mouth gentled beneath his. And as he slowly introduced himself to her body, her sleek fluid eased him deeper.

Her tongue tangled with his. The jolt of heat shot down to his erection, and instinctively, Gray flexed his hips, driving deeper into her. Her moan vibrated between their mouths. He felt Sky's body begin to fully accept him, and then he thrust slowly, establishing a rhythm for them. More than anything, Gray wanted Sky to orgasm with him. He could feel her breathing change as he quickened his thrusts, felt her lower body contract. Sliding his hand beneath her hips, he angled her upward just enough, creating maximum pressure against that knot of nerves within her.

He held her prisoner, pumping deep and swiftly. Sky's breathy groan, her hands gripping his upper arms, told him she was going to come any second. Gritting his teeth, holding back, Gray buried his head beside her neck and shoulder, driving powerfully into her. And then he felt her contract, felt the rush of heat and scalding fluids surrounding him, and he was lost. A ripping, burning heat tore down his spine, ignited in his tightened balls and exploded out of him. He gripped the covers on either side of her head, heard Sky cry out, felt her meet and move against him, prolonging the pleasure for both of them. Sweat popped out on his wrinkled brow, his eyes tightly shut, his breath jammed in his throat as her sweet hips swallowed him whole, milked him and made his entire body go limp.

Gray swam in a world of heat, light and edgy pleasure that caused an intense throbbing in his lower body. He released the covers, pulling Sky close to him, hearing her breathe just as raggedly as he was. Her heart was racing against his heart, her hands moving restlessly across his back.

She felt so damned good to him. She fit him like a tight glove. Her small, slender body lay juxtaposed against his tall, lean, muscular frame. Every cell of protectiveness bled out through him and into Sky. She was trembling in his arms, soft little sounds in her throat telling him how good she felt, how much he'd been able to give back to her.

Raw, beautiful feelings flowed like the colors of the rainbow throughout his sated body. She was warm and soft beneath him. Her curves fit his angles. Their hips were fused. Nothing in Gray's wide array of sexual experiences could compare to this one time of loving Sky, which unlocked him body, mind and heart. Nuzzling her slender neck, the pulse beneath his lips, Gray groaned and slowly eased off Sky. He got up, got rid of the condom and came back to the bed. Drawing Sky into his arms, he wrapped his body around her, their legs entangled with one another, and he held her close. He held her in his heart.

## CHAPTER SIXTEEN

GRAY LAY AWAKE a long time into the night as Sky slept trustingly in his arms. He'd pulled up the covers, tucked her in beside him, her head resting on his shoulder, her brow against his jaw. He stared up at the darkened ceiling.

Sky lay on his left side, her arm draped across his belly. He felt each soft, shallow breath she took. Absorbed the moistness of her breath as it caressed his neck and chest. His brow wrinkled. Gray had never wanted a woman like he'd wanted Sky. Not even in his marriage. The joke was, he waited on Sky and had been patient. Something he'd never done before. SEALs were meat on the hoof for a certain kind of woman who liked bedding a real warrior. There was danger involved, and the woman scented it like a wolf did his prey. At that time in his life, Gray had liked the competitiveness of the chase between himself and the woman he wanted. It was all about conquering her, giving her pleasure, listening to her cries as she orgasmed and then walking away, satiated and fulfilled. Except his heart had never been in play with those one-night stands. He'd given his heart to Julia, and she'd been torn out of his life. Now Gray was giving his heart again. And he couldn't stand a second loss.

Gray closed his eyes, inhaling Sky's sweet scent, her silky hair tickling his cheek. He tried to logically understand what had just happened. Why he'd approached Sky differently. *Saw* her differently. Was it her tragic story?

No, he didn't think so. Did he feel compassion for her?
Absolutely. But that wouldn't make him think about sex
and bed with her in the same sentence, either. Their con-
nections were their shared military and PTSD experiences.

Gray admired Sky's courage in the face of what had
happened to her. She was a fighter. She didn't give up, and
she didn't give in. She'd come further faster in her healing process than he'd seen with other men who wrestled
with PTSD, too.

Sky felt so damn good in his arms. Her belly, that
soft, rounded part of herself, could carry another human
being. Gray absorbed the sensation of her breasts against
his chest. Her left leg was crossed over his. *Soft strength.*
Yeah, Sky had that in spades. Her beauty was natural and
needed no makeup. Her honesty felled him.

He lifted his hand, sliding his fingers through the clean
silk of her hair. Sky stirred, moaned a little, nuzzling beneath his jaw in her sleep. He cupped her head, leaning
over, kissing those sleek strands. Gray allowed his hand
to trail across her naked shoulder and skim down her arm
until his hand covered hers across his belly. Had he ever
felt this content before?

Opening his eyes, he stared hard at the ceiling. No.
Never. Oh, he'd felt wrung out and drowsy after good sex,
but this experience was different. He held women in his
arms before and after sex, but his heart wasn't in the mix.
His mind was on other things, like when to leave or the
training coming up for his team. With Sky, he wanted to
wake up in the morning and watch her slowly awaken. See
those glorious blue eyes of hers reveal how she felt toward
him. A half smile curved one corner of Gray's mouth. He
remembered Kell Ballard, his LPO for his team, telling
him that one day, the right woman would come along,
and he would fall like a tree to her feet and never get up

again because he was in love. Gray remembered scoffing at Kell's teasing, saying love was a hyped-up thing found in romance novels, that it didn't really exist in real life. Love always died anyway.

Gray moved his hand slowly up the velvet smoothness of Sky's lower arm. When he'd turned fourteen, his father, a Marine captain in black ops, was killed in Iraq. He saw his mother become a ghost of her former self for several years after his death. Saw what love did to another person who had lost their mate. And he had repeated the family curse by losing Julia to a drug runner's bullets. By the time he went into the Navy at eighteen with the intent of becoming a SEAL and following in his father's black-ops footsteps, his mother had rebounded. He remembered one time, coming off deployment, going home to visit her. He was in his twenties and matured far beyond his years. They'd talked one night after dinner, and he asked his mother if she would ever think about getting married again. Isabel had smiled a little and shook her head. She told Gray that his father was the love of her life. That there would never be another man like Jacob. And she'd compared all men to him, and none would measure up. She was a widow to this day and seemed at peace with her lot in life. Gray had found no such peace.

Was he built the same way? Was Kell Ballard right? When the right woman came along, he'd know it? That his heart would fly open like his mother's had with his father? His mouth quirked. When he laid eyes on Sky, he'd felt emotions twisting through him, so alive, bright and scalding that it took his breath away. Gray had no experience with this kind of love. His feelings for Sky were so damned special, almost ethereal, as if they might disappear because they were so sacred to his heart.

Gray closed his eyes, absorbing the softness and warmth

of her naked body against his. He wanted to wake up every morning with Sky in his arms. Could it happen? A desperation wound through Gray's chest. He couldn't read Sky's mind or heart. But he'd been with enough women to know when a woman was committed to him wholly and without any agendas. Sky had initiated this. She had come to him. And God help him, he'd more than welcomed her with open arms. He wasn't sure who wanted the other more.

Gray was almost afraid to wake up tomorrow morning. How would Sky react to tonight? It complicated everything, especially since they worked together, and Sky had intense issues to work through. All he could do was wait and see what tomorrow morning would bring.

GRAY AWOKE SLOWLY, feeling drugged. He automatically reached out, trying to find Sky. When his exploring hand met nothing but the coolness of the sheet beneath his hand, he opened his eyes. Light was peeking in around the curtains. What the hell? He raised his head. The clock on the dresser read 0700.

He was late! Gray leaped out of bed, scowling. The drowsiness and good feelings of being sexually satiated disappeared. The door to the room was closed. He had left it open last night. Frowning, he grabbed a quick shower, shaved and put on a set of clean clothes. By the time Gray left the bedroom, a half hour had passed. The wolf pups were used to being fed at this time. He entered the living room. There was soft music on in the background, and Sky was nowhere to be seen. Inhaling, Gray could smell coffee that had been recently made. Where was Sky?

His heart cringed in fear as he quickly poured himself a cup, pulled on a denim jacket, threw on his baseball cap and headed outside. The sun was coming over the peaks to the east of the valley, the sky a light, clear blue. To his right, he saw all six families trundling to the wrangler dining room, where breakfast would await them. He turned his attention to the wildlife center and strode in that direction, hoping to find Sky feeding the pups.

SKY TURNED AS she heard the main doors to the center open and close. The puppies had just been fed and were racing around her, leaping over her thighs as they frolicked. Her heart bounded in her chest. Gray looked incredibly handsome, dangerous and powerful. Her body automatically contracted with heat, reminding her once more of his skill in loving her.

His gaze found her. She smiled and waved in his direction. As he drew near, she noticed turbulence in his eyes, but he had his game face on. There was relief in his expression as he came closer. He opened the door and stepped inside with his cup of coffee.

"I decided to let you sleep," she told him. She had awakened at 5:00 a.m., and to lie there propped up on her elbow, watching Gray sleep, had made her almost weep with joy. In sleep, he was utterly vulnerable to her inspection. She'd wanted to lean over and kiss him awake, make love with him once again, but she'd been too scared to do it. Sky wasn't certain how Gray would feel toward her this morning. Trying to tamp down her nervousness, she added, "The pups are fine."

Gray licked his lower lip. "I'm making breakfast," he offered, sipping his coffee. The wolf pups raced toward him, leaping up, yipping and cavorting around his cowboy boots.

Easing to her feet, Sky felt achy in all the right places. No sex for a year made her body stiff and sore, but Sky didn't regret one second of it. She pushed her damp hands against her Levi's. "I'd like that," she said softly. Picking up the food supplies, she walked out with Gray, shutting the door behind them. As she stored the food and bottles, Sky sensed his presence nearby. How she wished she could read Gray's face.

She walked out with him, the coolness of the morning surrounding them. She stuffed her hands in the pockets of her down coat. Gray walked easily beside her.

"Do they teach all SEALs to have expressionless faces?" she wondered out loud, giving him a quick look. "Or does it just come naturally? You come out of the womb like that?" She saw his mouth curve upward. Enough that it gave her hope.

"It's taught, yeah," Gray murmured. "Why?" He looked down to see her blushing. Gray forced himself to keep his hands at his sides. He could still smell her scent, and it made him become hard all over again. Did Sky realize the powerful effect she had on him?

Sky looked across the street and saw the wrangler dining room filled with the families. "I…um… I was trying to see how you were feeling this morning about last night. With me…"

He opened the door to their house for her. If nothing else, Sky confronted issues head-on. She had a set of invisible titanium balls. That was probably why she was so far along in her own healing process. Gray closed the door and shrugged out of his coat and cap. He took Sky's jacket and hung it on a peg next to his.

Turning, he said, "I woke up missing you this morning, Sky." Gray owed her the truth, no matter how scared he was of her answer. Or her possible rejection.

"Really?" The word was blurted out, and Sky cringed inwardly. She sounded like a starstruck tween in the presence of her favorite rock star. Gray's expression warmed.

Instantly, her body responded. Her nipples tightened against the soft cotton bra she wore.

"Really," he murmured, smiling a little. In that moment, Sky was excruciatingly vulnerable. There was turmoil in her eyes, but when her lips parted, every cell in Gray's body screamed for contact with her once again. "Is that okay?" He tilted his head a little, holding her unsure, nervous gaze.

Sky stood very still, feeling the heat radiate off Gray. He was so tall, confident and sure of himself. All the things she presently wasn't. "I guess I sound terribly immature," she whispered. "Surprised."

Gray shook his head. "Sky, you've been through a lot. Our making love last night probably wasn't in either of our game books."

She shook her head, staring down at her boots for a minute. "No, it wasn't, Gray." Lifting her head, she met his hooded stare, feeling that same powerful and bubbling connection that always surrounded them. "But I'm not sorry."

"Neither am I."

The silence thickened.

"I've never been here before," Sky admitted hoarsely.

"Where?" Gray frowned, not clear on what she meant. Her cheeks were a dull red now. And he saw the confusion in her blue eyes.

"I've never had a relationship with a man I had to work with."

Gray hooked his thumbs into the pockets of his Levi's. "Is that what has you spooked?"

Nodding, Sky didn't move. Gray's expression was available to her now and she saw the kindness linger in his eyes.

"This changes nothing regarding your employment here," he told her. "What we do on our time off is our business. Are you okay with that?"

"I just worry, Gray. I've had such a tough time finding a job and keeping it. And I love it here." Sky fought back tears. "I love everyone here. We're like a big, sloppy family, and I miss my family so much."

Gray reached out. "Come here."

Sky dragged in a ragged breath and walked into the circle of Gray's arms. The instant he pressed her against his tall, hard body, a trembling sigh of relief shimmered through her. Automatically, she slid her arms around his waist, feeling him kiss the top of her head. He understood her crazy seesaw world of emotions. Pressing her cheek against his shirt, she whispered, "I was so afraid…"

"I was afraid of your rejection, Sky." Relief shot through him. She felt so damned soft and smelled so good. She'd taken a shower earlier with her almond soap. "And I'm glad you told me. If we don't talk, we won't know where the other is at." Easing her away just enough to snag her gaze, Gray saw her eyes glisten. "What are the tears for?"

Sky shook her head. "I don't know. Before being tortured, I was so confident and sure, like you. Now there are hours…days…that I feel confused and unable to make one decision. And when I do, I'm never sure of it…or myself."

Gray caressed her flaming cheek. "Stop being so hard on yourself, Sky. It's normal to feel that way." He held her unsure gaze. "Last night for me was very special. I couldn't go to sleep for a long time afterward because I was worried you wouldn't feel the same toward me in the morning."

"I woke up scared, too, Gray."

"That I wouldn't want you this morning? That what we had couldn't stand the test of time?"

"Exactly." She smiled wryly and shook her head. "But you didn't shun me."

"That would never happen," Gray said. "Probably just the opposite," he teased, watching Sky relax, the tension

dissolving out of her features. Slipping his hands beneath
her upper arms, holding her a few inches away, he added,
"I'm not sorry, Sky, about what happened between us last
night. Not one bit." *Not ever.* But he couldn't say that. At
least, not yet. Because Gray could see how tentative Sky
was this morning. *Fragile.*

"I'm not sorry, either, Gray, but I don't know about
today or tomorrow."

"Sky, I'm not going to pressure you. I can see you're
worried about it."

"We live in the same house. I'm sorry, Gray, but this is
new to me. I don't know the rules."

He shook his head. "We both agree to make up the rules
as we go, Sky." He gently released her. "Look, we work
at a fast, steady pace around here. By the end of the day,
we're both tired as dogs. You're working to heal. I have responsibility for the wildlife center." He opened his hands.
"My personal rule regarding a woman in my life is that she
has to come to me. She has to speak up and tell me what
she wants. I'm not the type of man to chase a woman, Sky.
It doesn't work well that way. Are we clear about this?"

Sky dragged in a ragged breath. "Yes. Thank you, Gray.
I needed to hear that."

"Everything's in your court, Sky." Her anxiety seemed
to ebb. He wondered if some man had hounded her in the
past, made it difficult for her, but that was a discussion for
sometime in the future with her. "I don't know about you,
but I'm starving to death. Are you up for a Denver omelet
if I make them?" he teased.

Sky smiled a little. "I can dice the onions and green
peppers up for you."

"You've got a deal," Gray said, walking past her and
into the kitchen. She watched him stroll by her with such
male grace. Her body took off in heated, burning memory

of Gray's hands, mouth and lips upon her. Sky followed him into the kitchen. "How are your ribs and shoulder this morning?" she asked, pulling an apron from the drawer.

Gray drew a carton of eggs from the refrigerator. "Better." Hell, the truth was, he'd felt no pain last night, only awareness of Sky, her sweet, hot body, her warm lips sending him over the edge. "But I'm still going to the E.R. this morning after breakfast and getting examined for the assault and battery charges that Cade is drawing up on those two. Let the nurse take photos of my injuries for proof."

"Good," Sky murmured, relieved.

It wasn't easy to get to sleep that night. Sky was exhausted from the day's activities, plus not getting enough sleep the night before. She hadn't seen Gray most of the day. He'd been gone to see the sheriff in the morning hours. At 1:00 p.m., Justin had asked for her to go along on a pony ride to a nearby trail, and her afternoon had melted into joy with the autistic boy. They'd stopped in a flowery meadow and spent the time looking, touching and smelling many of the flowers. His parents were so grateful for her attention to their son, but Sky was exhausted.

And it was Justin's birthday, so Iris had planned a birthday party for all the children and the adults in the wrangler dining room after dinner. She'd briefly seen Gray, and he'd nodded in her direction as he walked through the dining room with Wes, Kam's husband.

There were a thousand loose ends on a dude ranch that had to be attended to. Only at dinner tonight did Gray tell her about the hospital examination. He had bruised ribs. Photos were taken and then sent by computer over to the sheriff's office. Gray had then gone with Cade Garner to Ace Trucking. He picked out the two men who had attacked him, and they were arrested on the spot and were now in jail awaiting trial. He didn't return home until late afternoon.

All day, Sky had waffled between her need for Gray and being scared out of her mind over her body's suddenly coming alive. It was a shock, almost too much for her to absorb. Closing her eyes, Sky was going to ask Dr. Jordana McPherson for help with her PTSD. She couldn't even stand herself and the way her emotions swung wildly one way and then the other.

Aching for Gray to hold her, feeling his warm breath across her skin, Sky shut her eyes. She was grateful he'd backed off, seeming to understand her dilemma. Unable to stop remembering his mouth upon hers, the strength, the tenderness as he took her lips, Sky thought it was better than nightmares. Would she ever sleep tonight? Would she not have a nightmare? Sleeping in Gray's arms last night was as close to heaven as Sky had ever felt. He made her feel safe, protected and loved.

*Loved?*

Her eyes flew open. Her pulse amped up as she thought more about it. No, it couldn't be love. It *had* to be lust. Before, Sky had enjoyed sex and being an equal partner in the best of ways. No man had pleased her more than Gray. His skill showed in every touch upon her body. Sky felt dampness collecting between her thighs as she replayed his hands moving across her, sending sheets of throbbing pleasure through her.

Sky groaned softly, turned over and pressed her face into the pillow. She wanted to walk down the hall and knock on Gray's door. Ask him if she could come in. But then, what did that make her? Wasn't she the one who'd asked for space? Her roller-coaster emotions were driving her crazy. Worse, Sky couldn't trust her own feelings where Gray was concerned. He was steady, quiet and patient. He clearly knew himself. She used to know herself. Now a wild, insane woman lived within her, jerking her feelings like puppet strings, her emotions overreacting to everything. It took so much of her daily energy not to allow the constant war taking place within her to be unleashed on people in her outer world. She acted normal although she didn't feel anywhere near normal. Like a nursing friend of hers wryly told her once, *normal* was a knob on a dryer.

## CHAPTER SEVENTEEN

SKY COULDN'T QUELL her nerves as she walked into Dr. Jordana McPherson's clinic. It was a beautiful turn-of-the-century house on a side street near the hospital. As she pushed her damp hands against her Levi's, hope warred with anxiety within her. Could Dr. McPherson really help her PTSD? When she'd gone over to the office and talked to Iris Mason earlier in the day, Iris was sure of it. And she'd seemed happy to give her a couple of hours off to see the physician.

Dr. McPherson stood up from behind her desk, offering Sky her hand. "Sky, it's nice to meet you. Come on in." She smiled warmly.

Taking the doctor's long, spare hand, Sky liked the kindness in Dr. McPherson's eyes. She was about the same height as her. The glint in her dark blue eyes told Sky that she was sincere. "Hi. Nice to meet you, Doctor."

Dr. McPherson had shoulder-length black hair. She had it tamed into a ponytail at the nape of her neck.

The doctor waved her hand toward one of two chairs out in front of her desk. She picked up a notebook. "Call me Jordana. Come have a seat, Sky. I understand you have PTSD and would like to get some help for it?"

Sky had worked with many physicians over her years in the military, and right away, Jordana was in her top-ten list. She was at ease, smiling, and exuded a maternal nurturing that Sky instantly soaked up.

"Thanks," she murmured, sitting down. Jordana sat nearby, legs crossed, her notebook across the lap of her green scrubs. "Did you just come from surgery?" she asked.

"I did," Jordana said. "I'm sorry to have kept you waiting."

"No problem. I know how surgeries can go."

Tilting her head, Jordana looked at Sky. "And you know this how?"

Sky had no problem telling her she was an R.N., in the military. She rushed through that information until Jordana held up her hand.

"Sky, you have a full hour with me, so relax and slow down." She held up her pen. "I have a computer at my desk and could be madly typing all this in, but I'm old-fashioned and like to handwrite in the information." She smiled.

"I thought it was only a fifteen-minute appointment."

Shaking her head, Jordana lost her smile and became serious. "Not for my PTSD patients. I have to understand how the symptoms occurred, and we need that kind of time. Are you all right with that?"

For a moment, Sky hesitated. Gray had urged her to see Jordana, saying she was someone she could trust with all her secrets. That she had counseled and helped a number of returning military vets with the same issues. Sky knit her fingers in her lap, feeling ambivalent. Jordana was patient and kind. She wasn't arrogant or rushing her along like so many doctors did when they had a short time schedule with a patient. "Okay," she said in a subdued tone.

"Then," Jordana said, "let's start at the beginning. Was your PTSD from one event, or was it an accumulation over time in a combat zone?"

Her softly spoken question made Sky freeze for a moment. Only a few people knew a little bit about what had happened to her. Gray knew how she'd gotten her symptoms. Biting down on her lower lip, her voice became strained. "You can really help some of my PTSD symptoms?"

Jordana remained serious. "I'm sure I can. It's just a question of how much, Sky. I know you're nervous about divulging your story, and I'm here to tell you that it's sacred and secret between us. I need to know in order to help treat you."

"You aren't going to try and drug me up, are you?"

"Absolutely not. All it does is suppress your symptoms," Jordana said.

"Gray said there was a night-and-day difference in his symptoms after he saw you."

Jordana gave her a kind look, folding her hands in her lap. "Every case is different, Sky. Being an R.N., I think you know that."

"I do." She felt edgy and nervous. "I just... Well... I was hoping against hope you might help me is all."

Reaching over, Jordana placed her warm hand across Sky's clasped ones. "Tell me everything, and then I'll know where we need to go next to get you some relief."

*Relief.* God, if only! Sky took a deep, serrated breath and dived in, leaving nothing out. By the time she was done, she was sweating and feeling nauseous because it brought it all back so vividly to her.

Jordana got up and poured Sky some water and handed the glass to her. "The worst is over, Sky," she reassured her quietly. "And your secrets are safe with me." She went over to the examination table and patted it. "Come on over. Let me listen to your heart and lungs."

The hour passed swiftly. Jordana gave her a saliva test box that she'd take home with her. Blood was drawn. Sky knew her lungs and heart were fine. Her blood pressure was borderline high, but then Jordana smiled and said that coming in to see her and relive her PTSD event was enough to make it amp up. It was nothing to worry about. She was young, healthy and strong. Clutching the cardboard box that contained the items for the saliva test, Sky sat down with Jordana afterward. The doctor wrote some notes and then lifted her head.

"The sooner you take that saliva test and send it in, the faster I can help you, Sky."

"You really think you can?"

"I do. Your anxiety stems from high cortisol, a hormone that works hand in hand with adrenaline. When a person lives through a protracted event, the pituitary gland, which is the master switch to turn hormones off and on, stops working to get it shut down. The threat to your life is ongoing, so adrenaline and cortisol are constantly flowing into your bloodstream. At first, the master gland struggles to try and shut it off, but the terror you experienced never let up or stopped. It was constant."

"So," Sky said, "my fight-or-flight hormones were like an open faucet that couldn't be shut off?"

Nodding, Jordana handed her a bottle. "That's right. The saliva test will show me when your cortisol is outside normal bounds. It will be at those times when I prescribe you this adaptogen. This medicine will literally plug the cortisol receptors at those times and stop it from continuing to flow into your bloodstream." She sat back as Sky looked at the bottle. "It takes thirty days to retrain the pituitary to control and stop the cortisol from firing off into your bloodstream 24/7. After that, you won't take it again."

"Thirty days?" Sky murmured in disbelief. The bottle she held in her hand was a thirty-day supply.

"Yes, in most cases. In some extreme cases, it might be a bit longer." Jordana sat relaxed in her chair, holding Sky's questioning look. "You should see a change in seventy-two hours after taking this adaptogen, Sky. For most people, it works, and they feel like a miracle has taken place." Her lips lifted into a smile. "And it is a miracle."

"But once this particular symptom is stopped, will it come back, Jordana?"

"It can," she told her. "If, for instance, you have another trauma or experience another shock, it could trip open the uncontrolled cortisol release again. If it does—" Jordana shrugged "—I prescribe another round of the adaptogen for perhaps a week, and it will control the cortisol again and shut it off."

"I don't want to be on drugs the rest of my life," Sky muttered, frowning. "I refused most of the meds at the hospital when I was returned to the States."

"I understand," Jordana said gently. She took the bottle when Sky handed it to her. Setting it on the desk between them, she added, "I'm not into drugs unless it's a last choice. The adaptogen is a specific regulator to the body, not like a traditional drug. There's no addiction to it, either. It just goes in and does its job, and you'll feel the change fairly quickly."

"If only," Sky murmured. "I'm afraid to hope, Jordana."

Standing, Jordana said, "I know you are, Sky. It sounds too good to be true. But if Gray shared his experience with you, then you should feel hope that it can help you, too."

"He said he doesn't feel anxiety anymore." Sky stood up and slipped the strap of her purse over her left shoulder. "He's made an amazing recovery."

Jordana patted her shoulder. "One of the reasons I became a physician was to give hope to the hopeless, Sky. I love what I do to help vets with PTSD. It's very fulfilling to see them take back their lives and live without the hell of anxiety and a jumble of wild emotional reactions."

Her fingers tightened on Sky's shoulder. "You've suffered terribly, Sky. And you're so very brave and strong. Keep your hope. I'm here beside you. We'll walk this path together...."

Sky left the clinic gripping the test box in her right hand. She didn't try to fight the hope soaring through her because Jordana had been so positive and confident about being able to help her.

Taking in a deep breath, she walked down the sidewalk, admiring the old wooden houses that had been built in the early 1900s in Jackson Hole. They were blue, green, white and yellow colors, the lawns neatly trimmed, bright flowers in boxes along the windows. The trees that lined the street were mature, their spreading branches lending shade as she walked to where she'd parked the ranch truck along the curb.

For once, she was hungry, and as she climbed in, Sky decided to stop at Mo's Ice Cream Parlor on the main square for lunch. Iris didn't need her back until 1:00 p.m., when she was to take Justin and his family over to the wildlife center and walk with them through the amazing one-hundred-acre facility.

The sun was warm and bright as Sky climbed out of the white truck. On the side of the doors was a burgundy design with an elk with a rack of antlers enclosed by a circle.

"Sky!"

She turned as she heard Gwen Garner's voice behind her. Smiling, Sky lifted her hand. "Hey, Gwen. How are you?" Gwen owned the quilting store two buildings down from Mo's, and she'd been one of the first people to welcome her to the town. The older woman with gray-and-brown hair grinned.

"Going to lunch, Sky?"

"I am. Want to join me, Gwen?"

"Love to," the woman said, smiling up at Sky. "You look better. Life must be agreeing with you out at the Elk Horn Ranch."

Sky grinned. "It's like heaven, Gwen. I'm glad you pushed me into answering that ad after I got here to Jackson Hole."

Sky had met Gwen at Mo's, and they'd shared a booth during the busy lunch hour and become acquainted. She knew that Deputy Sheriff Cade Garner was her son, and Gwen had given Sky a rave review about trying for the job out at the Elk Horn Ranch. As Sky opened the door for Gwen, she felt nothing but gratitude and love for this woman who knew everything about everyone in this town.

Inside, a waitress guided them to a leather booth along the window so they could see the foot traffic along the boardwalk out in front of the restaurant.

"So," Gwen said, sitting down and putting her bright quilt purse beside her on the seat, "I haven't seen you at all since you got hired by Iris. How goes it?"

Gwen was motherly, and she made Sky feel as if she were one of her many children. Taking the menu, Sky sat opposite the woman, who was dressed in a bright red quilt vest, white long-sleeved shirt and a bright blue quilted skirt that fell to her ankles. "Honestly? Like a dream."

"A dream come true?" Gwen teased, after giving the waitress her order.

Nodding, Sky gave her order for a hamburger and French fries. When the waitress left, she folded her hands on the table and said, "It is."

"I hear through the grapevine you're working with Gray and the wolf puppies."

Chuckling, Sky sipped her ice water and said, "*You* have the ears of a wolf, Gwen. How did you know?"

Giving her a sly look, Gwen sat back. "Oh, you know… I hear things…"

"Yes, and I'll bet even the sheriff's department visits you at your quilt store to get the latest on someone." She grinned.

"Sometimes," Gwen hedged humbly. "Why are you in town?"

"Just saw Dr. McPherson," Sky admitted. Being around Gwen was like being around her own mother. There was such maternal love that surrounded the quilter, and right now Sky desperately needed that kind of care.

"Ah, good, good."

The waitress brought them over their drinks.

Gwen sipped her lemonade. "Did Gray, by any chance, urge you to see her?"

Sky nodded. Gwen knew she'd been in the military. She just didn't know about her PTSD. It wasn't something Sky wanted many to know about. She didn't want to lie to Gwen, but she didn't want to expand on the visit with her. "Iris has an amazing medical plan for her employees, and she urged me to get my yearly physical." That wasn't a lie, thank goodness, because Sky wasn't good at lying. Not that she did it often, but she really liked Gwen and wanted an honest relationship with her.

"Iris treats her people like they are her own children," Gwen agreed, smiling. "You look like you've gained some weight. It looks good on you."

Touching her pink blouse, Sky smiled shyly. "Gray and I do the cooking at the employee's house. You're right. I'm regaining weight I lost." She saw Gwen become more somber.

"It's all over town about Gray being attacked over at the Horse Emporium barn a few days ago. Is he doing all right?"

Some of Sky's happiness faded. "Yes, he's okay."

Shaking her head, Gwen said, "I wish with all my heart Ace Trucking had disappeared when Curt Downing was murdered. I was hoping it would fold up and disappear."

"I guess it's common knowledge that a drug ring is trying to get a foothold here?"

Gwen grimaced. "Yes. And it's all because of Curt. He was the one who originally signed on with the Garcia drug ring. Now Chuck Harper is the owner, and he's a snake in the grass, too."

"Ugh," Sky muttered. "Him."

Gwen's brows rose. "You know him?"

"Not by choice, believe me." Sky told her about Harper sneaking up on her at the drugstore where she was buying medical items. Gwen's face grew dark.

"Curt Downing was suave and hid what he did from others. Harper doesn't have Downing's capacity to get along with others here in town. He's pure evil in my book. You just be careful, okay? Because once he spots a woman he wants, he stalks her."

"Gray warned me," Sky said, feeling some of her hope eroding. Gwen was sincerely worried, and that caused a spike in Sky's anxiety. "I've never seen him since that run-in at the pharmacy."

"But now Harper has two men in jail with assault and battery charges against them. And I know Gray is going forward with those charges. But I worry what Harper will do. Those men truck drugs all around the western United States. I know there's ATF and FBI hanging around, trying to get into the trucking end of it, but Harper is slick."

The waitress brought their meals. Sky put ketchup on her fries and her hamburger. Gwen was upset and worried. "Has Harper had a man or men brought up on charges before?"

"No," Gwen said, spearing some romaine lettuce from her huge Caesar salad. "My son Cade is worried about what Harper will do, too."

"Oh?"

"Harper strikes back. He came from Miami, Florida, shortly after Curt was killed by that escaped convict. Legally, he's clean as a whistle, but the sheriff's department keeps an eye on him."

"What do you mean he strikes back, Gwen?" Sky picked up a French fry.

"Harper has a penchant for pretty young girls, Sky. In the time he's been here, he's stalked two women." Her mouth thinned. "Neither wanted his attentions. When they each put out legal restraining orders on him, both of them disappeared." She snapped her fingers. "Just like that. And no one has found them. Cade knows that Harper did one of two things with these women. Either he sold them as sex slaves to Eastern Europeans or he had them killed."

Her stomach lurched. "Oh, God, you're kidding me."

"I wish I was." Gwen's voice lowered. "You need to be really careful about this snake, Sky. He saw you. He approached you."

"But," Sky stammered, "Gray saw it and pushed him away from me."

"And now Gray has been attacked by two of Harper's men. You see the pattern here, don't you?"

Sky completely lost her appetite and set the hamburger on the plate. "Harper gets even."

"Yes."

A cold shiver went down Sky's spine as she sat contemplating the pattern Gwen was drawing for her. "And Gray's going ahead with the charges." Her mouth went dry. "What will Harper do?"

Gwen shrugged. "I wish we knew. Cade is on pins and

needles about it. The whole office is. Harper hires outsiders to do his dirty work. I think he made a mistake having two of his drivers attack Gray. Now that implicates him even if there's no proof he ordered those two jerks to do it."

"Do you think Harper will try and kill Gray?" Sky hated even saying the words or thinking it out loud.

"I don't know. But those other two women disappeared."

Her hands trembled as she wiped her mouth with the paper napkin. Wadding it up, Sky put it aside. "But you know Gray is an ex-SEAL? That he can take care of himself? Wouldn't that make the difference?"

"I knew he was a SEAL. But he was injured," Gwen said softly. "Black-ops men aren't immune. They're terribly human just like the rest of us."

Swallowing hard, Sky stared at Gwen. She was the mother of a deputy sheriff, and she knew a lot more than Sky did about illegal activities in the area. "Then…do you think Harper would put out a hit on Gray?" The thought terrorized Sky. Her heart was in the mix. She couldn't forget how he'd loved her so tenderly, cared for her, protected her.

"No one knows for sure," Gwen counseled, "but the possibility is always out there."

"Has Cade or someone talked to Gray about this?" Sky managed, her voice growing strained. She couldn't lose him! Not this way. Gray was so incredibly confident in his abilities. He lived life with a vitality that she'd never seen in others. He seemed unafraid of anything, unlike her.

"Cade did warn him," Gwen said with a nod of her head.

Frowning, Sky muttered, "He never said anything to me." And then she realized her mistake because Gwen gave her a kindly look.

"You're sweet on him, aren't you?"

Sky wasn't going to deny it. "Yes. I— It just happened, Gwen. Over time…"

"I'm not surprised," Gwen told her quietly. "Gray is a man's man. He stands out. There've been plenty of women interested in him since he came here, but he never paid them any attention." Her eyes sparkled. "Until now. Until you came along."

Heat rushed into Sky's cheeks, and she groaned, hating the fact she blushed so much. "He's a good person, Gwen. He does right by others." Gray had done right by her, and now she was falling in love with him. The thought startled her. Made her feel afraid and, at the same time, made her yearn for his arms, his voice and his protection he bestowed so easily upon her.

Gwen gave her a warm smile. "When I met you here at Mo's and you were looking through the want ads for a job, and I pointed you toward Iris to get an interview, I thought about Gray and you."

Gwen Garner's perception of people staggered Sky. Her eyes rounded. "You did?"

"Yep. You're both ex-military. You share certain things that few others will ever experience, Sky. Gray isn't the kind of man who wants a wilting lily or a shrinking violet as a woman at his side. He needs someone strong and his equal. You're all of that."

Sky didn't feel as if she was that strong, but Gray's words came back to her. He had repeatedly told her she had incredible resilience despite her trauma. She believed him because she trusted him and how he saw her. Gray had never been an enabler to her; rather, he supported her at key moments when she felt too exhausted to continue fighting the battles raging within her. She moistened her lips and held Gwen's gaze. "You can't be in the military and be a wimp," she said half-jokingly.

"Cade was in the military, too," Gwen said, "and I agree. The military draws a certain kind of individual. Strong people with strong convictions. You are all heroes, Sky. I hope you know that." Gwen reached out and patted her hand. "And I so much admire you. I know you've had a rough patch while you were in, and I don't need to know what it was. But you're clearly a warrior." She smiled.

"I don't feel like a warrior," Sky murmured. "Maybe 'a survivor' is a better term to use…"

Gwen pulled out her billfold from her quilt purse. "Gray likes you a lot, Sky. I hope you'll let him be in your life. He's a man who will do right by you."

Sky felt heat rush up her neck and face again. She had hoped that with her teenage years, she'd have left blushing behind, but it stayed with her, showing the truth. Sky was protective of her relationship with Gray, but she could see the sparkle in Gwen's eyes. "He told me the other day that no one gets through life by themselves."

Gwen nodded and put the money down on the table. "Gray is right. So you keep trusting him, all right?"

Sky left Mo's in a quandary. Gwen hugged her good-bye and walked back to her quilt store. The wooden walk was filled with hundreds of tourists. The plaza buzzed with activity. As she walked down the porch to where the ranch truck was parked, she felt the need to talk with Gray.

Sky looked around, like she always did. PTSD did have some fringe benefits, she supposed. She would never again not pay attention to what was going on around her. It wasn't a bad habit to have, she decided, tossing her purse into the truck and getting in.

On her way out of town, climbing the long hill that would yield out to the valley floor, Sky felt hope more strongly than ever before. Jordana was someone who was confident and clear. It didn't hurt that Sky understood the medical side of what an adaptogen did. Her knowledge of hormones would aid her fight to heal. As she crested the hill, the blue granite flanks of the Tetons rose into the afternoon sky. White snow still clung to the tops of the sharp, jagged peaks. It was a sight that Sky would never get tired of seeing. Ten miles farther down on the right was the turnoff for the Elk Horn Ranch. Looking at her watch, she saw she'd be just in time for Justin and his walk with his parents through the wildlife center.

Sky's heart warmed toward the autistic boy. He was blooming here at the ranch, and she knew it was in no small part to her. To give the boy's mother credit, Judy was carefully watching how she worked with her son. Sky had a good feeling that when the parents flew back to New York City to resume their life, the mother was going to make efforts to get Justin more involved through the things he loved.

As she drove into the driveway of the employee house, she saw Gray coming out of the wildlife center. Her heart leaped and began a slow pound. Even though he had been born in Wyoming, he stood out. Sky could see the military bearing in Gray, the way he walked with his shoulders squared, his posture proud and his walk balanced. She would never tire of watching Gray move like the soundless cougar he was. In the warmth of the afternoon sun, he was wearing a black T-shirt that embraced him like a second skin, Levi's and scarred cowboy boots. That black baseball cap was always in place, the bill low, shading his eyes. A soft smile pulled at the corners of Sky's mouth. She felt full of joy, of nonstop happiness.

As she climbed out of the truck, she waved in his direction. He saw her immediately and lifted his hand, changing his direction toward her. Sky stood by the truck, pulling the strap of her purse over her left shoulder. The look in

Gray's green-and-gold eyes told her he was happy to see her. He smiled as he approached and slowed.

"Good timing," Gray said, taking off his cap and running his fingers through his short hair. "How'd everything go with Jordana?"

"It was all good, Gray." Sky held up the cardboard box containing the test material. "Saliva test is next."

"That's great. In about three weeks, Jordana will have the test results. And then your life is going to change remarkably," he assured her. "In the best of ways."

Sky followed him into the house. She had to get into her ranch uniform of a white blouse, jeans and cowboy boots. Gray opened the door for her and stepped aside. Being this close to him was making her body turn hot and melting. The look in his eyes, that green-gold gaze burning and silently telling her he wanted her, lifted Sky and made her believe in a happiness she had never known to exist. Until right now. With Gray.

## CHAPTER EIGHTEEN

SKY SENSED A problem before they even got to the barn area where the trail ride would begin. There was a family trail ride the next afternoon that had been scheduled. She would be riding with the Bradford family. She spotted Judy Bradford with a wild, worried look on her face. Pete, her husband, was scowling and looking around. There were fourteen horses saddled and patiently waiting in the corral for their riders. All the families were standing near the lead wrangler, who would take them on the trail ride.

"Something's wrong," Sky quietly warned Gray.

Gray felt her hand on his, as if to caution him. Her fingers were warm, and his flesh tingled over her welcomed but unexpected touch. "Where's Justin?"

That was it. Sky noticed Iris Mason, Rudd and Wes moving around the corral area, as if looking for something.

"Oh, no," Sky whispered. "I wonder if Justin's hidden somewhere?" Her emotions leaped and went into frenzied, terrorizing answers. Had Chuck Harper done something to get even with Gray for pressing charges against two of his men? Sky pushed those terrifying thoughts out of her head and peeled off from Gray, heading for Judy, who was pale and anxious.

"Judy?" Sky called. "What's wrong?"

Judy rushed over to her, gripping her arm. "Oh, Sky, Justin's disappeared!" She held her hand against her mouth, trying not to sob. "H-he was in our cabin, and in the next moment when I looked around, he was gone! We were getting ready to come down here to the corral to all go on that ride with you and the others."

Placing her hand on the mother's shoulder, Sky soothed her. "He's got to be around here, Judy. How long have you been looking for him?"

"Just a few minutes." Tears splattered down her cheeks. "H-he does this all the time, Sky. It scares me out of my mind. I—I didn't think he'd do it here. Justin seemed so happy here...."

Gray came up, hands on his hips, listening. "Judy, has anyone searched the barn over there?" He pointed toward the three-story red barn that housed the hay and feed for the horses.

"N-no, not yet. Pete thought he might be playing hide-and-seek around the corral. That's why everyone is looking there right now." Her hands trembled, and she gave them an embarrassed look. "I'm so sorry this happened...."

"Hush," Sky murmured, sliding her arm around Judy and giving her a quick hug. "Justin is curious. He's never been to a ranch before." She twisted a look up at Gray, seeing his gaze settle on the barn. It was her thought, too. "Listen, walk over to Iris. Tell her Gray and I are going to start at the bottom level of the barn and work our way up. When all of you get finished around the corral area, and if you don't find Justin, come join us. We both think he might be in the barn."

Judy gave a jerky nod, hugged Sky quickly and headed toward the group down at the corral. Nearby, wranglers stood with the horses, who were saddled and patiently waiting within the corral for their riders.

"Let's go," Gray said, slipping his hand across the small of her back. Just getting to touch Sky, even briefly, was life-giving to him. Every look she gave him, that gener-

ous smile of hers, fed his heart and soul. He'd missed her
in his bed. He understood her backing off. Sky was han-
dling a lot, and Gray was sure their unexpected coming
together hadn't been in the cards. But it was now, and he
was wrestling as to how best to deal with her under the
same roof. Did she want him as much as he wanted her?
Gray wasn't sure. Not yet.

"What do you think?" he asked her.

"I think he's probably playing in the haymow up on
the third floor," Sky said, giving Gray a rueful look. "Tell
me what kid doesn't love playing in loose hay?" She saw
a grin edge the hard line of his mouth. Though she was
rattled, she tried to tamp down her wild emotions, feeling adrenaline spurting into her bloodstream, making her
jumpy and restless. Her legs weren't as long as Gray's, and
he shortened his stride for her sake as they approached the
barn. "Good call," he congratulated her, guiding her into
the barn. Their footsteps echoed on the graying wooden
boards of the floor. The barn was nearly a hundred years
old and filled with hay and grain for the animals. There
was a buckboard and a wagon on the lowest floor.

Sky practically ran over to the wooden ladder that led
to the second floor, which was packed with baled alfalfa
and timothy hay. Gray looked up. The third and highest
floor contained loose hay.

Gray watched the movement of Sky's sweet rear, her
hips swaying. More heat plunged through him. He remembered cupping those rounded cheeks of hers, remembered
those flared, curved hips beneath his hands. He didn't even
try to shove away any of those burning memories, not
wanting to forget one honeyed moment with Sky.

He took the ladder quickly with his long legs. Sky was
already heading up to the wooden ladder against the west
wall of the barn that led to the third floor. Her hair was

loose and swayed with her body as she climbed up it. Hair
that Gray wanted to feel sliding through his fingers once
again.

Sky was breathing hard when she walked across the
dusty wooden floor of the haymow. There were huge
clumps of sweet-smelling timothy and alfalfa hay here
and there.

"Justin?" she called out, halting, her gaze ranging across
the four huge mounds of grass hay. "Justin? It's Sky. Are
you here?"

Her voice echoed around in the large interior. Below,
Sky heard the voices of the rest of the people hunting for
the boy. She narrowed her eyes, looking for movement or
maybe a hole dug into the tufts of timothy. She felt Gray
halt near her, feeling the heat of his body, her mouth growing dry. Sky couldn't be around him and not feel shaky,
needy and as if she wanted to make love with him again.

"Look," Gray said in a rasp, pointing to the left of where
she stood.

Frowning, Sky followed where he was pointing his finger. Her breath caught. *There!* Small footprints, or what
appeared to be footprints, scattering the hay here and there
across the floor. She twisted a look up at him, nodding.
Gray smiled down at her and moved his chin in that direction.

"I'll stay here. The boy trusts you," he growled softly.

Gray's physicality was palpable. Sky swore she felt him
reach out and graze her cheek with his hand. Just with one
look of those dark gold-and-green eyes focused solely on
her made her knees mushy. She managed a weak nod and
moved forward.

"Justin?" Sky called, following the trail through the
scattered hay. The prints led to the largest mow. "Sweet-
heart, come out, come out wherever you are," she sang out,

keeping her voice light. If Justin heard anger, she knew he'd hide and not say a peep. Getting down on her hands and knees, Sky saw the mow had been burrowed into. And then she caught sight of Justin's little red cowboy boot. "I see you, Justin," she sang out softly, laughing. She heard Gray moving toward the ladder to tell everyone that Justin had been found.

The mow shook like a shaggy dog. Sky heard Justin's high-pitched laugh. The dried timothy hay trembled again with the boy's laughter, the dried grass falling here and there. Sky eased closer. "Justin, isn't it fun to hide in there? Are you warm?"

"It is," Justin whispered. "It smells so good!"

Sky laughed with him, resting her elbows on her thighs, now seeing Justin fully. He'd burrowed into the hay like a bear ready to hibernate. "Hey, honey, your mommy and daddy are looking for you. Would you like to come out and let them know you're okay?"

"Yes," Justin called. He unwound, moved around and crawled out on his hands and knees, a huge smile plastered on his face.

Sky sat up, grinning with him. Justin was covered with grass hay! It was tangled in his hair, around his shoulders and arms. The child was smiling so widely that Sky laughed and held out her hand.

Justin stood up, shook himself dramatically, watching the grass hay fall off all around him. "That was fun!" he said, throwing up his arms and smiling up at Sky as she rose to her feet.

"I know it is," she confided in a secret whisper. "Come on. Let's climb down and surprise your parents. I know they'll be so glad to see you. And—" she gave him a conspiratorial look "—you can tell them all about conquering the Hay Men who live in this barn!"

Justin's eyes rounded, and he slowed as they approached the ladder. "Hay Men?" he asked, curious.

Sky got on the ladder first and then guided Justin over to the rungs, making sure his small hands had a good grip on them. She wanted to be below him in case he fell or slipped. "You mean," she whispered, "you haven't heard about the Hay Men?" She watched Justin's cheeks flush with excitement. His eyes danced with anticipation.

"No."

Gray stood below them, watching their progress. He helped Sky step aside, and then he lifted Justin off the ladder and into her awaiting arms. Below, all the adults were standing and waiting; relief was written on everyone's faces. The moment he gave the boy to Sky, his heart wrenched. Justin grabbed ahold of her, wrapping his thin little arms around her neck, squeezing her tight. The laughter rippling out of Sky's throat nearly totaled Gray's heart. She was so damn good with children. For a split second, Gray felt his world shift. Sky was there with their son in her arms instead of Justin. Shaking his head, Gray turned, scowling. *What the hell?*

As Gray led the way down the last ladder to the main floor, it wasn't possible to keep telling himself that Sky didn't matter to him. Dammit, she did. In so many large and small ways. He stepped aside and helped Sky off the ladder. They allowed Justin to climb down on his own.

"Mommy! Daddy!" Justin screeched, as he jumped from the last rung of the ladder to the floor, a show of confidence. "I was with the Hay Men!"

Sky felt tears sting her eyes as she watched the reunion between the worried parents and their excited child. Gray moved closer to her, as if sensing she was close to crying. Her vision blurred for a moment over the heartwarming welcome that Justin gave his relieved parents. Everyone else grinned at one another, shook their heads and took off toward the corral of awaiting horses.

"Come on, everyone," Iris called, settling her big straw hat on her flyaway silver hair. "We got a trail ride scheduled. Time to saddle up!"

Sky felt an invisible release of worry lose its grip on the group. She'd never seen Justin so animated. Judy had him sitting on her thigh, and she was patiently picking out grass hay from her son's ruffled hair. Gray's hand curved around her shoulder.

"I've got to get back to work," he murmured, holding her gaze. Jesus, she looked so vulnerable and beautiful in that moment. Her eyes glistened with tears, that soft mouth of hers parted. She swallowed several times, battling back the tears. Her neck was so elegant, so accessible, that Gray wanted to lean over and kiss and lick each spot along its expanse. He wanted to hear those delicious sounds that caught in her throat that told him how much pleasure he had given her, again. Knowing others might be watching them, he lifted his hand off her shoulder.

"Yes," Sky whispered. "I promised Justin I'd ride with him."

"Good. You can tell him a story about the Hay Men as you ride."

Feeling heat fly up into her face, Sky had the good grace to grin. "When I'm with kids, all kinds of wild stories just come popping out of my head," she admitted, a little breathless.

Gray wanted the world to stop right now. He wanted to turn and haul Sky into his arms and kiss her until she melted like the sweet honey she was, into his arms and flow down across his hard, throbbing body. "Well," he growled, so only she could hear, "maybe tonight, in bed, you can tell me more about them?"

Sky's throat tightened and words just blanked out in her mind as she drowned in that heated male stare. Oh, yes, she wanted to be in Gray's arms. In his bed. Her whole body quivered internally, the scalding heat going from simmer to boil inside her. She watched him walk away with that confident walk of his, then forced herself to go back to work. Their personal time would come later.

Sky walked over to Justin. The boy was beside himself with joy. He told his parents how he'd climbed those ladders all by himself. Sky could see the bleak look in their eyes, worried to death he might have fallen. A warm love for Justin flowed through Sky. The child was blooming right before their eyes and had become courageous and less imprisoned in his head. She felt tears come again, deeply touched by the miracle she was seeing take place. She saw the same expression and awareness in the eyes of his parents, as well.

As Sky walked out of the barn with the Bradford family, heading for the awaiting horses in the corral, she saw Gray entering the wildlife center. He would feed the wolf pups. Very soon, they would be turned out into their new home, able to explore the ten-acre enclosure and continue to grow strong and healthy. Her heart somersaulted as she reran Gray's gritty tone, telling her he wanted her in his bed tonight. Sky couldn't wait to get home at 5:00 p.m. to be with him. But then, she was also in turmoil. So much was happening so quickly.

GRAY WAS IN the kitchen when Sky entered the house at 5:00 p.m. She hooked her cowboy hat on a peg and unbuttoned the cuffs on her white blouse. As she rolled the sleeves up to her elbows she said, "Whatever you're making smells good." The afternoon trail ride had been hot, and she felt the grit of dust on her skin.

"Beef Stroganoff," Gray murmured. He felt like staring like a hungry wolf at Sky. Her ginger-colored hair had been drawn into a ponytail. She looked lean and graceful. He couldn't help remembering all her curves beneath his exploring hands. "Want to get washed up? Dinner will be in about thirty minutes."

Wrinkling her nose, Sky said, "I definitely need a shower."

"You have time," he said, trying to ward off the desire to join her. He had a vision of lifting Sky up against the tiled shower, her slender legs wrapping around his waist. But he forced himself to focus. It didn't help that his erection was thick and hard, pressing painfully against his Levi's.

Damn. The woman was certifiably sensual and sexy, flipping him on like a light switch. One look into her face, though, and Gray felt doused with ice-cold water. This wasn't about him. It was about Sky. He could see she wasn't having the same fantasy as he was. Testosterone brain, he warned himself. "I'll be back in a few," she called, hurrying across the living room.

Gray tried not to stare at Sky when she returned twenty-five minutes later. Her hair had been washed and hung in damp, drying strands around her face. Chest tightening, he liked the soft blue T she wore. Gray knew Sky didn't like wearing a bra and wouldn't wear one unless she was riding a horse. Even with a bra beneath the tee, he could easily see the swell of her small breasts, the nipples puckered teasingly beneath the material. She'd worn a pair of soft gray sweatpants, and her feet were bare. Watching her thread her fingers through her loose ginger hair sent a frisson of heat down through him. And as she came into the kitchen to lend him a hand, Gray could smell the scent of her almond shampoo.

"About ready?" Sky asked, feeling heat beneath his dark scrutiny.

That was an understatement, Gray thought wryly as he handed her the bowl of salad. "Yes."

"I'll get the dressing from the fridge," she said, carrying the bowl to the table. Sky liked the way they worked with one another in the kitchen. She inhaled the scent of the Stroganoff sauce. "Mmm, that smells so good. I'm starved."

Wincing internally, Gray smiled a little as he took the pasta out of the boiling water in the sink. "Yeah, I am, too." *But for you. Not the food.* Sky was sustenance for his heart, his soul. Once he brought over the pasta, Gray transferred and mixed it with the sauce. In no time, it was ready for the table.

"I smell garlic bread in the oven," Sky said, mouth watering as she picked up pot holders.

"You do," Gray said, taking the casserole dish to the table.

"You'll never be without a job, Gray," she teased, pulling out the lightly browned French bread that had been slathered with butter, parsley, salt and bits of garlic. "Your mom sure did a great job teaching you how to cook."

He gave her a heated look as he brought down a plate and helped her put the garlic bread on it. "My mother is one hell of a chef. And I did enjoy being in the kitchen with her. I saw it as chemistry. She saw it as loving a dish with certain herbs and spices."

Sky took the bread to the table and sat down. Gray poured them each a glass of water. "Chemistry? Is that a boy thing? This all smells so good," she admitted with a smile.

Gray sat down at her elbow and took her plate, ladling

out the beef Stroganoff. "I saw all those bottles of spices and herbs as chemistry," he admitted. "Enough?" he asked.

"Plenty," Sky said, taking the plate. "Thanks." Their fingers touched, and she eagerly absorbed the brief contact.

"How's Justin doing?" Gray asked, filling his own plate.

"Great. I didn't believe it but he rode his pony between his parents' horses, and he wasn't silent as usual." Sky smiled warmly. "It was an amazing shift, Gray."

"Do you think he'll stay open, or will he close down again when he goes home?" He passed her the garlic bread. Sky was eating well tonight, Gray observed, pleased. She was still at least ten pounds under her normal weight.

Sky shrugged. "I don't know. I hope for his sake, he stays open."

"Maybe this kind of stimulation is what he needed."

Sky poured some blue-cheese dressing over her salad. "I don't know. I'm an R.N., not a psychiatrist. But I can hope this ranch experience helps Justin be more open."

He shot her a look. "It's you, you know. Anything you touch, Sky, is better off for it." Gray sure as hell was. Pink stained her cheeks. Tonight, he could feel how vulnerable and open Sky was.

"That's why I love being an R.N.," Sky admitted. Her appetite was back, and everything Gray had made tasted delicious to her. Sky wanted to admit having Gray at her side made her feel so much stronger. More confident. She was never this way before, but now Sky knew the high cortisol was playing havoc on her emotional state. "I had lunch with Gwen Garner after I saw Jordana."

"Oh?" Gray smiled a little. "Was that by accident?"

Sky laughed a little. "I met Gwen when I was walking to the door of Mo's. Thought I'd catch a quick bite of lunch before coming back here." Her smile dissolved, and her brows gathered as she looked over at Gray. "She told me some things that have me concerned."

*Damn.* Gray knew exactly what Sky was referring to. He'd wanted to keep that intel away from her because he could see the worry reflected in her eyes. "Gwen told you about Harper," he said flatly, deciding not to play coy about it. That would only stress Sky out more because he could clearly see Sky was troubled.

"Yes." Sky held Gray's dark gaze. He was unhappy. "Were you trying to hide the rest of the story from me because you thought it would stress me out?"

"Busted," Gray muttered, digging into his food. "Sometimes, I wish Gwen would be more careful about what she told people."

"Oh," Sky said, raising an eyebrow, "I think she's very careful, Gray. She's got a nose like a wolf. She somehow senses that I like you, that we…uh…like one another." It was much more than *like,* but Sky was afraid to go there yet. Her voice dropped. "Have you told anyone here at the ranch that Harper might possibly put out a hit on you?"

Gray laid down his flatware and held her distressed gaze. "No. We talked about it, but Cade cautioned me not to say anything. At least," he sighed, "not yet."

Sky lost her appetite and pushed her plate away. "This is serious, Gray."

"No one knows better than me, Sky." He saw her face go pale and cursed to himself. "Look," he said, picking up her hand and holding it in his, "I don't want you going there, Sky. Don't think the worst."

She tangled her fingers in his. "I already am," she admitted sourly. "This afternoon when Justin was missing, I was wondering if Harper had kidnapped him to get even with you." She saw his eyes flare with disbelief. "I know my emotional responses are over the top, especially when I think someone is threatened. I didn't say anything to anyone. I kept it to myself."

Gray closed his fingers more tightly around hers. "I'm sorry Gwen told you that." But Gwen didn't know anything about Sky's past, her torture or the fact she had PTSD. Giving Sky intel like this was bound to snap back on her and create paranoia. Because that was what cortisol's job was in a human body: it kept the person alive. What better way than to create mild paranoia within them so they were more watchful, more alert?

"I'm not," Sky said stubbornly. "Okay, so I tend to go overboard sometimes, Gray. I know I do. I compensate for it. I wish… I wish you'd told me." She gave him a hurt look. "I'm mature. I've handled this hormonal crap inside me so far."

Gray wrestled with his feelings. Looking up, he rasped, "Sky, the last thing I ever want to cause in you is hurt. I'm sorry. I've been where you are. I know how upsetting news about someone I cared about affected me. It affects you the same way. I just…" Gray sighed, his gaze pleading. "I didn't want to pile anything more on your plate right now, Sky. God, you've got enough. I didn't want to add my shit to it was all."

"I forgive you," Sky whispered, staring at their hands entwined with one another. "But, Gray, what if Harper *does* try to get even with you? I was in the military, too. I know a little about strategy. Gwen said Harper gets even. If he couldn't kill you the other day with those two guys jumping you, what do you think he'll do next? Don't you think Harper would consider attacking you here at the Elk Horn Ranch?"

Grimly, he studied her. Gray had never made the mistake of underestimating Sky's intelligence, but now his respect for her rose even more. The glint in her eyes wasn't fear. It was a woman who was in a protective mode toward those she cared about. Those she loved. His mouth quirked.

"Yes, I've considered it, too. I've waffled about telling Iris and Rudd about it. But it's a fine line, Sky. It could send everyone in this place into a tense mode. Is that what I want? No. There's a two-mile asphalt road into this place. It's the only entrance/exit point. I've been watching the road more closely for vehicles I don't recognize since I got assaulted."

She rubbed her wrinkled brow. "God, I don't know Harper that well, Gray, but Gwen was really concerned. Shouldn't we be, too?"

"I'll take care of it," he soothed, seeing the tension ratchet up in her face. Her soft mouth was now thinned with worry. The truth was, Gray was more concerned with Harper stalking Sky. He didn't want to tell her that. "I'll go to Iris and Rudd tomorrow morning. I'll see what they think should be done about it, if anything."

"Gwen said the whole town is edgy because of what happened to you. That this was a step up in Harper's getting even. She told me how the two women, whom he'd stalked, are now missing."

*Double damn.* Gwen was giving Sky way too much information. He could see the fear deep in her blue eyes and would do anything to remove it.

"Look," he rasped, running his hand slowly up and down her lower arm in an attempt to soothe her worry, "we do need some kind of commonsense plan in place. And I'll see that it happens, Sky. What I don't want is for you to go on high alert."

"Too late," Sky admitted wryly, her skin feeling like tiny electrical shocks of pleasure where he traced her lower arm. "Gray…" She glanced away for a moment, trying to recapture her emotions. "I like you a lot…and I know we've only met, but I don't want anything to happen to you." She gave him a pleading look.

"I like you, too, Sky." Hell, he couldn't take two breaths without thinking about her, rerunning that hot, sexual encounter with her. Gray knew deep down that it was more than just sex. "Look," he said, trying to keep his voice light, the anger toward Harper removed from it, "we'll get through this together. I won't leave you out of the loop again. If anything comes up, you'll be the first to know about it." He pinned her with a dark look. "Okay?"

"Okay, because I don't want to learn this secondhand again, Gray." She wanted to blurt, *Because you're so important to me, my life, my heart....* Instead, she said, "I know you're trying to protect me, and I'm appreciative, but I'm a big girl. Do I have issues? Yes. But I was in the military. When things get bad, I get stronger, not weaker. You need to know that about me. I don't fall apart."

# CHAPTER NINETEEN

SKY TRIED TO control her yearning for Gray. Throughout dinner all she'd wanted to do was kiss him. She could tell that he wanted to do the same thing. Only there was a table between them and good food that shouldn't be wasted or go cold. Getting up afterward, she carried the dishes to the sink to rinse them off. It was impossible not to feel Gray's masculine presence when they shared the same space. He seemed in thought, and Sky wondered if her strong response earlier had made him upset.

After putting all the pots and pans in the dishwasher and turning it on, Sky picked up a small terry-cloth towel to dry off her hands. As she turned, Gray halted in front of her. Looking up, she saw that familiar green-gold color in his eyes, her breath hitching as he lifted his hands and settled them on her shoulders. Even through the thin blue T fabric, she could feel the latent strength of his fingers.

"What?" she asked, her voice a little breathless, the towel between them.

"I'm sorry," Gray said simply. "Every once in a while I need some reminding that women are strong by nature, Sky. I was—just sensitive to your situation, the PTSD." His fingers moved in a caressing motion across her shoulders. "I don't want you in the line of fire between me and Harper, that's all." His mouth thinned. "I care a lot for you, Sky. I want you happy. I don't want you feeling more fear."

Sky relaxed her hips against the counter behind her, setting the towel next to the sink. She slipped her hands over his hard, muscled forearms, feeling his skin tense. The light dusting of dark hair only made him more masculine. "Thanks for that," she whispered. "I know you care, Gray. You show it in so many ways every day to me." Some of the tension dissolved from his face. He lifted his hand, catching several strands of her hair and tucking them gently behind her right ear.

"I'm new at this, Sky."

She tilted her head. "What are you new at?"

Gray's mouth curved a little. "Us. What we have. I made it a point when I was in the SEALs to not get into a serious relationship with a woman. I saw too many of my buddies get married and then watched the divorce tear them apart." He grimaced. "It wasn't pretty, Sky, and I didn't want to drag a woman through that shit. That life is very hard on wives and even tougher on families."

Her whole body vibrated with need of Gray. She was lost in his voice, hotly aware of her flesh feeling alive beneath his restless fingers. "Black ops is harsh on everyone," she agreed quietly. "So? You're feeling like a fish out of water, Navy guy? That you have no skill set in relationship building?" she teased him, wanting to erase the wrinkles that had gathered on his brow as he'd spoken about his SEAL friends.

"Consider that I'm in the training-wheels stage." His marriage to Julia had evolved much differently. Someday, he would share that six months of his life with her. But not right now. Gray absorbed the amusement dancing in her eyes. He saw heat in them, and arousal. Sky had relaxed in his arms, inches separating them. "I'm going to put my foot in my mouth plenty," he warned her. "And I've got this thing about being very, very protective toward others who can't defend themselves."

Sky placed her hand on his chest, feeling the muscles leap beneath her fingertips, the heavy thud of his heart beneath her palm. "Gray," she whispered, "I'm stronger than I look. I'm not as tall as you are, or as heavily muscled, but that's not the real test or core of a human being." She slid her fingers slowly up the center of his chest. "It's a person's heart, Gray. Their spirit."

"And you're all heart," he rasped, leaning down, brushing Sky's lips, tasting the sweetness of the tart cherry pie they'd had after dinner.

A soft sound caught in Sky's throat as his mouth grazed hers, inviting her to participate. As hard and tough as Gray was trained to be, his hands were gentle, his mouth taking hers as if she were fragile. Her knees felt weak as his arm slid around her waist, drawing her solidly against his body. Heat flared in Sky's belly when she felt the strength of his erection. It set her lower body on fire, and she felt dampness gathering rapidly between her thighs.

Why had she backed away after he'd made love to her the first time? Her mind went blank as he flooded her with delicious sensations, kissing each corner of her mouth. Then it hit her, called her back. Sky knew she'd been afraid at first.

Pulling away from Gray's mouth was the last thing Sky wanted to do, but it had to be done. She breathed unevenly. "Gray," she whispered unsteadily, "are you sure?"

"Sure?" he growled, feeling her hesitation. "Of us?"

She framed his face with her hands, choking out, "I'm not whole, Gray. I've got so far to go to get well…." Sky almost said she was damaged goods. What man wanted someone like her in this present state? Gray had said he wanted a serious relationship with her. She saw his face grow thoughtful, and he shared a tender smile with her.

"You need to know from the first day we met, I lay in

that bed at night thinking, wanting you, Sky." Gray captured her hands into his, pressing them against his chest. "I found myself looking forward to getting up every morning because I knew you would be out here. I could have breakfast with you. I found myself starving for whatever you thought. I'd feel my soul smile when you smiled. Your laughter, Sky, is healing to me. I live for it."

Her heart melted. "This isn't going to be easy, Gray."

"From my side, it is, Sky. I like you in my life just the way you are." He kept her hands captured beneath one of his and cupped her cheek with the other. "I know you struggle minute by minute, day by day. And you are getting better with time. So am I. We share something most people will never have to suffer through, baby, but we'll gut through it together. And I want you here, with me. Does this help?"

Did it? She blinked, feeling the tears rush into her eyes. His calloused palm sent tiny jolts of electricity across her jaw as he held her so she couldn't draw away or turn her head away from his hungry, searching gaze. Giving him a jerky nod, Sky whispered unsteadily, "I didn't want to become a burden to you, Gray..."

He snorted and hauled her into his arms. "A burden? Who the hell put that word into your vocabulary?" And then he knew the answer: her father. Anger burned deep in Gray. How a parent could say that to a child was beyond his imagination. Leaning over, he pressed small kisses across her hairline.

"You are my sunlight, Sky. Your laughter is music to me. I can't ever get enough of you. I won't ever get enough of how you see the world, how you touch a child or hold a baby in your arms. I want you by my side for as long as you want to be there, no questions asked."

He tipped her chin up just enough to catch her glistening eyes that held unspilled tears in them. "I don't care if you're injured emotionally or mentally. I am, too. We can turn a disadvantage into an advantage, Sky. Since we both have PTSD, we understand on a much deeper level what the other is going through. Haven't I shown you patience and understanding?"

"You always have," Sky admitted, her voice strained.

"And you've shown me the same consideration," Gray said. "You are strong enough to hold those symptoms inside of you, Sky. There are so many people who can't do that. To anyone else looking at you, baby, you're normal in every possible way. You can turn around and love others without hesitation. You're unselfish, and you're giving." His mouth thinned for a moment as he considered his words. "Look, Sky, you know how I feel. The only question is, do you want me in your life the same way or not?"

Fighting back the tears, Sky felt her heart open, a rush of rich, deep emotions washing through her, erasing all her fear that she was too damaged to love. "Yes...yes, I do, Gray."

"Good," he said, releasing her and walking her out of the kitchen beneath his arm. "Let's go get undressed and then I want to love you...."

So many of her quelling fears about Gray finding her an encumbrance in his life dissolved. In his bedroom, she quickly divested herself of her clothes, allowing them to drop where they pooled around her feet. This time, Sky had no shyness as she stood naked in front of Gray. The look in his eyes was of a man who thought she was beautiful and priceless.

As he stood before her, incredibly masculine, it was easy to see how much he wanted her. His glittering eyes never left hers. Literally, she salivated, wanting to get her mouth, her hands, her body, against his.

Gray walked up to her, sliding his fingers across her jaw, tangling in her hair as he drew her to him. "I need to be in you," he rasped against her lips opening beneath his.

He lifted her and positioned her in the middle of his large bed, the sheets cool against the heat of her back. Smiling up at him as he lay at her side, feeling his calloused hand range from her shoulder, down across her rib cage and coming to rest along her hip, she pressed her belly against his erection. The low, growling sound in his chest feathered through her as she leaned up, kissing him hungrily, moving her tongue across his lower lip.

Instantly, his fingers dug into her hip, holding her tightly against him. Sky wasn't about to let him take the lead this time. She knew how to love a man and was his equal in this scalding dance throbbing wildly between them.

He lifted his mouth from hers. "I like that you want me," he rasped, sliding his fingers across her belly as he pressed her back onto the mattress.

Sky raised her brows, feeling the utter joy of his fingers spreading across her belly, splayed out, holding her gently in place. Her core ached with wanting him deep inside her. "Let me love you this time, Gray…please…" She slid her hand up his arm, feeling his biceps contract beneath her skimming fingers.

"Baby, you always will be first when it comes to you and me," he growled.

She was about to protest, but his mouth fit hotly across her own, his tongue moving boldly within her. Sky couldn't think, only feel. A moan echoed in her throat as he cupped her breast, his thumb moving across her hardened nipple. Heat exploded through her, her hips coming forward to meet his. Her breathing grew ragged as he left her mouth, positioning his lips over the captured nipple. Any protest she had was blown away because he knew how to give her raw, wild pleasure. Squirming beneath him, she felt him part her thighs, and she eagerly complied, wanting his touch that she knew would send her panting for more of him.

Her inner thighs tensed with anticipation as Gray trailed his finger teasingly through her soft, damp folds, finding her entrance.

"You're so wet," he murmured against her mouth, taking her, finding that knot of nerves just inside her entrance, teasing her until she moaned and kissed him with a ferocity that made him want to take her even more quickly than he'd planned.

Sky arched, her back bowing upward as he brought her to orgasm, the warm fluids flooding her lower body, her channel contracting. Her cry of pleasure drowned in his mouth, and as he slid a second finger into her, prolonging that fiery release, all she could do was freeze for a second against him, imprisoned in a scalding heat that sent her tumbling through oblivion. As Gray lifted his mouth from hers, she barely opened her eyes, drowning in the glittering gold and green of his. He was smiling down at her, pride in his look that he could please her. She felt helpless, like a weak puppet beneath his skilled hands. The amusement lingered in his face as he leaned over, brushing her wet lips.

"You're always first, baby. Never, ever forget that…."

Oh, she couldn't! Her whole body hummed as if being electrified. He finally eased his fingers from within her and positioned himself between her legs. Her flesh was damp, and her body ached to have Gray within her. Finding her strength returning, she spread her thighs wider, her fingers curving around his thick shoulders as he lay across her. After rolling on a condom, Gray kept most of his weight off her, elbows planted near her upper arms.

When he nudged her wet entrance, her lashes swept downward, and a small cry caught in her throat in anticipation.

"Yes," she pleaded. "Please... Gray, get inside me. I need you... I need you so badly." Her fingers were frantic against his hips, trying to pull him forward, pull him into herself.

He hissed between his gritted teeth as she bucked her hips upward, sucking him into her body. For a moment, she felt him tremble. It was as if a minor earthquake surrounded her. His hands framed her face, his mouth crushing hers, taking her as he thrust deeply into her. Her body was so small to accommodate him, but the burn of stretching so widely, so quickly, disappeared beneath the thick, hot fluid of her body responding to his thrusts. It was such a sweet, pleasurable invasion that Sky willingly surged forward to take more of him into her, so close to orgasming once more.

A fine quiver rode through her as he began to move swiftly with hard, deep plunges. Her fingers gripped his narrow hips, and she arched against him, feeling the scalding fire explode between them once again. Yes! This was what she wanted! What she'd yearned for. And when Gray slid his large hand beneath her hips, angling her just so, she gave a little, keening cry. The orgasm released, flooding her, contracting her walls, sending her into a boneless orbit of a raw inferno of satiation.

Gray groaned, his face almost in agony as he prolonged her release. And when he came, he rasped out her name, crushing her mouth against his, pumping hard into her, her body willingly accepting the power of him as a man. She was still floating as she felt Gray suddenly freeze, understood he was unleashing himself within her. She wrapped her legs around his hips, bucking against him, continuing to establish the rhythm he'd set, milking every last bit out of him.

She heard him utter a groan, suddenly sinking heavily against her. Eyes closed, she smiled softly, her arms sliding against his massive, damp back. His face was pressed against her jaw and shoulder, his breath moist and ragged. Sky felt as if she were beneath a hot, living blanket, the thud of his powerful heart slamming against her breasts.

She'd been able to satisfy him equally, and happiness soared through her. There wasn't any better feeling in the world than partners being able to please one another just like this.

"You're incredible," Gray said huskily, his lower body still burning with raw pleasure combining with fiery satisfaction. He lifted his head and forced himself off her, afraid he was going to crush Sky with his weight. As he opened his eyes, he saw the careless smile across her wet, lush lips. The words *I love you* nearly tore out of his mouth. It caught him by surprise in one way, but in another way, Gray had known that the feelings he held for Sky were special. One of a kind. Only for her. He gave her a weak smile and pressed small kisses against her damp hairline.

"So are you." Sky slid her fingertips across his sandpapery jaw. Her body felt full, felt expanded because he was not the average man in any way. Where their hips were fused, she sighed. "That was—incredible...wonderful.... I never want it to end...." And she didn't. Her emotions were scintillating and bright. Right now, Sky felt as if the most beautiful rainbow in the world throbbed with life within her. "You make me feel so good," she whispered, closing her eyes, absorbing each of his small kisses, cherishing the intimacy between them.

Gray eased away from her. "Hold that thought," he said. "I'll be right back."

Sky missed his weight upon her. Missed Gray. Within a minute, after getting rid of the condom, he settled back at her side, easing her back into his arms, his large hands against her hips, drawing her against him. Sky smiled softly because Gray's erection was still there. Still wanting her. Opening her eyes as he lay above her on his elbow, his hand ranging almost tenderly from her hip, up to her rib cage and back, she whispered, "I don't want to ever not share this bed with you."

Gray's heart expanded until he could barely breathe. Sky's trembling words, breathless and soft, totaled him. He leaned down, gently kissing her mouth, absorbing her as a woman, someone he never wanted to release again. Lifting his mouth, their lips still touching, he replied, "I want the same thing, baby. We're good together...."

Languishing in his arms, Sky drowned in his burning, narrowed eyes. Gray was part predator, fully alpha male and yet he treated her with such tenderness. Only a man who was confident in himself could do that, and it was so rare in Sky's limited experience. She closed her eyes and turned into his hand as he cupped her breast. Instantly, as he pulled the taut nipple into the heat of his mouth, she pressed restlessly against him. Good together? They were like a fire, wild and out of control.

"You taste so good," Gray rasped, lifting his head, meeting her aroused eyes. "And you are so damned hot and responsive."

"I like loving you, Gray."

He curved his fingers around her taut breast, the pink nipple begging to be suckled once again. "If we keep this up, I'm going to have to put on another condom," he warned her, his mouth curving as he held her dark, smoky stare.

"Let me put it on you," Sky whispered, sliding her hand

down between them, fingers wrapping around his already hard erection. "This is more than about me, Gray. I told you, I want to love you, too."

Her words inflamed his entire body. The fearlessness in Sky's gaze made him grin. "You're an alpha female wolf, baby."

"Which you'll find out, my very handsome alpha male wolf…."

DAWN LIGHT BARELY peeked around the heavy, dark curtains of Gray's room when Sky slowly eased out of some badly needed sleep. Her body was still pleasantly heavy, still pulsating with the memory of Gray within her. They had loved each other almost nonstop, so hungry for one another. She lay against him, her body slanted across his, their legs tangled. Her head rested on his chest, her slender arm across his rock-hard belly.

Closing her eyes, Sky listened to the slow beat of Gray's heart beneath her ear, felt the shallow rise and fall of his powerful chest. The dusting of dark hair across it tickled her nose. Inhaling his male scent, the aphrodisiac fragrance of the sex shared between them earlier, Sky never wanted to come out of this mindless pleasure. The man knew how to love a woman, no question. Her body flexed sweetly in memory as she had lost count of how many orgasms he'd coaxed from her. Barely able to move, so satisfied, Sky couldn't ever remember feeling this good, this pleasured, in her life.

Best of all, none of the anxiety that normally inhabited her was present. Good sex was the antidote to PTSD symptoms in her case. For that, Sky was grateful to be given a reprieve from those grating, constant feelings. She nuzzled her cheek against Gray's chest, his flesh warm and hard beneath her. It was then that she felt him awaken, his arm slowly sliding around her shoulders, holding her close to him. Sky wanted to wake up like this every morning. Wanted to go to bed with Gray at night knowing that love waited in his arms.

"Good morning to you," Gray said, slowly rising up on his elbow, pressing Sky onto her back. In the shadows her slender body, those small, perfect breasts, was outlined. He saw the curve of her waist and those flared hips. Most of all, he noticed the sweet swell of her belly, and he laid his hand across it, feeling the soft velvet of her flesh beneath his palm. The lustrous, drowsy look in her eyes made him want to love her again. Sky was open and vulnerable to him on every level. The trust between them was solid.

He leaned down, cupping the side of her belly and pressing a kiss near her belly button. She smelled of sex, of her own unique fragrance as a woman, and he licked her skin, tasting the salt from it. Instantly, he heard her moan a little, her fingers digging into his arm, her hips automatically lifting toward him because it felt good to her.

Gray wanted to always hear those sweet sounds coming out of Sky's mouth, feel her fingers pressing frantically into him, telling him she liked it and wanted more. He felt in a daze, somewhat groggy due to lack of sleep, but in another way, so damned hungry for her all over again. He lifted his head and smiled up at her.

"Are we ever going to get enough of each other?" Her answering smile tore at his heart, made him feel the love that had guided him all of last night with her. Gray wanted to tell her about his love for her, but hesitated. Did he dare? Didn't they need more time? He already knew that he wanted to marry Sky and make her his wife, his partner and his best friend.

However, last night had shown Gray clearly that Sky was the woman he wanted. *Forever.* But to tell her all of this? He studied her sleep-ridden blue eyes, his gaze resting on her slightly swollen, so well-kissed lips. His realizations would be too much for her right now. Her plate was full at this point, and Gray had no desire to make it even fuller. Maybe Sky would interpret his admission right now as a stressor.

"I don't know," she admitted in a wispy voice, meeting and holding his burning gaze. Already, she could feel his erection growing, thickening insistently against her hip. Her heart felt euphoric, and she knew these feelings were because of Gray. His shadowed face, the dangerous darkness that made her feel damp between her thighs once again, that crooked masculine smile on his well-shaped mouth, made her smile. "You're my dessert."

"Okay, I'll settle for being your dessert, baby," he said, kissing the lobe of her ear, feeling her breath rush out from between her lips. He licked the skin behind her ear and felt her shiver, her fingers dancing across his biceps. Sky was so damned sensitive, so easy to please. Gray wanted what they had found to last forever.

"We have to get up," Sky sighed and eased out of his arms. She pointedly pouted at the clock on the dresser opposite Gray's bed.

Gray liked her pout. He sighed and agreed. "Duty calls."

She leaned over, kissing his mouth languidly, absorbing the taste and feel of his lips beneath hers. "And if nothing else, being in the military, we will always do our duty. Won't we?"

Sliding his hand up along her hip, Gray answered, "You're right, but after 5:00 p.m. every night, we're off duty, and you're mine."

His low, animal-like growl vibrated through Sky, making her lower body begin to burn brightly all over again.

"I'm yours," she promised him, giving him one last, lingering kiss on his mouth before forcing herself off the bed.

Gray caught her hand as she turned to leave his bed. "Want to shower together?"

Sky laughed and slipped out of his grasp. "No. And you know why, Grayson McCoy. We don't have enough time…" Standing beside the bed, pushing her fingers through her mussed hair, she met his very appreciative male look. She liked the arousal in Gray's glittering eyes. Felt his wanting her. She wanted him, but time was working against them.

He feigned ignorance. "I don't know why."

Rolling her eyes, Sky muttered, "Oh, yes, you do, Navy guy. A shower is just another way to love one another, and I know that's not lost on you."

He raised a brow. "Okay," Gray drawled, slowly moving off the bed. "I'm up for it. Are you?"

Giving a very ladylike snort, Sky walked around the bed and quickly picked up her clothes. Gray reached out, hooking his arm around her waist, drawing her up against him. She laughed and tried to squirm free, but her nipples rubbing against his chest only weakened her resolve. "Gray…"

He took the clothes from her fingers, feeling her arousal, feeling her nipples hardening against his chest. Glancing at the clock, he looked at her. "We have thirty minutes, baby. Are you game?"

How could she resist his low wolf growl? That predatory look of hunger in his eyes for her alone. Sky relaxed in his arms. "All right… I'm having such a tough time telling you no," she admitted with a soft sigh, sliding her arms around his shoulders, feeling the strength of him against her.

Giving her a pleased look, Gray whispered against her smiling mouth, "Because what we have is going to stand the test of time, sweet woman of mine."

## CHAPTER TWENTY

IN EARLY JULY, Sky watched the three wolf puppies gallop and frisk around in their new enclosure. Gray stood with her near the den as the pups eagerly smelled and investigated their new home. They were now about ten pounds apiece, long and lean, their tiny whippet tails growing, as well. Their once puglike noses had changed dramatically, growing longer and taking on a more wolflike face. Gracie's eyes remained blue and had not changed color yet, but the other two pups now had yellow eyes. Sky wondered if Gracie might mature with blue eyes, thinking that with her white coat she would be a disarmingly beautiful wolf.

The warmth of the overhead sun brought out the scent of the pine in the surrounding area. Gray and Sky were crouched close to one another, one knee on the earth, watching the pups. Should she tell him? Biting down on her lower lip, Sky didn't want to spoil this wonderful moment.

Gray had worked with a crew for six weeks to prepare this state-of-the-art enclosure for the wolf puppies. It had been off-limits to the dude-ranch visitors, but within a month, after the pups got used to their new digs, it would become an educational part of the wildlife tour at the center, as well.

Gray smiled over at her. "Think they're happy?" Hell, *he* was happy because she was in his arms every night. And now she looked so beautiful with her hair in a set of braids.

Three weeks ago, Sky had willingly come to his bed. Every night, they slept together. On some nights, Gray was so exhausted from the push to get this new wolf enclosure completed, he fell asleep in her arms. Other nights, they loved one another with a hunger and fire that never seemed to dim. And he knew without a doubt, he loved Sky. Did she love him? He thought he saw it in her eyes sometimes, especially after lovemaking, the intimacy tender between them. But she never said it, never alluded to it. Was she still afraid she would become a burden to him? Gray couldn't accept it. Just couldn't.

She'd been tested by Jordana, and yes, Sky had high cortisol. No surprise there. Sky had been taking the adaptogen for two weeks since then. Had it made a change for the better in her? He made a point to remember that tonight when they got back to the house, he'd ask her about it.

"Gracie loves this," Sky whispered, hands clasped to her breast. "Look at her!"

Gray chuckled and watched the white female squat and pee along the fence. And then she would gallop and leap, then stop farther down along the cyclone fence and pee again. "Yeah, she's the alpha female of this group. She's scent-marking the fence line, letting everyone know inside and outside of it that she owns this place." He turned, giving her a teasing look. "I like the way you scent-mark me."

Sky rolled her eyes. "Really, Gray," she sputtered, her mouth curving ruefully.

"What? It's true." He helped Sky to her feet. "You're an alpha female wolf in disguise."

"Well, I certainly don't pee around your bedroom, scent-marking it," she laughed.

"Granted, that would be messy," he admitted, drowning in her laughter. Sky was happy. He could see it in her upturned face. She exuded a silent joy that he lapped up like the starving wolf he was.

"Remember? An alpha female chooses her alpha mate, and she will only mate with him. That's what I was referring to about us. You've claimed me," Gray murmured, slanting her an amused glance.

Sky shook her head. "Well, that part is true." Her lips drew away from her teeth as she studied his hard, weathered face shadowed by the trees surrounding them. There was such strength in Gray. Her heart opened fiercely, and Sky almost whispered, *I'm falling in love with you....*

But she didn't. She was afraid. Why, she wasn't sure. Maybe because in another month the trial with Harper's two thugs would occur, and Gray was the primary witness. Secretly, Sky worried about Harper. What he might do to Gray. She was unable to shake Gwen Garner's warning that Harper always got even. Was she afraid of losing Gray? *Yes.* Sky absorbed every minute with him, burning it into her memory, her heart. She knew Gray would tell her not to worry, that he was a SEAL, that he could handle whatever was thrown at him. *Maybe.* But the somber look in Gwen's eyes and her warning had dug into her fear.

They stood quietly watching the pups explore, pee and sniff around their new home. The three pups gathered near their new den and lifted their little muzzles upward, doing a group howl. At four weeks old, wolf pups began to howl. It was a way to celebrate the pack and keep it tight. Gracie, as always, led the howling, her blue eyes shut, her little nose thrust up to the sky as far as she could get it.

"Gracie is something else," Sky whispered, glancing up at Gray. He had a smile on his mouth, and she wanted to turn, stand on her tiptoes and kiss him.

Gray sensed her need and lowered his head, brushing

her lips gently. "You're a human version of Gracie," he murmured.

Sky chuckled, relishing his mouth skimming hers. She leaned away and caught the merriment in his hazel gaze. "What? I howl a lot, McCoy?" She saw his mouth tug into a grin.

"Well, maybe not howling," he granted. And then his voice dropped to an intimate growl. "But I do like the sounds in your throat and listening to your cries when I'm making love with you."

A streak of heat bolted down through Sky's body as she leaned against him, watching his smile deepen. The warmth in his eyes toward her made her heart fly open with fierce feelings for Gray. "Okay," she muttered, "you got me there." She slid her hand up across his shirt, caressing his jaw. "But I don't howl."

Chuckling, Gray kissed her hair and gave her a quick squeeze. "Baby, if you want to howl, it's okay by me." He saw her cheeks stain pink, her shyness always touching his heart. "You look beautiful when you blush. You know that?" he whispered against her ear, kissing her temple.

The wolf pups stopped howling, did a few last little yips and then raced around their legs, leaping up on them, whining and begging for food. Sky looked down at them, petting their broad heads. "You aren't hungry, you little beggars," she told them. They had been weaned at eight weeks and were now on meat instead of milk. Their little bodies were growing at a tremendous rate. Their tummies were always full.

"Come on," Gray urged. "Let's let them have some fun finding out just how big their new home is." He led her out a gate. There was a second gate to go through, and as Sky waited for Gray to lock it, she knew it was time. As he turned, she pulled him to a halt.

"I have something to share with you."

For a moment, Gray wasn't sure it was good or bad by the solemn look in Sky's eyes. "Okay."

Her hands fluttered nervously and she said, "I feel different, Gray. I've been on that adaptogen that Jordana gave me two weeks ago. Three mornings ago when I woke up—" she took a deep breath and whispered "—the anxiety was *gone*. It hasn't returned in three days." Sky looked at him almost pleadingly and asked, "Did it take your anxiety away like that? Suddenly? Out of the blue? And it never came back after that?"

Gray rested his hands on his hips, seeing the fear clashing with hope in her face. "Yeah, it took me a week of being on it, and one day, I woke up and the anxiety was gone. Totally. Blew me away. So," Gray said, smiling a little, "your anxiety is nowhere to be found?"

"Whew… Yes, it's gone." Sky licked her lower lip, her voice strained. "God, tell me it's going to last, Gray? That the horrible anxiety is not going to come back?"

He whispered her name and cupped her face. "Baby, it's all good. Okay? Once my anxiety left, it hasn't returned. It's solid. You can count on it." Gray saw her eyes swim with tears of relief. Leaning down, he kissed each of her lids. "You can stop holding your breath, Sky. This is real. The adaptogen has plugged those cortisol receptors in you, and that damned hormone is no longer spilling uncontrollably into your bloodstream twenty-four hours a day to make you feel that constant state of high anxiety and always feeling a threat."

"Oh, Gray," she whispered tremulously, throwing her arms around him. And Sky began to sob because profound relief flowed through her. She buried her face against his chest.

Gray's heart melted as he embraced Sky tightly, allowing her to cry. It was the first time she'd wept like this in a long, long time. He knew they were tears of utter relief from no longer experiencing the sawing anxiety that tore everyone up who had PTSD. The adaptogen didn't stop him from cringing when a car backfired or someone shot a rifle or pistol without him knowing about it in advance. The adaptogen's area of cure was centered on the cortisol hormone receptors, but for Gray, it had made a night-and-day difference in his life.

Kissing her hair, he slid his hands down Sky's shaking shoulders, wanting to soothe her. Love her. There just wasn't any question left in Gray's world that he didn't daily think about telling Sky he was in love with her. Patience told him to hold off. Sky had just taken the largest step of getting her PTSD under control. And it was going to take her months to adjust to no longer being anxious, alert and seeing a threat at every turn. Gray knew he had to wait, not wanting to put more pressure or stress on Sky right now. They had the time, and he was going to enjoy watching her step out from beneath the dark cloud of PTSD and take even more exciting steps toward healing herself.

Sniffling, Sky pulled a tissue out of her jean pocket and stepped out of Gray's embrace to blow her nose. She blotted her eyes and looked up at him through her lashes. "I so want it to stay away," she managed brokenly.

Gray's voice became thick with emotion. "It will," and he used his thumbs to dry the last of the tears on her cheeks. "This stuff works, Sky. Jordana is on the cutting edge of helping military vets, and others who have suffered abuse, with this particular symptom." He saw her hope conflict with her worry. "Listen, in the next few days, you'll see. You don't have to believe me. It will just happen." Her lower lip trembled, and Gray placed a soft kiss on her mouth, wanting her to believe a miracle really had happened. Because it had. His heart swelled with tenderness toward Sky because she'd been such a fighter to try to get back to normalcy. "Come on. Let's walk back to the center," he told her. "We have a group coming in shortly."

In the second week of July, Sky got to take care of another young baby for a couple who had come for a vacation to the Elk Horn Ranch. Sam and Becky Cooper had been worried at first. Could Sky really take care of their red-haired four-month-old daughter, Adeline, or Addy, as they called her? They were less anxious when they found out from Iris that Sky was an R.N. During the day, if the parents were on a ride or taking a raft trip down the Snake River, Sky got to take care of Addy. And was it all right if Sky took the baby to the employee house across the street to care for her? Becky came to check out the premises and walked away happy, knowing her baby girl was safe and in caring hands.

Sky placed the baby bassinet in the living room. She could hold the baby, feed her, rock her, and when Addy fell asleep, Sky would gently place her in the bassinet. Every day, she would get to be with Addy for a few hours. It also gave Becky a chance to rest because new babies kept parents up quite regularly for the first three or four months of their lives. And once Becky entrusted her with her green-eyed little daughter, Sky watched the dark circles disappear from beneath Becky's eyes.

Sky had just finished feeding Addy and burping her over her shoulder at her medical-dispensary office when she heard the snorts and whinnies of horses in the nearby dude corral. Becky and Sam were going on a long three-hour ride into the mountains with several wranglers. "I wonder if you're going to be horse crazy, too, Addy?" she asked with a smile, sitting down in the rocking chair with her.

The baby's eyes were barely open, her tiny bow mouth moving, emulating the sucking motion of a bottle between her lips. Sky laughed softly, cradling Addy in her arms, resting her elbows on the arms of the rocker, the baby snug against her body. Sky closed her eyes, feeling abnormally tired. Maybe because she no longer felt the anxiety.

Gray had told her after his anxiety left, he found himself sleeping longer, as if to catch up on all the sleep-deprived years he'd had the symptoms. The anxiety had kept him restless, sleepless, and he'd been lucky to get three or four hours a night. Sky grimaced. It had been the same with her. Constant sleep deprivation had worn her down, too. Now without that terrible anxious feeling, Sky had found herself sleeping eight hours without interruption. Or, she thought with a soft smile hovering on her lips, sometimes she needed more sleep because Gray and she couldn't keep their hands off one another. Slowly rocking the chair, Sky sighed, the baby tucked safely against her, soundly asleep in her arms.

GRAY HAD MOUNTED the steps to the medical dispensary when he spotted Sky rocking the baby in her arms. His gut tightened. His heart bloomed with a powerful feeling of love toward Sky. God, she looked so beautiful. Warmth drenched Gray as he stood there, motionless, watching as she leaned over, placing a kiss on the infant's tiny brow.

Her smile flooded him with new feelings. Throat tightening, Gray felt such a powerful wave of love and protectiveness toward Sky that it left him stunned. He swallowed hard and quietly backed down the steps, not wanting to disturb her or the baby. He didn't want to interrupt the cherished moment. Gray turned and walked down the sidewalk to the main office instead.

Opening the door, Gray stepped in and saw Rudd behind the desk.

"Hey," Rudd called, "did you get a call from Deputy Cade Garner earlier? He's been tryin' to reach you."

Frowning, Gray halted at his desk and pulled out his cell phone. The battery was dead. "No. What does he want, Rudd?" Gray remembered last night after dinner he'd taken Sky to his bed for dessert, and he'd forgotten to plug in the phone to charge the battery beforehand.

Rudd held up the landline phone to him. "I'll dial, and you can talk to him directly. He didn't say what he wanted, just that it was important to speak with you."

Thanking him, he heard Cade's deep voice answer at the other end.

"Sorry I didn't get your message. What's up, Cade?"

"We had a jailbreak this morning, Gray. Those two men of Harper's who assaulted you are gone," he told him grimly.

Gray's gut churned. His mind spun. Who had bailed them? And how? He had a lot of questions, and Cade sounded harried and frustrated. "How did that happen?"

"Someone, and we don't know who, got past the guard, knocked him unconscious and stole the keys. I was made aware of the jailbreak at 5:30 a.m., and that gave those two convicts a half an hour's head start."

"You've put out an APB on them, haven't you?" Gray demanded, his fingers tightening around the phone.

"Immediately."

"Dammit," Gray whispered. "This is Harper's doing. I know it."

"Wouldn't disagree with you," Cade said wearily, "but there's no fingerprints, no nothing, to prove our theory. The man or men who came in here sprayed paint over the cameras so we have no video footage of who they might have been. There's no foot or boot prints anywhere, either. We've basically had our hands tied. I have several deputies canvassing the area, talking to surrounding neighbors who might have been up at that time this morning. So far, we have no leads."

"And so Harper springs them so they aren't around for their trial."

"That's what the commander and I think. Yes."

As he rubbed his face wearily, Gray's mind leaped in several directions. "What's your best bet on them? They leave the county? For good?"

"Most likely," Cade said. "Probably are long gone over the Idaho or Utah border in a car provided by Harper. I've alerted Idaho, Utah and Montana police about the escape, sent photos and fingerprints to them. But they're probably in a car, in civilian clothing, and they'll never be identified unless they're accidentally pulled over for a traffic stop."

Mouth thinning, Gray looked out the front screen door of the office. "Or Harper could have paid them to come after me. To get even."

"Doubtful. What would Harper stand to gain from that? His two guys screwed it up with you in the first place. Why would he send them after you again?"

"Makes sense," Gray muttered, still feeling uneasy about it. Something was wrong, but he couldn't put his finger on it. This wasn't over.

"I'm going over to pay Harper a visit right now, interview him. Of course, he'll play dumb and claim he didn't know anything about it and wash his hands of it."

Snorting, Gray said, "That sounds about right." He worried about Sky. Harper was still in town. And Sky was in Jackson Hole several times a week by herself. He felt very protective of her knowing the two men had escaped.

Would Harper send them after Sky to get even with him? The thought chilled him to his soul.

"Look, nothing for you to do on your end. You might clue Iris and Rudd in and let them know. You have a two-mile-long asphalt road from the main highway to your ranch. It's the only entrance and exit to the Elk Horn, so ask them to keep their eyes peeled the next couple of weeks for unknown vehicles coming in?"

"I'll do it," Gray promised. "Anything else?"

"Not right now. Get your cell charged, eh?" Cade chuckled.

His teasing broke the tension in Gray. "Yeah, I'll do that. We'll be in touch," he promised, handing the phone to Rudd.

SKY WAS AT the stove preparing their nightly meal when Gray walked in. She sensed rather than saw he was concerned about something. His mouth was set, his eyes hard. When she saw his game face in place, Sky knew something was up. It was just a question of what. She briskly stirred the red and green peppers along with the onion in the skillet. "Hey, are you up for beef stir-fry with noodles tonight?" she called, smiling over at him.

Gray threw his baseball cap on the peg and shut the door. "Sounds good," he said.

Dammit, he didn't want to have to tell Sky about the jailbreak, but he knew he had to. He wandered into the kitchen, absorbing her. The yellow apron was tied askew around her slender waist. Sky usually, when coming home for the night, would get a quick shower to wash off the sweat and dust of the day. Her hair was still slightly damp, framing her profile. She'd changed from Levi's into a pair of soft, cream-colored sweats, a favorite of hers. Her small, bare feet stuck out from beneath them. She was heart-stoppingly beautiful.

Coming to a halt, he slid his hands across her shoulders, leaned down and kissed her temple. "Mmm, smells good, and so do you…"

"Iris gave me some elk stew meat before I left the office," she said, turning and giving him a warm look. Her heart took off as she relished his large hands skimming her shoulders. Sky would never tire of Gray's touch. Not ever. "She was cleaning out her freezer, so I told her I'd take it home and figure out a way to use it creatively tonight."

Leaning over her, he looked into the skillet. "Makes me hungry."

"You smell sweaty," she murmured teasingly. But he smelled good to Sky.

Grumbling, Gray released her. "Yeah, I was out helping a crew of wranglers dig a ditch over at the main corral. That last rain we had washed part of it out, and we need that area to drain and dry. Do I have time for a quick shower?"

"Yep," Sky answered, grinning. "Go for it."

Gray waited until after dessert, pineapple upside-down cake and coffee, before he broached the jailbreak with Sky. He urged her to come into the living room and sit down on the couch with him. He chose a corner, and Sky came and settled into his arms, a look of contentment on her face. Her hair was dry, and he took a few of the strands, moving them away from her cheek as he held her warm gaze. God, he loved her. So damn much. His hand stilled on her shoulder, and he slid his other hand across her hip as she rested her head against his chest.

"Mmm, this is even better than pineapple upside-down cake," Sky teased softly, moving her hand languidly up across his chest.

"It is," Gray sighed. He wanted to forget Cade's phone call and just sit here with the woman he loved in his arms. Gnawing worry forced him to speak. In as few words as possible, he told Sky about the jailbreak. Instantly, she tensed in his arms. When he was finished, she pulled out from beneath his arm and sat up, her hand on his thigh, studying him worriedly, her eyes filled with fear. Dammit anyway. Anger toward Harper simmered within him.

"What does this really mean, Gray?"

Hearing the fear in her husky tone, he slid his hand against her jaw. "Cade thinks they're gone." He scowled and dropped his hand. "I've already told Rudd, who will alert the other employees about strange cars coming into the ranch. We have rental cars in and out of here all the time because of the families vacationing here. Rudd said everyone will be a lot more alert."

"Because those two men could drive in here?" She felt her heart beginning a slow pound of dread. *And come after Gray again.*

"Yes," Gray reluctantly admitted.

Sky had tucked her lower lip between her teeth, worrying it. A sign he'd come to realize was an unspoken red flag that Sky was far more upset than she appeared. He moved his hand gently up and down her bare arm. "Look, I don't need you to fret about this. We've got it handled."

Sky's brows fell, and she held Gray's darkening eyes. He had his game face on. He always had it on when things weren't going right. "Really," she said. "It's Harper. They were his drivers. He's behind all of this, and although no one can prove it, he's the one who hired those two guys to jump you, Gray."

"No disagreement with you on that." He took a deep breath and tangled his fingers through Sky's hair. This was the part he hated saying. "Sky, you need to be more careful when you have to drive into town on errands. Neither Cade nor I think this is over. Harper *is* behind this, but there's no proof. At least, not enough yet to get his ass in jail, where it belongs."

Shaken, she stared at Gray. "But—"

"No, listen to me, baby. Harper saw you in the drugstore. He came in, walked up on you and scared the hell out of you." His fingers tightened around hers that had grown damp and cool. "He's a stalker. Cade and I both agree that Harper could go after you. It's now common knowledge to everyone that we like one another. Harper would pick up on that."

Startled, Sky whispered, "Me? Why?"

"Because it's no secret in town that you and I have a relationship, Sky. People see us holding hands or having lunch at Mo's together..." His mouth thinned. "It's an angle, that's all. Cade is the one that brought it up to me. I honestly hadn't even thought in that direction. The attack was focused on me, not you. And Harper hasn't tried going after you since that one time he stalked you in the drugstore." He squeezed her fingers and brought her hand to his lips, kissing the back of it. "I just need you to be more alert, Sky, that's all. I don't want you driving into town alone while this is ongoing."

She sat very quiet, absorbing the information. At least she still felt calm even though this was a potential threat. That amazed Sky, and she was glad that the cortisol had been tamed and no longer made her feel that sort of dreaded threat. But this was a genuine threat, and Sky saw the worry banked in Gray's eyes. "Okay," she promised him huskily, "when I go into town, I'll make sure one of the wranglers comes in with me."

"Yes. Rudd agrees that you should have a bodyguard of

sorts around, another man if I can't do it myself. This is just a precaution, Sky. You aren't the target. I am."

"That doesn't make me feel any better about this, Gray." She held his unhappy gaze. Suddenly, Sky wanted to tell him she loved him, but withheld the words. If she admitted her love for him, it could become a distraction. It might make Gray feel even more responsible. More agitated. No, Sky decided, she would wait until this dark cloud was no longer hanging over them.

"How long do you think we should be more alert?" she asked.

Gray shrugged. "Cade has an APB out on those two in four states." He slid his hands around her face, looking deep into her eyes. "This is just temporary, Sky. Nothing's going to come of it, but you need to know, and we need to put some protection for you in place." Because Gray couldn't conceive of ever losing Sky. He'd lost his wife, Julia, to drug runners. Now he was thrown back into what seemed a tortured repeat of what had happened in Peru. Harper was a drug runner, too, and Gray knew his type would kill without a second thought. He didn't want Sky in the line of fire as Julia had been caught in. And died.

## CHAPTER TWENTY-ONE

THE MID-AUGUST SUN was hot, heating up the valley and making everyone sweat. Gray had a few minutes to spare after showing another group of families through the wildlife center, and he wanted to touch base with Sky. Above him, to the west over the blue-flanked granite Tetons, clouds were gathering. By late this afternoon, thunderstorms would start rolling across the wide valley, giving life-affirming rain to everything.

He hadn't seen Sky since breakfast, knowing she was busy babysitting several young boys, ages seven and eight, over at the wrangler dining room. Sky had created a play center for the children in late July, and it was proving to be a highly popular place for restless little boys. Was she at the house yet? Or still over at the dining room? He saw the parents of these boys who had come back from the ride with their charges across the street.

Gray's heart lifted as he pushed open the door. "Sky?" he called. Usually, near noon, if she could pull away, she would be over here making them sandwiches. Then they could spend a quality half hour or so with one another. Something he needed like breathing air. As he turned to close the door, he heard the bathroom door down the hall open. Frowning, he saw Sky coming out, wiping her mouth with a washcloth. What the hell?

"Hey," he called, walking toward her, frowning. "Are you all right?"

Sky halted and lifted her head. "Gray...oh, I'm fine."
She managed a part grimace, the washcloth in her hand.
"I must have a touch of summer flu." She wrinkled her
nose, her stomach still roiling.

Concerned, Gray halted, sliding his finger beneath her
chin, lifting it a bit. Sky's blue eyes were dark. Her golden
skin was pale, and he could see perspiration on her brow.
"You have a fever?" He pressed the palm of his hand gently against her forehead. "Nope, no fever."

Making a disgusted sound, Sky slid her arm around his
waist and urged him to walk down the hall. "Maybe food
poisoning, but the cooks are so careful with the food prep."

He slid his arm around her shoulders and guided her to
the couch, getting her to lie down. "Are you cold?"

Sky felt better lying down, her head on a pillow that
Gray provided. "I feel better now that you're here," she
murmured.

Gray sat on the edge of the couch, his hip against hers.
Frowning, he nudged strands of hair sticking to her damp
brow. "I'll tell Iris and Rudd you're not feeling well. You
need to rest, Sky."

Sky nodded. "I'd like to take a few hours off and let my
stomach settle," she whispered. Looking up into Gray's
shadowed face, her gaze resting on his mouth, remembering the hot, scalding love he'd shared with her last night,
she managed a partial laugh. "Maybe we aren't getting
enough rest at night," she suggested as she slid her fingers around his lower arm that was deeply tanned. "Maybe
months of sleep deprivation has caught up with me?"

Gray grazed her brow with his thumb. "Maybe it is.
You've been through a lot of stress with those two guys
on the loose." Gray knew it had weighed heavily on Sky,
her worry that he'd get attacked in town by them. "I just
think you're fretting too much, baby."

"Oh, those two guys still on the loose?" Sky sighed. "Maybe…"

"You're a natural worrywart," he accused, watching her tenderly. She was a natural mother, Gray thought, her attention always on others, not on herself. And all of August, she'd been heavily involved in major babysitting with little boys and girls. Sky was like a mother hen, and these children were her chicks. Gray knew how much focus and energy that took, and Sky was still healing.

"My mother said that growing up I was like a brooding hen." Sky laughed softly, absorbing Gray's touch, watching the green and gold in his eyes chase away the brown.

"How so?" Gray asked, watching her mouth. No one kissed the way Sky did. She could barely graze his lips, and his entire lower body exploded to vivid, throbbing life. The woman was certifiably hot and sensual.

"Well, being an only child," Sky said, giving him a fond look, "I didn't have any siblings to play with. My mother had a chicken coop. I made it my business as a little kid to help the hens that had chicks, to help herd them around in the yard." Placing her hand across her belly, she felt the nausea lifting. It had to be Gray's powerful, quiet presence that made the difference. "My mom would find me out in the yard using my hands to herd the chicks here and there. I thought I was doing a good job, but my mother would always pick me up and take me out of the coop. She would hold me and tell me that the mother hen would always take care of her babies without me acting like a herd dog." Sky sighed and closed her eyes. "A really happy memory of my childhood."

"You had a lot of them," Gray agreed, grazing her pale cheek with his fingers. "You look tired, Sky."

Lifting her lashes, she made a face. "Can I blame you?" She grinned up at him.

Gray nodded. "Sure can." He frowned and searched her cloudy-looking eyes. "Having you in my bed, in my arms, is like being constantly teased. You touch me, kiss me, and I need you, Sky. I'm never not hungry for you, baby."

"Well," she murmured, raising her brows, "I think that makes two of us." She shook her head. "And I like it. I don't grow tired of it, either." Her lips twisted upward.

Gray grinned and shook his head. "Me, neither," he rasped, trailing his finger down the long curve of her slender neck. "You make me happy, Sky, in every possible way, on every level of myself," Gray confided, serious and holding her softened gaze. "Maybe I need to leave you alone and let you get more sleep."

Sky shook her head. "I'm *fine,* Gray. I saw Jordana last week, so don't even go there. I can't stand the thought of you ignoring me in your bed. I love having your body wrapped around mine. I love the way you touch me, make me feel good. I've never been so well loved as by you."

Gray leaned down, placing a chaste kiss to her brow. "Thank you, but I think you're tired because you're not getting decent enough sleep. Your body is still healing." He slid his hands around her face, holding her shining eyes that held what he was sure was love for him in their cobalt depths. "I'll never not hold you in my arms or curl around you and hold you while you sleep."

The calloused warmth of his hands made her sigh. "Okay, so long as you don't send me back to my room. Because if you did, McCoy, I wouldn't sleep at all." She made a sound of disgust. "The nightmares would probably come back."

Gray released her after kissing the tip of her nose. "Try and leave my bed," he warned her, giving her a mock look of sternness. "And you're right. Since we've started sleeping together, you haven't had one nightmare." That, in and of itself, to Gray, was startling. It was the nightmares that frequently kept him awake and caused his sleep deprivation.

"Because you make me feel safe, Gray," Sky whispered, sliding her hand up across his jaw. "In your arms, I feel the world melt away. I always feel safe when you're near me, bed or not."

"I'm a big, bad guard dog." He chuckled, understanding. Threading his fingers through her hair, he asked, "Is there anything I can get you? Some water? Juice?"

"Some orange juice with ice in it sounds really good."

He patted her hip. "Okay, stay where you are, and I'll get you some."

Sky felt incredibly happy as she lay there, hands across her belly. No man had ever shown her such kindness or sensitivity. Beneath that hard SEAL game face of his was a man who could be tender. And that was something Sky had never known existed before Gray. Closing her eyes, Sky listened to him putter around in the kitchen, never feeling more fulfilled. Or happier.

GRAY WAS COMING into the house with a bouquet of red roses to celebrate the end of the dude-ranch season at the Elk Horn Ranch. The last six families had left Sunday morning. Now, beginning on September first, the entire ranch would swing its full attention to branding and vaccinating cattle and taking care of many other ranch demands. The cattle would be trucked south for the winter because Wyoming had such harsh winters they wouldn't survive it. The buffalo that occupied part of the ranch would survive without a problem. Bales would be taken out to them by a tractor hauling a flatbed. The rugged, thickly furred beasts would handle Wyoming blizzards and survive. The cattle, however, would not.

Gray was looking forward to getting back to ranching work. Opening the door, he stepped in, looking for Sky. Worry ate at him because since that bout with flu she'd had two weeks ago, she'd never really bounced back from it. He found Sky in the living room with her knitting needles, working on a blue-and-gold afghan that she'd wanted to make for him. It was to celebrate the Navy colors as a reminder of his time in service. She looked up as he came in the door.

"Wow," she said, putting down the needles. "What's this? Flowers?"

Grinning, he closed the door and walked into the living room, handing them to her. Sky's face, always looking tired since the flu, smudges beneath her beautiful eyes, lit up with pleasure. She took the bouquet, making a happy sound, her lips curving upward as he sat down next to her. "Celebration time," Gray said, looking at the huge afghan spread across her lap. "We survived the dude-ranch portion of our lives here at the ranch."

Her cheeks colored slightly as she inhaled the scent of the roses.

"Mmm, these are beautiful, Gray," Sky sighed, her hands on the bouquet in her lap. "Thank you. They're lovely."

"What I'm looking at is lovely," he said. Worried, Gray nudged some strands from her cheek. "Didn't you sleep well last night? Bad dreams?" Because the purple shadows beneath her eyes concerned him.

"I did," Sky protested. "I'm just...well...feeling tired, Gray, that's all."

"Maybe you should get checked out by Jordana?" He picked up her slender fingers and pressed a kiss to them. "Maybe you need a B12 shot? Or have anemia? You've been working nonstop since you got here. It could be catching up with you." Since she'd been sick, Gray had forced himself to give Sky more sleep. If they made love, he didn't keep her up all night, loving her a second and third time. And some nights, he stilled his own hunger for her sake, drew her into his arms to allow her to sleep deeply for eight healing hours. She looked fragile. Almost haunted. He knew PTSD was a multipronged monster that lived within a person. Was another facet of Sky's torture raising its head of late?

Making a noise of protest, Sky said, "She just saw me, Gray. I'm fine." Sky gave him a beseeching look not to worry about her. She gently touched one of the red rose blooms. "These are gorgeous." She leaned forward, sliding her hand against his jaw, placing her lips against his. "You always surprise me in the best of ways, Gray."

She slid her mouth against his, feeling his lips part, drinking her into him. The moments were heated, and she felt her body respond as he groaned, taking her into his arms, the roses and afghan crushed between them. She drowned in the heat and tenderness of his kiss with her. Gray was treating her as if she were some fragile flower that might wilt if handled too roughly.

The phone rang.

Groaning, Sky lifted her lips from his, breathing unevenly, feeling her womb bubble with need once more. "Do you want to get it?" she asked him. The phone was on the kitchen wall.

"Yeah," he grunted, unhappy. "Stay put." And then he shared a warm look with her. "Smell your roses."

Laughing softly, Sky rearranged the afghan, folding it up and setting it aside on the couch. She loved to watch Gray walk, that boneless male grace of his, shoulders broad and thrown back with natural pride. Sky inhaled the fragrance of the bouquet as he reached out to answer the jangling phone.

"Gray McCoy," he answered.

Something was wrong. Sky saw his light mood disappear in a second, his game face coming into place. Automatically, she tensed, her hands tightening around the bouquet in her lap. And when Gray turned, looking directly at her, his eyes dark and stormy, her throat tightened. He gestured for her to get up and come over. Her heart took off in a thudding beat as Sky rose and walked quickly to the kitchen. Gray handed her the phone.

"It's your mother," he said, his voice heavy. "Your father's in the hospital again."

Brows lifting, Sky took the phone, instantly feeling terror rivet her to the spot. "Mom? What's wrong with Dad?" she asked, her voice off-key, fear in it.

"I'm sorry to call you, Sky, but your dad just went into the hospital. The doctor said he has a blood clot in his lung."

Sky felt as if the earth had just been yanked out beneath her. She heard a gasp, not realizing it had come from her. Gray came up behind her, steadying her with his hands on her shoulders. "What's his condition?" she whispered, her voice strained.

"Critical."

Sky heard tears in her mother's low, pained voice. "Okay," she whispered, her mind whirling with the medical information. "I'm coming home. I want to be there for him and you."

"Your dad asked for you, Sky." Balin sniffed, her voice tremulous. "The doctors don't give him much of a chance. You need to get home as soon as you can."

"I'll be there," she promised her mother firmly. Right

now Sky knew her parents needed her to be strong. "I'll call you with airline information as soon as I know."

Gray watched the color in Sky's cheeks leach out. She hung up the phone and turned in his arms. Wincing internally, he saw the terror in her eyes.

"It's my dad, Gray. He's got a blood clot in his lung," she choked out.

"Life threatening?"

Licking her lips nervously, Sky nodded. "Y-yes. If the clot leaves his lung and goes to his heart, he'll die. It's bad. Really bad. Oh, God…" She pressed a hand to her brow, trying to think clearly. "I—I don't want to lose him, Gray. I know we've had our differences, but he's my dad…."

"Shhh," Gray rasped, feeling her tension, the terror and grief tunneling through her. "Let me call the airport. You get packed. Or do you want me to help you pack?"

Sky's gaze moved restlessly as she tried to harness her emotions and think logically through this crisis. When he eased her away from him, he saw Sky doing just that. After all, she was an R.N. She'd spent years in the emergency room where coolness, calmness and detachment were essential in order to care for her wounded patients.

"Y-yes, can you do that for me?" Sky took a swipe at her hair, pushing it behind her shoulder. "I'll go pack." She left his arms, hurrying down the hall to her bedroom.

Cursing softly, Gray pulled out his cell. He had an iPhone and was able to quickly search Google for the airlines that flew in and out of Jackson Hole. Within a minute, he had their schedules, and he picked up the phone, calling the airlines. The good news was a flight was leaving in an hour for Casper, where her parents lived. He made a round-trip reservation, paid for it by credit card and got her seat assignment. By the time he hung up, Sky was carrying a small overnight bag. She was traveling light, and Gray couldn't blame her.

"I've got your flight. One hour from now. I'll drive you to the airport." He picked up his baseball cap and settled it on his head. "First, I need to see Rudd or Iris and let them know what's going on."

"Good," Sky whispered, suddenly bereft. She felt so alone when Gray stepped out of the house. The silence surrounded her and made her feel abandoned. Sky knew it was her PTSD, the part she continued to work with. That sense of abandonment had been one of her deepest wounds. Abandoned after the helicopter crash, taken prisoner, tortured for two weeks with no hope of rescue.

Shaking her head, she snapped into action. One of the many things Sky had learned over the past year was to never allow such feelings to overtake and run her. She knew better than to suppress the feeling. And now she let it sit there, but she didn't give it any more emotional energy. Her detachment as a nurse was coming in handy and had helped her become stronger as a result. And right now she needed to call on every reserve she had to be there for her mother and father.

Gray stepped back into the house, his game face on. Sky moved toward him, picking up her purse. "I'm ready," she murmured.

"I wish I could go with you," Gray said, sliding his arm around her shoulders, leading her to the door.

"You can't. No one else knows the feeding schedule and care of all the animals at the center, Gray."

He scowled, his mouth thinning. That was the one caveat in running the center; only Gray knew the animals enough to feed and medically monitor them. Sky was learning from him, but now she was leaving him, and there was no way Gray could be with her as much as she needed his company. She walked out the door and down the walk to the garage where the silver pickup truck with the Elk Horn Ranch logo on the doors was parked.

"I wish someone else did know how to take over my job," he grated. He opened the door for Sky and took her "go bag," as she called it. Once Sky was in, Gray handed it to her and shut the door. His mind whirled with worry for her. Sky hadn't been doing well the past two weeks, for whatever reason. As he climbed in and started the truck, Gray felt the fine, raw edge of fear starting to stalk him.

He glanced over at Sky. He could tell by the set of those lips of hers that she was steeling herself against emotions to come. Who wouldn't under these circumstances? He wanted to howl out his frustration as he backed the truck out of the driveway and aimed it down the two-mile road to the highway.

"What can I do to help?" Gray demanded, picking up her hand. Her flesh was cool and damp.

"Just be here for me," she whispered, feeling tears burn in the backs of her eyes. Sky swallowed convulsively. "I'll call you the minute I land."

He squeezed her fingers gently. "Keep me in close touch." He gave her a swift glance. "You aren't going through this alone. All right?"

His low, grating words vibrated through her pounding heart, cut through the terror that her father might die. Gray's hand was warm and dry around hers. She wanted to absorb his calm and quiet strength right now. "Yes, I understand," Sky said, her voice low. She wanted to cry so badly. "God, I don't want my dad to die, Gray. I—I need to make peace with him about…"

"About his reaction to your PTSD symptoms," Gray growled. He felt desperation curl in his tightened gut. "Listen, your father loves you. You know that, Sky. He was never like that with you before this. I *know* in my gut, he's got PTSD himself. Maybe—" his voice dropped with barely held emotions "—maybe he's going to talk to you about it."

Her fingers trembled as she touched her closed eyes, fighting back the need to weep. "I—I think you're right. He couldn't stand having me live under the same roof with him having those awful nightmares." She sniffed.

"Hang in there," Gray murmured. "I'm with you, baby. All the way. You know that, don't you?" He wanted to pull the truck over, stop and hold Sky. Keep her protected for just a second, but he couldn't. They were up against a looming deadline to get her to the airport and get her through security in order to catch that flight to Casper.

"I—I know," Sky whispered, her voice raw. She lifted her hand away and pushed the tears off her cheeks with trembling fingers. The anguish she saw burning in Gray's eyes lanced through her. There was no question he loved her. She loved him.

"We'll get through this, baby. I'm there for you. No matter what happens," Gray promised her thickly, seeing the airport road sign coming up. His throat ached with tension, with so many things left unsaid between them. Swallowing hard, pain in his knotted stomach, Gray worried this crisis could rip Sky apart. It was a test. One hell of a test.

## CHAPTER TWENTY-TWO

SKY SAT IN the plane, on an aisle seat, wrestling with so many emotions that threatened to swamp her. Lips tingling from Gray's long, powerful goodbye kiss, she absently touched them, her heart torn over her father's condition. A phone call to her mother, who was sitting in the ICU with her father, did nothing but hammer home her terror that he was going to die. *God, no...* She pressed her hands against her face, struggling not to cry. Wishing Gray was here to be the support he'd always been to her. But she was alone.

The captain came on announcing that everyone had to return to their seats, that they'd be landing in Casper in twenty minutes. Allowing her hands to drop into her lap, Sky leaned back, closing her eyes. God, from somewhere, she had to pull herself together. Her mother's wobbling voice at the other end tore at her stability. Balin, her mother, was Cheyenne, a strong woman warrior, a woman who was seen by her tribe and friends in Casper as indomitable.

But less than an hour ago, her mother had been reduced to a puddle of tears, and Sky had barely been able to make out what she was saying. Her fierce love of her father was never more on display. Balin wasn't given to many emotional displays, always the serious one, the one who didn't smile that much or that often. It had been her father, lean, lanky Alex, who had always provided comic relief.

Sky grew up remembering his laughter, his tickling

her ribs, playing with her as her stern mother looked on. It wasn't that Balin didn't love her; she did. Sky knew her mother's inherited strength was what had gotten her through the torture. As broken as her soul had been, Sky had reached so deep within herself to maintain hope even when there was none she ever expected to arrive to save her. It was Balin's toughness that she'd genetically passed on to Sky that had helped Sky survive. Now...

Taking an uneven breath, Sky closed her eyes, feeling the movement of the jet, being slightly jostled in her seat as it continued to lower in altitude. Now her mother was shattered, fearful that her husband, whom she loved with a fierceness Sky had never seen before, was slipping away. *Oh, God, give me strength. Give me the right words.... Let me be someone my mom can lean on....*

The plane landed, and soon they arrived at the terminal. Sky was one of the first people off, thanks to Gray's thoughtfulness. He'd bought her a first-class ticket, and she was only steps away from the door, able to quickly leave the plane.

She needed to hurry. The urgency overwhelmed her as she practically trotted up the long tunnel that led into the terminal. She was so glad she didn't have to wait an hour at baggage claim to get a suitcase. As she hurried out of the terminal to hail a taxicab, she called her mom on her cell.

"I'm here, Mom. How's Dad?"

"He knows you're coming, Sky. He's rallying. It's so important for you to get here. He says he has to talk to you soon."

Gulping, tears in her eyes, Sky saw a yellow cab pull up. She quickly opened the door. "I'll be there in just a little while, Mom. Tell Dad I love him, that I'm on my way...."

Sky asked the woman cabdriver to get her to the hospital. She sat back, immune to the sunny afternoon, the puffy white clouds in the sky above the city of Casper. Opening her iPhone, she put in a call to Gray, who she knew was hanging on tenterhooks, too.

"Hey," she said as he answered his phone. "I'm here in Casper. I'm in a cab on the way to the hospital."

"Good. Your dad?"

Choking, Sky whispered, "My mom is falling apart, Gray. She said to hurry…" She fought to remain steady, not melt into a pool of tears.

"Okay, baby, just take a couple of deep breaths. You know the drill. Get yourself calmed down. You can do this. I've seen you do it before."

Just listening to Gray's calm, deep voice, the care in it, she did as he instructed. Taking slow, deep breaths always helped. As a nurse she understood it was getting more oxygen into a person's body, feeding the cells, calming every system down and keeping things stable. Sky looked out the window as the cab sped along the freeway. In the distance, she saw the hospital. Her throat ached with unshed tears. "I'm so glad you're here with me," she whispered unsteadily. "Thank you…"

"Listen, keep taking those breaths. Sky, you're a lot stronger than you realize. I've always told you that. Now, you need to pull down and grab that strength that's always been there that's available to you. You have two people you love most in the world in the worst crisis of their lives. You're an R.N. You blossomed in the emergency room. Just consider this an E.R. crisis. Fall back into that muscle memory. Let it come forward to support and protect you. Okay?"

His words triggered something deep and knowing within her. *Muscle memory.* SEALs knew those words and understood them better than nearly anyone. It meant that a person had gone through the motions so many times that they no longer had to think about it. Their body, their central and peripheral nervous systems remembered it. All of it. Taking a gulp, she rasped, "That helps me so much, Gray. The cab is almost at the hospital. I'll call you as soon as I can...."

"Good. I'm there in spirit with you, Sky. Just feel me with my arms around you, holding you..."

Sky swore she could feel his arms, his protection, enclosing her as he spoke those gritty words. Reluctantly, she shut off her iPhone and pocketed it into her purse. The cab pulled up to the front entrance of the hospital, and she paid the driver, getting out. Looking up at the three-story building, her heart beginning a ragged pound in her chest, Sky refocused, visualizing herself back in the E.R. of the Bagram hospital. A calm descended upon her and her body, her mind and emotions slid into that old, familiar emotional detachment. Sky couldn't do her job with chaos around her, if she hadn't detached and allowed that unique calm to guide her in every way.

As she stepped into the opening doors of the hospital, Sky felt strong enough to cope, and that was all she needed. Just endure and be a quiet center in the storm surrounding her beleaguered, shocked parents. Stepping into the elevator to go to the second floor, where the ICU was, Sky leaned back against the wall, eyes closed, picturing Gray smiling. He didn't smile often, but when he did, his entire face changed and became unbearably beautiful to Sky. His laughter was like rolling thunder through his massive chest, and she allowed the memory of that to flow through her, feeding her, soothing her, giving her even more strength than before. Gray was only a phone call away. She had a lifeline....

Sky spotted her mother standing near the waiting room of the ICU. Up ahead, she saw the nurses' desk and six nurses in white uniforms behind it. Off to the left she saw the glass-enclosed ICU rooms. She was no stranger to any of this, and oddly, it calmed her some more. This was her other world, her other life. Sky knew it as intimately as breathing. Her mother sensed her presence, lifting her head, her eyes widening with relief as she spotted Sky.

Balin Pascal was a Cheyenne and proud of it. From the time Sky could remember, her mother had always proudly worn long black braids that hung nearly to her waist. She remembered her mother, every morning while sitting at her dresser, combing her thick, blue-black hair and gracefully plaiting it into the braids. She always decorated the ends with bits of raptor fluff and red yarn, to symbolize the color of an Indian's skin. But on a deeper level, her mother had taught her, the red yarn symbolized that red blood ran through all two-leggeds, and therefore, they were all brothers and sisters to one another.

Her mother looked weary with exhaustion as Sky moved quickly toward her. Balin was Sky's height, thin, her shoulders always thrown back, her chin lifted just enough to show her pride. Today her golden-brown eyes were marred with grief and worry. Her high-boned cheeks were glistening with recently spent tears. She was wearing familiar clothes of Levi's and a white blouse.

Her parents had a small, rural farm just outside Casper. Her mother had a huge garden, and she canned and froze fruits and vegetables to be eaten and savored during the winter months. To Sky, she was still beautiful in her mid-forties. That fierceness that was always a part of her was gone now, as if she were a balloon that had been punctured cruelly by a needle called Life Trauma. Sky had never seen her mother as hopeless-looking as she was right now. She heard Balin choke out her name, throwing open her arms to her.

"I'm so glad you're here," Balin whispered, hugging her daughter. She kissed Sky's cheek and held her at arm's length. Looking her over, she asked, "How are you doing?"

Sky settled her hand on her mother's slumped shoulder. "I'm okay, Mom. Dad?"

"He's awake. I just left his ICU room." She pointed to the one on the end. "Number six, the one closest to the nurses' station."

"Okay, good," Sky soothed. "Listen, I want to talk to the head nurse in charge on this shift. She'll give me information that might help me understand where Dad is at medically."

Balin glared toward the nurses' station. "They talk in a foreign language to me," she huffed. "I don't understand what they're saying. There's so many machines in Alex's ICU room. I don't know how to read them. It's so noisy in there. That's enough to kill a sick person, Sky."

"Mom," she whispered gently, kissing her damp cheek, "let me see what I can find out?"

Nodding, Balin muttered, "I'll be here in the waiting room."

Sky noticed all the ICU rooms were filled. The nurses were very busy. Some were watching monitors behind the long, crescent-curved desk; others were caring for their very ill patients in the different rooms. Sky slowed and almost stopped at the last one. Her heart dropped.

Her father was lying with his eyes closed. His face was gray. Gulping back tears, Sky forced her feet to keep going toward the nurses' desk. Knowledge was power. If she didn't get the latest stats on her father's condition, she wouldn't know if he was declining or improving. Or holding strong.

"Excuse me," Sky said, buttonholing an older blonde

nurse standing behind the other nurses at the desk. "I'm looking for the charge nurse?"

The blonde said, "That would be me. May I help you?"

Sky knew she was checking her out. She was a new face here in the ICU. Only family was allowed on this floor. "Yes, I'm Alex Pascal's daughter, Sky Pascal." She saw the nurse's name over her pocket of her uniform: C. Ramfort.

"Oh," she said, coming forward, "your mother, Mrs. Pascal, said you'd be arriving shortly. I'm Christine Ramfort. Is there any question I can answer for you?"

"Yes, there is. Christine, I'm an R.N. My speciality is E.R. I would deeply appreciate seeing my father's chart, the medications and his hourly information. Is that possible?" Sky knew that because she was a sister R.N., there was an unspoken fraternity between them. The nurse's dark brown eyes assessed her for a second.

"Your mother said you'd been a U.S. Navy nurse over in Afghanistan. Is that right?"

"Yes. Yes, I was." She saw Christine offer her a hint of a smile across her thin lips.

"I was a Navy R.N., too, for twenty years. Come on around here, Sky, and I want you to sit at this terminal. Your parents signed the consent forms for you to see the files. It has all your father's data on it."

Gratefulness flooded Sky. She reached out, gripping Christine's narrow hand. "Thank you," she managed, her voice cracking.

Christine grinned. "If any doctors show up, I'll have to ask you to quickly vacate yourself from the terminal. Okay?"

The glimmer of amusement in the charge nurse's eyes made Sky feel on the verge of crying. "Got it." Because Christine was putting her career on the line by letting someone not affiliated with this hospital read the raw records on a patient. But because she and Christine had both been in the Navy, there was a stronger, deeper military bond and sisterhood shared between them.

Sky quickly sat down at the computer terminal. Christine leaned over Sky's shoulder and brought up her father's records. Instantly, Sky's gaze narrowed on the numbers, the medicalese, the lab reports, the MRI showing the clot sitting in his right lung. In five minutes, Sky had a detailed understanding of it all. She quickly got up and walked to the other side of the desk. "Thanks," she said to Christine, who went and hid the information with a keystroke.

Nodding, Christine walked around the desk and stood next to her. "The good news is the blood thinner the doctor's given him is helping. You can see his pulse-ox is improving hourly."

"Yes, this looks better than I'd hoped."

"He's a fighter, your dad," Christine said, giving her arm a squeeze. "Your mother is an emotional wreck. I tried to ask if she'd like some sort of sedative, but she got really pissed off when I asked her."

Sky grinned a little. "My mother is Cheyenne. She hates white-man drugs. Refuses them for herself."

"Mmm, that explains it." Christine's eyes glinted. "Maybe a little chamomile tea for her nerves, then? That's an herb well-known to calm someone down. And it's natural. Would she be open to that?"

Sky gave the woman a warm look. "All good advice. I'll ask her if she'd like any. I'm going in to see my dad now. Do I have five minutes?"

"Give or take," Christine murmured, flashing her a grin. "As long as he doesn't look like it's tiring him out, stay with him."

"I will. First I need to talk with my mother."

"I tried to explain things to her," Christine lamented, "but she didn't understand."

"It's okay. My mom is a pretty fixed person. And English is her second language. Cheyenne is her first."

"Ohhh," Christine murmured. "Okay, got it. If you need anything else, come see me. Navy sisters stick together."

The sense of control over the situation, the knowledge, her years of experience as a trauma nurse were kicking in big-time. Sky walked to the lounge and sat down with her mother, who looked so broken and forlorn.

"Mom, Dad is better." She squeezed her hands. "The medicine is working. It's reducing the blood clot in his lung, and he's breathing easier. He's getting more oxygen into his blood."

Her mother frowned, as if the situation was still too complicated medically for her to understand.

Smiling, her voice hopeful, Sky said simply, "Dad is better. He's rallying. And those are all good signs."

Instantly, her mother's eyes lit up with hope.

"Really? Is this true, Sky?"

"Yes," she murmured, giving her mother a warm look, fighting back her tears.

"What does this mean, Sky? Will he live?"

Hearing the desperation in her mother's hoarse voice, Sky hesitated. "I don't know yet, Mom. It's too early to tell. But all things point in that direction."

"I've been praying so hard," Balin whispered, pulling her hands out of her daughter's hands, covering her face.

"I know, I know," Sky soothed, sliding her arm around her mother's sagging shoulders. "You keep praying because it's working, Mom." She leaned over to catch her mother's tear-filled eyes. "Okay? You know prayer is powerful."

"I asked our medicine woman from the reservation to conduct a healing ceremony for Alex. That was yesterday."

Nodding, Sky knew her mother believed in the medicine, the prayers of her people. And so did she. "It's working, Mom. Really, Dad is better. You hold on to that thought while I go see him."

Sniffing, wiping her cheek off with the back of her work-worn hand, Balin touched her daughter's cheek. "You know how bad he felt about asking you to leave, don't you?"

Her smile dissolved. "Y-yes, I do, Mom. I figured it was about that."

Balin gripped her daughter's hand. "Your father never told you what he did in the Marine Corps, Sky. He— well, he needs to tell you himself. I pray you'll understand more…better… Why he reacted the way he did."

Sky placed a kiss on her mother's furrowed brow. "Mom, I have a man in my life who has helped me understand why Dad did what he did. I think I already know, but let me go find out. In the meantime, will you go down to the cafeteria in the basement of this hospital? See if they have some chamomile tea? It's good for helping worry."

"Really? Why haven't I heard of this before?"

Grinning, Sky stood and helped her mom to stand. "You know, Nurse Ramfort is a very wise woman." Sky gestured toward the nurses' station, where Christine was. "She knows a lot about healing herbs. She's the one who suggested to me to tell you." She saw Balin's face change and grow respectful.

"Really?"

"Uh-huh. If you want, you might go over and ask Christine if she might know exactly where that tea is kept in the cafeteria. So you can go have a cup."

"I'll do that," Balin said, suddenly stronger, more confident. She pulled at her white blouse and straightened her long braids. "She's a good woman if she knows about healing herbs, Sky."

"Indeed," Sky murmured, hooking her arm through her mother's arm and walking toward the desk.

Sky released her mother and walked over to the glass door of her dad's ICU room. He appeared to be asleep, his long, work-worn hands across his blanketed belly. Quietly opening the door, Sky went in, feeling suddenly shaky and unsure. Muscle memory couldn't help her now. Her robust, vibrant father had never been ill. She'd grown up with him always being strong and caring for both her and her mother.

She crept closer, her damp hands resting on the bed that had been lifted up into Fowler's position so that he was at an angle that promoted better breathing for him. There was a cannula in his nostrils, delivering pure oxygen to his struggling body. Her eyes flicked to the monitors, reading each of them. Sky was so glad she knew how to read them and what they meant. Relief sped through her as she saw his blood pressure was normal. It meant he was resting well. The medication to melt that deadly blood clot in his right lung was doing its work. *Thank God.*

Her father had always had a rawboned face. His brown hair was cut military short. She saw the deep lines around his mouth, recognizing perhaps for the first time how much pain it showed he'd fought back and refused to release into the world. Sky had seen those lines so often in the black-ops wounded who came through her hospital in Bagram. The feathery lines at the corners of her father's eyes told her of his love of being outdoors.

When he wasn't on duty as a chef at their restaurant, he was chopping wood for the winter, hiking, fishing or hunting. He never killed anything they didn't eat. And Balin had taught him to pray over those lives he took, releasing their spirit, thanking them for giving their lives.

*Lines.* How much they told her as she observed her sleeping father. How much had he never told her?

Gently moving her fingers down his lower right arm, Sky was careful to stay away from the IV inserted into the crook of it. She saw his lids quiver. He was coming awake. Trying to steel herself, trying to be strong for him, Sky slid her warm fingers among his long, calloused ones. Slowly, his eyes opened. At first, Sky could see he wasn't aware, just in that in-between state. He'd been given other medications, among them, a sedative to keep him calm. If he moved around too much, he could dislodge the clot. It was a fine balance between keeping her dad quiet and then allowing him to move enough so that his limbs didn't become numb or circulation sluggish.

"Sky…you came…."

Her father's hoarse, broken voice nearly unraveled Sky. She smiled down into his drowsy-looking blue eyes. She had her mother's features but her father's blue eyes. His pupils were huge and black, indicating medication in his bloodstream. "Hi, Dad," she whispered unsteadily, leaning forward, placing a warm, lingering kiss on his wrinkled brow. She felt his fingers grow tighter around hers.

"Sky…" he croaked.

"Are you thirsty?"

He nodded. "Like a camel," he muttered, lifting his other arm and wiping his cracked lips with his trembling hand.

Sky looked at the IV drip. She also saw a pitcher and glass on a tray nearby. "Hang on. I'll get you some water to drink…"

Just getting to do something…anything…to help her dad made Sky feel better, more stable. As Alex settled back, giving her a weak look of thanks afterward, her heart opened with such love for him. Despite the past rocky months with him, he had been a wonderful father to her.

He'd helped put her through college, money out of his own pocket, to see that she got her degree to become a registered nurse. He'd sacrificed a lot and so had her mother so she could have the education she'd wanted so badly. Both her parents had given up a lot so that she could thrive.

"You're doing better, Dad," she whispered, leaning over and smiling warmly at him. A little color came into his cheeks. The spark of life slowly emerged from his cloudy-looking eyes. As she lifted her head to sweep her gaze across all the beeping and sighing instruments, she was hopeful. His blood pressure had dropped even more, indicating he was at peace. Maybe because she had come and she was here at his side?

"Thanks," he managed. Grimacing, he said, "Am I going to die?"

So typical of her father: straight and to the point. Gray had the same kind of bluntness. "From everything I see, Dad, you're better. The medication is melting the clot." She squeezed his hand. "You just need to lie still, rest and let it do its work."

"Damn clot. Who knew?" Alex moved his head slowly toward her, their gazes locking with one another. His eyes grew dark. "I wanted you to come, Sky. I need to say something…to own up to something…. I was wrong to tell you those things when you had those nightmares, when you were screaming in your sleep…."

"Dad, it's okay," Sky soothed, seeing how anxious he'd become. His blood pressure was rising. "I understand and I forgive you. I *was* a mess when I got home. And frankly, I don't blame you. I was waking you and Mom up every night, almost. Hindsight is always twenty-twenty. I should have rented a house in Casper, gone through that stage of my wounds—"

"No," he said flatly, his voice cracking. "No, Sky, you

should have been home with us, but I chased you off. I told you that you were messed up, that it was all in your head." He let out a broken breath, his chest heaving with exertion. "Dammit, it was my fault. I was projecting on you when I should have been holding you, listening to whatever you wanted to tell me, letting you cry." He gave her a pleading look, tears rolling out of the corners of his eyes. "I'm so damned sorry I hurt you like that, Sky. If anyone understood what you were going through, it was me." His lower lip trembled, and Alex squeezed his eyes shut, raw pain in his hoarse voice. "I was in black ops. I had PTSD, but never admitted it to anyone. I was strong enough to hold it at bay. Strong enough to not let it eat me alive, destroy Balin, destroy you..." He opened his eyes, staring up at her, begging her to understand.

"It's all right, Dad," Sky quavered. "I do forgive you. Please...you need to calm down now, all right?" She anxiously scanned the instruments, all of them climbing, indicating his distress.

Gently, Sky smoothed her hand across her father's chest, much like petting the wolf pups. "Dad, I want you to calm down," she whispered, holding his tear-filled gaze. "I want you to slowly breathe in and out. You don't want to move that clot around in your lung, and your breathing is ragged right now."

She put her hand up to his cheek, smiling with all the love she had. "Breathe with me. Let's breathe out our pain and replace it with the love we've always had for one another."

And for the next five minutes, she and her father began synchronous breathing, bringing down the climbing instrument readings, calming one another.

Christine came over and opened the door. "Sky? How is your dad doing now? Things look more normalized."

Glancing over her shoulder, Sky murmured, "He's going to be okay. Thanks for checking in."

She saw the worry in Christine's expression, but she nodded brusquely, said nothing and quietly closed the glass door, leaving them alone once more.

Sky smiled down at her father. "We're a good team, you and me. Your monitors are looking normal."

"You always had a magic touch with me," Alex whispered. "I don't know what I'd do if you weren't in our lives, Sky. I chased you away, but I want you to come back. We can heal one another...."

"Shhh, Dad, just close your eyes. You're so tired. You've been fighting so hard, you're exhausted. I'm here, and I'm not leaving. Do you hear me? I'll be here along with Mom. You're going to beat this. You're too tough, too stubborn, to give up now."

His hand curled around hers, weak but still strong. "Balin said you had a man in your life," he said, barely opening his eyes. "I hope he's good to you."

Her face crumpled with tenderness as she searched her father's glistening eyes still filled with tears. "His name is Gray McCoy, Dad. He's the one who figured out why you couldn't have me in the house. He's black ops, too...."

Alex grunted. "Tell me he's a Marine?"

Laughing softly, Sky said, "Sorry, he's Navy. He was a SEAL for nearly a decade."

"Well, it could be worse. The Navy cuts the paychecks to the Marine Corps. He's a sister branch, so he's okay."

Sky's softened laugh filled the ICU, and she felt her father's hand begin to relax in hers. His lashes fell against his cheekbones, his skin pulled tight across them. His skin was pale from the battle with the blood clot. She gently caressed her father's head. "You'll love him, Dad."

# CHAPTER TWENTY-THREE

"Is THERE SOMETHING wrong with you?" Balin asked her daughter as she came back from the bathroom. "You look terrible."

Nausea rolled through Sky, and she forced a weak smile she didn't feel. "I think it's something I ate," she offered, walking back to the waiting room of the ICU. She'd just filled her mother in on her dad's progress when Sky suddenly needed to vomit. She'd barely made it to the bathroom.

Feeling suddenly exhausted, she said, "I'm going to go to the house and get cleaned up, change clothes and rest for a while. Then I'll come back and spell you?"

Sky hated to see her mother's anxiety. The woman had enough to worry about.

Balin dug out the keys to her car. "Take the truck. Why don't you come back at six? You can spell me, and then I can go home for a bit, get a shower and something to eat?"

Nodding, Sky squeezed her hand and left. As she passed her dad, she slowed to a stop, studying the monitors, studying him. He was stable. And he was improving. With a sigh, she turned and nearly ran into Christine.

"Hey," Christine said, slipping her hand around her arm, "you don't look so well. Can I help?"

Sky grimaced. "Something I ate."

"Do you have a fever?"

Sky knew that would be death in an ICU, to come in here with a fever. It meant a virus or bacteria could easily be passed on to a struggling patient and potentially kill them. "No…"

"Just do me a favor?" Christine said, giving her a maternal look. "Come to the back room with me? I want to take your temp just to make sure."

Sky didn't fight her. She knew she didn't have a fever, but Christine was the front line of defense to keep her patients protected. They moved into a small examination room and Christine closed the door, motioning her to sit on the gurney.

It felt good to sit, and Sky could feel the emotional tsunami of today beginning to swell, getting ready to overwhelm her. She needed to go to her parents' house because her emotions were shredded. She needed some quiet time because of her PTSD, to get herself together once more.

Christine popped the ear thermometer into her left ear. "Hmm, you are normal." She placed her fingers on the inside of her wrist. Watching her clock, she pursed her lips. "You're 120, Sky."

"I've been through a lot in the last twelve hours," Sky grunted.

"You have been," Christine murmured, using her stethoscope. "Heart and lungs are great." She tilted her head. "How long have you been vomiting?"

Shrugging wearily, Sky sighed and muttered, "Three weeks, I guess."

"Got a guy in your life?"

She frowned. "Yes. Why?"

Christine moved her hand gently down Sky's left arm. "Protected sex?"

Her brows went up. "Well, yes."

"Honey," Christine said gently, "I don't want to alarm you, but from my viewpoint, you could be pregnant."

"Oh… I just figured it was nerves or a bug." And then, automatically, as if her body knew more than she did, she protectively moved her hand across her belly. "But we always have protected sex."

"Are you on the pill, sweetie?"

"No. He uses condoms," she said, realizing she'd been in denial. Oh, God, she could not be pregnant, not with all the turmoil in her life, even though she did have strong feelings for Gray.

Christine nodded sagely and gently patted her arm. Like a mother would an upset child. "One way to find out." She reached down in a drawer and pulled out a pregnancy test. "Why don't you go pee on the stick. I can run a blood test to confirm. Okay?" She gave Sky a kind look.

Sky's breath was ragged and her heart thrashed in her chest. Sky sat gripping the ends of the gurney where she sat, head down, trying to deal with the shock. The possibility.

"Are you in love with this guy?"

Closing her eyes tightly, Sky whispered, "No... I love him... I mean..." She lifted her head, shaking it. "I—I haven't told him yet. So much has been going on..."

"You've got a lot to deal with," Christine said quietly, her hand stilling on Sky's clenched hand.

It felt as if someone had gut-punched her. For a moment, Sky felt as helpless as she had on that wooden board she'd been chained to by the Taliban. "Y-yes, but I'm getting better."

"Are you on any medication, Sky?"

"No. None. I won't do that. I won't numb myself out—"

"It's a good choice. You're young, and you're strong." Christine gave her a wink. "Your secret is safe with me. Come on. I need a confirmation one way or another on this. Because you know I can't let you back into ICU even if you don't have a fever. The vomiting is coming from somewhere, and I need to know where." She gave her a gentle look. "You understand?"

"Yes," Sky whispered brokenly. She took the small box, staring at it. My God, what if she was pregnant? How had it happened? When? Gray always took precaution. Always. Her chest hurt with a primal scream she wanted to shriek out to the world. Sky knew it was her PTSD. Wrestling with it, she gave Christine a glance, slid off the gurney and said, "I'll be right back."

SKY STARED AS the color changed. She gulped. Tears rushed to her eyes. These kits were reliable. Her mind spun over the past months with Gray. Had a condom malfunctioned? It was known to happen. A tiny rip or tear in it? Oh, God…

Christine took a blood sample from her. "Listen, I'll rush this through the lab. Give me your cell phone number. If you are pregnant, you're more than welcome to come back up here to see your dad. If it comes up negative, I can't let you back in here. Understand?"

Sky wearily nodded. She wrote down her phone number. Reaching out, Sky gripped the nurse's hand. "Thank you, Christine—for everything." Because the nurse was nurturing and trying to be as supportive as she could to her right now. Sky was sure Christine sensed her emotional reactions even though she was presently sitting on them.

"Honey, if you love this guy, he's not going to walk out on you once he knows you're pregnant. I see that look in your eyes. As if he'll abandon you."

Sky nodded, the words jamming in her tightened throat. "I don't know what will happen, Christine." Lifting her head, she continued, "Right now, my dad is my priority." She touched her belly gently. "I can't handle any more right now."

"I know, I know," Christine soothed. "Come on. I'll walk you down to your mother's car. I think you could use some girl company right now…."

Sky sat out in the car in the late-afternoon summer sunlight, in shock. Christine had told her she was going to be all right, given her a sisterly hug and walked back into the hospital.

Needing to call Gray, she pulled out her iPhone. He would be waiting to hear about her father, his condition. Sky found a rush of emotions, both beautiful and terrifying, tearing through her. When she could be in a quiet place, not distracted, the R.N. in her knew the truth: she was pregnant.

Moistening her lips, Sky looked blindly out the car window, seeing nothing, wrapped in too many conflicting feelings to do anything but sit and let them subside. Rubbing her face, she held the cell in her right hand. Gray would be worried. He cared for her. He'd never said he loved her. And she hadn't told him she loved him, either. *God, what a mess.*

A powerful, overriding knowledge swamped Sky. She *needed* Gray. She was desperate to hear his voice. His calm counsel. His voice that feathered through her, quieting her, helping her to relax, to trust him as she'd never trusted any man in her life with the exception of her father.

Her mind churned over telling Gray about being pregnant. Sky couldn't tell him over the phone. She needed to see his facial expression to know truly how he felt about this bombshell suddenly exploding into their lives. Worrying that her PTSD would harm the baby she carried, Sky gnawed on her lower lip. She needed desperately to talk to someone who might know. Jordana would! After she called Gray, she would place a call to Jordana tomorrow morning. It was too late in the day to catch her at her clinic or at the hospital.

Gray... Her lashes swept down and Sky so desperately wanted him here, with her. Just hearing his voice would soothe her. Settle her. He would help her get through this in one piece, not shattered as she'd been when she had been rescued by the SEALs.

"Sky?"

Gray's deep voice flowed through her like sunlight in the darkness of her fractured soul. "Yes… Gray…" Sky's voice broke into a husky whisper as she shared all the information about her family with him. She was clinging to the cell phone, her brow against the steering wheel, eyes tightly shut. PTSD cut her off at the ankles. It made her feel incapable of sustaining strength for any long period of time. Gray had promised her over time, she'd get stronger, and the weakness she felt right now would one day no longer dog her heels. By the time she was done with the news, Sky felt like water spilled across a tabletop, no boundaries to stop her, nothing to halt her pulverized emotions.

"How are you doing, baby?"

Just his endearment rushed tears to her shut eyes. "I—I'm okay." She heard him give a short, wry laugh.

"Now you sound like a SEAL. 'I'm okay. Nothing's wrong.'" Gray snorted. "Tell me the truth."

Sky swallowed convulsively against a lump forming in her throat. "It's overwhelming me, Gray. I—I thought I could handle it, thought…"

Her voice broke. Tears dribbled down her drawn cheeks. "I just feel so weak…so damned inept…like I'm fragile in places I never used to be. God, I've handled screaming, out-of-their-head wounded men, and it never made me blink an eye. It wasn't that I didn't care, Gray. I did. It's just…that I knew if I couldn't put my own feelings away, they could die. And I could do it. I did it."

"Listen, baby, you're still healing. Stop being so hard on yourself. You need to draw the wagons around you right now. Go to your parents' home, draw a hot bath, relax and chill. Quiet heals you, Sky. This is just how PTSD works. You need to stop now and help yourself."

Sky nodded and sniffed. More than anything, she wished he could be here at her side, but she knew she couldn't say those words. Couldn't give it voice. No one at the ranch knew the feeding schedules, the type of food to give to the animals. "You're right."

"Dammit, I wish I could be there for you, Sky."

She bit down hard on her lower lip, wanting to say, *Yes, come. I need you so badly.* Never mind she was pregnant. Sky just couldn't grasp it all. "It's all right," she said, her voice strained. "You're needed there, Gray."

"I know," he growled. "But I'm not happy about this, Sky. You need support. You need me. And I need you. Damn, I miss you so much. I've done nothing but worry about you since you left."

His words fed her, infused her heart and smoothed the tears that still existed in her soul. "I miss you, too. I keep thinking about what you'd say or do here." She smiled softly, wanting to reach through that phone and touch him, feel his arms coming around her, rocking her, kissing her.

"I—I need to go, Gray."

"Can you call me tomorrow morning? Let me know how your dad is? How you're doing?"

She heard the thin veil of desperation in his tightened voice. Sky swore she could feel his love streaming through that phone, flowing into her and feeding her the badly needed energy to go on. "I promise," she whispered.

"Okay, get some sleep tonight."

"I'm going to be at the hospital, Gray. My mother is absolutely exhausted. If I don't stay to keep watch over my dad, she'll sleep on a couch in the waiting room of ICU. She has to get some sleep herself."

"I understand. Okay, just know I'm here. If you need to talk at 3:00 a.m., call me."

Her lips softened and parted, the tears running into the corners of her mouth. "I promise… I will…."

She reluctantly hung up, craving Gray's voice, his care. Was it love she was hearing in his voice? Sky wanted it to be so, but she wasn't sure. Tucking the iPhone in her pocket, she drove the truck out of the hospital parking lot, heading to her parents' home to somehow piece the broken puzzle of herself back together again.

ALEX PASCAL WAS alert when she slipped into his ICU room the next morning. Sky knew she looked pale and drawn, purple smudges beneath her eyes. Yet her father said nothing and slid his hand into hers.

"Hey," Sky said softly, leaning over and kissing his brow, "you're really rallying. Did you talk to Dr. Jonas earlier?"

He nodded. "Yeah, he said I was too tough to die." He smiled weakly. "Said the blood clot was dissolving well."

"I know. I caught him out in the hallway right after he saw you," Sky admitted. Her gaze swept restlessly across all the monitors. "He said maybe one more day in here and then you could be transferred to a private room."

Grunting, Alex said, "Thank God. All these damned tubes and needles in me is driving me up a wall."

Sky grinned a little. Her father was not one to sit in one place long. But knowing he'd been in black ops, these men were restless by nature. Gray had confided that he couldn't sit still longer than fifteen minutes. He had to get up and move around. Her father had always been the same way. "Patience, Dad."

"Not one of my finer points, is it, Sky?" Alex eyed her tenderly. "I need to talk to you some more. You look exhausted. Are you up for this or not?"

Sky brought over a chair. Her mother had just left after getting the good news about her father. She was going home to get a shower and then some serious sleep. She would spell Sky late this afternoon. "Sure," she said. Her father gave her a frown, his blue gaze digging into hers.

"Are you positive, honey?"

Sky warmed to his pet endearment for her. She squeezed his hand on the gurney. "I'm listening, Dad."

He nodded then looked up toward the ceiling, as if gathering his thoughts. The doctor had reduced the antianxiety medication, and her father was much more like himself this morning. Sky didn't see the cloudiness any longer in his eyes. Alex Pascal had always reminded her of a hawk who never missed anything. There was a ringing clarity in his eyes, and it suddenly struck Sky that Gray had that same look of a raptor. They shared more than she'd ever realized.

"Sky, I never told you about my time in the Marine Corps."

"I know..." she said softly. "Remember? I came along after you got out after four years and met Mom?"

"Yeah," he sighed. "Meeting your mother was the best thing to ever happen to me." His eyes lit up. "And when she got pregnant three months after our marriage, I was even happier. You slid into my hands because your mom birthed you at home, refusing to go to the hospital. She never trusted white man's medicine." He smiled fondly, holding her gaze.

Sky felt so loved in that moment, seeing the warmth in her father's eyes toward her. "Mom said I cried a lot at first."

"Yeah, we took turns rocking you at night and burping you. You did well on breast milk, but for whatever reason, you were a cranky little thing for a bit."

"Glad I've grown out of that," Sky said, smiling as she saw her father relax.

"Sky, I need to tell you why I reacted like I did when you came home." His voice dropped and so did his brows. He held her gaze, however. "I was a Marine Force Recon. In 1990, they sent me in with a group of Navy SEALs into Desert Storm, the first Gulf War." He scowled. "Recons do behind-lines reconnaissance, Sky. We're black ops for our branch of the military. I spent a month before Desert Storm ramped up in the Iraqi desert with a SEAL team. We were dropped into Iraq, and our job during Operation Desert Saber was to locate, find and give intel on where the Scud missile launchers were at. In February of 1991, my recon team was sent in to check out the Iraqi guard buildup along the Kuwait border." He grimaced. "Things got bad, really bad. The U.S. Army 1st Cav came across and entered Iraq. That was known as the Battle of Wadi Al-Batin."

Alex stopped, as if grappling with sudden memories and emotions. "Sky, I don't think I'll ever be able to tell anyone about those five days in February... The 1st Cav withdrew from Iraq on February 20th. We'd taken forty prisoners and destroyed five of their tanks."

"I didn't realize you were in Desert Storm," Sky admitted quietly, seeing the grief and terror deep in her father's eyes.

He sighed raggedly. "Honey, I never wanted you to know. It was gruesome and the stuff of nightmares. I never wanted to stain your life or the way you saw the world." Voice cracking, he added, "I had PTSD. Really bad. Back then, you said nothing or you'd get kicked out of the service. After four years, I quit. I had enough horror about what man can do to man to last me a lifetime." Alex squeezed her hand.

"When you came home, honey, and you had those nightmares, it stirred it all up in me. Your mother lived through years of me screaming in my sleep, launching myself out of bed, fighting ghosts. Thank God your bedroom was at the other end of the house because you never heard my screams." He gave her a pleading look. "I thought I was done with PTSD, but when you were captured…" He looked away briefly then turned back to his daughter. "PTSD lurks inside you like a poison, Sky. I never got help for it. I just jammed it down deep inside myself. I thought it was gone after twenty years, but when the Navy informed us you were missing in action, it all came roaring back at me."

Her heart broke. "God, Dad, this was torture of another sort for you, too."

"Not half as bad as what you survived, Sky. That's for damn sure. I couldn't force myself to go to the Naval hospital in San Diego to see you. God, I knew I should. I was your parent. It was my responsibility. I knew you needed our love, our help." Tears glistened in his eyes. "But I was a coward, Sky. I—I couldn't handle seeing my daughter broken like I had been broken at one time. It tore me up. I cried so much for you, but I didn't feel I had the guts, the strength, to see it through. See you…"

"It's all right, Dad," Sky whispered unsteadily. Tears blurred her vision, and she blinked them away. "I understand now. I really do. I don't have the emotional strength I used to have, either." She gripped his hand hard, giving him a beseeching look. "I do understand. There's nothing to forgive here. Gray has told me how many guys stuff their PTSD. And I'm sure when I came home, it was like staring at all that horror you'd seen, that you'd lived through and survived, all over again." Hot tears streamed down her cheeks. "I was a raw reminder, that's all."

Alex nodded, lifting his hand and grazing her damp cheek. "But you're my daughter, Sky. And when you needed me the most, I abandoned you. I chased you out of the house. God, I'm so sorry, honey. I didn't mean to. I really didn't. There's no excuse for what I did."

Closing her eyes, Sky felt the trembling touch of his hand against her cheek. Sniffing, she opened her eyes. "Dad, I know the monsters that live inside you. They live in me. I know how I've run in the past. Until Gray came along, I was lost. But he has PTSD, too, and he understood." She gave him a tremulous look. "Gray's dealt with his, is getting help, and he's much further along in the healing process than you or I."

Some relief came to his face. "Then...when I chased you away, you found Gray?"

"Sort of," Sky stumbled. "He was my boss where I got a job at the Elk Horn Ranch."

"He's a good man, Sky, if he's reached out to help you. I'd like to shake his hand, tell him thank you. He did my job for me. I should have been there for you." He grimaced. "Look, when I get out of this damned place, things are going to be different. Will you let me back into your life, Sky? I know I don't deserve a chance, but will you? Let me be there for you from now on. I'm a good listener, and I don't want you carrying this load by yourself anymore."

Sky stood up, her knees shaky with fatigue and overwhelming emotions. She kissed her dad's cheek. "In a heartbeat, Dad." Her voice fell. "I love you. I never stopped loving you. I just didn't understand at the time. Now I do. And it's okay. If there's one thing Gray has taught me over the months it's that we can always glue the shattered pieces of ourselves back together again with love, care and support."

## CHAPTER TWENTY-FOUR

SKY PUSHED OUT the door of the ICU, her mother having come and relieved her. Weariness plagued every step as she turned the corner to walk down to the bank of elevators. Maybe her midafternoon exhaustion was due to her pregnancy? That would make sense. She scrubbed her face, hoping to stay awake for the drive back to her parents' home. The elevator doors whooshed open, and she looked up across the green-and-white-tiled floor toward them.

Her heart jammed in her throat. Sky jerked to a stop, her mouth dropping open.

Gray stepped out of the elevator. "Hey, you," he called softly, opening his arms, "come here...."

Sky gave a strangled cry, disbelieving Gray was really standing in front of her. He flashed that thousand-watt smile of his, arms opening and quickening his pace toward her. She wasn't sure she could move, her knees feeling suddenly unstable beneath her. An avalanche of emotions, good and bad, flooded her. And then Gray was there, his arms enveloping her, crushing her against him, his voice flowing across her, his kisses against her hair as he held her.

"Oh, God... Gray..." Sky choked out, pulling back just enough to meet his smiling eyes. "How... I mean...you shouldn't be here!"

Gray smiled lazily and gently pushed strands away from her eyes. "I thought outside the box," he murmured. "I got one of the veterinarians in town to come out twice a day to feed the animals." He searched her upturned face, noticing how tightly her skin was pulled across her pale cheeks. Worse, purple smudges rested beneath her beautiful blue eyes. He felt the tension in Sky, saw it and understood.

"Were you leaving?" he asked.

"Yes, my mom just took over the watch." She gulped, giving him a relieved look. "Dad is much better. I was going back to my parents' home to rest."

"All good news, baby. Come on. Show me your car, and I'll drive you there."

Sky sank against Gray, her cheek against the rough weave of his chambray shirt, inhaling his scent, unable to move because exhaustion avalanched her. With Gray, Sky could be weak when she needed to be, and he wouldn't fault her as others would. "I'm so glad you're here," she quavered, shutting her eyes, holding him, never wanting to let him go.

"Want me to carry you, baby?" he whispered against her ear.

"Oh, no." For a moment, Sky felt giddy. Felt as if her whole world had reordered itself, and she was going to be all right. His hand slid against her jaw, guiding her chin upward. His mouth moved tenderly against her lips. The rush of love tunneled through Sky as he nudged the corners of her mouth open, taking her gently. It was all Sky needed. Finally, Gray eased his mouth from hers.

"I've missed you so damn much," he growled, allowing Sky to stand fully on her own feet. "I don't sleep well at night if you aren't there beside me."

She managed a sour grin as he tucked her beneath his arm, and they walked toward the elevators. "You? I don't think I've had four hours' sleep in the last two days. I feel wired, unable to sleep even though I'm exhausted."

Nodding, Gray took her into the elevator and punched the button to the first floor. "That's going to change right now," he warned her.

Sky seesawed between abject fear and euphoric joy that seemed limitless as Gray drove the car to her parents' rural farm. Her heart overflowed with love for him. Gray had come to help her. To be there for her. If that wasn't love, then what was it?

She hadn't even admitted her love to him, and now she was carrying his child. In some ways, Sky felt suffocated by all her feelings being stretched to the breaking point one way and then another. Her father could have died. She was carrying new life in her body. The extremes were wearing her down in ways she couldn't even begin to cope with. With or without PTSD, she wondered how anyone could successfully negotiate these kinds of perfect-storm events. More than anything, Sky needed a good cry. It always cleaned her out and helped her reboot herself in a healthy way.

Gray opened the car door for Sky once he'd parked in the driveway of her parents' home. The late-afternoon sun was hot and beating down on the Wyoming landscape. He eased her out of the car, keeping hold of her hand as she led him into the large farmhouse.

"So," he said, "this is where you were born and grew up?" He looked around and then smiled down at Sky.

"It is." Sky stumbled going up the wooden stairs. Gray caught her and slid his arm around her waist. They entered the large home.

Inside the living room, Gray gently pulled Sky to a stop, turning her around to face him. "What do you need first, baby? A bath? Food? Tell me."

Her heart twisted in her chest, and Sky looked up into his caring, dark eyes. "I'm ready to fall apart, Gray." She felt her throat tighten painfully. "I've had too many shocks in a row."

He tunneled his fingers through her loose ginger hair. "I can see that," he said. There was such a tortured look in her eyes, Gray was worried. He knew Sky loved her father deeply, that the wound he'd created in her earlier this year had come full circle. Alex Pascal had apologized, and Sky had agreed to mend fences with him. All of that had taken a horrific toll on her. And then Sky suddenly froze then tore away from Gray.

Tensing, he watched her run down the hall, confused. *What the hell?*

Sky barely made it to the bathroom on the first floor before heaving her guts out in the toilet bowl. She felt Gray's hand on her brow, gently holding her while everything came up. Her eyes watered, and her mouth burned with that terrible acid taste. On her knees, clinging to the porcelain, she found herself too exhausted to move. Gray quickly stood up, and she heard water running in the nearby basin.

Kneeling, Gray placed a warm washcloth in her hand. "Here," he murmured. Frowning, he noticed how her flesh was almost translucent, her eyes dark. Sky croaked a thank-you and wiped her mouth with a trembling hand. Gray then traded the cloth for a glass of water.

The shame and embarrassment of vomiting in front of Gray, of feeling the world grinding over her until she could barely function, made Sky feel paralyzed. After she cleaned herself up, she took Gray's hand.

"Come on," Gray grunted, drawing her into his arms. Worried, he knew something was very wrong with her. She was limp in his arms, and he slipped his arm beneath her legs and hoisted her up against him. Her head nestled beneath his jaw, her arms limp in her lap.

"Where's your room?" he asked, taking her out of the bathroom.

"Last door on the left down the hall," she whispered. All she could think about was what Gray would say when he found out she was pregnant. There was no way to hide it. He wasn't dumb. In time, he'd put together her midafternoon exhaustion and vomiting sessions. Sky simply couldn't fight anymore, just needing him to hold her, if but for a little while.

Gray nudged the door open with the toe of his boot. The room was beautiful, a pale lavender with flowery drapes and bedspread. It was a girl's room, for sure, and he smiled as he laid her gently on the queen-size bed. Sky curled up on her side, in a fetal position, burying her head into the goose-down pillow, as if she wanted to hide.

He sat down on the other side of the bed after he removed her shoes. Getting out of his boots, Gray rolled over on the bed and brought Sky against him. He heard her whisper his name as he turned her over, bringing her into his arms and against him. This wasn't about sex. It was about loving her in a moment of crisis. Gray knew Sky would heal in his arms. She always had. He kissed the top of her ear, strands of her hair tickling his nose.

"Better?"

"Um…" It was the last thing Sky remembered saying before she tumbled over an abyss and fell into the deepest sleep she'd ever experienced. Gray's arms were around her, holding her safe, holding her together when she felt as if she were being torn apart in slow motion with no way to stop it.

Gray closed his eyes, feeling his worry recede as Sky, even in her sleep, snuggled as deep as she could against him, her breath soft and shallow against his neck. God, this was what he needed, too. He needed Sky. For the rest of his life. Exhaustion claimed him shortly afterward, and Gray slept deeply, the woman he loved like breath itself safe in his arms.

WHEN SKY SLOWLY AWOKE, Gray was propped up on one elbow beside her, watching her. The tenderness in his eyes made her feel incredibly desired. "What time is it?" she asked thickly, rubbing her eyes.

"6:00 p.m."

Sky started, but Gray reached out, his hand on her shoulder, keeping her on the bed. "I called your mother and told her you were worn-out. She understood and said for you to come to the hospital tomorrow morning."

Relief fled through her, and she relaxed. "And Dad? How is he?"

"Improving to the point to where your father's bitching got him sent out of ICU to a private room," he said with a grin. "Your mom said the blood clot in your dad's lung is gone. The doctor wants to keep him in the hospital for another two days for observation."

It felt as if a huge weight had suddenly been lifted off Sky's heart. Tears leaked into her eyes, and Gray's face blurred for a moment. "That's the best news ever," she quavered. Her dad was going to live! And then a sob tore out of her, and Sky felt Gray bring her into the shelter of his arms.

"It's okay, baby, go ahead and get it out," he urged thickly, kissing her hair and smoothing his hand across her shaking shoulders. He knew her father's admissions of being in black ops had torn her up. Gray wondered if it had brought back the terrifying memories of her own torture again. Sky looked so damned fragile that it scared the hell out of him, as if she were barely able to hold it together. "It's going to be all right, Sky," he rasped against her ear. "Everything's going to be all right. You have me, and I love you, baby.…"

Gray didn't even realize he'd whispered these words until they were out of his mouth. He doubted Sky heard them; she was weeping as if she'd lost everything. Moving his hand gently up and down her back, he understood that one trauma could domino-effect the inner PTSD trauma in a person. Judging from Sky's tense phone calls to him last night about her mother and her father, she had been strung too thin. Everyone had a breaking point.

He moved her silky hair aside, kissing the nape of her neck, whispering words he hoped would be healing for her. Gray knew he couldn't take away Sky's pain even though he wanted to. Every person had to walk that damn gauntlet alone. What he could do, the reason he came, was to be a safe harbor for her.

SOMETIME LATER, SHE QUIETED, hiding her face between her hands, nestled against him, her breath jerky. The tension had left her, and Gray could once more feel the relaxation of her shoulders beneath his hand. He kissed her cheek and felt the velvet softness of her fragrant skin. Her scent drove him crazy with need. He wished he could put into words how good, how clean, she always smelled to him. That honeylike sweetness to her flesh. Gray inhaled her fragrance deeply into himself. He gently moved her tousled hair aside, uncovering her face. Sky slowly allowed her hands to drop away, her eyes reddened and swollen.

"Better?" he asked, kissing her hair.

Giving a nod, Sky whispered, "Thank you.… I needed you so badly, Gray. You must have felt me or something."

He slid his thumb across her damp cheek, drying it. "I heard it in your voice last night, baby. I knew I had to do something. We all need one another every now and then."

Gray slid his finger beneath her chin, lifting it enough so that their eyes met. "I love you, Sky."

His thick, emotional words fell over her like the warmest blanket in the world. Reaching up, she took his hand, wrapping it in her own against her chest, over her heart. "I love you so much, Gray," she quavered.

But how would he react to her news, that they were going to have a baby? At the worst, Gray could be upset and walk out of her life. But that didn't seem likely. A baby changed everything, though, and Gray might not want this new responsibility. Sky felt her stomach tighten with a fear so devastating, it took her breath away. She closed her eyes, burrowing her head against his shoulder, her palm against his heart, desperate for the calm he always fed her.

Gray frowned. "Sky, talk to me," he whispered against her cheek. "There's something wrong. I can feel it. What else is bothering you, baby?"

Sky took a deep breath and slowly extricated herself from Gray's arms. She sat up, her hair tumbling across her shoulders as she crossed her legs. She faced him. "There's no other way to say this, Gray." Sky held his gaze and swallowed painfully. She whispered, "I'm pregnant. I found out yesterday at the hospital."

Gray slowly sat up, his eyes never leaving hers. "Are you happy about it?" he asked, slipping her cold, damp hand into his.

She gave a painful nod, her voice unsteady. "You know how much I love children…the babies…"

He smiled tenderly and reached out, bringing her into his arms. "Then I'm the second happiest person in the world, Sky." Gray looked down into her eyes that glistened with such love for him. "Must have had a condom accident," he teased, wanting the fear to leave her eyes.

Nodding, she said, "It must have been."

"How far along are you?" Gray slid his hand gently across her belly, allowing it to stay there, wanting her to know he wanted her, wanted the child she carried within her.

"I talked to a doctor yesterday afternoon. She said I'm three months along."

"And you have morning sickness?"

"Yes," Sky whispered. Searching his face, seeing the curve of his mouth, she asked, "You aren't upset, Gray?"

He moved his hand tenderly across her belly. "Shocked, yes. Unhappy? Never." Gray cupped her cheek, guiding her mouth to his. "I love you, Sky. I don't care when we have children. I always knew you'd be a good mother, and now I get a chance to try and be half as good a father." His mouth closed over her soft, opening lips. Gray felt his heart expand until he thought it might burst with blinding joy. No wonder she'd been so emotional the past few months. It all made sense now.

As Gray kissed her, he felt her melt into his arms, surrendering utterly to him. She was pregnant. Carrying his child. A flood of raw, jubilant emotions tunneled through Gray as he realized their loving one another had created a new, living being. The child was a symbol of the goodness they had brought to one another, the healthy love that could only happen when you saw the world through the other's eyes.

"I love you," he rasped. "Sky, no matter what happens in our lives, you hold on to that." He opened his eyes, staring into her gold-flecked blue eyes. Now there was happiness glistening in them. The fear was gone.

LITTLE BY LITTLE, Sky felt life dripping back into herself. Gray had drawn her a hot bath and then carried her down to the bathroom, telling her that he could carry her when she felt tired. And then Gray left for the kitchen and found enough food to make them a late-afternoon snack.

They sat at the table afterward, and Sky could actually feel herself reawakening. It was a strange sensation, one that she'd experienced once after being rescued by the SEALs. She had pulled her hair into a ponytail as Gray served them turkey sandwiches on whole-wheat bread. He'd thoughtfully made a salad, too. Grabbing the chair, Gray sat down at her elbow.

"Did you talk to the gynecologist about prenatal vitamins? What you should be eating?"

Sky smiled a little. "Yes, she gave me some. I told her I'd see Jordana when I flew home."

He arched a brow and jabbed a finger at the salad beside her plate. "Then all the more reason to eat lots of raw veggies in your diet. Good nutrition in them for you and our baby."

Her smile widened, and she shook her head.

"What?" Gray teased. "You think I'm going to become a helicopter father hovering around you? Asking if you took your prenatal vitamins every day?"

Warmth flowed through her as never before as she took a small bite of the sandwich. "I wasn't expecting this kind of reaction from you, I guess."

"No?" He dug into his salad with gusto. "You were worried I'd walk away?"

Sky felt ashamed. "Gray, there were a hundred different reactions you could have had, including that one." She saw him lift his head, his eyes warm with love for her. How could she have ever questioned Gray about his reaction to her being pregnant? He'd always done the right thing by her. *Always.*

"I imagine you had a list," Gray teased her lightly. Reaching out, he grazed her wan cheek. "You're human,

Sky. You went through a helluva lot with your parents before you found you were pregnant. If I were in your shoes, punch-drunk from so many emotional hits, I wouldn't be clear about it, either."

"Right now," she admitted, "all I want to do is go home and rest. I feel tired to my soul, Gray."

"You've run an emotional marathon by yourself," he told her quietly. "I've already got plane tickets for tomorrow afternoon. What you need is some downtime, Sky. Some fresh Wyoming air, a certain little white wolf to come and lick your hand and then to just lay around with your feet propped up."

She forced herself to eat for her baby. Sky had no appetite, but she'd seen this pattern in herself before. In time, it would leave, and she was sure she'd start eating for two. "Are you going to spoil me even more rotten than you do already?" she teased softly, watching his grin widen.

"Baby, you have no idea of how much I'm going to spoil you. I want you and our son or daughter to have a peaceful six months."

"Well," Sky said, managing a short chuckle, "this happened three months ago, and these have been the happiest months of my life, Gray." She held his gaze that told her how deeply he loved her. "My parents don't know yet…."

"We'll swing by tomorrow morning before we leave for the airport, and we'll tell them." Gray saw a little color coming back to Sky's cheeks. There was relief along with hope in her eyes, thank God. He knew how wicked PTSD symptoms could be. They distorted normal human reality and emotions.

"Yes, I'd like that."

"How do you think it will affect your father?"

"I think he'll be happy. He's desperate to patch things up with me."

"Nothing like becoming a doting grandfather to strengthen the ties that bind."

"He's been a really wonderful dad to me, Gray, except for this one episode. And I know he feels so guilty about it."

"Then," Gray said, "holding his grandchild in his hands six months from now is probably going to be one of the most healing things that could have ever happened between you two."

"It's already helping me," Sky admitted. "Now that I understand why I was getting so tired, my breasts enlarging, feeling even more exhausted than usual, I can relax. I thought I was getting some kind of a disease or something."

Gray chuckled and nodded. "So much for being an R.N., right?"

It felt so good to laugh instead of cry. To hear that rumble in his chest and see that wide smile of Gray's that changed his face in a remarkable way. "Bingo," she said, matching his smile. She told him about Christine and how she'd sized up the situation and pronounced her pregnant.

"Christine's good," Gray agreed, finishing off the salad and putting the bowl aside. "Really good."

"The best," Sky murmured. "She was very kind toward me."

"You R.N.s are all the same," he said. "Big hearts and endless love for the rest of us poor bastards."

Sky laughed again, feeling lightness invading her, chasing away the darkness. "How do you think Iris and Rudd will take all this?"

With a shrug, Gray said, "Knowing them, they'll feel like cosmic grandparents to our little tyke."

"But I worry she won't let me work."

Gray gave her a flat look. "Baby, you are not working.

You're going to live with me, let me make you happy and pursue hobbies like knitting while you're pregnant. I don't want you stressed right now, Sky. You've been through enough." He saw her considering his arguments. "Look, you just got handed a left hook with your father's two illnesses that occurred months apart. You're still in the middle of healing from your PTSD. Don't you think you deserve a little R and R? A chance to recoup?"

"I never looked at that yet, Gray. Being told I was pregnant yesterday threw me into a completely new loop."

He reached out, covering her hand. "Then let me think outside the box a little for you. I want you focused on yourself, Sky. And our baby. I make more than enough money. And Iris is not stingy when it comes to hiring good people and paying them well for their knowledge. Baby, you don't have to lift a finger to make another dollar if you don't want to."

Her world was changing so quickly, Sky couldn't absorb it all. Threading her fingers through Gray's, she said, "There's a lot to think about, Gray. I just need some time to sort through it all."

"Yes," he agreed gently. "About now you probably feel like a shuttlecock being batted back and forth in a badminton game."

She grinned a little. "That pretty much sums it up."

"First things first," Gray said. "Finish your sandwich, and then I want you to go lie down and get more sleep."

"And what will you be doing?"

"Making a few phone calls," he hedged, giving the back of her hand a kiss, his eyes sparkling with mischief.

# CHAPTER TWENTY-FIVE

SKY AWOKE SLOWLY. Her nose twitched. She smelled fresh coffee. Warm and snuggled into the pillow, she cracked open her eyes. Sunlight was pouring in around the drapes in her bedroom.

*Gray?*

Automatically, she turned over on her back, her arm moving outward to touch him. His side of the bed was empty. Drowsy and feeling almost drugged, Sky forced herself to sit up, her hair mussed around her face. The clock read 9:00 a.m. She hadn't meant to sleep that long!

"Hey," Gray called from the open bedroom door, "want some coffee, sleepyhead?"

Sky instantly relaxed, seeing him lounge casually against the entrance, a cup of coffee in his hand. The sleep must have done her a lot of good because as she gazed over at Gray, who was dressed in a black T-shirt that outlined his broad chest and shoulders, she felt her body grow warm with yearning. Pushing the hair off her face, her voice thick, she said, "That smells wonderful."

"Figured you'd want some," he said. Gray entered the bedroom and sat down, their hips touching.

Never had he wanted to love Sky more than right now. Her eyes, once red and swollen, were back to normal. As Gray handed her the cup, he saw there were no longer smudges beneath her eyes. Sky felt solid, like her old self, and he breathed an inner sigh of relief.

He was content to sit there in the silence of the warming bedroom, the song of a robin somewhere outside the open window, which allowed fresh air to flow into the area. Laying his hand on her blanketed thigh, he asked, "Better this morning?"

She managed a nod. "Much." Drowning in his hazel eyes, the green and gold telling her that Gray wanted to love her, she smiled a little. "I feel like I've been run over by a Mack truck. I'm so drowsy. I can hardly get out of that sensation of wanting to sleep more."

"You slept deep." Gray looked at the watch on his wrist. "From 8:00 p.m. last night to 9:00 a.m. Thirteen hours." He slid his hand slowly up and down her thigh, giving her a warm look. "You needed every hour, Sky. You look good this morning."

"Do you really think I'm going to sleep like this throughout my pregnancy?"

"Well, you do need your rest. You just went through a major life test under your own power, and now you need time to get back on your feet."

"Mmm," Sky whispered. "I feel like a boxer that's gone fifteen rounds—bloody, reeling and stunned."

Gray smiled a little and nudged some strands of her uncombed hair across her shoulder. The lace of her white nightgown made Sky look so damned feminine. Vulnerable. A Madonna. "I can't imagine what you went through," he told her, serious.

"Has my mom called yet? How is my dad?"

"I called her earlier this morning, and she's fine. She said your dad is starving to death, wanting a big breakfast, but they're giving him gruel instead." He grinned a little, watching her eyes alight with relief, the worry dissolving in them. "She said to take your time coming over. Your mom realizes how tired you are from everything."

Sky crossed her legs beneath the covers, resting her elbows on her thighs, the cup cradled between her hands. "I wonder how they'll take our news."

"After getting over the shock, they'll probably be two of the happiest people on the planet." Gray touched her chin and leaned forward, grazing her lips. "Except for us, of course."

Heat skittered right to her core. She felt her breasts growing taut. Her nipples hardened instantly, feeling supersensitive against the soft cotton of her nightgown. Now Sky understood why her orgasms had felt more intense, her nipples far more sensitive to Gray's touch than normal. "I hope you're right. I just worry it's one more shock on a bunch that my parents have had to deal with."

"This is a good shock," Gray soothed. "Ready for a hot bath?"

She handed him the emptied coffee cup. "Yes, but I can walk, Gray. Really, I can."

He rose and smiled down at her. "I want to do it for you, baby. Let me draw the water for you, all right?"

She sat there enveloped in the warmth burning in his eyes, that careless smile curving his delicious mouth she wanted to kiss again. "Thank you, Gray."

"Want some breakfast?" he asked, hesitating at the door.

"I'm not really hungry," she murmured, automatically moving her hand across her belly. "But I have to eat...."

Nodding, he said, "Bacon? Two eggs? Toast?"

"Sounds wonderful," Sky agreed. Pulling the covers aside, she pushed her legs across the mattress, the floor feeling cool beneath her feet. "Now," she teased him, "you are going to let me walk on my own two legs to the bathroom, aren't you?"

He shrugged. "This time. But you never know when I just might pick you up in my arms and carry you." He grinned broadly and pushed away from the door, disappearing silently down the hall.

Sky sat on the edge of the bed, absorbing the silence in the farmhouse, the place where she'd grown up happy and loved. The robin outside her window was singing, and it made her feel a sense of peace she'd not felt since being tortured. Being home, having Gray here with her, the fact her father had dodged a bullet that could have killed him, all moved slowly around in her bruised heart. Looking around, she smoothed the sheet she sat on with her hand, feeling the material beneath her fingertips.

She was happy. Happier than she could ever recall. Lifting her chin, Sky stared at the empty doorway. And it was all because of Gray. Her heart swelled so powerfully with feelings of love for him, she sat there with her eyes closed, simply absorbing those wonderful emotions. In a span of three days, her life had been turned on its head, and she'd found herself nearly out of control, the threat of losing her father, the terrible things that lay between them unsaid and misunderstood.

With a sigh, Sky pushed off the bed. She slid her fingers through her uncombed hair and slowly walked toward the door. It felt as if she were walking through another door, another chapter in her life. A much better one. Filled with hope and love.

GRAY'S CELL PHONE rang when she was climbing out of the tub. She could hear Gray's deep voice beyond the door, and she wondered if it was her mother calling about her father. Worried, Sky brushed her teeth, combed her ginger hair into some kind of order and got dressed. She padded out of the steamy bathroom and into the hall. The air was filled with the scent of bacon frying. Aiming herself toward the kitchen, she found Gray working over the stove.

"Who called?" she asked, stepping over to the counter, watching him lift the bacon out of the skillet and onto a plate.

"Good news," Gray said, giving her a glance. "That was Cade Garner from the sheriff's office."

Frowning, Sky had completely forgotten about the other threat hanging over their lives. "Oh?"

Gray shrugged. "Well, maybe not good news, but it's an end to our problems with Harper and his gang." He put a paper towel over the bacon, absorbing the grease from it. "Cade said that Chuck Harper was found this morning at Ace Trucking with a bullet in the back of his head."

Gasping, Sky stared at him. Automatically, her hand went to her belly, as if to protect her baby. "What?"

Gray took her by the arm and led her over to the table. He pulled out a chair. He had the plates on the table, two eggs on each one, toast ready to be buttered. "It was a professional hit." He went to the stove and picked up the platter of bacon and set it before her. "Cade thinks the Garcia drug ring was really pissed off at Harper. He'd sent those two guys after me, and it failed. And then they had to spring those two from jail." He sat down, holding her stunned expression. "Cade said drug-ring lords don't give people like Harper a second chance when they screw up that badly."

"God," Sky whispered, her hand against her throat, staring at Gray. She swallowed hard. "What does it mean for you, Gray? Will that ring come after you now?"

"No," he rasped, gripping her hand, seeing the fear come to her eyes. "I'm in agreement with Cade on this one, baby. The ringleaders don't want this kind of high profile where they're trying to house and distribute drugs. They want this all to go away. By taking out Harper, they'll install another lieutenant in their organization to take over Ace Trucking." He patted her hand, seeing the fear subside in her eyes. "And I'm sure they're wanting a guy who will keep a very low profile, not be on the sheriff's list like Harper continued to be. Come on. Eat up."

Sky barely tasted the salty bacon, but she ate. Her mind whirled with the implications of the news. "So, Cade thinks you're safe now?"

"Yes." Gray cut up his eggs. More important, Harper wouldn't be a blight in Sky's life every time she went to town. He didn't have to worry about the bastard following her, threatening her. Gray would never tell Sky, but he was damned glad Harper was dead. It solved all their problems, as far as he was concerned. In Sky's present condition, he wasn't going to discuss it with her. He could see another kind of relief in her expression, however, understanding she would be safe to go to town by herself now.

"Wow," Sky murmured, buttering the toast on her plate. "So much is happening all at once."

"We can hold on to one another during this storm," he said. He saw her cheeks begin to flush, her flesh no longer translucent and tense. "And this morning when I got up, I called Iris."

Sky stopped eating for a moment. "You told her I was pregnant? That my father pulled through?"

"I did." Gray saw more relief in her eyes, understanding Sky was fragile, and she wouldn't be up for the Elk Horn Ranch family coming and visiting her, hugging her and making a fuss over Sky. "Iris is ecstatic that you're pregnant. She said that she would hire another woman to take your place right away because you needed to rest." He saw her relax and close her eyes for a moment. When she opened them, he added, "Iris isn't upset with you, Sky. She's happy for all three of us because I told her I would be taking care of you from now on."

"I'm just so glad she's not upset with me, Gray."

"Your PTSD makes you think the worst, not the best," he said, cleaning up everything on his plate. He pointed his chin in the direction of her plate. "Keep eating."

Grinning a little, Sky made a real effort to eat everything. "You really are a helicopter father, McCoy."

"Guilty as charged," Gray said. He wanted Sky to smile a whole lot more. And he silently promised her he would move heaven and hell to give her that kind of space and environment. He wanted Sky to flourish.

"What time is our flight back to Jackson Hole?" she asked, finishing off the second piece of toast.

"3:00 p.m."

"I want to see my parents."

Gray stood and cleared the plates. "We'll leave in about an hour," he said, putting the plates in the sink. Sky had chosen a pale lavender T that beautifully outlined her upper body, the fabric hugging her small breasts. She wore a loose-fitting pair of gray gym pants, and he wondered if her waist was expanding, the elastic giving her relief from the tightness of wearing the jeans she normally wore. He sat down at her elbow, holding her soft gaze that shone with love for him alone.

"We have one more very important thing to address," he told her. Gray pulled a small box from his hands and set it before her. Taking her hands, he rasped, "Will you marry me, Sky? Be my best friend? My lover? My life?"

Her eyes widened in surprise. Her lips parted and then she looked down at the red velvet jewelry box and then up at him.

"Gray…" She whispered unsteadily, staring at him, feeling tears prick her eyes.

Releasing her hands, he gave her a smile and slowly opened the box, revealing a wedding ring set. "I'd been holding on to these for the last two months, baby. I was waiting for the right time to ask you. Every day, I'd get up, thinking this was the day. And then something would happen, and I knew it wasn't the right day. And then your father falling ill, possibly dying, really was more important, so I just packed the rings with me, hoping against hope he wouldn't die."

A soft sound caught in her throat as she stared in disbelief at the rings. The engagement ring consisted of seven channel-cut diamonds set into the ring. The wedding band was thin gold and engraved with a floral pattern around it. "Gray…" She reached out, her fingertips barely brushing them.

"Well?" he prodded with a grin. "Want to marry me, Sky?"

"Yes," she said, her voice catching. "Yes."

Gray eased the engagement ring out of the bed of the box. "I wanted something that was practical for you, Sky. The diamonds are cut to lie in a channel on the ring so they can't be torn out and lost." He took her left hand, hoping like hell it would fit. Gray had had to guess. The ring slipped on her finger as if it were meant to be there. When he saw Sky lift her hand, looking at the ring, Gray knew she liked it. And it was beautiful, like her.

"I— It's stunning, Gray. And you knew two months ago?"

Gray felt relief because Sky clearly loved the rings. Sitting back in his chair, he said, "In truth, baby, I knew it the first day I met you. I had a hell of a tug-of-war with myself because from the get-go, I was so powerfully drawn to you, I didn't know what to do. What to make of it." He opened his hands and held her glistening gaze. "I need to tell you about my first marriage to Julia."

Sky nodded. Gray had told her early on he'd been married before and that Julia had died. He hadn't told her how.

Seeing Sky's eyes darken and become serious-looking, he pushed on. "Like you, Julia was an R.N. She worked for Healing Hands Charity, a global NGO, nongovernmental organization. Julia had devoted her life to the Quechua people of Peru. I met her because Liz Standsworth, the owner of the charity, wanted someone like myself who could protect her out on the trail. There was a lot of drug running in the area." He frowned. "Six months after we met, we fell in love. I tried to get Julia to leave Peru because the drug war was heating up in the area. She refused. And then she started getting personality changes. She went back to the States for a checkup. Came back." He shrugged, his voice lowering. "She had an inoperable brain tumor and was given six months to live."

"Oh, no," Sky whispered, her hand pressed to her lips, seeing the pain in Gray's expression.

"I wanted to marry her right away." He shrugged. "I would spend the last six months with her. So we did. We were flown into a village, and when we landed with medical supplies, a Russian mafia gang hit us. I was shot and went down. Julia ran between where I fell and the gunmen in the jungle." He slowly rubbed his hands and remained silent for a moment. Looking up, he held Sky's pained-looking gaze. "Julia died instantly. I recovered and came back to the States. That was two years ago."

"Were you over her before you met me?" Sky wondered, feeling deeply for Gray, for his tragic loss.

"I didn't know it, but I was," he admitted quietly, rubbing his hands along his thighs. "I fell for you hard, Sky. I didn't have a relationship in my mind, but when I saw you, things happened." He gave her a slight smile. "It was then I realized my grieving for Julia had run its course. I'll never forget her, Sky." He touched his heart. "She'll always be a part of me."

"As well she should," Sky agreed, her voice strained because she realized other things now. "When Harper hit on me, this must have caused you a lot of worry."

Gray sighed and nodded. "It did. And then when his men tried to kill me, I felt like I was doing a rerun of what had happened down in Peru."

"You were afraid you'd lose me to a drug runner's bullet, too?" She stared at him, seeing the anguish set deep in his eyes. His mouth had tightened, as if he were barricading himself against the truth.

"Yeah, something like that."

"Why didn't you share this with me earlier, Gray?"

"Because," he said gently, giving her a loving look, "you were combating PTSD. This would have been just one more load for you to carry, Sky. I wasn't about to put it on your shoulders."

"Okay, that's fair. I guess if I were in your shoes, knowing how hard I was struggling, I'd probably have made the same decision."

"Thanks for understanding."

"Promise me one thing?"

"Anything," Gray said.

"If there's ever anything you need to get off your chest, you come to me? We talk it out? I don't want you seeing me as someone who can't handle real life. Because I can, Gray."

He saw the spark of determination in Sky's set expression and grinned. "That's a promise, baby, that's going to be easy to keep from here on out."

She nodded, satisfied. A marriage was about sharing, partners helping one another, not one spouse carrying all the loads by himself.

"But you fell in love with me anyway. Even after what happened to Julia?"

Gray nodded. "Yes. I figured it out a month into our relationship." He extended his hand, drawing her right hand into his. "I wasn't sure you loved me, Sky, but I got the rings made, and I held on to them, hoping that someday, you would tell me you loved me."

"And I never did."

"Well, I didn't, either. For obvious reasons now."

"Because I was afraid, too, Gray. I knew I loved you early on. We were good in bed, and you were helping me thrive. I was afraid that I was a yoke around your neck, that my PTSD symptoms were going to eventually destroy what we had." Sky shook her head and gave him a look of apology. "I was so scared of losing you, Gray. And I was even more scared of admitting how I felt about you."

He snorted and shook his head, his fingers growing more firm over hers. "And here I was understanding your first priority was getting your life back and in some semblance of order after what you went through. I held off saying anything, baby, because I thought by me telling you I loved you, it could be seen as one more stress on you. One more brick on that load you were carrying already."

Sky lifted his hand and kissed the back of it. "We are really a pair, aren't we?"

"And then some," Gray agreed, sharing a slight grin with her. "I told you I loved you last night when you were crying, but I didn't think you heard it."

"I'm sorry. I didn't."

"Just as well," Gray said, getting up. He pulled Sky into his arms, feeling her body against his, her arms sliding around his neck. He leaned down, taking her mouth with all the tenderness he had in his heart for Sky. That wonderful sound caught in her throat, and she melted like hot honey into his arms. She was his. She would be his wife!

Suddenly, Gray's entire world shifted and refocused as

he felt her smile beneath his lips. He had a treasure beyond his imagination. Sky was so courageous, always a
fighter, always trying to get well. His admiration for her
inner strength, her ability to reach out to love him despite
her tragic wounding, never ceased to amaze Gray. She
whispered his name, reached up on her tiptoes and kissed
him with all her womanly love.

ALEX AND BALIN PASCAL traded looks of shock. Not only
had Gray McCoy appeared out of the blue, but Sky had
just revealed that she was pregnant and that they were
going to get married.

Balin burst out into tears, her hands against her face as
she sobbed. Alex slid his arm around his wife, tears in his
eyes, too. But they were tears of happiness. Balin stood up,
going over to her daughter, enfolding her gently. "This is
so wonderful, Sky. I'm so happy for you…for Gray," she
said, eyeing her future son-in-law warmly.

"Thanks, Mom. It means so much to us that you're
happy for us."

Gray held Alex Pascal's gaze. Was the man happy? He
seemed somber. Maybe thoughtful. Gray had never met
him until a few minutes ago, when he'd shaken the man's
hand. He could see the telltale marks of a black-ops warrior in Sky's father, even though Alex looked pale and was
recovering from a near-fatal illness. He noticed how Sky
got her blue eyes from him.

Tension raced through Gray because above all, he didn't
want her father to rail about how his daughter had gotten
pregnant out of wedlock. A lot of people nowadays didn't
care about that, but military people were more conserva-
tive. And maybe Pascal was one of them. Gray didn't mind
if Pascal took him on, but there was no way he was coming
after Sky again. Alex had already wounded his daughter

so deeply that she almost hadn't survived his emotional and verbal assault against her.

Balin patted Sky's shoulder, sniffing and smiling through her tears. "Do you know yet? A boy? A girl?"

Sky shook her head. "No, I won't find out for a while. I have to get to Dr. McPherson, and when we know, we'll let you know, okay?"

Balin smiled and slid her arm around Sky. "I'm so happy, Sky. This is a good surprise."

"A happy ending," Sky agreed, sniffing, too. She took a tissue out of her pocket and blew her nose. With Gray standing tensely at her side, she felt the energy between the two men in her life. Their gazes were locked with one another. Like two alpha wolves circling one another, sniffing one another out, testing one another. She slid her fingers into Gray's hand. And then she gave her father a longing look.

"Dad? Are you okay with this?" He was so hard to read. But he'd been that way all of Sky's life. She felt tension radiating off Gray, as if he were getting ready to go into battle. He didn't know her father like she did, and she was sure Gray didn't trust him. Not after what he'd already done to her.

Alex held out his hand to his daughter. "Come here, Sky. Let me hold you and your baby."

Relief tunneled through Gray as Sky left his side, smiling like the sun itself as she rushed to her father's side. He watched Alex embrace his daughter. Sky hugged her father gently, her face buried beside his. That hard, unreadable look on Alex's face disappeared, and Gray saw tears in the man's eyes. It was going to be okay. The last potential problem had been bridged and turned out to be nothing more than the four of them smiling at one another, happiness infusing the hospital room.

Balin slid her arm around his waist. "Welcome to our family, Gray." Her eyes shone with hope. "You've been so good for Sky. There's such a positive difference in her." She squeezed him. "Thank you."

"Your daughter, Mrs. Pascal, is so very strong. I didn't do much at all except when she fell, picked her up. She's the one who dusted herself off and forged ahead. She has heart." God, did she have heart. A huge heart that wrapped itself around Gray, around those who were fortunate enough to be in Sky's orbit whether at work, at Mo's or with the children who came to the ranch.

"My daughter," Balin said proudly, "is half Cheyenne. She has the people's blood and bone. And she is strong." And then she smiled, watching her daughter and husband continue to hug one another. "We are so proud of her. And we're so glad she has found a man, a warrior, equal to her."

Gray remembered that Balin's Native American name meant "mighty warrior," and there was no doubt in his mind that Balin had raised Sky to be strong, resilient; she had that warrior blood in her veins. All of those things had made her who she was right now, and those genes had pulled her from the edge of hell and back to being gifted with an almost normal life. Sky had him. She carried their child. They were a family. And he loved her so damn much that he couldn't conceive of one day without waking up with Sky in his arms. Where she belonged…with him.

## CHAPTER TWENTY-SIX

SKY STOOD QUIETLY in the ankle-deep snow, watching Gracie bound around her den. The early-February sky above her was partly blue and partly cloudy. The valley was just digging itself out of a two-foot snowstorm from last week. She smiled at Gracie, who was now nine months old, as she came over, wagging her tail and champing. She then licked Sky's fingers with her pink tongue. The late morning was quiet, the green of the pines scenting the air. She loved the silence broken by a melodic gurgle from a raven somewhere nearby.

"Gracie," she said, petting the wolf's broad, white head, "in about a week, I'm going to be giving birth to a baby girl." She leaned down, the wolf licking her face. "I hope she has blue eyes just like yours...."

Gracie whined and nuzzled her neck and jaw with joy. Sky knew it was the way wolves greeted one another. Gracie saw her as her mother. Crystal, the black female, came trotting up, waiting her turn because Gracie was the alpha female. Chert had been sent to Canada, to another wildlife center, where he was to share a huge enclosure with a young female wolf. The hope was that they would like one another, breed and eventually have wolf pups. Crystal's yellow eyes followed Sky as she straightened. She was just as big and healthy as Gracie. They were truly sisters, happy to have one another's company, Sky thought as she saw Crystal champing as Sky extended her hand toward her.

The wolf whined, made chomping sounds with her mouth, showing Sky that she was being subservient as well as happily greeting her. A beta wolf in the pack was always showing its status so that the alpha wolves would not punish it for getting out of line. Sky moved carefully, her gloved hand against her swollen belly. She found her center of balance was no more, and she'd taken great care in walking out here to visit the wolves she'd help save last June.

Crystal whined, licking Sky's fingers, her yellow eyes dancing with what Sky interpreted as happiness.

Suddenly, both wolves raised their heads, looking past Sky, their ears up and alert. Sky slowly turned, hands protective on her swollen belly. She smiled, watching Gray trudging through the snow, his hands jammed in the pockets of his black goose-down jacket. He wore that SEAL baseball hat of his. He was never without it when outdoors, and Sky felt warmth flow through her heart. Gray might be an ex-SEAL, but in his soul, he was still one. He would always be one. Her lips curved softly as she saw him meet her gaze. Lifting her hand, she waved.

"What's the matter?" Gray called, his words turning to breathy frost as he spoke. "You have cabin fever?" He grinned and opened up the first door and then turned and locked it.

"You could say that," Sky answered drily, moving over to allow him in the second door. "I left you a note. You must have got it." Gray had been in town earlier helping the wranglers with a load of grain for the horses. They were almost out, and the blizzard had shut down the county for three days.

"I did." Gray gazed down at Sky. Her cheeks were ruddy, her mouth soft, and he felt himself going hot with need. It was the look of utter happiness in her eyes that made his heart swell. All Sky had to do was smile, and Gray felt like the luckiest man on the planet. He came over and dropped a quick kiss on her smiling mouth.

Gracie came over, whining and leaping up on him, her paws smearing snow across his jacket. Gray roughed up Gracie's ears and gave her some healthy pats. He took Gracie's paws off him and ruffled her fur across her strong back. "How long has it been since you came out here to see them?" he asked, moving out to welcome the shyer Crystal.

Groaning, Sky said, "Far too long."

"You got bored."

"I hate staying in all the time, Gray. You know that."

He chuckled and came over, sliding his arms around his wife. She looked as if she were carrying around a twenty-pound watermelon, her belly resting between them. "You could have slipped," he said, kissing her temple. Her nose was slightly red. It was in the twenties right now. The good news was there was no cutting wind to make it even colder. Snowflakes danced and glittered in the sunlight, falling off the surrounding pine trees.

Sky snorted. "Oh, don't start, McCoy. I was careful, very careful, coming out here." She saw him give her a teasing grin, leaning into his strong body, his arms holding her as close as she could be under the circumstances. She sighed and absorbed him, his masculine scent, the smile in his half-closed eyes as he rocked her gently in his arms.

"Now, now," he teased. "Lately, Mrs. McCoy, you've been getting to be a little crabby...."

Sky made a sound of protest. "If you were carrying this bowling ball around inside you, you'd be a little irritable, too!" And then she laughed because she knew he was trying to make her feel better. Yes, the ninth month, she'd turned testy. It was tough finding a comfortable position to sleep in. Sleep deprived, her body stretched to the max, Sky knew Gray's patient personality had made her suffering less. Somehow, he could feel when she was uncomfortable or worried.

"True," Gray whispered, his white breath joining hers as they laughed. She felt so good in his arms. She had bundled up well, and Gray knew she needed to get outdoors, to be in fresh air and sunshine. He couldn't fault her. "I just wished you'd waited until I got home. I could have helped you out here."

"It was a whim or maybe sheer desperation," Sky admitted. "I just missed the wolves." She watched them as they lay down near their den, panting and watching Sky and Gray. After all, they were their alpha parents in their wolf minds.

"And we've had one hellacious blizzard after another since Christmas," Gray agreed, leaning down, kissing her cheek. He caught her glance. "You know what? I think you're more beautiful now than ever before."

Groaning, Sky muttered, "I feel ugly, Gray! Ugly!"

He grinned. "You'll get your body back in about two weeks. I was talking about how angelic you look." He grazed her cheek, feeling the coolness to her skin. "I see it. Don't you?"

Pushing some snow with the toe of her boot, Sky muttered, "No...not right now. I just feel..." She gave a frustrated sigh.

"Like an elephant?" Gray teased, laughing with her.

"Yes!" Sky buried her face against his jacket, feeling his hand move through her loose hair. "I miss sleeping in your arms. I'm so restless. I toss and turn. I can't get comfortable anymore."

"I miss that, too," Gray rasped. "And I miss loving you..." He leaned down, claiming her pouty lips, hearing her moan with need, her gloved hand curving around his neck for a moment. Sex had gone off the table at six months. Gray took it in stride. He looked forward to the time when they could sleep in one another's arms again, and he could love her, hear those sighs and sounds of pleasure spilling out of her soft lips once again.

"I'll be so glad when this is over," she griped, easing away and getting her feet under her again.

Gray nodded. "I couldn't do it," he admitted, giving her a proud look. He skimmed her brow, erasing the small frown. "Your strength amazes me." And it did. The past six months had been a major change in Sky's PTSD symptoms. At first, she'd reluctantly followed his suggestions of resting and doing things she only really wanted to do. Her work ethic had had to be reined in. And Gray had been right because as a quiet and new rhythm of life established around them and inside her, Sky made swift progress. Now she was calm in a way he'd never seen before. And lighter. Happier.

"Next lifetime," she grumped, "I'm coming back as a man."

Gray chuckled. "This will be all over soon, baby." He met her mutinous look. "Have you settled on a name yet?"

They'd tossed a lot of them around, but none seemed to strike Sky. Gray didn't care what his daughter would be called. All he wanted was a safe delivery for Sky and a healthy baby girl.

Sighing, Sky said, "I'm not sure…. I'm still waffling. I think it's my hormones."

"Can't disagree with those wild woman hormones of yours."

"I'm wild all right. Wild about getting this baby girl of ours born and out of me." She gently patted her belly.

Gray kissed her brow. "You're going to be one incredible mother. You know that?" There was no question because Sky was maternal and nurturing by personality.

In the past six months, she'd had only two nightmares. Just two. It was an amazing change, and Gray was glad for Sky's sake. Whether it was the pregnancy, their marriage or something else, he didn't know. But Sky was healing at a phenomenal rate. He saw it in large and small ways every day.

He was sure when her parents came and visited them at Christmas, joining the Mason family for a huge holiday celebration at the main ranch house, had helped, too. The wound between Alex Pascal and his daughter was closing and healing. In part, Gray knew it was due to the strong love they'd always had before the incident occurred.

PTSD could tear a family apart in so many ways. It was a lethal, invisible and toxic disease created by war, by abuse and trauma. And Gray had watched it and how it had affected Sky and her family. Now he was once again relieved that Sky's father had the courage to confront his own combat horror, too. He'd gone to see Jordana McPherson and was stunned that his anxiety was gone. To Gray, he looked like a man who had just been set free from a prison that'd held him for half his life.

"Let's go in?" he asked, meeting her eyes.

"I'm getting a little chilled," Sky admitted, slipping beneath his arm, absorbing his closeness, his always protective demeanor.

"I'll make you hot chocolate. With all the marshmallows you want." Gray raised his brows, watching her respond to his care.

"I'd like that." Sky walked through the two gates, waiting for Gray outside the compound. The two wolves got up, going over to the cyclone fence, watching them, wagging their tails in a friendly fashion.

"If you're good," Gray teased, sliding his arm around her shoulders, "I'll even add a little whipped cream to it." He knew Sky was watching her weight, but she also loved rich hot chocolate, too. Today she deserved something to make her happy, to draw her out of her cranky disposition. "Well?"

"Sounds good," she whispered, leaning her head against his shoulder as he moved them slowly down the snowy path between the trees. "I love you so much, Gray."

Her words caressed his heart, made him feel strong and good for her sake. He squeezed her gently, leaning down and kissing her temple. "I love you, too, baby. Every day is better than the last…"

ON FEBRUARY 14, Valentine's Day, little ginger-haired Emma Jordana McCoy was born at home. She slipped out of her mother and into Gray's awaiting, gloved hands with two midwives and Jordana McPherson in attendance. Just like her mother, who had had her at home, Sky had wanted to have her baby without hospital walls surrounding her. The day and a half of labor had been worth every second as Sky had watched the expression on Gray's face as his daughter quickly slipped into his large, awaiting hands. The warmth in his eyes, the softening of the line of his mouth, the look of awe as he lifted his tiny, red, wrinkled daughter up for Sky to see for the first time, had made her cry with joy.

And when Cindy, the primary midwife, had cleaned squalling Emma up, bundled her in a new soft pink blanket that Sky had knit for her, Sky felt a surge of euphoria race through her. She forgot the excruciating pain of childbirth and stared at her baby. Emma was nestled into her arms for the first time, her red face all scrunched up with cries, and she relaxed as Sky began to coo softly to her. In moments, with the help of the midwife, she sat in her bed with lots of pillows behind her back, watching her daughter latch hungrily on to her swollen, milk-filled nipple.

It was then that Gray came to her side, that look of wonder still in his eyes as he sat down and faced her. Their hips touched, and he smiled into Sky's exhausted eyes. "You did it," he whispered.

"It was worth it," Sky whispered, her voice trembling as she met his gaze. But when Gray reached out, barely touching the light smattering of ginger-colored hair across his daughter's tiny head, she saw tears in his eyes. Tears of happiness. He skimmed her damp, mussed strands of hair so tenderly.

Gray eased upward, leaned over Sky, kissing her for a long, long time, letting her know just how much he loved her. And then Gray placed a kiss on his daughter's tiny brow.

"She's a hungry little thing," he murmured, grinning as he watched Emma suckle strongly on her mother's nipple.

Cindy came over, hands on her hips, grinning. "How are you feeling?"

"Tired," Sky murmured. "Like I could sleep for two weeks solid."

Cindy grinned. "Ain't gonna happen, New Mama. You and Gray are gonna be up every two to three hours. The good news is you can bring Emma to your bed, feed her, and then Gray can take her to the bassinet beside your bed. Breast-feeding really cuts down time to mix formula, warm a bottle and all that."

Gray gave Sky a teasing look. "She's really hungry."

"I would be if I'd been stuck in me for nine months."

Everyone laughed. Cindy came over and helped move Emma to her other breast and get the baby to suckle on the other nipple. "Okay, you're good to go. Jordana has already examined you and given you a thumbs-up, so the three of us are outta here."

"Thanks," Sky said, giving Cindy a look of gratefulness for her help.

"I'll drop in tomorrow and see how you're doing. In the late afternoon."

The room fell silent except for the suckling sound of Emma gorging herself.

Gray exchanged a look with Sky. "What can I do for you?" he asked, reaching out and sliding his hand briefly over her left arm that held Emma.

"I'd give anything to get a hot shower," she muttered wearily.

"When Emma's done, I'll put her in the bassinet and then get it ready for you. All right?"

"That sounds wonderful. Thank you…" Sky swore she'd never seen Gray as soft-looking as right now. His emotions were clear for her to read, and that stunned her. Gray was no less touched by Emma's birth than she was, she realized. The way he looked at his new baby daughter drove tears into her eyes for a moment. Fighting them back, Sky closed her eyes and wearily leaned back against the pillows. There was a special pleasure in feeding her daughter, and Sky couldn't think beyond the wriggling, hand-waving baby in her arms. Something soul-deep whispered to her as she almost drifted off into a light sleep that Emma could continue to help heal her. That one day, her trauma would be a memory without an emotional gut-punch behind it. Love had a funny way of doing that, Sky thought, feeling herself drift a little more toward sleep.

Gray's love had been her bulwark. He'd laid the foundation, the boundaries, to help her get on her feet again. And then, carrying Emma, feeling the profound love flooding her all the time, Sky had felt so much of the inner darkness dissolve because love was light. And light dissolved darkness, no matter what kind it was.

Gray moved to her left side. She vaguely felt his strong arm slide beneath hers to help cradle and hold Emma in place. His body felt so good against her bruised, beaten-up one. *Strong. Steady.* And when Gray eased his other arm behind her neck, coaxing her to lean fully against him, Sky melted into his embrace, trusting him. Always trusting Gray because he'd never not been there for her. Now he was here for her and their beautiful baby daughter. As a whisper of a weary sigh escaped her parting lips, she felt his warm, moist breath across her brow.

"Go to sleep, baby. I've got you and Emma," Gray rasped, kissing her hairline. He felt Sky surrender, so exhausted and in need of a safe harbor for herself. It was easy to have Sky in his arms, his left arm beneath hers, supporting their active little daughter, who drank even while her mother slept. The feelings moving through Gray were profound, anchoring, and he felt his heart expand so much he thought it might pop out of his chest.

He'd heard other teammates tell him that when their baby had been born, it changed them forever. Now Gray understood. It was too early to tell what color Emma's eyes would be. Or even who she would look more like. Gray would bet his paycheck that Emma would become a spitting image of Sky in every way. She already had Sky's ginger hair. With a smile, he watched Emma's tiny little arms slow down. And finally, Emma relaxed, her tiny bow-shaped mouth releasing Sky's nipple, sound asleep. He felt Sky take a deeper breath, but she remained fast asleep in his arms, too.

It would never get better than this. Not ever.

\* \* \* \* \*

**HARLEQUIN**

*Heartfelt or suspenseful, inspiring or passionate, Harlequin has your happily-ever-after.*

With new books published
every month, you are sure to find the
satisfying escape you know you deserve.